Quantum of Terror

I0563965

RON WILK

Ron Wilk

Ron Wilk

Chapter One

Wednesday, January 2, 2019

Temple Beth Emanuel

Miami, Florida

9 P.M.

Two years earlier, when the synagogue's renovation had just been completed, George, aka Schlomo Katz, had awakened to the sound of blood curdling screams interspersed with bursts of automatic weapons fire. Bodies had been strewn about the room, some draped over chairs, while others had writhed about on the floor calling for help, but he'd remained seated where boredom had initially brought forth slumber, with his head pitched forward as he'd reclined on a wooden chair pretending to have succumb to the massacre. It had been a horrific scene, the source of recurring nightmares, and a gruesome life changing event for thirty-two year old George.

George had been an only child, and he'd been raised with repeated tales of his grandparent's execution at the Bergen-Belsen concentration camp.

George's parents had met at a temple social while they'd been living in Minnesota, but Shmuel (Samuel), the elder

Katz, had been a shy boy, and it had taken considerable convincing on the part of his soon-to-be wife before Samuel had agreed to take Ethel's hand on the dance floor. They'd married five months later. But brutal winters had convinced the newlyweds to consider a warmer climate to raise their family, and a short time thereafter they'd moved to Miami Beach, Florida. In Miami, Samuel had gained initial employment as a butcher's assistant and had subsequently opened his own shop. Life had been good, but the planned family had been long in the coming, and it hadn't been until Samuel had approached his fifty-first birthday that Ethel, then forty-two years old, had informed him of her suspected pregnancy. It had been a joyous, yet fearful time for the Orthodox couple, as their advancing ages had threatened a complicated gestation. But almost nine months to the day, Ethel had called their butcher shop and had shouted that the time had arrived. Samuel had dropped the koshered beef that he'd been trimming and had beseeched a neighboring shop owner to drive him to his home.

Despite his Orthodox upbringing, at the age of eighteen, George had harbored serious doubts about religion, and during one particularly rebellious moment he'd visited a barbershop where his hair and sideburns had been cut to mimic that of a military recruit. His parents had been mortified, fearing that they'd be ostracized by their community, but a week later George outdid himself with a new, non-traditional wardrobe. The metamorphosis had been completed, and he'd no longer considered himself an Orthodox practitioner, having all but purged himself of religion, all religion. Needless to say, his parents had toyed with the idea of disowning him, but given what they'd gone through in the childbearing department they'd been loathe to do so.

To avoid the odd looks and the behind the back whispering that his neighborhood presence had provoked, George moved into his own, one bedroom apartment, away from the Orthodox community. And over time, the clandestine visits to his parent's home had became less frequent, having boiled down to weekly appearances at his almost eighty-year-old father's shop and occasional phone conversations with his mother. But George would come to regret the schism, as not long after his relocation the elder Katz slipped on the bloody floor of his butcher shop, his head striking the marble counter on the way down ... he'd never regained consciousness. Two months later, Ethel, severely depressed from the death of the only man she'd ever loved, overdosed on a prescription antidepressant and passed away. George was despondent and, having been shunned by religious acquaintances for obvious reasons, had no place to turn. And that's when he began to reconsider his theological heritage.

"George, you trippin'?" Marvin Freed asked, when he'd found his friend seated on a bench, staring off into space.

"No man, I was thinking about what had happened here."

"Sucks."

"Where's Freddie?" George sniffled, wiping his running nose with a handkerchief.

"You got another cold?"

"Nah, damn allergy. What about Freddie?" he repeated.

"He's gettin' our stuff."

George blew his nose and advised, "The Rebbe doesn't want us to meet here anymore."

"Why not?"

"Says we're not doin' the place any justice," he shrugged.

"What, our donation wasn't big enough?"

"Anyway, we need someplace less conspicuous."

"Your place or mine?"

"Neither. Did you fence the shit?" he whispered.

"Yeah, but the putz ripped us off."

"How much you get?"

"Nine K."

"What about the big rock?"

"Wouldn't take it."

"Seriously?"

"Said it was too easily traceable."

George exhaled and gazed up at his friend. "That thing should be worth at least a hundred K. We'll find it a home."

"There somethin' I want to talk about," Marvin mumbled, as a noisy vacuum made its way down the isle.

"Yeah?" George grunted, scratching the crotch of his rumpled khakis.

"I think we've been pushin' our luck. I mean, don't we have enough?"

George frowned, "There's never enough. But you're right, we need to change our profile to fit the goal."

Marvin exhaled and said, "Glad to hear that."

"Remember, what we've got planned is way more risky than our jewel heists."

"But more respectful."

"That's debatable."

Marvin yanked on the sleeve of his white, heavily

starched shirt to reveal a gold Patek, and said, "Almost time to meet up with Freddie."

George rose, brought his lips close to Marvin's right ear and warned, "Don't be showin' off that watch, someone might recognize it as their own."

They took a long and circuitous walk to an older apartment complex on Meridian Avenue, checked to make certain that they hadn't been followed, and knocked on a ground floor door. An overweight male in his mid-thirties opened the door a slit and, recognizing his friends, welcomed them inside.

"You're late," Freddie announced, finishing off the remainder of a candy bar.

"Sorry about that ... got the stuff?" George asked, as he locked the door and entered the small living room.

"Yeah, in the bedroom."

George took a seat on Freddie's tattered, mustard colored couch and inwardly cringed at the hideous green walls with its patches of white stucco bleeding through. His own apartment, a second story affair in an older low rise, had been freshly painted in an off-white shade to complement the terrazzo flooring. And his furniture, although rented for a reasonable monthly sum, was comprised of a collection of almost new, modern appointments.

Marvin, on the other hand, had made himself at home in the bedroom, and was busy toying with a Heckler and Koch MP-5 9mm submachine gun. Thinking that it had been left unloaded, he carried it into the living room with a big grin and handed it to George.

"That's it?" George exclaimed.

"There are six more plus ammo under the bed," Freddie advised.

George shook his head approvingly, hefted it with both hands and then lifted it into an aiming position.

"Don't touch the trigger," Freddie shouted, moving away from its muzzle.

"It's loaded?" George asked.

"Fuck yeah."

"This the safety?" he inquired, touching the lever with his index finger.

"It's on safe now, don't move it."

"How's it work?"

"Four positions. Safe, two round burst, three round burst and full auto."

"Cool."

"What about the handguns?" he asked, as Marvin steadied his breathing, having come to the realization that he could have killed both himself and his friends.

"Tonight, after midnight."

"Here?"

"No, I'm picking 'em up in SOBE (South Beach)."

Freddie walked to the kitchen and filled three shot glasses with schnapps. He handed one to each of the others and said, "This is the beginning."

They each swallowed the liquor in a single gulp, as George lowered his glass and rose from the couch, the MP-5 now resting on the floor near his right foot, and announced, "I've given our thing some considerable thought and I think we should call it Magen."

"Magen David," Marvin guffawed.

"Just Magen. Agreed?"

They all nodded affirmatively.

"Do we have a target?" Freddie asked.

"The synagogue attackers."

"I thought that was an open case," Freddie exclaimed.

"I was there," George said, adding, "I know who they were."

"And you didn't tell the police?" Marvin exclaimed, with obvious outrage.

"They wouldn't have done jack shit."

"Who was it?" Freddie asked.

"I heard 'em talkin'—called themselves the Fellowship."

Chapter Two

Thursday, January 3rd

7 A.M.

George had returned to his rental and, confident that Freddie would fulfill his promise to retrieve the remaining guns, he'd fallen into a deep sleep. But as his bedroom came alive with the morning sunlight his cell phone began to ring.

"Yeah?" he groaned.

"It's Freddie."

"What's up?" he asked, rising to a seated position at the edge of the bed.

"No guns."

"Huh?"

"The guy was a no show."

"Well, go find him."

"Not that easy."

"Did you pay him?"

"No."

"Find another source."

"I've tried, but the word's out."

"What the fuck does that mean?" he growled.

"They don't want to sell to Jews."

"Who the hell were you dealing with?"

"The Jamaicans."

"What about the Russians?"

"Don't trust 'em."

"Oh, but the Jamaicans were OK. And how did they know about your ethnicity?"

"They'd guessed, said I had a Jewish nose."

"And you'd agreed."

"I'll keep lookin'," he said, as George terminated the call.

I always knew that Freddie's deck was short a few cards, he thought, but I'd given the fucker a simple task. And now I'm not sure that he won't fall apart under pressure.

He walked the short distance to the bathroom, took care of business, and threw on the clothes from the night before.

Most of his local traveling had been accomplished on foot, and given Miami's traffic issues he'd rarely used his aging Volkswagen Beetle. But Marvin lived a distance away, so he fired up the faded red auto. It coughed a few times before the tiny engine settled down to a rough rhythm and he put it in gear.

Marvin lived in a North Miami condo. It was a three bedroom penthouse unit in a ritzy building with a doorman, maid service—the works. He was a trust fund recipient, and while he'd never flaunted his wealth or talked much about his deceased family, it had been crystal clear that employment was never going to be a necessity. George hadn't inquired, thinking that it had been none of his business, but he'd always wondered about the motive behind Marvin's decision to become a crook. He clearly had no need for the money, he'd pondered, but he'd guessed that boredom and the rush that accompanied a successful heist had been the attraction. As for himself, his father's meat market had been profitable, and while he did not have Marvin's perceived bankroll, his inheritance had been enough to temporarily keep him out of the job market, that is, until his quest for revenge had been fully accomplished.

He gave the car to the valet, had been announced by the concierge, and took the elevator to the penthouse level.

"C'mon in," Marvin said, a half eaten piece of toast dangling from his lips.

"Got any more of that?"

"Sure," he replied, leading the way to the kitchen.

George had been there before, but mostly at night, when he'd marveled at the brightly lit, multicolored Miami skyline. But today he could see the yachts motoring along the Intracoastal Waterway and, not far off in the distance, the dark blue Atlantic Ocean.

"Got any coffee?"

"Yeah," Marvin said, filling an empty cup with the steaming, black liquid.

George took a bite of his raspberry coated toast, downed it with a mouthful of coffee and announced, "We might have a problem."

Marvin smiled, scraped a slice of burned toast over the stainless sink, and said, "Freddie at it again?"

"Afraid so."

"What happened?"

"He screwed up the gun deal."

"Not surprised. In fact, I was amazed to see all those machine guns."

"Me too."

"He always has an excuse, what was it this time?"

"Some antisemitic bullshit."

"You think he's lyin'?"

"Not sure."

"I took the MP-5's home last night, got 'em in one of the bedrooms."

"Good move."

"There are cameras all over this place."

"You had 'em covered?"

"Yeah, in three, large canvass bags. Took me two trips."

"We need to know if he can be trusted," George said, wiping the jam from his lips with a paper napkin.

"Ask him for the gun money."

"That's too obvious."

"Then what?"

"The rock."

"Not if there's a trust issue."

"He only caught a glimpse, when I'd removed it from the safe."

"So?"

"We give him a fake."

"And he gets whacked for attempting a rip off."

"There's that."

"Well, if he's as good a liar as you think, he'll come up with an excuse. But how will it prove his sincerity?"

"Any good fence will know it ain't real. If Freddie comes back with one of his ridiculous excuses for not sellin' it, we'll know that he didn't try, and that'll be good enough for me."

"I've got the rock in my safe, want it?"

"No, you hold onto it. A fifteen carat cubic zirconia should do."

"They're not cheap."

George laughed, "Wasn't planin' on payin'."

"And if he fails the test?"

"Then we have a big problem."

"Yeah, he knows the plan."

"Exactly."

"So we off him?"

George shrugged.

"We've known him a long time."

"But we're too far along to have him screw things up."

"How would we do it?"

"Let's see how it pans out."

"By the way, the other day you'd mentioned a group called the Fellowship. I didn't want to sound like an idiot, but who are they?"

George's face assumed a quizzical expression, and he said, "The Muslim Fellowship."

"They did the temple?"

"Yup."

"Why?"

"Who the fuck knows. The Muslims have had it in for the Jews for over fifteen hundred years. Every now and then they come up with a new reason, but like the Hatfields and the McCoys, they probably don't remember how it really began."

"So they're the target?"

"The top of the list."

"And the others?"

"In due time."

"There are a lot of antisemites, we can't do them all," Marvin said, placing a dish in the sink.

"I get it, but we can send them a message."

"Have you considered that there are at most, just three of us?" Marvin said.

George hesitated, clenched his jaw, and replied, "I have a contact in the JPA (Jewish Protective Alliance)."

"And you're just getting around to mentioning that?" Marvin said, angrily.

"We need help."

"No shit. But they'll run us over like a Mac truck."

George scratched his unruly head of dark brown hair, and replied, "They're organized."

Marvin filled a glass from the faucet, downed it in one gulp and asked, "You suggesting we join them?"

"Not sure they'd have us."

"Reason?"

"We're nobodies."

"That could work in their favor."

"How so?"

"If things go south, we take the hit."

George considered Marvin's enlightening statement, gazed at the time on his cell phone, and hit a preprogrammed sequence of numbers.

***

The conversation with an assumed, low level member of the Jewish organization had lasted less than five minutes, but the result had been promising.

"What did he say?" Marvin asked anxiously.

"Has to speak with a superior."

"That's all, five minutes of blah, blah, blah and that's all you got?"

"If there's a deal, we'll have to meet with them."

"Where?"

"New York."

"Is your contact aware that we could be provoking a war?"

"Not exactly."

"For all the years that we've known each other, you've always been above board. Why didn't you tell him?"

"First of all, it's a she, and I couldn't be certain that my phone was secure."

"A woman?"

"Yeah, you got a problem with that?"

There was a moment of silence, and then, "Not really."

"Good, because she's got bigger balls than you."

"Where do you know her from?"

"Remember that two week trip I took to Israel last year?"

"You porked her?"

George laughed. "No, man. But I ran into her at a night club ... she was wearin' an IDF uniform."

"Shit."

"Yeah. She ain't a runway model, but her arm muscles are bigger than both of ours together."

"She moved to the States?"

George slid his cell phone to Marvin's side of the table, and said, "Look at the last number dialed."

"Damn, Israel."

George nodded in the affirmative.

"When do we hear back?"

"We're seven hours behind Tel Aviv—could be later today."

Chapter Three

Friday, Jan 4th

8 A.M.

The eight a.m. call had awakened him from a deep sleep.
George had fumbled with the cell phone until it had fallen
to the terrazzo floor with a crash. He'd jumped from the
bed and grabbed it, hoping that it was still functional.

"Hello?" he'd said, without checking the caller ID.

"George?" the accented voice had asked.

"Adina?"

"Yes. Sorry about the noise, I'm in a helicopter."

"Not too clear, but go ahead."

"My people are interested."

"Great."

"They want to meet."

"Where and when?"

"I'll get back to you when I'm off duty."

"Today?" he'd asked, but the line had gone silent.

That was quick, he'd thought. She must have some
pull with the JPA for them to accept a meet with total
strangers.

He'd dressed, stopped at a local cafe for black coffee
in a go cup, and made his way to a jeweler that he'd dealt

with in the past. He pressed the outside security button and was buzzed inside.

"Shalom," Izzy, the proprietor called out from the back of the store.

George replied in kind and took up position at a counter.

"It's not about that big stone, I hope?" Izzy said.

"Marvin brought it to you?"

"Why, is that a problem?"

"You know," he smiled, slyly.

"Yeah, I'm an honest man, but when business is slow well..."

"But you'd turned it down."

"It's too hot, my friend."

"The street been talkin'?"

He shook his head with a, yes.

George shrugged and said, "Got anything that looks like it?"

"A cubic?"

"Yeah."

"How realistic are we talking?"

"Just need to fool a friend."

Izzy walked to the back of the store and George could hear the sound of a heavy safe door slamming shut. He returned moments later with a wad of tissue paper in hand. He unraveled it and placed it before George on a square of dark green colored cloth.

"That it?"

"What you asked for."

"Looks real."

"To the uniformed."

"How much?"

"Three hundred."

"I'll give you one," George said, thinking that it was one hundred more than he'd planned on spending.

"Two fifty."

"One seventy-five."

"Two hundred, and that's my last offer," Izzy said.

George lifted the stone and moved it around in the light. Is Freddie worth two hundred bucks, he asked himself. We go way back, and if this will prove his loyalty it's worth the investment.

"OK, deal," he muttered, peeling off two hundred in twenties from a dwindling stack of bills.

"Want a box?" Izzy asked.

"How did Marvin present the real rock?"

"In a booger laden handkerchief," Izzy chuckled.

"No box."

He rolled the cubic back into the tissue paper, stuffed it into a pocket and waved good-bye to Izzy.

***

1 P.M.

The morning hours had oozed by nauseatingly slow. George had done some window shopping, searching for a new pair of athletic shoes. But after viewing an overwhelming variety of what he used to call sneakers, he fatigued, and stopped at a Cuban restaurant for something that his parents would certainly have disowned him for—a pressed pork sandwich. And as he swallowed the last savory morsel, his cellphone came to life.

"Yeah," he said, as he walked along the busy street.

"No more helicopter," Adina advised, gleefully.

George brightened. Despite the deprecatory description that he'd given Marvin, he'd been smitten by the young lady's intelligence and military expertise. And he hadn't found her appearance to be unappealing, either.

"Shalom," he said.

"Is this a good time?" she asked.

"Anytime is good," he replied, kicking himself for sounding too anxious.

"We have a representative in Boca Raton, does that work for you?"

"Of course. When and where?"

"Tomorrow, 10 a.m., Mizner Park. Are you familiar?"

"Yeah, no problem."

"What his name?"

There was a brief lull and then, "Virginia."

"An Israeli woman?"

"American. Not an issue, I hope. We fight wars, you know."

"I meant no offense, just surprised."

"She'll be waiting in the center island, directly across from Max's Grill. Been there?"

"Once."

George wanted to ask if there was any chance that she'd be coming to Florida, but he couldn't find the words, so he said, "Just me, right?"

"You've said that you were three. She will want to meet all of you."

Shit, he thought. Might not be enough time to deal with Freddie. "OK, we'll be there."

"You might not hear from me again," she cautioned.

"Why?"

"Maneuvers."

"But we can talk in the future?" he said, but she had already terminated the call.

I finally meet someone that interests me and she's thousands of miles away and I may never hear from her again, what a pile of shit, he thought. Well, at least things are looking up for our cause.

He shoved the phone into a back pocket and headed for Freddie's apartment. Freddie was a habitual late riser, and while the big hand was rapidly approaching 2 p.m., he figured that his corpulent friend would still be lazing around in his undies. Fifteen minutes later he stood banging on the front door.

"What the fuck," Freddie called out from within, "I'm comin',"

"You might want to cover up," George advised, as Freddie's junk was protruding from his boxers.

"Yeah, I was just..."

"Too much info," George interrupted.

"Want some eggs?"

"Freddie, it's past lunchtime."

"Not for me."

"Whatever. Take a seat, we need to talk."

They took positions on opposite sides of the living room and George wasted no time explaining, "I need you to fence the big stone, and it has to happen today."

"But Marvin said that..."

"He took it to Izzy."

"That wasn't cool."

"Agreed. Try the usual dirtbag."

"If the word's out he won't give us top dollar."

"Whatever, we need operating capital."

"No problem."

"Today, Freddie. I need to get it done before sundown."

"What's the rush?"

On the way over, George had deliberated about holding back the content of the conversation with Adina, but now he'd realized that it would not make a difference, especially if Freddie turned out to be the worthless piece of crap that he'd suspected. And if not, well, he would have to get his ass out of bed real early to make the Mizner Park meet.

"We have a meeting with the JPA in the morning."

"No shit," he shouted, obviously excited.

"You know who they are, right?"

"A frickin' army."

"Not exactly. But they can do things that we cannot."

"And they're gonna help us?"

"The opposite."

"So we're gonna join them."

"That's what the meeting is about."

"What time?"

"We'll pick you up at eight."

"In the morning?" he guffawed.

"You'd better be ready, or you're out."

Freddie let loose with a loud burst of air, an exhale that could have been heard in the adjoining apartment. "I'll be ready," he promised.

"Now, get some clothes on and sell this fucking diamond," George said, removing the tissue paper enclosed fake from his pocket and passing it to Freddie.

Chapter Four

Friday, 7 P.M.

TooJay's, Miami

SW 145th Street

As prearranged, the three men met for dinner at a deli and, as usual, Freddie was late. Rather than wait, George and Marvin had ordered their favorite pastrami on rye sandwiches with side orders of fries and soft drinks.

With a strand of pastrami fat hanging from his lips, Marvin asked, "You think he knows the score?"

"I gave him a fake to sell. Yeah, he might figure it out."

"That could be a problem."

"Only if he decides to talk."

"But it is a risk."

"What are you suggesting?" George asked, discarding the bread from his second sandwich half and picking at the meat with his fingers.

"I know that you two go way back, but he may have to be silenced."

George pushed back in the booth, grimaced, and replied, "Yeah, I've had the same thought."

Just then, Freddie came through the door and was

shown to the table by a hostess. George breathed a sigh of relief and motioned for Freddie to have seat.

"How much?" he asked, assuming that the answer would be zero.

Freddie lowered his head and replied, "I got an offer of fifty but I'd turned it down."

George gazed askance at Marvin and squealed, "Fifty thousand?"

"Yeah," Freddie mumbled.

"Our guy offered you fifty thousand dollars and you said no?" he repeated, incredulously.

Freddie shook his head as if to say, yes.

"Where is it?"

"In my pocket."

"Hand it over."

"You got a buyer?"

George fiddled with his drink and wondered if Izzy had screwed up by accidentally giving him a real diamond. After all, why else would anyone in their right mind offer 50K for a piece of glass, he thought. But he came back with, "Not right now, but I'll keep it safe."

"We still on for the meeting?" Freddie asked, checking out the available deserts.

"Yeah, and wear somethin' decent."

After their discussion, and following Freddie's devouring of a double portion of rice pudding, Freddie had wandered off on his own, while Marvin had piled into George's little red beetle for the ride home. And while they sat in silence for the first few minutes, Marvin opened with, "Do you think he was lying?"

"Probably."

"I think we should cut him loose."

"We've been down that road, if he's out he's dead."

"We don't have much time to decide."

George hit the brakes hard and put the red car into a 180 degree turn.

"What the fuck," Marvin shouted, the seatbelt cutting into the right side of his neck.

"We're gonna wake fat Izzy."

"What for?"

"To see if he screwed the pooch and gave me a real stone. If it's the fake that I'd paid for, Freddie's a liar."

They drove in silence to the jewelry store but, as expected, it had been closed for the night. Izzy lived not far away in an older, remodeled single family home that was lodged between two small commercial structures. George parked on the cracked, asphalt driveway but left the engine running.

"I'll leave the air on, stay here," he said.

He rang the bell, and following a longer than expected wait, Izzy opened the door in a pair of red and blue stripped pajamas, his belly protruding over the elastic waistband in a most unattractive fashion.

"Your girlfriend didn't like the diamond?" he laughed.

George grinned, held up the paper covered stone, and replied, "You sure you sold me a fake?"

Izzy offered a puzzled expression, but he took the stone and walked inside, signaling for George to follow. From a dining room credenza, he grabbed a jeweler's loop and brought it to his right eye.

"What do you want it to be?" he asked, lowering the loop to table.

"Whatever it is."

"OK. It's not the most convincing cubic, but it's a fake nevertheless."

George groaned.

"You were expecting a different answer?"

"Not really, but thanks, and sorry to have bothered you."

"Hey, no problem. I always entertain unexpected visitors in my pj's."

"Won't happen again," George offered, as he crossed

the threshold to the exterior.

He got into the car and sat staring though the windshield for a few silent seconds, and then announced, "We have to take care of Freddie."

"It wasn't real, was it?"

"What part of take care of Freddie did you not get?"

"Sorry. I was hoping for a free pass."

"You know, our plan involved three people. And that was hardly enough to accomplish anything other than getting ourselves killed. But two, I just don't know," he said, driving aimlessly over several oversized, jaw jarring potholes.

"That makes tomorrow's meeting all the more important."

"There's something I've been meaning to mention."

"Shoot."

"I'd never discussed our ultimate goal with my contact."

"So the JPA has no idea why we're going to meet?" he screeched.

"Not exactly."

"Lay it out for me."

"They want to meet to see if we're a good fit for their organization."

"And if so, we become their lackeys?"

"Maybe, but in exchange we ask for help with our thing."

Marvin pushed back into his seat and simmered, and as the red car drove up the incline to the front door of Marvin's condo, he said, "I'll do it, but about Freddie, we only have tonight to get it done."

"Got any ideas?" George asked, putting the car in neutral and waving off the valet.

"I've never killed anyone," Marvin trembled.

"Me neither, but that's what our overall plan is about. May as well get used to it."

"Shit."

"You wanna do it?" George whispered.

"You do it, I'll watch and learn."

"It's too close to home for me."

Marvin turned in his seat, aimed his watery eyes at those of his friend, and suggested, "We both do it, together."

"We never got the handguns."

"But we have loaded machine guns."

"That means noise."

"Got an idea."

"Listenin'."

"The cement plant. We sneak through the gate and off him in there."

"The big one here in Miami?"

"Yeah. I know how to get in."

"How do you … never mind. You sure we can enter?"

"Postive."

"OK. We'll tell Freddie that we set up a meet for the handguns that he never bought, but we tell him that we're going with him."

"Might work."

"Can you sneak two rifles down to my car?"

"The doorman will be suspicious, but I can get them into the garage and the trunk of my car."

"I'll wait here."

"No, park your car at the end of the street and we'll use mine."

"You want to take your brand new Porsche to a cement factory?"

"It's a lease."

"Oh, that makes a big difference," George cackled.

"Make the call."

"Hang on, Freddie doesn't have a car."

"He has a motorbike, right?"

George nodded affirmatively.

"Tell him to bring the gun money and to park his bike just outside the Cemex entrance. I'll get us inside."

"And the MP-5's?"

"I'll put them in a canvass bag and if he asks, the bag is for the handguns."

"I don't know, he ain't that stupid."

"We'd better hope that he is."

"Go get the guns, I'll make the call."

***

11 P.M.

Freddie had been reluctant, but he'd agreed to meet at the appointed time of eleven-thirty p.m.. Marvin had parked his dark blue Panamera several hundred feet from the cement factory's entrance, and Marvin, with the canvass bag slung over one shoulder, guided George to a key coded entry door. George stood back a few feet, while Marvin tapped at the buttons. Success was announced by a soft buzz.

"Where'd you get the code from?" George asked anxiously, as they walked through a dark office and headed for the yard.

"My uncle is an accountant, he does the books."

"So?"

"Last tax season his car quit. I gave him a ride to this place but the office had already closed, however, he knew the code. I was standing right beside him and the sequence stuck with me."

"Amazing."

"We have twenty minutes to pick a location and stash the guns."

"What about those three cement mixing trucks?" George said.

"That should work."

There were three large trucks parked side by side, as if they'd been waiting for a drive-in movie to begin. Marvin removed the two MP-5's from the bag and stood them up against the middle truck's right front wheel. He turned to George and said, "We'll tell him that the meet is back here, grab the guns and open fire."

"Here? What about the noise?"

"A couple of pops will go unnoticed, and we can shove his body under one of the trucks."

"Let's dump him in some cement."

"During my first and only visit, I'd noticed a bunch of cameras," he advised, nodding in the direction of one very obvious, dark tinted orb suspended from a light pole.

"If that's so, we're already on record."

"For doing nothing but trespassing, but if we take the time to do the cement thing it could get sticky."

"Ok, under the truck is a go."

Marvin removed his cellphone and checked the time. "We've got five minutes, probably a little more, since Freddie is never on time. Let's go, but keep your head down so the cameras can't record your face."

They sprinted toward the entrance, but this time they aimed for the gates that allow for truck traffic. There was a keypad similar to the one on the front door and, fortunately, the same combination of numbers unlocked it. They left the gate slightly ajar as they passed through and awaited Freddie's arrival. Twenty minutes after the anticipated arrival time, with no Freddie in sight, they turned to face each other.

"He's never this late," George advised.

"Yeah, I think he suspects."

"Should we wait awhile longer?"

"No. Let's recover the guns and get outta here."

They'd loaded the canvass sack into the Porsche's trunk and headed for Freddie's apartment. They'd concluded that the MP-5's would create too much noise, making an alternative solution necessary.

"Ever put someone in a sleeper hold?" George asked, as they'd approached the targeted neighborhood.

"No."

"It's not difficult, but holding on until they stop breathin' takes some muscle."

"How you gonna pull that off?" Marvin asked, parking the car a few hundred feet from Freddie's place.

"You distract him, while I come up from behind."

"You sure about this?" he said, as they sat in the car, engine extinguished.

"No choice. Freddie is a dangerous loose end."

"Dangerous?"

"He knows the plan and the initial objective."

They locked gaze for a few seconds, and then exited the vehicle.

Chapter Five

Saturday, January 5th

6 A.M.

JPA East Coast Headquarters

Broome Street, New York

The Jewish Protective Alliance had located their Eastern headquarters in a nondescript storefront on the lower East side. Masquerading as a functioning pawn shop had kept the curious at bay, but the backroom and basement would disclose an entirely different story.

The basement had been soundproofed, while the walls and ceiling had been outfitted with a copper screen that effectively negated the ability of even the most technologically advanced eavesdropping devices. Computer screens, a collection of six, thirty-inch color LCD's had been connected to the latest high speed computers that collected hijacked data from numerous law enforcement and Federal agencies. A separate link allowed for a secure, direct connection to Mossad headquarters in Tel Aviv. While the pawn shop kept the same operational schedule as other local establishments, the basement facility was manned on a twenty-four hour basis. Normally, three pairs of two Israelis alternated and occupied the space at all times, but four agents had been recalled, leaving only two people to man the site continuously. A small, stocked kitchen afforded them the opportunity to create whatever, within reason, their culinary fancies desired. A bathroom and shower completed the amenities.

Twenty-seven year old, First Lieutenant, Adina Faiola, well known to the Mossad, and a trusted member of the JPA, had contacted the organization's Tel Aviv office to suggest a meeting with the Miami trio. She had gone out on a limb to sponsor George Katz, with whom she'd had only a brief, but encouraging encounter.

The JPA had made it known that they'd been in the market for deniable, American pawns to be employed for as yet to be determined operations. Virginia Oden had been one such disposable individual, and her Boca Raton residence had offered the geographic flexibility that the JPA had considered desirable. Adina's new friend—George —had represented another potential prospect.

Virginia is a trust fund recipient, her parents having died during the crash of their privately owned Gulfstream as it had traversed the Sierra Nevada mountains en route to a California resort. She had been a Stanford University junior at the time, and the loss had been devastating. But with no other family to console her she had found solace from an unlikely source—a local synagogue's congregation —that had resulted in a second, life changing event; her conversion to Judaism. The occurrence of anti-semitic tragedies, both within the U.S.A. and abroad, had caught her attention and, searching for a method of personal retribution, she'd encountered and had joined with the JPA. And following a brief period of instruction that she'd likened to a James Bond script, she'd been left to her own devices, with the understanding that she would be activated in due time.

Having attended a party the night before, Virginia had been slightly hungover when the cellphone had begun to ring at 6 a.m. She fought with her sleep encrusted eyelids, willing them to part, as she reached to the nightstand and charging cellphone.

"Yes?" she said, not bothering to check for the caller ID.

"This is the Broome Street Pawn shop, we have several items of interest," the male voice advised.

Virginia hesitated, the morning cobwebs still clouding her thought, and she replied, "Pawn Shop?"

"Concentrate," the voice urged.

"Oh yeah, I get it. Describe them."

"Three males."

"Where?" she asked, her adrenaline flowing with the prospect of her first operation.

"Mizner Park, across from your favorite restaurant, 10 a.m.."

"How will I recognize these items?" she asked, trying to stay in character.

She could hear a sigh, an apparent sign of frustration, and she said, "Orders?"

"Confirm suitability."

"Criteria?"

"Your purview," the unnamed voice replied, as the call disconnected.

Wow, she thought. I've been activated, and that's a little scary.

She showered and dressed, downed two cups of the strongest elixir that her Keurig could provide, and headed for the lobby and the building's concierge.

"I need my Bentley," she said, smoothing the fabric of her all black pants suit and blood red, silk blouse in the granite wall's reflective surface.

"Right away," Miss Oden."

Five minutes later she witnessed the arrival of one of

her two owned vehicles, a silver Bentley Continental GT, smiled at the valet and took her position behind the wheel.

The oceanside condominium, as well as the automobiles, had been paid for in cash by a trust fund withdrawal. And as she drove off she engaged the window washer in an attempt to clear the salty residue, a slimy deposit that habitually accumulated on the surface of the garage's inhabitants.

The Bentley's clock had indicated that she'd be too early for her meeting, so after a few turns around the park she found a just vacated parking spot and headed for Starbucks for another jolt of something strong.

**

9:45 A.M.

The meeting was to take place across from Max's Grille. Her JPA training had cautioned her regarding the ills of being too obvious, and with that in mind she'd taken a stand behind a concrete column just outside of the restaurant, where she had a clear view of the intended rendezvous, the median. A quick glance at her diamond encrusted Rolex revealed that she had five minutes before zero hour. And as she nervously waited, flicking a errant strand of her long blond hair, she observed two males approaching from the North.

I have no means of identifying the targets, other than by their number and their appearance at the appointed time and place, she thought. Recognition was left up to my intuition, but there are only two men, not three. Should I let them pass, she wondered.

She continued observing their advance until they'd stopped directly across from her hiding place and stood immobile, looking about. Two, not three, she kept telling herself. But their apparent adhesion to the spot raised her interest and she'd decided to take a chance and approach.

"You fellas lost?" she said, hoping for some clue that they were, or were not her subjects.

"Nope, waiting for someone," George smiled, as he fidgeted in the beige sport coat over jeans that he'd never worn before.

"A friend?" she said, wishing that she'd asked a less inane question.

Marvin had been standing by George's side, and he took the lead by saying, "Any chance you're name is Virginia?"

She furrowed her brow and responded, "What happened to your third?"

"Couldn't make it?" George improvised.

She considered his response and, having been taught to roll with the unexpected, said, "Let's walk."

They began walking slowly along the parklike median strip, at first in silence, and then Virginia broke the ice with, "Why are you here?"

With his eyes still aimed straight ahead, George said, "We want revenge."

"For?" she asked.

"Crimes against jews."

"But I suspect you have something specific in mind?"

George turned briefly to face her, and replied, "A Miami synagogue."

She shook her head knowingly.

"We think it was the MF," Marvin chimed in.

"Excuse me?" she said.

"The Muslim Fellowship."

"You know that for a fact?

"Well, I was present during the attack," George claimed.

"And?"

"They took me for dead ... I heard them talking."

"So you don't have definitive proof."

"Proof enough for me."

"Not enough to start a war," she advised.

They continued walking until they'd reached the end of the park, where Virginia stopped, turned to face the pair and asked, "What do you want from us?"

"We're only two, and there's strength in numbers," George said.

"What's in it for us?"

"Plausible deniability," he said, repeating a phrase that he'd memorized from countless espionage movies.

"And what is it that we'd be denying?"

"Anything that we do on your behalf."

Virginia smiled and lowered her head, her long blond hair falling forward as she stifled a giggle. "I have yet to agree to anything," she said.

"Are you the decision maker?" Marvin asked.

"At this time and place I am."

"But you answer to others, I assume."

"Correct."

"So, where do we stand?" George asked.

"In Mizner Park," she laughed.

George turned to Marvin and said, "This is a waste of time, let's go."

"Are you that easily discouraged?" she jeered.

"We came with a serious offer and you're making

jokes."

"Today, this moment, is about who you are, not what you want or what you can do."

"Meaning?" Marvin asked.

"I'll discuss our conversation with my superiors and we'll be in touch," she advised, before crossing the street and disappearing amongst the strolling crowd.

Chapter Six

Saturday, Noon

Denny's Restaurant, Biscayne Blvd.

George and Marvin had driven south on Interstate 95 in silence. The road noise heard throughout the little red Beetle would have stifled any meaningful conversation, so they'd held off until they'd reached their destination, a Denny's on Biscayne Boulevard.

"What was your impression," George asked, once they'd been seated by a hostess.

"She was hot," Marvin replied.

"Not what I asked."

"Well, I guess she had to kick it up the ladder."

"Yeah. But I didn't get the warm fuzzies."

"We'll just have to wait."

A server appeared and they each ordered a hamburger plate and a soft drink. And as they awaited their lunch, George stared out of a near window, deep in thought. Finally, he locked gaze with Marvin and asked, "What if I was wrong?"

"About what?"

"The temple shooters."

"You heard them talking, right?"

"Yeah, but I could have misunderstood, or it could have been a frame up."

"You'd played dead, and everyone else was for real, so who would they have been addressing?"

"I didn't see them checking the bodies, so they could've thought that someone might have survived."

"Doesn't matter."

"Does to me."

"Whether they did our temple or not, we know that they've done others."

"But I don't want to give the real dirtbags a pass."

Marvin's demeanor turned dour, and he said, "I feel bad about Freddie."

"We've been over that—we had no choice."

"We could've convinced him to leave town."

"To a town without telephone, Internet, mail delivery or other means of communication?"

"Yeah, I get it. He could've screwed us good."

"Don't you ever forget that."

A few more people were led to booths near their own, so they stuffed the remainder of their burgers into their mouths, gulped down their soft drinks, paid the check and departed.

Back in the Beetle, George put his hands on the

steering wheel, prepared to leave the parking space, when he turned off the ignition and swiveled to face his friend, and asked, "What if the JPA isn't interested in us?"

"I guess we get rid of the MP-5's and live with our inability to fight back."

"No. Freddie would have died for nothing."

"We killed him."

George's eyes narrowed into a cold stare, and he replied, "I killed him, you just stood there, terrified."

"OK, but in the eyes of the law we're both on the hook."

He gave the wheel a hard turn and rolled out onto the poorly maintained road heading for Marvin's condo. Halfway there his cellphone began to call out the tune from Star Wars, his personal ringtone. He removed the phone from a belt clip and, without recognizing the caller ID, hit the talk button.

"Yes?"

"It's Virginia."

He brightened and nodding at Marvin, replied, "Glad to hear from you."

"My people want to meet."

"They're interested?"

"We'll see."

"Where and when?"

"New York, tomorrow afternoon."

George had been caught off guard by the request and he whispered, "Shit."

"What's wrong," Marvin mimed.

Waving him off, he returned to the phone and said, "It's short notice."

"That's how we roll," she replied.

"Can I get back to you?"

"No. I need an answer, now."

"Hold on."

"They want to meet in New York, tomorrow," he said to Marvin.

"Wow."

"She wants an answer," George pressed, the phone resting on his thigh.

"I'll make the arrangements and put it on my credit card, will we need a hotel?"

He lifted the phone to his ear and asked, "How long will we be there?"

"That depends," she said.

"So we'll need a hotel?"

"I'd make a reservation, just in case."

"OK, can you text me the address and time?"

"On its way."

The call ended, and a few moments later the incoming message tone dinged. He handed the device to Marvin so that he could find a hotel not far from the address.

George left his beloved Beetle with the Valet and they made their way up to Marvin's penthouse.

"Want a drink?" Marvin asked, as they both stood in a daze, looking out over the ocean.

"Too early for me," George replied.

"Not for me," Marvin breathed, as he walked to a free standing bar and poured himself two fingers of Grand Marnier.

"Better get going on the reservations," George encouraged.

"I'm on it," Marvin agreed, lowering his glass and removing a cellphone from his pocket.

While he made the call, George availed himself of the bathroom, and when he'd returned five minutes later his friend directed him to a seat on the couch.

"We have a direct flight leaving Miami at six this evening. Go home, pack a bag and meet me back here at three p.m.."

***

* * *

Manhattan, New York

9 P.M.

They'd taken a taxi from the airport and had checked into the Crowne Plaza Times Square hotel. The room provided two separate beds, a narrow bathroom that could accommodate only one at a time, and an office building view.

"Smells like mold," Marvin observed, as he tossed his overnight bag onto his chosen bed.

"Check out the bathroom ceiling, water stains," George called out.

"That explains the stink."

"Suck it up, we won't be here long."

"Should have paid for a better place," Marvin mumbled, kicking off his shoes and stretching out on the bedspread.

"Uh, I wouldn't do that if I were you," George advised.

"What's wrong?"

"Let's check for bedbugs."

Marvin flew from the mattress, whipping off his overnight bag in the process. And twenty minutes later, after having stripped both beds and having examined the mattress seams, pillows and anything else that could

potentially harbor the critters, they congratulated each
other for the negative results. The successful inspection
had led to a search for a place to dine, and following a few
calls to the desk they'd settled on the Piccola Cucina
Enoteca on Prince Street. The food and service had been
better than anticipated, but the mistake of the evening had
been the bottle of Cabernet that Marvin had insisted upon.
It had been a costly choice that, while having met with
Marvin's somewhat snobbish, palatal appeal, sported a
higher than normal alcohol content that had dictated their
return to the hotel for bedtime. They had planned to scope
out the meeting address that Virginia had supplied, but the
wine had scrubbed that idea as well. And to make matters
worse, the outdoor temperature had dropped precipitously
and snow was a real possibility. Neither of the men had
arrived with adequate, cold weather attire.

The meeting had been scheduled for one p.m.,
Sunday, at Salud Soho, on Thompson street. George set
the clock radio's alarm for eight a.m., tossed his shoes
across the room, hopped onto the bed and passed out fully
clothed.

Chapter Seven

Sunday, January 6th

8 A.M.

Scattered snow flurries drifted past the window, as George hit the alarm's snooze button. But Marvin, having awakened ten minutes before the appointed time, had steamed up the bathroom with his morning hot shower, and the noise from the water cascading down upon the thin metal tub had erased any thoughts of further sleep.

A blast of moist, warm air accompanied Marvin's exit from the bathroom and George recoiled to the opposite side of the room. "Use up all the hot water?" he sneered.

Marvin grinned, pulled a fresh pair of jockeys over his thighs, and replied, "Not accustomed to sharing my bathroom."

"You really should have that looked at," George advised, gesturing toward Marvin's left thigh and a prominent, black mole.

"It's nothing."

"Your funeral," he said, disappearing behind the restroom's closed door.

Marvin had continued dressing, his mind focused on finding a restaurant to quench the rumbling coming from his gut, when there was a knock at their door. He approached, but before he could call out, an envelope zipped across the floor from beneath the door. Assuming that it was their bill for the one night's stay, he ignored it and returned to a brochure advertising various local breakfast joints. Moments later, George exited and, noticing the yellow envelope, bent to retrieve it.

"What's this?" he asked.

Marvin shrugged, as he continued to flip through the glossy pages.

With the envelop in hand, George took a seat on the bed and tore it open. It contained a single, printed page, the content of which sent chills down his spine.

"We're in deep shit," he gasped, clutching the paper and beginning to sweat.

"What?"

"They know."

"Know what?"

"That we killed Freddie."

Marvin rocketed from the edge of the bed and stood staring, speechless, at George and exclaimed, "No way."

"This message," he advised, holding the paper above his head, "makes it clear … they know."

"We weren't followed when we'd dumped him, I'd

made sure of that," Marvin said.

"Apparently, not sure enough."

"Who sent it?"

"No signature, but I'm guessing the JPA."

"Makes sense, no one else would know our location."

"There's no mention of the meeting being cancelled, so I guess we go and listen to what they have to say."

"Maybe they'll view it as a good thing."

"How so?"

"Shows that we can take care of business."

They'd dressed and wasted as much time as possible at a local breakfast cafe. At twelve noon, unfamiliar with Manhattan, they took an Uber to SOHO and walked down Thompson Street until they'd spotted Salud.

It was a small venue that sold wraps, watermelon juice and other health food offerings. But glancing inside they'd suspected that the meeting was not going to take place within, so they waited just beyond the entrance. At exactly one p.m. a white Maserati SUV came to a stop just beyond the curb and a nattily dressed, middle aged man exited. In his gray, pinstriped suit, white shirt and flaming red tie, he seemed out of place for the not so ritzy neighborhood, but he aimed straight for them.

"Is that our guy?" Marvin asked, as the man walked

slowly in their direction.

George shrugged a, maybe.

When the man was within earshot, he extended his right hand to George and said, "Rafael."

"You are from...?

"Yes," the man interrupted, "let's walk."

George began to follow and added, to the back of the man's head, "This is Marvin."

"I know all about you both," he advised, turning to face the men, his small, tightly wrapped ponytail swinging ever so slightly.

As Rafael turned to continue walking, George took note of his firmly swept back, graying, black hair, and he wondered why a man with a Spanish sounding name would be connected with a Jewish organization. But they caught up with him and walked side-by-side.

Suddenly, Rafael said, in a soft voice, "We own you."

Startled, Marvin stuttered, "What do you mean?"

"We have photos of the body, the disposal site and the both of you making the deposit."

"But..." George started to complain.

"You will do our bidding," Raphael cut in.

I was afraid of this, George thought, responding, "What is it you want from us."

"It is my understanding that you had sought our assistance?"

"Yeah, that's right."

"We may be likeminded in that regard."

"And what does it involve?" George asked.

"Something that you've already demonstrated competence for."

"Freddie?" he said, not knowing if Rafael had been aware of the deceased's name.

"Precisely."

George glanced at Marvin, who was walking only inches from Rafael on his opposite side, and said, "Are there others in your organization?"

"Of course," Rafael chuckled.

"Do we get to meet them?"

"No."

"But..."

"We require deniability, even this meeting represents an exception to our normal mode of operation."

"You will remain our contact?"

"Depends."

"On what?" he asked, as they rounded a corner without stopping.

"Geography."

"I don't understand," George said.

Rafael stopped in the middle of the sidewalk, turned to face George and asked, "When was the last time that you'd read about us in a newspaper?"

George thought for a moment, as he gazed at Marvin's blank expression, and said, "Never."

"Exactly. We exist in the great ether."

"But the geography thing?"

"We have operatives all over this county, as well as others. To avoid exposure we employ them as go-betweens or, as your CIA terms it, controls."

"So it's Virginia."

"For the time being."

"So now what?" Marvin said, finding his voice.

"You go home and wait for orders."

"What about our thing?" George asked.

"The synagogue shoot up will have to wait until we have confirmation about the perpetrators."

"But..."

"You work for us now. Your personal vendetta must sit on the back burner."

"It's hardly personal," Marvin bristled.

"A poor choice of words, perhaps, but our needs take precedence."

Neither George nor Marvin had taken note of the white SUV trailing from behind. And Rafael, without a word, turned, waved his right hand in the air, stepped off of the curb and entered the vehicle. So quickly had it disappeared in traffic that neither man had had the time to record the tag number.

"We traveled twelve hundred miles for this?" Marvin whined, shivering from the chilly weather made worse by occasional gusts of wind.

"Not sure who came out ahead in this deal."

"It sure ain't us. But let's call an Uber and get the hell outta here."

They'd returned to the hotel, packed what little they'd arrived with, and made arrangements for a flight leaving several hours later.

Chapter Eight

Monday, January 8th

8 A.M.

The flight back to Miami had been met with considerable, and at times violent, turbulence. And immediately upon arrival at Miami International the pair had taken a taxi back to Marvin's condo, where George had hopped into his Beetle and returned home. He'd gone straight to bed, hoping to sleep away the effects of the flight, as well as his newly anointed status of JPA puppet. But nightmares of downed aircraft burning in the Everglades, along with visions of being carted off to prison for deeds done while acting as a JPA proxy, had made for a restless night.

The first streaks of morning light had found him seated at the edge of his bed, wondering how he'd allowed his life to go awry, when it'd struck him that a black cloud had appeared the moment he had found himself the only survivor of the temple massacre. I'd been meant to die, he said to himself. What other explanation could there have been, he thought, unless, revenge wasn't my idea and I was preordained to be the tool of retribution.

With a nagging headache, a frequent wakeup companion, he trotted off to microwave a cup of water, poured in a packet of instant coffee and, shirtless, leaned against the kitchen counter wearing only a pair of tattered Jockeys. A few sips and he realized that he'd left the cellphone in the bedroom and, with the cup still in hand, he padded back and retrieved it to check the morning news. It had suddenly become apparent that he'd slept through a notification indicating that a text message had arrived sometime during the early morning hours, and he sat down at the edge of the unmade bed to investigate.

The text said: *We have to meet. Ten a.m., same as last. Do not reply. V.*

He checked the cellphone's clock and realized that there wasn't enough time to notify Marvin, dress and get to Boca, so he lowered the cup, threw on a pair of jeans and a T-shirt, and brushed his hair on the way to the car.

He arrived ten minutes early, parked his car in one of the garages and quickstepped to the meeting place. He could see Virginia's blond hair blowing in the breeze as he approached—a thin, black leather portfolio dangling from her left hand—and he slowed his pace, so as not to appear overanxious.

"Where's the other guy?" she asked, when he was within earshot.

"Had a time conflict," he lied.

"What I have requires the both of you," she advised, motioning for him to walk with her.

"Not a problem."

"You sure about that?"

"Absolutely."

She stopped and removed a sealed envelop from within the case. "The details are inside," she instructed.

"Any hints?" he asked.

"Haven't got a clue," she said.

"They don't tell you?"

"I'm just the messenger, and the fewer heads in the loop the better."

"Anything else?"

She shook her head, as if to say, no, as she turned and crossed the street without so much as a wave good-bye.

Another wild-goose chase, he said to himself, as he slid the folded envelop into a pocket and walked back to the garage.

Seated in the Beetle, he removed his cellphone and hit the speed dial for Marvin.

The phone rang five times before a groggy sounding voice responded with, "Yeah?"

"You still asleep?"

"Rough night."

"Good thing I hadn't awakened you when I'd gotten the message."

"What message?"

"We've got a job to do."

"A job?"

"Go drink some coffee and I'll be at your place within the hour."

***

11:30 A.M.

North Miami

Begrudgingly, George handed the Beetle over to the valet and made his way up to Marvin's apartment. Two knocks later he was seated on the living room couch beside his friend.

"What's up," Marvin, now more awake, inquired.

George removed the folded envelop from his pocket and said, "This."

Marvin frowned.

George, who had yet to view the contents, broke the seal and removed two printed sheets of paper, as Marvin moved in close to join in the discovery.

"It's a friggin' list of names and addresses with

pictures," Marvin exclaimed.

"But the first two are in bold print."

"And?"

George lowered the first page to his left knee, his jaw dropping wide as the words on the second page struck home. "It's a termination list," he breathed.

"Shit, not what I'd signed up for," Marvin squealed, leaping from the couch, as if the pages were somehow toxic.

"Remember, they've got us by the short hairs."

"Killin' Freddie was one thing, but this is fucking crazy."

"I don't know all of these names, but a few are in the news every other day."

"Even if I agree, we don't have the intel or skills to pull it off."

"The two in bold are probably the priority marks, the others I'd guess are targets of opportunity."

"You'd guess? You make it sound like a board game," Marvin shouted, nervously wringing his hands.

"Look, there's no timeframe. We take it one at a time."

Marvin took a deep breath, paced around the living room, and then turned to face George and said, "Our thing is and was about revenge, not meaningless assassinations."

"Obviously not meaningless to the JPA."

"I don't give a shit."

"You'd better, because we either do what they ask, or we go straight to jail and do not pass go."

"Either way we're going to get busted."

"What do you suggest?"

"We run."

"Forever, because that's what it'll take."

"Are they offering protection?"

"Didn't say, didn't ask."

"I need some assurance."

"We're just pawns..."

"Speaking of which," Marvin interrupted, "are they paying our expenses?"

"Page two, last line says, call this number for materials."

"Tell them I want a bulletproof vest."

"Yeah, good luck with that."

Marvin walked to a window and locked his gaze onto the expansive, dark blue Atlantic. A cruise ship could be seen just approaching the horizon, and he wished that he could will himself aboard. A life of murderous crime had not been on my bucket list, he told himself. I have enough

money to keep myself going until I die, why in the world
did I get involved in George's revenge plot, he wondered.
And then, he answered his own question with the
realization that boredom had been the catalyst. Shit, I
should have found a hobby, or anything other than life as
an assassin, he thought, as he turned to George and
mumbled, "Where's number one located?"

"Not sure."

"What does the address say?"

"Minnesota."

"So?"

"Congress is in session."

"Wait a minute," Marvin bristled, "are you saying that
number one is a member of congress?"

George nodded, yes.

"Hell no, I'm not doin' it."

"Makes no difference to me."

"They have bodyguards."

"Not necessarily."

"And what do we do, walk up and shoot the person?"

"Maybe something more subtle."

"Like what, shove 'em in front of a bus?"

"Might work."

"There are cameras all over the city."

"We avoid them."

"From the looks of that list," Marvin advised, gesturing toward the two sheets of paper resting on the couch, "we'll never get it done."

"Explain."

"We're amateurs, we're gonna get caught."

"OK, here's a thought."

"Listenin'."

"What if we string them along, make it look like we're devising a plan that we never put into action."

"If that gets out, the Feds will take us down just the same."

"Well, that's all I've got."

"We could turn whistleblower," Marvin suggested.

"They have deniability."

"We have the list."

"It could have come from anywhere, and you can bet that the phone number is not traceable."

"Shit, shit, shit," Marvin mouthed, shaking his head in disgust.

"Ever been to D.C.?"

Chapter Nine

Wednesday, January 10

Washington Dulles Intl. Airport

10 A.M.

George had called the unlisted number that had been noted on the presumed, JPA kill list. A male, mechanical sounding voice had responded with instructions to visit an airport luggage storage facility, and to use the key that had been provided. When he'd indicated that he possessed no such key, the voice told him to check his pockets and had promptly disconnected.

For the Washington trip, the pair had dressed appropriately, with overcoats, leather gloves and a few sweaters. In addition, each man had packed a suit, or in George's case a sport coat, as well as dress shirts and a few ties. The out of character attire had come about as a result of Marvin's insistence, and had been justified by the need to assimilate.

With his hanging bag lying on the floor of the arrivals building he pocketed the cellphone, and it was at that moment that he'd become aware of the mysterious key.

He turned to Marvin and asked, "Did you see anyone stick their hand into my pocket?"

"No man, why?"

"How did this key get in there?"

Marvin shrugged and suggested, "Our coats were in the overhead bin."

"Hmm. I guess someone on the flight could have accessed it."

"What's it for?"

"A luggage locker."

"How do you know that?"

"Pay attention, the phone call."

"That means that we've been followed," Marvin acknowledged, suspiciously.

"These people are pros, and we're a pair of clowns."

They'd been directed to the storage facility, and after a few minutes of searching they'd located the numbered locker.

George gazed left and right, as Marvin blocked one side from any potential onlooker's view. He unlocked the cabinet and slowly removed a beige canvass suitcase.

"It's heavy," he observed.

"Open it," Marvin said.

"Here, where there may be cameras? Not gonna

happen."

They'd reserved a double at the Airport Marriott and had hailed a taxi for the brief ride. Once through the checkin procedure and safely behind their room's locked door, George hoisted the beige bag onto his chosen bed and proceeded to unpack the hanging bag.

"Aren't you curious?" Marvin questioned.

"Hell yes, but I don't want my clothes to crease."

"We're here for, you know what, but creases take front and center," he guffawed.

"OK," he breathed, reaching for the latch and flipping it open.

"Damn," they both exclaimed simultaneously.

Inside the bag were two, suppressed, .22 calibre Walther semiautomatic handguns with fully loaded magazines. In addition, wrapped in hand towels, were a pair of .40 caliber Glock 27 Gen4 pistols with fully packed 15 round magazines. Stuffed in the four corners, and held in place by strips of velcro, were four flash bang grenades.

"Are they expecting all out war?" Marvin gasped.

"What the hell are these for?" George marveled, rolling a flash bang in his right palm.

"Put that back," Marvin urged, it could explode.

George quickly returned it to its resting place, moving

a few feet away, as if it were infectious. "What the hell is it?" he asked.

"Seriously? It's a grenade," Marvin explained.

"Holy shit."

"Why...?"

"It gives off a blinding flash of light along with a loud bang. It's not supposed to be lethal, although it could wipe out your eardrums."

"We won't be needing them."

"Might be useful for a quick escape."

George lowered his body to the edge of the bed and asked, "Where did you get this knowledge from?"

"ROTC. Anything else in the bag?"

"A box of .22 caliber, long rifle, hollow point bullets, a box of .40 cal. hollow points, and ... wait, fake ID's and two thousand dollars in hundreds."

"Oh goody. Who am I?" he exclaimed, ignoring the cash.

George frowned at the one sporting his photo, and wondered where and when the picture had been acquired, as he tossed Marvin's New Mexico driver's license across the bed. "Do you recall being photographed?" George asked.

"No, but this is the same picture that's on my Florida

driver's license. Should have used it for check in."

"Shit, they must have hacked into the DMV."

"Did you expect any less?"

"You know what this means?"

Marvin offered a quizzical expression and George returned with, "They've got us on a tight leash, and they can yank it anytime they please."

With the firearms containing suitcase still open, Marvin said, "I guess we should talk about technique."

"Since when are you the expert?"

"I've done a lot of reading, and the .22 calibre pistol is a favorite of Israeli assassins."

"Bullets are kind of small," George observed, taking one out of the box.

"Those are hollow points, and they expand or fragment upon impact."

"But they're still small."

Marvin rose and jabbed his right index finger against the base of George's skull, saying, "Fire two or more rounds in here and it's all over."

"You sure?"

"That's what I've read."

"How do we get that close to a target?"

"Not sure."

"And these?" George asked, hefting one of the .40 caliber Glocks.

"Shoot someone with that and they're out of the game."

"Dead?"

"Depends on where the bullet lands."

"I've fired some handguns at the indoor range," George said.

"And?"

"I'd barely hit the target at twenty-five feet."

"That means we get up close and personal."

"We need a disguise, like a mask."

Marvin shook his head, no.

"Why not?"

"We'd stand out like cherries on whip cream."

"But we'll be identifiable."

"That's why we'll need to pick the right time and place."

"Gonna take some surveillance."

"That's a big word for you," Marvin laughed.

George frowned.

"Start with the top of the list."

"It's a woman."

"Got a problem with that?"

"A little."

"Get over it."

"Maybe we should rent a car to check her out, where she lives and all that."

"Food first."

***

Following a quick restaurant break, they'd located the Thrifty Rental agency and had driven off in a dark blue ford Fiesta. The list had provided the home and office addresses for the targets, and the first stop was a rental apartment building on North West Harvard Street. The six story, red brick structure loomed before them, as they sat with the engine running alongside of a blue postal box.

"Got an apartment number for her?" Marvin asked.

"Nope."

"Let's park and check out the security."

But as they neared the entrance it became apparent that the door was coded, and short of breaking the glass there was no way in.

"Now what?"

"We wait for someone to come or go."

"And if they ask where we're going?"

"We use the congresswoman's name."

"And why didn't she let us in?" George sneered.

"OK smart ass. We work for her and she told us to wait at her door."

"See that black dome up there?" George mentioned, nodding to an area above the door.

"Yeah, a camera. But who knows if anyone's watching."

"I don't see any guards and there's no concierge."

"Let's go," Marvin said.

"What happened to waiting for someone to open the door?"

"I'm putting this together on the fly, George. I don't think we should whack 'er in her apartment."

"There's no place to do it out here. "

"Yeah, could be a problem. We could take out the camera with a can of spray paint, but it's a long run to the getaway car."

"So we forget this place?"

"Think so."

"And her office?"

"Office buildings have people coming and going—too risky."

"And that leaves squat," George moaned, as they

walked back to the car.

"Not necessarily. We come back here before sunup and track her moves."

"You got all this from reading crime novels?"

"Pretty much."

Chapter Ten

Boca Raton

1 P.M.

Virginia had passed the morning hours on the telephone. Several of the calls had been to and from her trust fund administrator, and yet others had been related to a charity that she'd been forming that had just received a stamp of approval from the IRS. The organization had been created under the guise of an international healthcare entity, for the alleged purpose of providing superior nutrition to children of underdeveloped nations. But the charity had little to do with diet and everything to do with the funneling of money to a little known Palestinian group with a questionable background. The loosely organized body had distanced itself from the region's controlling political and military authority, Hamas. The schism had come about, not as the result of ideological differences but, rather, as a consequence of Hamas' unwillingness to allow them free will to deal with the *Jews* as they'd seen fit. The group had badged itself as the Palestinian Organized Front, or, POF.

Her role with the Palestinian plight had begun during her senior year at Stanford University. Despite the fact that she'd been taken under the wing of a local synagogue following the untimely death of her parents and had converted to Judaism, she'd been torn by the devastating picture that had been painted by a professor officiating a course in *Ethics in Society*. The lecturer had presented the case for the total subjugation of the Palestinian peoples, but while he had intimated that the Israelis had been the responsible agents, he'd deftly neglected to include the role that had been played by Hamas in the subjection of its own people to their control. And given the extremely liberal history of her chosen university, no one had ever questioned the professor's dubious facts. As such, Virginia had mentally separated the people who had supported her during the darkest hours, from those who resided in a nation thousands of miles away.

Her association with the JPA had come about in a rather circuitous fashion. During the final months of her senior year she had been befriended by a young woman of Middle Eastern origin. Devra, a nineteen year old alleged Palestinian, had occupied a chair close to that of Virginia's in her societal ethics class. And apparently, the nature of Virginia's class questions had signaled a potential willingness to assist in her uncle's cause, the POF. Due to her Stanford indoctrination into the world of extreme political correctness, in concert with an element of loneliness, Virginia had been ripe for the picking and a friendship had been formed. At first, it'd been the simple matter of two friends sitting together at the cinema, and then dinners together several times per week, followed by the escalation to evenings at Virginia's apartment studying for finals. And then, down came the hammer. Devra began to slowly propagandize her uncle's and her own common cause, that being the purported Palestinian occupation. The bond had grown, and Devra's influence had increased to the extent that together they'd devised a plan to subvert the so-called occupiers by any means possible.

Virginia had begun to once again frequent the same synagogue that had carried her through emotional times. One Friday evening, following Shabbat services, she'd approached the rabbi with a question.

"Rabbi, is there some way that I can repay you for all that you and your congregation have done for me?" she'd asked.

"You can make a donation," the Rabbi had suggested.

"Of course, but I was hoping for something more personal," she'd said.

The rabbi had stroked his greying beard and motioned for her to follow him to his sanctuary. Once behind closed doors he'd offered her a chair, and asked, "How far are you willing to go?"

"Distance?" she'd asked.

The rabbi shook his head, and replied, "No. I mean in terms of your actions."

"Within reason, I have no limits."

"There are some people who might be interested."

"In what way?"

"That's for them to explain."

Two days later she'd received the call that the rabbi had told her to expect.

"Hello?" she'd said, tentatively, noticing that the caller ID had indicated, UNKNOWN.

"You are Virginia?" the man had asked.

"And you are?"

"Rafael."

"How can I help you?" she'd asked, still unsure of the caller's purpose.

"The rabbi had spoken highly of you."

"Oh, yes. I've been expecting your call."

Rafael had kept the call brief, but had indicated that over the following weeks she would be tested with menial tasks of increasing complexity. And apparently her actions had been deemed acceptable, as she'd been told that at some point she'd be called upon to act on their behalf. And after nearly a year of silence the request had come in the form of the meeting with George Katz and Marvin Freed.

Her college days had ended, but her friendship with Devra had endured, and although the Palestinian had relocated to Minnesota, they'd kept a regular conversational schedule, replete with innuendos and coded words. During one such conversation, Devra had congratulated Virginia for her ingenuity in establishing a connection with the JPA. Virginia had asked for suggestions regarding this new association and had been told to work her way into a position of trust.

Chapter Eleven

Wednesday, January 10th

3 P.M.

New York, N.Y.

Aaron Tapiero, a sephardic jew, code named Rafael, aka Andrew Cosgrove, had just balled up the waxed paper covering from his already consumed jumbo, Italian sub, aimed, and had thrown it across the room to a waiting trash bin. "Bulls eye," he'd called out, as the projectile drifted into the pail.

"Too bad your toilet aim isn't so good," his Israeli accented female counterpart, Bina, sneered.

"You're just jealous that you have to sit," he laughed.

"But you don't have to clean up after me," she giggled, continuing the folly.

Rafael belched, finished the last of his diet coke, and asked, "Anything from those two schlimazels (inept) from Miami?"

"No, I've been told to sit on them."

"They'd seemed a little anxious when we'd met."

"Wouldn't you?"

"I guess if I were a schmuck from the south looking for revenge, and I'd turned a dangerous corner, I'd be a little leery."

"They have no idea what awaits them," Bina mumbled.

"You know something I don't know?" Rafael asked, swiveling his chair to face her.

"Just a suspicion."

"And?"

"Well, when the Mossad allows a puppet's strings to fall slack, they're usually preparing to yank them taught."

"I get it, giving them a false sense of security."

"Or time to accept the inevitable."

"Meaning?"

"They're on the hook for a homicide, no reason to stop there."

"So who's next?" he asked, with a big grin.

"I have no fucking clue."

The secure telephone rang and they both stared at it.

"Are you going to answer that?" Bina said.

Rafael grimaced, reached for the receiver and replied with the scripted, "Yes?"

"Romeo, alpha, Foxtrot, alpha, echo, lima," the voice quickly droned, the phonetic spelling for Rafael's code name.

"Affirmative," he replied, the required response.

"We have traffic."

"Receiving," he said, reaching for a cellphone like device that was spitting out an encrypted message.

"Confirm," the voice demanded.

Rafael read the message twice, his eyes widening as he glanced at Bina for support, and replied, "Confirmed."

The line went silent.

"What the hell was that about?" she asked.

"Looks like we have a mole," he said, with a surprised expression.

Bina leaned over to read the damning message and asked, "Who do you think?"

"There's only the two of us, and I know it's not me," he claimed, his eyes aimed at her's.

"It isn't me, " she bristled.

"Then we have to start looking elsewhere."

"The two schmucks?" she chanced.

"Unlikely."

"Then whom?"

"There are other operations like ours," he advised.

"But the message came to us, not San Francisco or elsewhere."

"We don't know that."

"Call one."

"That's against protocol."

"Then what?"

"We have to assume that the message was meant for us alone."

"OK, who else do we have in our network?" she asked.

"You know the answer."

"The Boca chick," she breathed.

He nodded a, yes.

"So we bring her here?"

"And then what?"

"We break her down."

"What, waterboard her?"

"That's too easy," she said.

"I think we should play this safe."

"No. The military has taught me to be quick and silent."

"What if the home office is wrong, you want to neutralize an innocent?"

"Better than have our purpose compromised."

"I have an idea," he offered, tapping a pencil on the desktop.

"Oh, I can't wait," she ridiculed.

"Let's activate the two schmucks."

"Without consulting Tel Aviv?"

"We'd been given leeway to act before."

"This is different."

"The message didn't tell us how to ferret out the mole, just that we had to do it."

"Shit. We can burn for this," she said.

"And if we don't get it done?"

"We burn just the same."

***

At that same moment in time, George and Marvin were seated in a rental car, preparing to leave the location of number one on their list. George had just released the parking brake when his cellphone began to play a jingle. He took his foot from the accelerator and reached for it.

"Hello?" he said.

"This is your lucky day," a voice claimed.

"Who is this?" George asked, glancing at his front seatmate .

"Rafael."

"About this list..." George began to say, when he was cut off.

"List?"

"Yeah, the list you people made up."

There was a moment of hesitation and then, "What kind of list?"

"You don't know?"

"Answer my question."

"Not sure I should be discussing this on the phone."

"OK, give me a hint."

George thought for a second or two and then replied, "It's a list of sick dogs that need to be put down."

"Where are you?" Rafael asked, with a tone of concern.

"Seriously? Washington, D.C."

"Go home, immediately," Rafael ordered.

"But..."

"We did not compile that list."

"Are you kidding?" George said, his face contorted to the extent that Marvin leaned in closer.

"Then who?" he shouted.

"Take the first flight out and we'll contact you in the morning," Rafael demanded, and hung up.

"What's going on?" Marvin asked, anxiously.

"We've been played."

"What do you mean?"

"Someone else created the list."

"But the Boca babe gave it to us."

"Yeah. I think we're in some real deep shit."

"What the?"

"You've read spy novels, what does it sound like to you?" he said, his tires squealing, leaving black marks on the concrete as he pulled out into traffic.

"She's a double agent?" he said, with a shocked expression.

"Would seem so."

"Now what?"

"We get the hell outta Dodge."

"What about the guns?"

"We leave 'em."

"They have our ID's."

"What time is it?"

Marvin gazed at his gold Patek and said, "Three-thirty."

"We'll remove the ID's an' stuff the suitcase in the utility closet near the elevator. It'll be found, but we'll be gone by then."

"OK, step on it."

Back at the hotel, they packed their overnight bags, shoved the firearm containing case into the mop closet and checked out. There was a flight leaving for Miami scheduled to leave at six p.m., and they'd secured two first class seats, the only pair available. Rather than sit around the hotel and risk being nailed for leaving the gun containing suitcase behind, they went directly to the airport to await their flight. And as they nervously anticipated the boarding call, Marvin's cellphone rang.

"Who's calling?" George asked.

"Says, unknown."

"Don't answer it."

But Marvin, ever the curious one, hit the accept button on his iPhone and said, "Hello?"

"We're watching you," the metallic sounding voice said.

"Who is this?"

"You will do as told and fulfill your task."

"What task?" Marvin said, as George urged him to hang up.

"The list of names."

"Who are you?"

"You know."

"I want to hear it."

"Not on the phone."

"Then where?"

"Over your left shoulder."

Marvin lowered the phone and turned, but the only

person visible was an elderly woman cradling a small dog.

"I don't see you," he said, but the phone had gone dead.

"Are you fucking nuts," George said, "I told you not to answer."

"Wanted to find out who set us up."

"By getting us killed."

"We're in a public place."

"Planes can be made to crash, you moron."

"I didn't say anything to anger the caller."

"What did he say?"

"That they're watching us."

"Then they already know that we're bolting."

"We're dead meat."

Just then, the overhead intercom called out their flight and they took off running.

Chapter Twelve

Miami International Airport

8:45 P.M.

The two men had sat in silence throughout the flight, each engulfed in his own version of terror. But they had arrived on time and without incident, and as they waited for the car service to bring them both back to Marvin's condo, George finally spoke up. "What the hell have we gotten ourselves involved in?" he said, to no one in particular.

"Been asking myself the same question," Marvin replied.

"Not sure its worth the effort anymore."

"Doesn't look like we have a choice."

"It began as a simple vendetta. Find the temple perps, kill 'em and take off."

"Yeah, a fantasy at best."

"But this shit is so confusing that its giving me a headache," George moaned, as he nodded toward the ride that had just pulled to the curb.

They gave the driver their destination and sat back for the trip. They had already decided to avoid any conversation until they were safely ensconced in Marvin's apartment, and other than responding to the driver's questions, they'd suffered through his ear shattering Hip Hop music in silence.

Back in Marvin's living room, George stretched out on the couch and suggested, "The caller who'd said that they'd been watching us, hit the redial."

"You sure?"

"Nothin' to loose."

Marvin produced his cellphone and did as requested.

"Anything?" George asked

"Not a working number."

"Big surprise."

"Who do you think they are?" Marvin asked.

"No clue, but I'd bet that the Boca babe knows."

"Let's set up a meet."

"Too risky."

"Why?"

"If she's in cahoots with whomever sent the list, we could walk straight into an ambush."

"Not in a public place."

"So they follow us to a not so public place."

"OK, forget the meeting."

George removed his right sock and began to knead his toes, and in the process had a thought. "If we've made the connection to Virginia, the JPA has as well," he said, matter of factly.

"How does that help us?"

"It's their mess, let them deal with it."

"Have you forgotten where we stand with them?"

"No, but we don't have their resources."

"What if they simply decide to take her out and call it a day?"

"First of all, we really don't know what they're capable of. But if my initial contact wasn't blowing smoke up my ass, the JPA won't allow this incident to pass unanswered."

"And that gives me an idea," Marvin exclaimed.

"Go for it."

"Call your Israeli contact."

"And tell her what, exactly?"

"You're good at conversation, something will come to mind."

"I'm not sure we can trust anyone right now."

"What have you got to lose?"

George sat back playing mental chess for a few minutes and then withdrew his phone and dialed. He'd already decided not to leave a message, and after nine rings was about to hang up, when a sleepy voice mumbled, "Shalom."

"Adina, it's George, from Miami."

"Nice to hear from you," she yawned.

"Hope you're well?"

"Yes, I'm home recouping."

"An illness?"

"Slipped into a trench and fractured a tibia."

"Ouch."

"Got a big ugly cast on my leg."

"Sorry to bother you."

"No bother. Actually, all I've been doing is sleep, so conversation is good."

"I've made contact with your friends."

There was brief interval of silence, as if she'd been waiting for more, but she replied with, "Oh, yes, my friends in America."

George analyzed the tone of her voice, and it appeared to him that she was either stalling for time, or was trying to avoid mention of the organization over the phone, so he asked, "Is it OK to talk?"

"I hear that Florida can be chilly in January," she said.

George moved the phone an inch away from his ear and shook his head for Marvin's benefit, but replied, "It can be. You must be in pain, should I call again later?"

"I'll call you back," she said, and terminated the call.

"What was that all about?" Marvin asked, pouring

himself a glass of Merlot and offering the same to George.

"I think there may be a problem," he said, sipping from the offered glass.

"Oh shit, now what?" Marvin breathed.

"Her phone may be bugged."

"Or maybe it's our phones that are compromised."

"Either way, she didn't want to talk about the JPA."

"Then she's out of the picture."

"No, said she'd call me back."

"But if our phones are...," he began to say, when his wall mounted, kitchen landline began to ring.

"Answer it," George said.

"I don't give out that number," Marvin informed, his face morphing into a worrisome expression.

George rose, gave his friend a disgusted look, and walked into the kitchen. He grabbed the receiver and said, "Yes?"

"It's me, Adina."

"How did you find this number?"

"I'm not the person that I've appeared to be, George."

"That's becoming apparent," he said, waving for Marvin to come hither.

"Your cellphone's GPS allowed me to pinpoint your location—don't ask me how—the telephone number was the easy part."

"You're not in the army?"

"Not in the conventional sense."

"Then what?"

"Use your imagination."

"Mossad?"

"Something like that," she admitted.

"And your friends at the JPA?"

"Let's just say that we talk."

"They work for you?"

"Not important. But what is important is that you and your friend are in danger."

"We'd figured as much."

"The real problem is that we do not have a handle on their origin."

"What should we do?"

"Rafael will be in contact."

"Will the JPA offer protection?"

"Are you familiar with your CIA's designation of NOC?"

"No."

"It means non-official cover and, among other things, it implies the deniability of a NOC's existence. As it pertains to deniability, you are both NOC equivalents."

"You're hanging us out to dry?" he exclaimed, with a soft whine.

"We'll try to shield you, but we cannot acknowledge engagement with American citizens."

"What if we come to you?"

"Your status remains the same."

"So, we're fucked."

"You had to know that your original quest had been dangerous."

"But this has nothing to do with our revenge."

"As you Americans say, it is what it is. We have to deal with the present, and it means that you keep a low profile until Rafael calls."

"Are our cellphones being bugged?"

"Don't know, but Rafael will call on your number and provide a secure means of returning his call."

"Anything else?"

"Yeah, good luck," she said, as the line went dead.

"So?" Marvin asked.

"We need new phones."

"That's it?"

"And we sit tight until the guy from New York calls."

"What about protection?"

"There is none, we apparently don't exist."

"Great. I'd been planning on getting laid before I die," Marvin admitted.

"Do what you always do, call for delivery."

"I'm gettin' tired of escorts, I want something real."

George chuckled and came back with, "What we're facing is real enough for me. But I need to go home for a change of clothes."

"I'm not goin' anywhere."

"I won't be long."

"Not sure I want to be alone with this shit hangin' over our heads, hurry back."

George had reluctantly left his car with the valet, and as he waited for it to arrive from wherever they'd stored it, he realized that he was a living character from the many spy movies that he'd watched on late night cable. But unlike those actors, he had no script and no idea what might be around the next corner.

"Your car, sir," the valet said, as he extended his right hand for the anticipated tip.

George reached into his pocket and removed a five dollar bill, and as he did, the airport luggage locker key fell to the ground, an all too real reminder of the kill list and what he'd been willing to do.

He slammed the Beetle's door shut with a bang,

stepped on the accelerator and headed for home.

Chapter Thirteen

Thursday, January 11th

7 A.M.

George had fallen asleep upon arriving home the night before. He had intended to pack some clothes and head right back to Marvin's place, but fatigue had ruled and he'd collapsed on his couch, shoes and all. Marvin had called several times, and in his stupor, George had explained that an immediate return trip had been out of the question. But awakening at sunup on the couch had served as an ugly reminder of their predicament, and he'd reached for his cell phone.

"Marv?" he said, when a hoarse voice responded following a few rings.

"Yeah. Think I'm gettin' a cold."

"I'm comin' over."

"Mind stopping for some bagels and lox?"

"No problem," he said, and slipped the phone into a pocket.

But as he closed the door and turned the key to set the lock on his apartment, the phone began to vibrate against his thigh. He reached for it and checked the caller ID. UNKNOWN caller was displayed on the screen. He hesitated, but tapped the talk icon and waited for a voice.

"Rafael," the voice announced.

George quickly slapped the phone to his ear, and said, "Been waitin' for your call."

"Look under the passenger seat of your vehicle."

"For what?"

"A package."

"Containing?"

"You'll figure it out."

"What about protection?"

"Follow the instructions in the package."

"And?"

"We'll see about protection."

"Can you tell me what's really going on?"

There was a moment of silence and then, "You're in the game."

"What the fuck does that mean?" George shouted, angrily.

"Cat and mouse."

"Don't understand."

"You will," Rafael said, and terminated the call.

It gets more confusing by the minute, George said to himself, as he scurried to the car, checked for onlookers and boarded the driver's seat. Convinced that no one was watching, he leaned over and reached beneath the passenger seat. His fingers met with an overstuffed, Manilla envelop and he pulled the weighty package from beneath the seat and sat with it in his lap for a few seconds. Following another look about, he opened it. His jaw dropped, when a fully loaded, noise suppressed 9mm Glock slipped between his legs, along with what appeared to be a well used Samsung cell phone. He'd yet to have noticed the single, printed sheet of paper that had remained within the envelop, and he shook the presumed empty package. The paper floated to the space beneath his feet and he reached for it and began reading:

The phone is encrypted, a single telephone number is in its memory. Call that number when the mission is complete.

What mission, he wondered, as he was about to crumple the page, when the sunlight piercing the windshield revealed several more lines of print, more an impression than typical, dark lettering. He struggled to read it but its intent was clear. They were to terminate a threat—the Boca contact, Virginia. Holy shit, he thought. I can't do that. On the other hand, she clearly played a role in setting us up with that list of names.

He'd almost forgotten the bagels and lox, but he'd

hit the brakes and made a u-turn. Squeezing into a parking space a few feet from the deli, he hid the gun and phone back beneath the passenger seat and rushed inside.

Twenty minutes later he'd arrived at Marvin's high-rise, but rather than give the car to the valet and risk discovery of his newly acquired tool of dispatch, he parked down the block, locked the car and rode the elevator to the penthouse.

"Where the hell have you been, I'm starving," Marvin exclaimed, dislodging the bag from George's fingers.

"Rafael called."

At the sound of the man's name Marvin lowered the knife that he'd been using to lather a layer of cream cheese on a bagel half and frowned. "And?" he asked.

"You're not gonna like it."

"Spit it out."

"We have another target to hit."

"You're certain that it was Rafael this time?"

"Yes."

"OK, who's the victim?"

"The Boca babe."

Marvin almost choked on his own saliva, and when his coughing fit had subsided he cried out, "No way."

"She'd given us the kill list."

"It had been in a sealed envelop, maybe she didn't know what was in it."

"Think about it. She didn't get it from the JPA, so who gave it to her?"

Marvin took a bite of his bagel and lox combo, chewed, swallowed and replied, "OK, confirmed, she's a double agent."

"She had to have known that we were being set up."

"Alright, how do we do it?"

"Rafael sent a few gifts or, rather, one of his disciples put them in my car."

"Gifts?"

"A silenced gun and an encrypted cell phone."

"Shit, where are they."

"Still in the car."

"Is there a timeframe?"

"ASAP."

"And I suppose you asked about protection."

"Yeah. He said, mission first."

"Sounds like the carrot and the stick."

"But it's all we've got."

"We could leave the country," Marvin suggested.

"I don't have the resources to run for the rest of my

life."

"Yeah, and we don't even know who we're running from."

"I've been thinking about that."

"Me too, but I've come up blank."

"I think that we were in the wrong place at the wrong time."

"Meaning?"

"The meeting with Virginia might have been entirely opportunistic, for her."

"Still not gettin' it."

"I'm guessing that whomever she's working for needed leverage with or against the JPA, and we're it."

"But we're nobodies."

"Consider this. They, whomever they are, make up a list of targets, knock off a few and then plan to blame it on the JPA. But along come you and I, with no real connection to the JPA, but one that can be attested to by Virginia, or even Adina..."

"Wait, I thought that the Israeli woman was your friend?"

"Right now, we can only trust ourselves. Anyway, we take the fall for the hits and the JPA gets blamed. Sound good?"

"Too good. But there could be another explanation."

"I'm listening."

"I don't have one, just saying that something less obvious may be in play."

"Suppose so, but right now I'm going with my story."

"Getting back to the mission, we have to arrange a meeting with her and it has to be somewhere private."

"Yeah, we need to work on that, as well as a compelling reason for the meet."

***

12 P.M.

George had retrieved the pistol and phone from his parked vehicle and had hidden both in Marvin's apartment. They'd called a local pizza delivery service for their lunch, and as George sat opposite Marvin, removing pieces of pepperoni from his pizza, he noticed a sticky note adherent to the bottom of his slice.

"You believe this?" he squawked, "they left a piece of paper on my slice."

"Sucks—wait a minute," Marvin advised from across the small diameter table, "what's that writing on it?"

George shook off a few drops of red sauce and

examined the yellow sticky. "It says, abort."

"Abort? Lemme see that."

George passed him the square and Marvin scrutinized it with the eye of a wannabe detective. "This was meant for us," he said.

"You don't know that."

"What else could it mean, abort a pizza?" Marvin exclaimed.

"Maybe pizza boy had knocked someone up."

"And accidentally stuck it in our box. You answered the door, who delivered the pie?"

"Some guy."

"A little more detail would help."

"OK. Forty or so, white male, thin, black hair. That's all I've got."

"I order from Pudgies Pizza all the time, and the delivery person is a young girl."

"Maybe the note was for her?" George said.

"If she'd been pregnant her father would have killed her, he owns the store."

Marvin reached for the wall phone, punched in a speed dial number and waited. "Angelo, it's your favorite Penthouse customer. Yeah, yeah, the pizza's fine, but who's the new delivery boy?"

"Really. Your daughter's boyfriend is forty years old?"

George could hear the sound of rage coming across the line, as Marvin moved the receiver away from his ear and then replaced it, responding with, "Sorry, I could have been mistaken."

As he returned the phone to the wall, he raised one brow, stared down at George and admitted, "Something's not right."

"Meaning?"

"His daughter has the flu and her fifteen-year-old boyfriend is helping with deliveries."

"Well, that was no fifteen-year-old."

"OK, you have to use Rafael's phone and confirm the abort."

"But I was specifically told to call only upon mission complete."

"There may not be a mission, so make the call."

George retrieved the phone from its hiding place, hesitated a few moments and then hit the speed dial. It rang once, and then, "Speak," a voice demanded.

"Are you Rafael?"

"And if I am?"

"There was a message in my pizza..." George began

to explain, immediately realizing how ridiculous he sounded.

"You are to stand down," Rafael cut in.

"So, no mission?"

"Not now."

"Is there an explanation?"

"Yes, but you are not entitled."

"What about the promised protection?"

"There'd been no promise," he said and terminated the call.

George pocketed the phone and walked back to the kitchen, where Marvin was anxiously waiting. "As they say in the movies, we're out in the cold," he advised.

"And the mission?"

"I was told to stand down."

The two men sat at the round table staring at each other, until George piped up with, "I'd asked for an explanation and he'd said that I couldn't have one."

"Maybe it's need to know shit," Marvin suggested.

"Yeah, but we need to know."

"I'm Ok with not having to kill someone."

"Doesn't make sense. They put a gun in my car, tell us to kill a specific person and then quickly change their minds."

Marvin shrugged, as if he really didn't care.

"Well, we have bigger problems to think about," George breathed.

"Without their help there's no way we can figure out who set us up."

George considered his friend's observation and replied, "Yes, there is."

"How?"

"Our mission just changed."

Chapter Fourteen

2 P.M.

With no support forthcoming from the JPA, the two men had concluded that their lives depended upon finding the person, or persons responsible for creating the kill list. And while they had been told to scrap the plan to terminate the Boca representative, they had not been denied the ability to organize an operation of their own.

"OK, I'll send her a text and tell her that we have to meet," George said.

"Make it a very public place."

"Agreed."

"And tell her that it has to happen today," Marvin suggested.

"What's the rush?"

"Less time for her to set a trap."

"Good point."

"But tell me again why we can't just forget about the list and get on with our lives?"

"The connection."

"Huh?"

"Boca babe gave us the list, she knows who we are and approximately where we reside. If she knows, the list makers know. And unless they're a bunch of halfwits, they'd have to assume that we'd want to know where the list came from. That's the connection."

"Shit. We're loose ends."

"Exactly."

"So why haven't they taken us out already?"

"Good question," George admitted, as he reached for his cell phone and paused, adding, "where should we meet?"

"Tell her the same place as before, but when we're a few minutes out we'll send her another text with a different location."

"OK. That should minimize the chances for an ambush, but we need a second, public location."

"Abe and Louis steak house on Glades, that place is alway buzzing."

"That'll work," George agreed, as he sent off the text for her to meet them at 3 p.m.

The response—*will meet at 3:15 p.m*—came back several minutes later.

"We're on," George said, "let's get going."

Before they'd left the apartment, George had collected the suppressed pistol and had hidden it inside of a black leather *man bag* that Marvin had supplied. Rather than take his old VW Beetle, they'd taken Marvin's Porsche and had made their way to I95 North.

***

2:50 P.M.

They'd arrived sooner than anticipated, and rather than risk being spotted in Mizner, they'd gone directly to the steak house, self parked and waited in the car. At exactly 3:05 p.m., George sent off another text indicating that there had been a change of plans, and for her to meet them at Abe and Louis. As they waited with the engine running, George stuck his right hand inside of the man bag and gently wrapped his fingers around the pistol's grip. He had no intention of using it unless their lives appeared to be in danger, but the cool metal against his hand offered some degree of comfort. At 3:20 p.m., a white Mercedes 550SL pulled into the parking lot and slowly rolled to a stop fifty or so feet from their vehicle.

"Is that her?" Marvin asked.

"Not sure. I see long blond hair covered by a big green hat."

George twisted in his seat and squinted. "That's her," he said, as he reached for the door release and exited, followed by Marvin. They could hear her car's engine idling as they approached, a sign of her readiness for a quick escape. And when he was within a few feet of the driver's side window, George grinned and waved. She motored down her window.

"What's this meeting about?" she asked, in a business like manner.

"You really want to have this discussion out here?" he replied.

She smirked, and said, "Let me park."

Together, the trio entered the relatively empty restaurant and were guided to a large, half-moon shaped booth.

"Why am I here?" she insisted.

George gazed briefly at Marvin and replied, "The list."

"What list?" she said.

"Don't play dumb, you had to have known what was in the envelop that you'd given me."

She hesitated, bit her lower lip and replied, "I was just the messenger."

"Right, and I'm the Golem."

Her face took on an expression of confusion, but she appeared to ignore the statement and said, "The JPA had provided the envelop."

"We both know that's a lie."

"No, I'm telling the truth."

"Then why were they surprised to hear about its contents?"

"Once again, I was just the messenger."

Marvin nudged his friend and offered, "Who else are you working for?"

"I've said all that I'm prepared to say," she replied, as she rose to depart. But George had grasped her right wrist and she thundered back down into the banquet.

"We're not finished," George informed.

It had been barely perceptible, but Marvin had noticed that the apparently rock solid Virginia had begun to sweat, and she reached for a cloth napkin and patted her upper lip. "I could call out … the police would be summoned," she advised.

"Great idea," George said, "I'm sure that they'd love to see the kill list that you'd supplied."

"You can't prove that it came from me."

"So you were aware of its existence," Marvin pressed.

She pushed into the seat, her back erect, and she whispered, "I had nothing to do with that list."

"You'd presented it to me and that makes you an accessory," he said, not knowing if his taunt would hold up in a court of law.

"What do you want from me?" she hissed.

Just then, a male server arrived and asked about their orders. Marvin said that they needed more time and the server disappeared.

"What I want from you is the origin of the document."

She exhaled a blast of air that was felt across the table, and said, " I can't do that."

"Can't or won't?" Marvin growled.

"The latter."

"Unacceptable," George warned.

"Either you let me go, or I start screaming, your choice."

George had carried the small leather bag into the restaurant and had placed it upon his lap. As he glared at Virginia, he unzipped the case, removed the pistol and draped his napkin over the top of its slide. "Pretend that you'd dropped something and look under the table," he advised.

She appeared confused, but did as requested. When her head had risen above the tabletop, her now crimson cheeks glowed with the intensity of a heated branding iron. "OK, stay calm," she breathed.

"You know where it's aimed, so answer the question."

"It came from a competing group."

"A name, gimme a name."

"They don't have a name," she lied.

"If we," he nodded toward Marvin, "know that you're a double team player, the JPA must know. And I understand that they're not big on second chances."

"That's my problem."

George had not been expecting that answer, and he'd been taken by surprise, as he watched the leverage that he thought that he'd held dissipate like a puff of smoke.

Marvin had remained quiet throughout the brief discourse, but his mind was a whirl with rage, and he said, "We can take you out anytime we want."

"But that's not our goal," George assured her.

"What is your goal?" she stuttered.

"Your people set us up for a fall," he explained, working on his hunch regarding the list and the impossibility of completing all of the requested kills, adding, "and since we haven't carried out the request, we assume that we've become targets ourselves. We need to know who's after us."

Marvin leaned in closer and whispered into George's ear, "It's the JPA that we'd assumed were to be the fall guys."

"And by extension, the low hanging fruit, you and I," he whispered in reply.

The pistol's muzzle was still pointed at Virginia's crotch, and although she couldn't see it from her vantage point, she visibly squirmed in her seat. "I really need to leave," she said.

"Make her an offer," Marvin whispered.

George considered the possibilities, and finally decided to use the trump card that the JPA had unknowingly provided. "There's a contract out for you," he said, a half truth, given the original JPA order.

She smiled, and replied, "Very funny."

"Not funny at all."

"You're serious?" she asked.

He nodded a, yes.

"How would you know that?"

"Because we'd been given the job."

"If that's true, why am I still alive?"

"We'd turned it down," he lied again.

"OK, I get it," she moaned, "you want an exchange of information."

He nodded affirmatively.

"You first," she said.

George gazed at Marvin for support, but none was apparently forthcoming, so he swung for the bleachers with, "You're on the JPA's radar."

Her brows furrowed and her lips puckered, but she exhaled and replied, "It was bound to happen, and you've already implied that."

"Why was it bound to happen?"

"Trust is like a carbonated drink, it's great until the fizz is gone."

"What exactly does that mean?"

"You figure it out,"she laughed nervously, rising to leave.

Marvin shot from his seat and blocked her path, provoking a wary stare from a nearby server. "Family argument," he fibbed, as Virginia slid back into the booth with Marvin now seated at its outer edge, preventing another attempted departure.

"We had an agreement," George growled.

"Oh, what the hell," she breathed, "how many times can I be killed."

"We're waiting."

"The POF, that's who you should be looking at. Can I go now?"

"Who the fuck are they?"

Another nervous giggle escaped Virginia's lips, and she replied, "The Palestinian Organized Front."

"You're a Muslim?" he said with a tone of incredulity.

"No."

"Then what the hell are you doing?"

"Helping some needy people."

"You're disgusting," Marvin blurted.

"That's your opinion."

"It's no wonder they wanted you dead," George said.

"You used the past tense," she observed.

"Just a slip of the tongue."

"No, you've been very careful with your language. I'm guessing that they've cancelled the contract."

George ignored her speculative statement, and said, "You can go, but watch your back. There may be others on your trail."

Chapter Fifteen

Thursday, 6 P.M.

Broome Street, New York

Rafael had spent the night monitoring the computer screens and recording the occasional communication traffic that had originated from the Mossad's Tel Aviv headquarters. Both he and Bina had been alternating seventy-two hour shifts in the chilly, red bricked basement facility, and while they'd shared the facility during the daytime, the nights belonged to whomever's name appeared on the schedule. It was nearing the end of his watch, and as usual, fatigue was beginning to wield its ugly head.

Tel Aviv had set up a fairly regular communication schedule, and when the traffic had come through at six-thirty p.m., Rafael had temporarily ignored it in favor of the stuffed cabbage that he'd been defrosting in the microwave. Having consumed his dinner, he'd just placed the reusable plastic dish in the sink, when it'd occurred to him that he hadn't acknowledged receipt of the transmission, so he dropped the soapy sponge and rushed to the screen. The messages were automatically encrypted upon transmission and unencrypted by the receiving hardware/software, and usually contained information regarding the arrival and departure of agents within the U.S., financial data pertinent to their New York operations, and occasional operative orders. But this message represented such a departure from the norm that it had required several reads:

Flash. Operative V compromised. Allegiance in question. Control unclear. Acknowledge.

That's she's been compromised has already been established, he said to himself, wondering why the repetition. But the fact that Tel Aviv has not established who she's working for is troublesome. They've got tentacles everywhere, determining her loyalty should be a simple matter. Either there's something they're not telling me, or she's really deep cover, he mused, typing the word *acknowledged* and hitting send. Shit, she could be working for any number of bad actors.

He glared at the computer screen, hoping for an addendum to the communique that offered some direction, even an unreasonable demand, but the machine did not comply. They know that she isn't with us, why was I told to stand down, he wondered. I'm a fucking intelligence agent, I should be able to figure this out, he screamed at himself. But I'm stuck in this ass smelling basement without a view of the outside world—I can't think straight.

Drumming his fingers on the computer desk he had a thought. He reached for the encrypted cellphone that the pair had used to communicate with each other when out of sight, and dialed his partner.

"Bina?"

"Ugh, don't tell me you ran out of toilet paper again," she groaned.

"No," he chuckled, "we have a problem and I need your help."

"I still have a few hours of fresh air to breathe," she complained.

"There's stuffed cabbage," he cooed.

"Fuck the cabbage, I hate that dungeon."

"C'mon, it's important."

"Tell me."

"Not over the phone."

"We're encrypted, Rafael."

"As far as we know."

"You mean?"

"I'll explain when you get here."

"Don't keep me waiting in the dark when I get there, come upstairs and unlock the damn door."

"I'll be there just as soon as you text me."

There had been an established routine for re-entry during off hours. The Pawn shop closed for the evening, just like all of the other nearby businesses. And when either of the pair had left at closing time, they generally did not return to the site until the next day's start of business, in order to give the impression of a normal operation. For that reason, a procedure had been established for those emergency situations where dark hour re-entry had been deemed necessary. It consisted of the encrypted call that Rafael had already made, and receipt of a one word text message—*shalom*—that would alert the nightshift person to their counterpart's arrival for the purpose of unlocking the outside security gate and front door.

The text arrived twenty minutes later, and Rafael rushed up the stairs to allow Bina's entry.

"What's so important that I had to cut my time off short?" she sneered.

"Virginia," he said, as they entered the basement.

"She's a turncoat, is there something else?"

"Read this," he said, pointing at the computer screen and the message that he should have deleted upon receipt.

"Would have expected something more concrete from Mossad," she admitted, adding, "where's the stuffed cabbage you'd promised?"

Rafael grinned, walked to the refrigerator, removed a plastic tub, slid it into the microwave and returned to his chair. "Four minutes should be enough," he advised.

"Where'd you get it from?"

"The Deli."

"Ugh, so it's been sitting in the freezer for a few days?"

"Afraid so, but let's focus on the message."

"I've been with Mossad for five years, and I've never heard them admit to uncertainty about an operative's loyalty."

"Me neither."

"So that makes her something special."

"And not in a good way."

"What do we do?" he asked.

"The communique did not specify an action."

"That's where I'm confused. First they authorize extreme prejudice, then they scrub the order, and now this?"

"What are you thinking?" she said, rising to the ding of the microwave.

"Like you said, she's something out of the ordinary."

"I know you've got more than that," she complained, stuffing a steaming chunk of cabbage into her waiting mouth.

"Tastes good, right?"

"Don't change the subject."

"Alright. We know that she's a double, but we don't know for whom. And for Tel Aviv to cancel the kill order there had to have been a compelling reason."

She swallowed and said, "Maybe they're working on a way to make her useful."

"Or, she's working with an ally."

"That should be easy enough to ascertain," she said, adding, "got any more of this?"

"No, that's the last of it."

"For the original order to have been sent there had to have been powerful evidence. But what if she's playing more than two sides?"

"That's like three dimensional chess, it takes an expert."

"I agree, she doesn't fit that profile, but a pro would be able to create whatever persona the situation called for."

"I'm getting a bad feeling, like the time I'd been left behind in a Gaza neighborhood," Rafael admitted.

"Yeah, I'd heard about that. The Army had a good laugh, but they went back for you."

"Sure, after I'd shit my pants trying to avoid a Hamas

hit team."

"Too much information," she guffawed.

"Anyway, we need to figure this out."

"Why is it our responsibility?"

"I vouched for her."

"Oh."

"And unless I want to spend the rest of my life in this shithole basement, I need to figure out what's going on."

"That's not going to be easily accomplished from this dungeon."

"Understood."

"And your plan?"

"For you to cover for me while I do what's necessary."

"Tel Aviv won't like that."

"They don't have to know."

"What if they want voice contact with you?"

"I'll have the encrypted satellite phone."

"Risky."

"I don't see another option."

"You could allow them to figure it out."

"It's my responsibility."

"And it's my ass that'll be on the line."

Chapter Sixteen

Thursday, 7 P.M.

Aventura

The pair had returned to Marvin's condo, their new headquarters, to flesh out their next move. Virginia had spilled the beans on the POF, but there had remained the task of verification and localization. They had just polished off a large pepperoni pizza and a six pack of Pepsi, when they'd retired to the living room. Marvin opened his laptop, connected to the dark web via Tor, and initialized a search for the Palestine Organized Front (POF). It hadn't taken long, before references to the organization had begun to appear, some in isolation and several tagged to articles about Hamas.

"Bingo," Marvin exclaimed, as George leaned in to view the screen.

"OK, so they exist," George said, "see if they have a presence in the U.S."

Marvin began scrolling and entering search schemes, but he kept coming up blank. "Nothing here about a presence," he said.

"Here's an idea, plug in the phrase, associates of, or associated with."

Marvin frowned, but did as suggested. And much to his surprise, a few names came into view.

"What's that?" George said, his right index finger thumping the screen.

"Three names."

"Just names, no addresses or countries of origin?"

"Not on this page."

"Type in the first name on the list and see what happens."

"Huh," he exclaimed, adding, "Devra, sound like a code name to you?"

"Is there a last name?"

"No."

"Location?"

Marvin smiled, and replied, "Minnesotta."

"And the other two?"

"The dark web has no data on them."

"One's better than none, but we need to find her."

"That might not be her real name, and finding one person in that state could take forever."

"We won't have to, chances are that Virginia knows who she is and where we can find her."

"She's not gonna want to meet with us again," Marvin said.

"Time for good cop, bad cop."

"We're not cops."

"Yeah, whatever. But one of us has to play the good guy, presumably acting in her best interest."

"And what would that be?"

"Information about the alleged contract."

"She didn't believe the existence of the contract the last time we'd met."

"But she's bound to be curious."

"So who?"

"You."

George retired to the kitchen in order to allow Marvin some space and time to make the call. But she had responded on the third ring and had remained on the phone for less than a minute. Marvin called out for George to return, and he did so with a large, yellow fruit sticking out from between his lips.

"Where the hell did you get this banana from," George complained, "tastes like shit."

"That's because it's a plantain."

"Yuck," George groaned, successfully tossing it across the room into a trash can.

"She's agreed to meet," Marvin advised.

"No reluctance?"

"Not really."

"Not a good sign."

"A trap?"

"Maybe, but I'll be there, out of sight, to back you up."

"When?"

"Tonight, 10 p.m., Flanagan's parking lot."

"Where the hell is that?"

"Federal highway, Boca."

George checked his wristwatch and said, "Just enough time for me to get there and find a place to hide."

"Not a big parking lot," Marvin explained.

"I'll figure it out," he said, reaching beneath the couch for the noise suppressed pistol.

***

9:55 P.M.

Flanagan's Seafood Bar and Grill

George had arrived thirty minutes early, and as the meeting time approached he crouched behind a row of hedges. Virginia's Mercedes SL rolled into the parking lot a few moments later and he froze, as he watched and waited. But as she parked, it soon became apparent that she too was waiting for something, because she'd made no effort to exit the vehicle. However, the moonless night had hidden the fact that she'd carried a rider who'd quietly slid from the passenger side of the small, white car and had nonchalantly walked off a short distance.

Not good, George thought, she brought backup.

The Mercedes' headlights had been extinguished by the time Marvin's Porsche entered and, as had been prearranged, he rolled slowly, searching for a parking spot not far from the road.

George watched from his uncomfortable perch, but something told him to be ready, so he withdrew the pistol from beneath his shirt, his hand beginning to sweat around the grip.

Marvin was now out of his vehicle and approaching Virginia's car, and when he was within ten feet of the bonnet, she exited.

"Don't have much time," she advised, "what's this all about?"

"Out in the open?" Marvin chanced.

"Spit it out."

Marvin had no idea that her backup was lurking in the distance, pretending to be a customer out for a smoke, so he approached and leaned against her car. "I have another trade offer," he said.

"What have you got that I'd want?" she jeered.

"The name of the person out to kill you."

George stiffened at his friend's fabrication. Not following the script, he thought.

She giggled and replied, "If you're still trying to sell that bullshit, I'm leaving."

"It's the real deal."

"I'm listening."

"Does the name Devra ring a bell?"

What the fuck is he doing, George said to himself, giving away the farm?

She hesitated and came back with, "No."

"C'mon, you know who she is and where she is."

"Not."

And then George really did wet himself when he heard Marvin take a flier with, "She's your POF contact, right?"

Virginia turned vicious and snarled, "Who told you that?"

"I have my sources," he smiled.

Marvin had missed the brief tilt of her head to the left, followed an instant later by a jet of hot air whizzing past his right earlobe. George watched his friend as he reacted to what he would later liken to a large bug flying by his ear, but it was followed by a second, more accurate shot that grazed his left shoulder, and he dropped to the ground. George hadn't heard a gunshot, but he instinctively knew what had transpired, and he raised his pistol in the direction of the muted, muzzle flash that he'd noted originating from one side of a parked vehicle. Without considering the safety of pedestrians or exiting customers, he fired a suppressed round that struck the windshield of the shooter's cover vehicle, causing the wraithlike individual to run off. And with the exchange ongoing, Virginia had re-entered her car, engaged the engine and had put it in gear, barely missing Marvin as she attempted to leave the lot.

George, taking note of her escape effort, fired two more lucky rounds into her right front and rear tires, bringing the car to a grinding halt. As he approached, she pointed the business end of a Walther PPQ 45 pistol toward his torso.

"The police will be here any second," he advised, "you want to explain what happened?"

"What do you propose?"

"Leave the gun and follow me."

She jumped from the car and ran toward his VW, as Marvin, his shirt sleeve turning red, screeched from the parking lot, the Porsche leaving behind a trail of black rubber.

"Where are we going?" she asked.

"Away from here," he said, the pistol resting peacefully across his lap.

"But my friend..."

"That's his or her problem."

"Her."

George gazed at her askance and said, "She work for you, or on you?"

"You fucking asshole, you have a problem with the gay movement?"

"I don't care if you're a rug muncher, but you are going to tell us how and where to find Devra."

"Good luck with that," she growled.

George drove in the direction of Marvin's condo, but several miles away he began to have second thoughts. If I take here there, we'll have to dispose of her afterwards, he thought. Nope, not a good idea. He changed direction slightly and headed for his own dwelling, thinking that he needed a change of address anyway. And after her interrogation he'd simply vacate the premises and move elsewhere.

It was now 11:30 p.m., and he parked the Beetle in his

usual spot and exited. The darkness served to conceal the pistol that he now aimed at the still seated Virginia, as he commanded her to exit. She hesitated a second too long and he grabbed her by the right upper arm and dragged her from the seat.

Once inside his apartment, he shoved her onto his well worn couch, Zip Tied her hands behind her back, slapped a length of silver duct tape across her lips and called Marvin.

"You OK?" he asked.

"Yeah, just a deep scratch."

"I'm at home."

"I'll come."

"Not yet."

"Why?"

"Got a visitor."

"Gonna pound her?"

"Are fucking kidding me? No, I'm not gonna do that."

"Then what?"

"Not sure."

"Hide your car."

"Shit, I hadn't thought of that."

"Use the ugly car cover you bought at the flea market."

Chapter Seventeen

Friday, January 12th

Friday, January 12th

1 A.M.

George had decided to perform the interrogation by himself, without the assistance of his friend and accomplice. To that end, he had removed the duct tape from Virginia's lips and, later, the zip ties from her ankles so that she could relieve herself with the bathroom door left open. But under his watchful eye, with the pistol held menacingly close to her head, she'd returned to the couch.

"What I need from you is Devra's contact info and location," he calmly advised.

"Fuck you," she spat.

"Not on your life," he chuckled.

"The cops will trace me to my car," she warned.

"But not to this place," he returned, gesturing about the room with his pistol.

"I think I'd spotted a camera on the edge of the restaurant's roof."

George shrugged, "So they recorded a VW rolling down the street."

"You're dead meat," she growled.

"And that's the reason for this exercise."

She turned her head into the couch's age softened fabric, and then aimed her eyes back at George and said, "I don't know how to contact her."

"Nice try."

"Really, she calls me when she needs something."

"Someone in your business would trace the call."

"She uses burners."

"And her location?"

"She moves around."

"What about her primary address?"

She shook her head with a, no.

"You're wasting my time. I already know that she resides in Minnesota, so cut the bullshit."

"That's her family's city," she said.

"Tell me about them."

"I don't know anything."

George's level of frustration was gradually accelerating, and he lifted the pistol and racked the slide, a live round hitting the floor, as he aimed the muzzle at her forehead. "I guess that you're no longer useful to me," he cautioned, as he moved the gun several inches closer to her head. But when she did not respond to the implied threat he found himself at a loss. I have no experience with interrogation methods, he realized, and I don't know how far I should go.

"You're not gonna shoot me," she jeered.

"You're right, I'm not gonna shoot you, here, it would make a mess. So get up."

"What?" she squealed.

"I'm taking you to where a mess won't count and where no one will notice."

"Wait a minute. I did my homework, you guys are not killers."

"Nice fantasy, but no cigar. Get movin'."

"OK, OK, you were correct, she lives in Minnesota."

George allowed his fingers to drop from the front door handle, and he said, "Address, I need an address."

"I'm telling the truth when I say that I don't know, but I can get a message to the POF."

"How?"

"They have a P.O. box in Manhattan."

"Not sure I'd believe that a terrorist group uses an easily identifiable mailing address."

"It's hiding in plain sight."

George nudged her in the direction of the couch, and she plopped onto the cushion. He took note of the fact that he'd not replaced the zip-ties that had secured her ankles, but decided to leave them off. Her hands were still secured behind her back, so escape wasn't going to be an easy chore, he surmised, and he was pleased with her apparent attempt at cooperation.

With the pistol still in hand, he took a seat beside her on the couch and wondered how he could use the postal box to his advantage. Marvin and I could travel to New York, send them a package and wait to see who picks it up, he mused. And then what, he wondered. Following that person back to their hideout would be the equivalent of handing them a gift of our heads on a silver platter. Just like the revenge plot that got me into *this* pile of shit, I haven't thought the process through. I don't know for certain that they're out to kill us, but if they are, they're surely biding their time. And even if I can locate their headquarters, do I ask for a sit-down to discuss a way out, he asked himself. If I were them, and I'd given someone a list of people to eliminate, I'd be thinking about cleaning up loose ends, lest the culpability fall back upon me. This is going to require a different approach.

"Ever been to their center of operations?" he asked.

"Once."

"Then you know where it is?"

"It was nighttime and I'd been blindfolded."

"How many people did you see there?"

"Three."

"Names," he demanded.

"They never used any."

"Do they have other locations?"

"They'd claimed to."

"Which one did the list come from?"

"Not sure, but I think it was New York."

"No postmark on the package that you'd received?"

"It had been hand delivered and shoved beneath my condo's front door."

"You live in a secure building, right?"

Yes, she nodded.

They'd either paid the concierge or they'd circumvented security. If the latter, it had been delivered by a pro, he told himself. So, New York is the nexus, he pondered, mentally thumbing through the thesaurus that he'd been reading on a daily basis in order to expand his vocabulary. And that's where the JPA lives as well. Maybe we can organize a block party, he laughed to himself.

"Was it your idea to give us up to the POF?"

She hesitated, then replied, "Yes."

"Why?"

"I'd figured that you'd be gullible enough to do what was asked without questions."

"So you'd tagged us as a pair of morons."

"Pretty much."

And then a thought popped into his head, and he asked, "Do you have any Israeli contacts?"

"Just the people in New York."

By the slight crack in her voice, he wasn't sure that she was telling the truth, but he let it go for the moment. And while she had turned uncharacteristically cooperative, he was running out of questions.

Her eyes widened when he reached for the roll of duct tape, tore off a piece and was about to seal her lips, when she cried out, "I gave you everything."

"That doesn't mean that I trust you," he replied, gently applying the tape, followed by the application of a single, large Zip Tie around the circumference of both ankles.

He left her alone, visited the bathroom for a long overdue pee, and dialed Marvin.

"She cracked," he said.

"You got the name and address?"

"Sort of."

"Meaning?"

"She gave me the postal box for the POF, but not the address of her contact."

"Worthless."

"Not entirely, but we haven't discussed what we'd do if we'd made contact with the list makers."

"We whack 'em."

"Not the least bit rational, Marvin."

Marvin's exasperation could be heard in the form of a breathy expulsion of air, and he responded with, "That means you already have a plan."

"Just the seeds, just the seeds."

"I'm listening."

"And so might everyone else, so we need to talk in person."

Marvin yawned and inquired, "Your place?"

"Yeah, still dealing with the Boca babe."

"Can it wait 'till morning?"

"I know it's late, but I don't know what to do with her," he admitted, looking back at Virginia from the kitchen.

"OK, I'll be there in a bit."

***

2 A.M.

Virginia had fallen asleep on the couch with her head

resting on the seat back cushion. And the sight of her apparent state of slumber had begun to take effect on his sleep deprived body. Seated on a kitchen chair, with a clear view of the living room couch, he'd been heading off into dreamland when Marvin had knocked on his front door. He rubbed his eyes, took a quick glance at Virginia, and walked to the door.

Marvin entered, a large, white bandage just visible beneath his short sleeve shirt, and George led him to the kitchen.

"How's the arm?" George asked.

"Probably could have used a few stitches, but that would have meant questions."

"Yeah. Got any ideas about her?" he said, gesturing toward the couch.

"We could do a Freddie."

"I don't know, killing a woman doesn't sit right."

"She could get us killed a dozen different ways."

"Remember, we'd been told to stand down. If the JPA finds out about what we've done, we're toast."

"Damned if we do and damned if don't."

"Seems that way."

"What if it looks like she offed herself."

"Might give us some leeway. What do you have in

mind?"

"Drugs. Happens every day of the week," he whispered.

"I don't have any."

"This is Miami, man, you can buy them on any street corner."

"Still doesn't feel right."

"You can't keep her trussed up forever, we need to decide."

George paced about the small kitchen, pulling on the craggy, black beard that he'd been meaning to shave off, and said, "There must be a way that we can use her for our benefit."

"I haven't gotten laid in awhile," Marvin grinned.

"That ain't gonna change."

"What about a trade, like in the movies?"

"Trade for what, magic beans?"

"Our freedom."

George considered Marvin's suggestion. On the surface it appears naive, he thought, but maybe there is something the other side wants. However, a ransom demand via a postal box is not practical. On the other hand, I do have a way of contacting the JPA.

"The only relationship we have is with the JPA, and

it's shaky at best. But what if we could come up with a reason for taking possession of the Boca babe that would not look like we'd defied orders?"

"That's gonna require some heavy bullshit."

"Right up your alley."

"Gimme a few," Marvin said, as he helped himself to a swig from a bottle of Amaretto that George had forgotten to store away.

Chapter Eighteen

Friday, 5 A.M.

Boca Raton

Following the shootout at Flanagan's, Sandy Barrick, Virginia's significant other, had jumped on a Harley soft tail motorcycle whose owner had carelessly left the key in place, and raced back to the Boca Raton condo that they'd periodically shared. Sandy maintained an apartment in Pompano Beach, not far from the ocean, but she'd assumed that her girlfriend would be heading home to regroup. And while George's poorly aimed gunshots had missed her entirely, she'd been struck by shards of glass that had flown from the windshield of the car she'd used for protection.

The concierge had been made aware of her existence and the fact that she would occasionally require access to the building in Virginia's absence. And she'd taken the elevator to the unit and used her key to open the front door. But her pulse began to race when her search of the apartment had revealed Virginia's absence. Her girlfriend's favorite fragrance still permeated the air, and she filled her nostrils. Calming some, hoping that Virginia had not been apprehended by the Boca PD, she walked into the bathroom and examined her injuries. Her striking, long black hair, bright red lips and green eyes stared back at her from the body length mirror. A three inch gash, the same one that had ruined the white silk blouse that she'd forgotten to remove before heading out that evening, was still oozing blood, some of which had found its way down to her right wrist. The rest were simple scratches that had required little, if no attention. Tearing open a gauze pack that she'd found while rummaging through the drawers, she cleansed the wound with an antiseptic solution and applied a large square, secured it with a length of white duct tape that a plumber had left behind and marched into the living room to wait for her lover.

When she'd awakened following what she'd thought had been a brief period of rest, she was astonished to find that hours had passed. She'd slept through the night and into the next morning. But after relieving herself in the bathroom, she began to panic when it had become apparent that Virginia had yet to return.

The jeans that had remained affixed to her hourglass body were still wearable, but the silk blouse was ready for the trash, so she ventured into Virginia's bedroom to borrow another. And that is when her world turned upside down.

"Who the fuck are you?" she growled, at the fully

clothed, dark skinned male stretched out across Virginia's king sized bed, his black pistol aimed at her torso.

He smiled and, with a British tinged accent, replied, "The grim reaper."

Her martial arts training surfacing, she immediately assumed a defensive posture, but quickly realized that her skills were no match for a speeding bullet, especially given the twelve foot distance that separated them. "Very funny," she snarled, adding, "how'd you get in?"

He waved the gun back and forth and said, "I ask, you answer—clear?"

She nodded, OK.

"Where is your wife, husband or whatever?"

She gritted her teeth and bit her lower lip at the obvious slur, but said, "I might ask the same of you."

"Right. Here's how it's going to go. Each time you give a smart ass answer I'm going to fire a round into some useful part of your body," he smiled, while screwing a long suppressor onto the pistol's protruding barrel.

"Look, I came home last night expecting to find her here and, as you can see, she hasn't returned," she calmly offered.

"But you know where she went."

Sandy hesitated. The pistol was aimed at her right

shoulder, and while she did not relish the thought of getting shot, she did not want to connect either herself or Virginia with the Boca shootout. "She was here, in town."

"Not good enough," he said, thumbing back the gun's hammer.

"Wait," she shouted, adding, "she was to meet some friends at Flanagan's."

"To what end?"

"Social, I guess."

"Aren't you two a couple?"

"We lead our own lives."

"She has a cellphone, call it," he demanded.

"I've been trying her number all night, but no answer."

With the pistol steadily aimed where it shouldn't have been, he reached to the nightstand for an apple and took a noisy bite.

"Am I allowed to ask something?" she said.

"Take off your clothes."

"What?" she squealed.

"You heard me."

"I'm not into men," she screeched, backing up as far as the near wall would allow.

"Makes no difference, get 'em off."

Sandy was frozen in place. She knew that she was about to be taken forcefully, and while it wouldn't have been the first time, the prospect was still loathsome. But close quarters combat was her specialty, and feigning compliance would get her to where she needed to be, so she began undoing the belt on her jeans, the bloody blouse having been left in the bathroom.

"The bra first," he demanded.

She allowed the belt to dangle, as she reached behind to undo the clasp. The light blue bra fell to the beige, marble tiled floor, while her ample nipples began to extend uncontrollably in response to the constant flow of cool air from the overhead vents.

"Now the pants," he called out, gripping the apple's remains with his front teeth, as he kicked off his own khaki slacks and undershorts, revealing a bobbing, eight inch erection.

Sandy fixated momentarily on his penis, then slowly slid her jeans to the floor, leaving her with only a narrow, dental floss wide piece of cloth between her buttocks and a small triangle of white covering her pubis.

He rose slightly to evaluate his prize, and said, "Now the rest."

She, like many other women in today's world,

habitually shaved her pubic hair, and as she stood in place the man grimaced and complained, "What the hell is that?" aiming the gun at her crotch.

"I shave."

"That sucks," he said.

"Sorry."

"Come over here."

She kicked the thong free from her ankles and began the slow and deliberate journey towards her captor, all the while planning his demise from the best of her Israeli trained, Krav Maga (a form of martial arts designed to kill one's opponent).

When she had reached the bed, she placed her right knee upon the edge of the mattress, while he reached forward with his left hand and grasped her near breast.

"Get on it," he demanded, gesturing toward his erect manhood.

That was her cue, she slapped the pistol free from his grip and with lightening speed spun around in such a manner that her naked thighs surrounded his neck in a viselike fashion. He coughed, grunted and kicked in the air, as his hands flailed, attempting to loosen her hold, but she began pummeling his face, causing a stream of blood to trickle from his eyes and nose.

"Who sent you?" she demanded, the flesh of her thighs deforming his face.

"Ask your girlfriend," he grunted.

"I'm asking you, scumbag."

"The organization," he wheezed.

"What organization?"

"The front," he barely managed, as his color turned ashen.

"What front?"

"Palest ...," he began to say, before he lost consciousness.

She eased her grip, as a few drops of her own urine dripped down his forehead, and said, "Yeah, piss on you."

Sandy lurched from the bed and turned to feel for a pulse, and finding that his heart was still pumping she ran to find something to tie his hands and feet. And rather than waste time going through a series of closets, she removed the sashes from four of Virginia's silk kimonos and hogtied him face down on the bed. Stark naked, she yanked on the bindings to make certain that they were secure and, for a moment, considered smothering the intruder with one of the several pillows but relented, thinking that she might need him as a bargaining chip.

With the Brit no longer a threat, his pistol now lying

on the kitchen table, she borrowed the necessary items from her girlfriend's closet and dressed.

Seated in the kitchen, a cup of steaming coffee in her right hand, she attempted to make sense of the prior twenty-four hours.

Virginia had never really told me why she'd needed backup, and I hadn't questioned her, but maybe I should have. She's always been a tad secretive about her outside of the bedroom activities, she thought, but with my head between her legs the world disappears, and I need the world to disappear. But the douchebag in her bedroom is causing me to wonder what she's been up to and, from the sound of his last partial word, terrorism comes to mind. Five of my twenty-seven years had been spent on a Kibbutz —not the usual vacation spot for a non jew—and I thank my deceased parents for sending me. If it hadn't been for that trip I would never have learned the ins and outs of Krav Maga and wouldn't have been able to subdue the dick in the other room. But none of that helps with Virginia's whereabouts, or where I should go from here.

Chapter Nineteen

Miami, 6 A.M.

Marvin had arrived at 3 a.m., and together they'd taken up watch in the kitchen, while Virginia had been passed out on George's couch. She had awakened briefly at around 4 a.m., and had squirmed about, leading George to assume that a trip to the bathroom had been in order. But she'd quickly drifted back to slumberland and the two friends had returned to a discussion about her future.

"I say we take her to the cement factory and put a bullet in her head," Marvin had argued.

"Disagree," George had said.

"She's a major liability, man."

"There's that. But look at her," he said, gesturing toward the sleeping prisoner.

"OK, she's hot, but she knows where you live and could bring all kinds of hell down upon us."

"We're already on the POF's shit list, and the jury's still out on the JPA, so what else can she do?"

"There's the shootout at Flanagan's."

"I'd say that she's on the hook for that, since the PD must have impounded her car," George had pointed out.

"Given any thought to the backup shooter?" Marvin

had asked, shifting the conversation slightly.

"Not really."

"Whomever that was is still on the loose."

"And that's another reason not to kill her," George had suggested, adding, "the shooter could have come from either side."

"Oh fuck, that's just too confusing."

"You're the one whose read all those spy novels, this shit should be a no brainer for you."

"The books hand you facts and clues, but all we've got is a fistful of nothing."

"Not entirely. We know that the JPA gets its orders from Israel and, while they may be open to some unsavory acts, they're probably not terrorists. But we don't know much of anything about the POF. And considering the organization's name, we can pretty much assume that they're terrorists."

"How does that help us?" Marvin asked.

"I don't know yet."

"And the Boca babe, she's gonna awaken soon and then what?"

George grinned, and said, "Before you'd arrived, I'd played around with her cellphone and I think that I can track it."

"Show me how."

George removed his own phone, tapped the screen and explained, "I found an app called mSpy and I downloaded it to her phone. I can track where she goes, who she messages and so on."

"Won't she notice the strange new app?"

"No, it's hidden."

"And if she changes phones?"

George shrugged, "We're shit out of luck."

"So your plan is to let her go?"

"Yeah. She's more useful to us alive than dead."

"The JPA obviously feels the same, but the Palestinians might not."

"Not our problem."

At 6 a.m., Virginia began to move about—as much as her restraints would allow—and George approached with a pair of wire cutters in hand. He sliced through the Zip-Ties and freed her hands and ankles a second before her eyelids shot open.

"What are you doing?" she snapped.

"You can go," he breathed.

"Go where?"

"Wherever."

"What's the catch?" she asked, rubbing her ankles

with reddened hands.

"No catch, just tired of babysitting."

She glared at him, and hissed, "They're waiting for me, aren't they?"

"There's no one outside, see for yourself," he informed, pulling back the shade covering a living room window.

"They're out there somewhere, I can feel it," she trembled.

"Of whom are you afraid?" Marvin asked, as he entered the room and stood before her.

She shifted her gaze from one to the other, and replied, "Never mind. I'll need my phone to call for a ride."

George handed it to her without hesitation and backed away to unlock the front door. Virginia paused, pursed her lips and departed.

With the door closed, Marvin peered from behind the living room shade and said, "She photographed your place from across the street and kept walking."

"I guess it's time to leave this apartment behind."

"You can stay with me for a bit."

"Just for a few days, I'll need a place of my own."

"OK."

"Is she still in view?" George asked.

"No."

George whipped out his phone and began to track her movement. "She's two blocks down, and stationary."

"Waiting for a ride?"

"Maybe. You think she's called the shooter?"

"Gimme your phone," Marvin said, "I'm gonna follow her."

"Not without me."

"OK, but stay low in the front seat."

"She might notice your car."

"Cars like mine are a dime a dozen in Miami."

They drove past Virginia on their way to a loading zone a few hundred feet down the road. Marvin pulled into the unoccupied space and kept the engine running.

"I can't see her from here," George complained.

"Your app says that she hasn't moved ... wait a minute, she's on the go."

A silver Toyota Prius passed them, and Virginia could be seen in the front passenger seat just before it had left their field of view.

"Did you notice the driver?" George sneered.

"No, was focusing on the Boca babe."

"Chick with long black hair and red lips."

"But we don't know if she's the shooter."

"We do know that the babe is a rug muncher."

"And the black haired girl is the rug?" Marvin chortled.

George shrugged, and chuckled, "Everybody shaves, no more rugs."

The two friends had a good laugh, the first since the beginning of their debacle, and then Marvin had a thought. "What's the plan once we see where they're going?"

"Don't have one."

"So we mark the location and keep moving?"

"No, we park and wait."

"Oh great, a stakeout."

"Boca babe kept saying that they're coming for me. Let's see whom they are."

"Two options."

"That we know of."

"If there's a third I'm gonna shoot myself."

"Save your energy, they might do it for you."

"Haven't we had enough of this cloak and dagger crap?" Marvin whined.

"Enough for a lifetime, but we can't just call game over."

"I get it, we're the pieces on their board."

"Exactly, we don't get to roll the dice unless..."

"What?" Marvin asked excitedly.

"We need some leverage, something they can't resist."

"We don't even know whom *they* are."

"There's a common denominator."

"Right, the babe that we'd just let go."

"And now we can snare her again with her girlfriend."

"Have you paid any attention to the time of day, we can't snatch her right in front of her building."

"We're not there yet, but we can cut her off when she leaves the highway."

"She can try to take off ahead of us."

"In a Prius?" George guffawed.

"If my Porsche gets damaged in the chase, you're paying for it,'" Marvin scowled.

"If we don't figure this mess out your car will be the least of our problems."

As is often the case with I95, a construction crew had slowed traffic to a crawl and the pair were getting anxious. The Prius was two car lengths ahead of them and off to their side in the right lane when George thought that he'd noticed the driver adjust the rearview mirror.

"We might have been made," he exclaimed.

"Not much either of us can do about it, we're stuck behind that frickin' Publix eighteen wheeler," he said, pointing at the truck's tailgate, roughly three feet ahead of their car.

"Maybe it was my imagination."

"So we cut 'em off, drag them out of their car and put them where?" Marvin said.

"Back seat."

"And all of the crap I have back there, we toss that to the curb?"

"OK, change of plans. I'll carjack them and use the Prius."

Marvin sighed and rolled his eyes, countering with, "A broad daylight carjacking at gunpoint. Yeah, great idea."

"OK, you're right, we should never have let Virginia go."

"We? Remember, I voted for bullet in the head."

Traffic began to move again, they could see the exit sign coming closer, and George suggested, "A diversion, I need you to create a diversion while I jack them."

Marvin burst out laughing and when he'd calmed some he suggested, "I'll drop my pants in the middle of the road, that should get some attention."

"Works for me."

As they rolled through the Ives Dairy Road exit, the two cars separating them from the Prius pulled away leaving them directly behind. And while there had been some earlier indication that they had been recognized, the Prius driver had given no sign of awareness.

"I thought they'd be going on to Boca," George observed.

"Maybe they're avoiding it."

"Where are they taking us?"

"Looks like the Aventura Mall."

"So much for a secluded car jacking."

"If they head for the garage we still have a chance," Marvin announced, backing off of the accelerator in order to create some distance.

"There's the parking garage," George observed.

"And they're aimed right for it."

Marvin maintained a good distance between the two cars, and once inside the garage they slowed to a crawl. The silver Prius was inching into a narrow space and Marvin came up from behind and stopped inches from the car's rear bumper, effectively blocking any attempted escape. George jumped from the Porsche's passenger side, took a quick gaze about for onlookers and cameras, and ran to the driver's side door and pressed against it with his body.

The driver rolled down her window and growled,

"What the fuck do you want?"

Leaning across toward the driver, Virginia frowned and snapped, "Change your mind?"

With his pistol clearly visible to both women, he replied, "Sorry for the inconvenience, ladies, but you're shopping trip has been cancelled."

Virginia reached for her door handle, but Marvin had already left his vehicle, tapped on her closed window and with his extended right index finger signaled for her to stay put.

"What do you want?" Virginia asked.

"Not going to introduce me to your friend?" he smiled.

"No, I'm not, and mall security will be here any minute," she advised, gesturing upwards, toward a ceiling mounted camera that had gone unnoticed.

"We're just a few friends having a conversation."

"With a gun pointed at us?"

Shit, he thought, this isn't going as planned. I need a good story. He slid the gun beneath his shirt and decided to hit them with a fabrication, by claiming, "The people you'd thought to be on your tail? They are."

"And you're my Knight in shining armor?" she sneered.

"Not exactly. But I do have a proposal."

"Listening," she replied, while Sandy sat stone faced behind the wheel.

"We bait them."

"I suppose that I'm the bait," she smirked.

"We'll be there to catch 'em."

"You must think that I'm a fool. You expect me to trust my life to a pair of amateurs?"

"Is there someone else?"

Sandy spoke up for the first time and through clenched teeth said, "She's got me."

"I'm guessing that you were the Flanagan's shooter," he chanced.

"What of it?"

"Here's the plan," he droned, ignoring Sandy's implied threat, "You go back to your condo, both of you. Shooter here can cover your ass from inside, and we'll grab the perps before they can get to you."

"Great plan," Virginia ridiculed, "we have no idea what they might look like."

"And that's why we'll all enter the building like two couples..."

"My concierge won't go for it," she interrupted.

"Why not?"

"You know the answer," she said, as Sandy launched an *if looks could kill* facial expression.

"We need to stakeout your floor and stop anyone who approaches your door."

Virginia hesitated, and then asked, "Why do you even give a shit?"

"Self preservation," he replied truthfully, sidestepping his intent to use her as a bargaining chip.

"Give us a minute," Virginia muttered, as Sandy motored the window closed.

George and Marvin stood on either side of the Prius, waiting for their decision. But whatever their decision, the two men had already set a plan in motion, and the women were going to comply, like it or not.

Sandy's window lumbered down and George asked, "Well?"

"Follow us," she said.

Chapter Twenty

Friday, 8 A.M.

Fort Lauderdale-Hollywood International Airport

Despite a bout of last minute turbulence, Rafael's flight had arrived on time. He'd made a reservation at the Hyatt Place Boca Raton, the nearest location to Virginia's last known address. After acquiring a rental car he'd driven to the hotel and checked in. Since there had been no reasonable means of transporting a firearm by air, and in anticipation of same, he'd sent two, unloaded semiautomatic pistols; a .40 caliber, and a small .22 caliber Walther, both equipped with suppressors, as well as a .38 calibre Smith & Wesson snub-nosed revolver, via FedEx overnight to be delivered to the Hyatt under the name of Andrew Cosgrove, a pseudonym that he'd been using and for which he carried valid, yet counterfeit identification. He knew that purchasing ammunition would not present a problem, as there were a plethora of gun shops and shooting ranges where ammo could be purchased with limited, if any interrogation. And to that end, his first stop had been to a Boca Raton firearms retailer where he'd purchased the required ammo.

Once inside his room he tore open the FedEx box,

removed the Glock 27 that had been modified to
accommodate a suppressor, and loaded the magazine. He
then retrieved the encrypted satellite phone from his
overnight bag and punched in the number for the JPA
office's corresponding device.

"Bina? I'm here."

"You got the package?" she asked.

"Have it in hand."

"Any inquiries?"

"Not so far."

"Be careful. Make a ruckus and Tel Aviv will hear."

"Shalom," he said, before terminating the call.

Wearing a pair of blue jeans and a white collared
shirt, he pulled on a beige sport coat and wedged the Glock
between the waistband and the small of his back, slipping
the satellite phone into an inner jacket pocket. He'd
packed the sport jacket for the express purpose of
concealing the weapon, although he knew that January
evenings could be unpredictably chilly, making it a dual
purpose choice.

Following breakfast at the Hyatt he'd retrieved the
rented, dark grey Chrysler 300 and set out to do some
reconnaissance. Virginia's home address had been known
from the beginning of their relationship, and not long after

leaving the hotel he'd found himself on A1A rolling past her high-rise condo. Other than a narrow soft shoulder, parking had not been a viable option, so he'd made several U-turns, affording him the ability to repeatedly pass by her building. And during his last pass he'd slowed to a crawl and thought, I need to get a closer look before I can formulate a plan of action. To that end, he'd decided to park the rental on a side street off of Camino Real Road and walk the distance back to the condo. It had taken a good fifteen minutes to reach the building on foot, and as he'd approached he'd observed two vehicles entering the driveway traveling almost bumper to bumper.

That's odd, he thought, as his eyes were drawn to the vehicles moving with the precision of a pair of circus elephants. But suddenly, he was walloped by the unexpected. Two women exited from the silver Prius, one of whom fit his distant recollection of Virginia, but even more surprising was the appearance of George Katz and Marvin Freed, as they left a dark blue Porsche. Wiping a few beads of sweat from his brow with the back of one hand, he remained fixated on the four people passing through the building's entry doors.

There had been no equivocation in my order to stand down, so what the hell is he doing there, he wondered. And the second woman is clearly a puzzle. But four people, that's going to complicate matters, and unless I can separate Virginia from the others I may have to take them all.

He crossed A1A and stood at the edge of the driveway leading to the valet's podium. Getting through the main entrance could be a problem, he pondered. I could pretend to be a delivery person, but I would require a specific recipient, and using Virginia might raise some suspicion. No, a better option would be to find a way to circumvent the inevitable security and take her by surprise, he considered, as he waited for the valet to turn his head away from street, while he ventured around the side of the building toward the ocean.

A strong, unanticipated breeze struck his face as his shoes sank into the moist sand of a narrow stretch of beach. From there he surveyed the building's rear, searching for an area of weakness that might be vulnerable to penetration. He kicked the sand from his shoes and walked onto the concrete, poolside area with the flair of an owner/resident just returning from a jaunt on the beach. Smiling at a few elderly couples who were firmly ensconced on a row of webbed, recliners and who viewed the sport jacket attired newcomer as if he'd just exited from an alien spacecraft, he kept moving decisively in the direction of a well marked entrance. Above the door was a sign that read: *Please shower off all sand before entering.*

While management had thoughtfully installed a keypad, rightfully assuming that beachgoers would not be carrying their keys, the last person to pass through had left one edge of a rubber mat curled beneath the door, to the extent that it had not closed sufficiently to lock. He smiled inwardly, grabbed the handle and passed through to the cool interior. A bank of elevators stood before him and he entered the one whose door flew open upon approach. Alone in the marble adorned cubicle, he perused the liquid crystal display that had replaced the traditional buttons and reached for the icon corresponding to the penthouse level. That's odd, he thought, as he took note of the absence of the secondary level of security frequently afforded penthouse residents, and tapped the appropriate icon. The door closed with a whoosh and the lift quickly carried him to the uppermost floor, but not before he'd observed the surveillance camera staring at the top of his head from the elevator's ceiling.

You're getting careless, he thought, chiding himself for not observing the camera, and the fact that his presence was now on record. But he walked down the corridor with the confidence of one who's existence was not out of the ordinary, just in case there had been other cameras that he'd overlooked.

There were just two units on the ocean side of the building, and Virginia's—the smaller of the two—occupied twenty-four hundred square feet. The entry doors were absent name tags, although a small, camera lens could be seen just above the door-frames, and he stood transfixed for a few seconds, realizing that he had a fifty-fifty chance of getting it right the first time. Putting his ear to one of the doors revealed the sound of a small dog's bark, and there had been no information in Virginia's profile indicating the presence of a dog, so he moved on to the remaining unit. The distant sound of indistinguishable voices could be heard and he backed away to decide on a course of action.

I can ring the bell, hope that someone opens the door and force my way in, he considered, or ... there is no or. The bell is my only option to catch them all in one place. But, despite the ease of my entry, this is a secure building and arrivals are probably announced. A ringing doorbell might act as a red flag in the absence of a call from the concierge. He patted the small of his back, making certain that the Glock was still in place, and reached for the doorbell button. With his ear to the metallic door, he observed only silence and assumed that he was being monitored via the surveillance camera. He kept his face obscured so that only the top of his head would be visible, and waited.

"Yes," a female voice called out from an intercom.

He had to come up with an on-the-fly response, so he called out, "Gas company, there's a leak in the building."

"Hold up your ID."

"Left it with the concierge."

"I'm calling him."

"There could be an explosion at any moment," he urged.

The person behind the door hesitated, but the sound of the latch moving prompted him to grab his pistol and aim it at the slowly opening door. But suddenly, a second female voice called out, "Don't open it, Sandy."

The door slammed shut, and Rafael was left with his face barely an inch from what could have been a bloody nose. He rang again.

"This is not a game," he called out.

A male voice responded, "No ID, no entry."

False identification had always been part of any spy or agent's tradecraft, and Rafael was no different in this regard. But he hadn't planned on that requirement and had brought with him an FBI Agent's ID and badge that he'd been loathe to use, given the consequences of impersonation. But he had arrived at a crossroad and had no option. Reaching into his jacket's inner pocket he withdrew the ID folder and held it high for the camera. "FBI," he called out.

"Since when does the FBI check for gas leaks," the male voice asked.

"Open the door, or I'll do it with my truncheon," he lied.

The door opened a crack, wide enough for Rafael to recognize George's bearded face, and he shoved inward with his entire body weight causing the door to cave. Suddenly, there were pistols pointing from all directions, as Rafael kicked the door closed with a backward tap from his right foot.

"Looks like a standoff," he smiled.

"I know you," George said, his gun aimed at Rafael's torso.

"And I know everyone here, except for that one," he said, nodding toward Sandy.

Sandy was seated beside Virginia on a couch, her fists clenched and ready for action.

"You're here for me," Virginia announced, her pistol now resting on her lap, "leave the others alone."

"There's a problem with that," he said.

"I could kill you where you stand," George snarled.

"And I could do the same, but here's how it's gonna go down..."

Virginia placed her pistol on the arm of the couch and slowly rose to a standing position. "There's something I have to tell you in private," she interrupted.

"Privacy is no longer an issue," Rafael barked.

"But it's something you need to hear, and if you kill me, well..."

Rafael considered her plea, and said, "Tell George to relinquish his weapon."

She turned to face George, who frowned but complied, as he handed his pistol to Rafael's receiving hand.

"We're not leaving this room," he advised, adding, "whisper in my ear. And if you try to disarm me there will be bloodshed."

She came forward and cautiously approached. Placing her lips within inches of his left ear, she murmured, "I've infiltrated a Palestinian terrorist group."

"Nice try, but my intel says otherwise."

"Your intel is flawed."

"Prove it."

She exhaled nosily and murmured, "This is for your ears only, but I'm a undercover Federal Agent."

"Highly creative, but no cigar."

"I can prove it."

Her statement gave him pause, and he replied, "How?"

"Call the State Department and ask for Herringbone."

"Who's that?"

"My code name."

"If you're not lying you've just blown your cover," he advised.

"You've given me no choice."

"And the others?"

"They have no clue."

"What about black hair?"

She grimaced and replied, "My girlfriend, and she's not part of this."

"OK, sit back down while I think."

With his back against the front door and the pistol aimed at the four people now seated on the couch, he palmed the satellite phone and punched the speed dial for the JPA office. It rang twice before being answered.

"Yes," Bina said.

"Call the State Department and ask for Herringbone."

"Joking, right?"

"Just do it while I hold, and use a burner."

"What's going on?"

"Later, make the call."

Chapter Twenty-one

Friday, January 12th

10 A.M.

Bina's call to the State Department had been received by an operator who had put her on a prolonged hold. But eventually, a calm, male voice had informed her that Herringbone was on vacation and could not be reached. Assuming that her call was being traced, she had used the suggested single use burner, following which she had tossed it into the trash compacter and hit run. She then grabbed the satellite phone that she'd placed on the table before her and said, "Herringbone is not available."

"Thank you," Rafael snapped, and terminated the call.

He motioned with his pistol for Virginia to come near. "OK, Herringbone's confirmed, but how do I know that you're Herringbone?"

"You're gonna have to trust me on that."

He scratched his scalp and said, "Tell me about the Muslims."

"Let the others go."

"Not yet."

"I have to pee," Marvin called out.

"Hold it," Rafael ordered.

"You got less than a minute before this white rug turns yellow," he complained.

"Shit. Where's the bathroom?" Rafael inquired.

"Off the kitchen," Virginia advised.

"What about the bedroom?"

"Yeah," she replied.

"Everyone, in the bedroom, now," he demanded.

Marvin entered the bathroom, leaving the door open as ordered, while the remaining three took a seat on the kingsized bed—the British accented intruder having been long since disposed of— and waited for the next demand.

Gazing out from the penthouse window, he realized that escape from same would be a no go, so with Virginia in tow he ripped the bedside phone's connection from the wall and sealed the triumvirate within.

"Time to earn your reprieve," he said, offering her the living room's white leather armchair.

"The POF, or Palestinian Organized Front, is an offshoot of Hamas. But they don't get along with each other."

"I've heard of them, they're marginal, go on."

"They've got plans to expand."

"Explain your involvement."

"It goes back to Stanford and a girl named Devra," she

went on to explain in detail.

"So you were with the State Department when you'd joined us?"

"Afraid so."

"You've made a fool out of me, I'd vouched for you."

"Sorry, but that's the bis we're in."

"Tell me about their plans."

"It gets complicated."

"The name of the game."

"I'd been given a list, people who'd been marked for disposal."

"And?"

"They were all members of either Congress or the Senate."

"I assume that there were no Muslims on the list."

She nodded in agreement.

"What was the proposed mechanism?"

"It had fallen upon me to find a few faithfuls."

"And?"

"I can't imagine that they'd anticipated success, but that's when I had the bright idea to engage the two numbskulls in the bedroom."

"Oy, they're amateurs."

"But with myself acting as the go-between, the POF

must have thought that they'd acquired deniability."

"And the list?"

"The morons had done some recon, but that's where it had ended."

"You know that I can't leave them to their own devices, too risky."

"But Sandy, my girlfriend, has no knowledge of any part of this."

"She's still a liability and you know that."

"I don't want her harmed," she insisted.

"Then she'll have to be read in and become part of the plan."

"What plan?"

"Workin' on it."

***

Noon

Virginia had used whatever food she'd had in her kitchen to feed the guests, and while Rafael had not holstered his pistol he was no longer brandishing it in a threatening manner. George and Marvin had succumb to their subservient positions, and Sandy had been provided with a few bits of information pertaining to her lover's real function in life, a fact that had the potential to sour their relationship well into the foreseeable future. But with the exception of Virginia, and under threat of extinction, they were all resigned to perform whatever tasks Rafael would require of them. Virginia, on the other hand, took her Federal Agent status quite seriously and had not relinquished full control to the JPA operative. Instead, she had negotiated an unlikely partnership that had not been sanctioned by either government.

Rafael swallowed the last bit of salami that had fallen from his sandwich, took a swig of water, and said, "It appears that the common denominator among us is the alleged, POF."

All present nodded in agreement.

"Like most terrorist groups, they likely harbor a sense of omnipotence and purity of cause. But it's all bullshit. They are all motivated by the scent of power and control."

"That should not come as a surprise to anyone," Virginia agreed.

"We need to turn the tables on them."

"Destroy them?" George asked.

"We are not the likely slayers, but we can blindside them."

"How so?" Virginia asked.

"The list. We make it public with emphasis on its origin."

"I can't prove that it came from them," she said.

"It appears that the American media doesn't require proof."

"Can't argue with that," Marvin interjected.

"So we leak some of the names to the press, they leak it to Congress, and the fire ignites."

"Interesting plan," Virginia observed, adding, "who's going to feed the press?"

"The Mossad."

"And then what?"

"We wait for them to run for cover," Rafael informed.

"They might just leave the country," Virginia suggested.

"If so, they'll probably seek sanctuary in Gaza, and any flight they take will land in Israel. We'll get them."

"But we don't know who they are or what they look like," George said.

"Leave that to me."

"So we're free to go?" George inquired, more a request than a question.

"Not quite. You and your accomplice have unknowingly acted as POF facilitators, and that fact is bound to put you both on countless intelligence agency's radars."

"Great. What should we do?"

"Hold tight and maintain a low profile."

"Wait a minute, no one outside of this room knows about the POF," George whined.

"That's about to change."

George exchanged glances with Virginia and realized that the tables had been turned, and that he and Marvin were the ones who'd been blindsided. "Virginia got us into this mess, she should arrange for protection," he blurted.

"If you recall, you were the ones seeking the JPA's assistance for revenge. This is of your own doing," she scolded.

"And you'd used us to your advantage," he said, angrily.

She shrugged, indicating that she couldn't care less.

"If things begin to look bad," Rafael offered, "we could offer you asylum in Israel—are you both Jews?"

"Yeah," Marvin replied.

"But before that happens, I may have a few simple tasks for you both."

"Can I have my gun back?" George inquired.

"Sure," Rafael agreed, dropping the magazine and

thumbing off its contents.

George glared at him, but took the offered gun, and said, "You do know that I can easily replace those."

"But not until I'm out of range. And keep in mind that until I say otherwise, the two of you belong to me."

Virginia and Sandy had remained seated on opposite ends of the couch. Sandy, for her part, had taken on the appearance of a statue made of stone and had not uttered anything other than an occasional sigh. Virginia, however, rose and approached Rafael, who was now standing with his right hand poised to grab the front door lever, and said, "I'll have to notify my superiors."

"As far as they know you're still undercover, right?" he replied.

"Yes."

"Leave it that way."

"But once you leak the list I'll be considered rogue."

He moved his hand away from the door lever and replied, "You'd told them about the list?"

"Had to, there were lives at stake."

"Fuck," he spat, "that changes everything."

Suddenly, an ear shattering blast, followed by a cloud of dust and the front door slapping against the marble floor stopped them cold. Three, medium height wraiths, clad from head to toe in black and carrying suppressed automatic rifles entered and shoved them all toward what remained of the couch. The blast had dislodged George's empty and Rafael's fully loaded pistol from their respective hands, as the two dazed men gasped for air.

"You," one of the wraiths ordered, gesturing with his rifle toward Virginia, "over here."

"Who the fuck are you?" she shouted.

"On you knees," the rifleman demanded, in broken English.

"Go fuck yourself," she spat.

The man fired a suppressed round into the floor by her feet, sending marble chips skidding across the room.

"You wanna shoot me, do it," she shrieked.

The intruders had yet to identify themselves, and Virginia's apparent non compliance had given them pause, but one of the three infiltrators stepped forward and placed the muzzle of his rifle against her left temple and repeated, "On your knees."

The cloud of marble and concrete dust had yet to settle and visibility was foggy, at best. Without warning, Sandy sprang from the couch and within an instant had her lover's assailant stretched out on the floor, writhing in pain, his rifle now firmly ensconced in her grip. She rang off a short burst in the direction of the man closest to the doorframe and he returned fire, quickly shredding one end of the couch, adding a few pounds of white foam stuffing to the room's murky atmosphere. The third man joined in, his wildly inaccurate shooting tearing up another few feet of marble flooring as well as Virginia's left shoulder. She cried out in pain, further infuriating Sandy, who emptied the remainder of the rifle's thirty round magazine in an around the room fashion. Rafael, George and Marvin had taken cover close to the ground when the shooting had begun and had luckily avoided Sandy's furor, but the two standing intruders had not been so fortunate, and their bloodied bodies lie stretched out on the beige marble floor like a pair of oozing jelly donuts. Sandy dropped the now empty rifle and ran to her friend.

"Is it bad?" she cooed.

"Hurts like a bitch, but I'll live," Virginia hissed through clenched teeth.

Rafael was the first to his feet, and he quickly and efficiently checked to make certain that the invaders had been incapacitated. "The bleeders are dead," he called out, adding, "but the one moaning and holding his junk has some questions to answer."

"Junk?" Marvin coughed.

"His nuts."

Sandy smiled from where she stood comforting Virginia, "Krav Maga," she advised.

Rafael gazed at her with an expression of admiration and said, "A topic for another time."

Chapter Twenty-two

Friday, 3:30 P.M.

Virginia's condo was a mess, and with the entry door lying flat on the living room floor there was no way to conceal the mayhem. Rafael had called in a favor from an FBI contact and arrangements had been made for the bodies to be removed and the apartment sanitized. Together, they had dragged the two dead infiltrators into the master bedroom in order to avoid detection from the outside corridor. In addition, Sandy had knocked on the only other resident's door to preemptively explain the absence of their door and the disarray within.

"There'd been a gas explosion," she'd explained.

"Hadn't heard anything, but anyone injured," the neighbor had inquired, nervously.

"Virginia, but she'll be OK," she'd replied.

"Do I need to evacuate?" the neighbor had asked, in a terrified tone.

"No, it was our error. One more thing, people will be by to tidy up and put things in order."

That conversation had occurred an hour earlier, at 2 p.m. It was now 3 p.m., as their FBI supplied panel truck approached a safe house that Virginia had secured one year prior, and which had never been put to use. It was an old, single family home on SouthEast 5th Street in Deerfield Beach. It had been purchased with State Department funds, and the electricity and water contracts had been assigned to a fictitious name.

"Stinks in here," George grunted, as both he and Marvin struggled to carry the survivor's hogtied body.

"Been closed up for more than a year," Virginia explained, on her way to the bathroom to have her wound wrapped by Sandy.

"You may require a trip to the hospital," Rafael called out.

"Bullet went clean through," Sandy advised, "but a few sutures wouldn't hurt."

"Just wrap it tight," Virginia was heard demanding from the bathroom, adding, "the hospital will ask questions that I'm not prepared to answer."

They'd lowered the still black clad intruder to the rust colored shag carpet and stood over him, like a mother guarding her chicks, when Rafael approached and waved them off.

"Pull that rag from his mouth," Rafael ordered.

Marvin bent, and with the tips of his fingers yanked the dishtowel from the man's nearly toothless mouth. He tossed it across the room, where it struck a hideous, green painted wall.

Rafael nudged the man with a shoed foot and demanded, "Who sent you?"

No response.

"You do speak English?"

The man glared at him.

Rafael said something to the prisoner in Arabic and the man had attempted to spit at him, but all that had come out had been a tiny blast of air.

"What did you say to him?" George asked.

"Asked if he ever wanted to see his family again."

"I heard him speak English back at the condo."

"Yeah, the pig understands."

"Now what?"

"We'll let him simmer for awhile, give him time to realize that his life is ours."

The three men, George, Marvin and Rafael, withdrew to speak privately. When they'd reached the opposite side of the room, Rafael said, "This clumsy attempt was probably the work of the alleged, POF."

"Then why do we need the asshole on the floor?" Marvin said.

"I need his conformation, as well as the location of his

commander."

"We're going after them?" George asked, excitedly.

"Maybe."

And then Marvin elbowed his friend, and suggested, "I think we're off the hook."

"Not from where I stand," George replied.

"They came for Virginia, not us."

George rubbed his beard thoughtfully, and answered, "Guess I'd overlooked that."

"Why not allow us to disappear?" Marvin asked.

"The big picture," Rafael replied, "you're not seeing the panorama."

"Oh, the shit that just went down," Marvin moaned.

"That and then some. To put it simply, you guys know too much."

"So you'll kill us in the end, like in the movies?"

"There may be a way out."

"But it won't involve a return to our prior lives, will it?" George interjected.

"Likely not," Rafael agreed.

Rafael left the two men to commiserate with each other, while he returned to the hostage. Kneeling, so that his face was only six inches from the man's scowling mug, he said, "This is when you start answering my questions."

The man turned his head away.

"You know who I am?" Rafael hissed.

The man quickly turned to face him and replied, "A dirty jew."

Rafael exhaled noisily and replied, "One word, Kidon (Hebrew word for bayonet)."

The man's expression turned to terror and he spat, "Assassin."

"Only when it is necessary. Tell me what I need to know and I will spare your family."

"And me?" he said, in perfect English.

"You are an enemy combatant, you knew the risks."

A single tear trickled down the detainee's right cheek, and he asked, "What do you want?"

"Your leader, where can I find him, or her."

"In Gaza."

"His time will come, but the person in charge in this country."

"Abu Alim."

"Family name," he demanded.

"Awad."

"Location?"

"New York City."

George had been whispering with Marvin and

watching Rafael at the same time. But he'd been startled by the appearance of a small, semiautomatic pistol in Rafael's right hand. He watched with detached amazement as the Mossad operative screwed a suppressor onto its barrel, and without hesitation placed the muzzle against the base of the captive's skull, firing three times in rapid succession. He then rose to a standing position, faced the two young men and called out, "Give me a hand with this corpse."

"Why did you kill him?" Marvin asked, in a tremulous tone.

"He'd served no further purpose."

"What had you said that made him so frightened?" George asked, as he grabbed the man's feet and began to drag.

"Not important."

"You said, Kidon," Marvin advised.

"You must have exceptional hearing, I'd whispered it," Rafael said.

"What does it mean?"

Rafael allowed the man's head to strike the floor with a bang, just as Victoria and her girlfriend had returned to the living room, and he replied, "Later."

"What's going on?" Victoria asked, as she glared at the

dead man on the floor.

"Got what I'd needed," Rafael explained.

"So you killed him?"

He shrugged.

"What do you plan to do with the body?" she snickered.

"FedEx it back to its owners."

"Very funny."

"Got a shovel?" he asked.

"How the fuck would I know."

"It's your place."

"Look in the garage."

He nodded toward Marvin, who had already taken the cue and was walking off to search. He returned five minutes later with a two long handled shovels and a rake. "I'm not a digger," he announced.

"Fine," George breathed, as he reached for a shovel and passed the second one to Rafael.

"Where are you going to plant him?" Virginia inquired.

"Back yard."

"Are you fucking crazy? This is a government safe house."

"Got an alternative?" he asked, standing calmly over

the body.

She seethed for a few seconds with Sandra standing silently by her side, and replied, "What about your FBI contact?"

"The two stiffs at your condo and the van ended his obligation to me."

"Fuck it, stick 'em in the ground."

Chapter Twenty-three

Saturday, January 13thI'll

6 A.M.

George had awakened at 5:45 a.m., his back sore and irritated from a night of thrashing about on the living room's shag carpet. Virginia and her significant other had occupied one of the two bedrooms, Rafael the other. Marvin, on the other hand, had staked out the entire couch, and he was still snoring when George arose to visit the bathroom. But as he walked through the living room, a nearby streetlight cast a moving shadow, and he stopped in his tracks to peer out from behind the closed curtain.

Something's outside, he said to himself, while trying to make sense of a dark amorphous figure that at first had appeared to be an illusion, but had become very real as it had shifted position. He dropped to his knees and nudged Marvin awake.

"Get up, something's not right," he whispered.

Marvin turned to face him and said, "Wake me when it is."

"No joke, we're being watched."

Marvin scratched his scalp and rose to a seated position. "It's dark out, probably just a jogger."

"Runners don't stand in one place."

Marvin crawled to the window, peeled back the curtain and quickly withdrew. "Shit," he hissed. "There's more than one."

"I'm going to wake the others," George advised, adding, "don't turn on any lights."

Rafael and Virginia, both fully clothed, slithered into the living room, positioning themselves a distance from the window. Rafael was the first to speak.

"Were you able to ID anyone?" he asked, facing George.

"Too dark."

"OK. If we've been compromised, the front door is the likely point of breach. The back door is inoperable."

George held up his empty pistol and said, "How about some ammo?"

Rafael disappeared for a few moments and returned with a box of cartridges, which he handed to George, saying, "You know what to do with them?"

"Yeah, one in each ear," he sneered, as he began loading an empty magazine.

Rafael pulled up his pant leg revealing a leather ankle holster. He removed a stainless steel, snub-nosed revolver and passed it to Virginia and said, "I have to make a call."

While Virginia disappeared to awaken Sandy, Rafael returned to his bedroom and dialed his encrypted cellphone. It rang several times before a hoarse sounding voice answered, "Shalom."

"Bina, it's me."

"Where the hell have you been, I feel like a prisoner down here."

"You don't sound well."

"It's damp and freezing in this shithole and I've got a cold."

"Sorry, but things have gone south really fast."

"Can you talk?" she asked.

"It's gotten complicated, and there have been some casualties."

"I warned you about making a mess."

"Didn't have a choice."

"Tel Aviv has called twice. I told them you were out with the flu."

"I owe you."

"Big time."

"What do you know about a group called the POF?"

"Wait a minute, there was some traffic two days ago," she said, as the phone went silent. She returned a few moments later and announced, "They're a breakaway group from Hamas. Tel Aviv claims that they're trying to achieve notoriety."

"By doing what?"

"Didn't say."

"They now have three less soldiers."

"I gather that's your complication?"

"Yeah, and they may be about to seek revenge."

"Run," she said excitedly, "you're not in Jerusalem."

"You're afraid of the non registered foreign agent crap?"

"No, you idiot, I'm afraid of your death."

"There are three of us with weapons, albeit, no match for what they're probably wielding."

"Remember your training—live to fight another day."

"Escape may not be an option."

"I could call our friends in Tampa," she offered.

"It's a few hundred miles away."

"Sorry, that's all I've got ... wait, I could call the local PD."

"Never get here in time, and they'd ask questions."

There were a few sniffles, and Rafael couldn't tell if they were a symptom of her cold or something else. Agents had been schooled to be aloof and to not establish any attachments to fellow operatives. But he and Bina had been working together in a confined space, in a country that was not their own, and they had established a bond that could have been likened to the best of marriages. So he softened his voice and said, "Don't worry. Assholes like me always make it through."

"You'd better. I'm not spending the next two years in solitary confinement."

"I'll call you when it's over," he said, as he hit the end button, pocketing the phone and walked back to the living room.

"They're still out there," George observed, a tinge of fear in his voice.

"Let's move the couch against the door," Rafael suggested, adding, "and see if you can find a length of wire."

"Wire?" Marvin questioned.

"I'd like to send line voltage to the door handle."

"Oh, I like that," Virginia exclaimed, returning to the room with Sandy in tow.

"Anything else useful in this place?" Rafael asked of her.

"What about shoving a few mattresses against that big window?"

"Not sure we have time for that."

"We could hide in the attic," she said.

Just then, Marvin returned with a six foot piece of wire and handed it to Rafael. "I had to yank this from the floor lamp in your bedroom," he advised.

Rafael glanced at Virginia who simply shrugged off the damage to her safe house. He then stripped the loose end with his front teeth, exposing five or six inches of bare wire that he proceeded to wrap around the inside door handle. Passing the plug mounted end to George, he said, "Energize."

"Hadn't taken you for a Trekkie," George mumbled, as he knelt before the wall socket and inserted the plug, resulting in a few sparks from the door lever.

"I'm a complex person."

"Why haven't they attacked?" Marvin said, anxiously.

"Go ask them," Rafael sneered.

"They'll come before sunup," Virginia advised.

"We'd better get ready, it won't be long," George moaned.

With the rear door hopelessly inoperable, no interior garage entry and the front door blocked by the couch, the electrified handle added a small modicum of deterrence, but nothing that a burst of automatic weapons fire couldn't overcome.

"There's room for all of us in the attic," Virginia said hurriedly.

"They know we're here, they'll figure it out," Rafael said.

"But they might not know how many of us there are," she suggested.

Rafael hesitated, and then said, "OK, Marvin and your girlfriend are good to go."

"Wait a minute," Virginia objected. "Whomever goes up should be armed, so we can take them by surprise."

"Where's the access?" he asked.

"Over there," she pointed, gesturing toward a covered opening in the ceiling just past the living room.

"Do we need a ladder?"

"It has pull down stairs."

"Alright. George and I will remain, while the three of you head on up. But make certain you don't shoot us in the melee."

Suddenly, Sandy moved in close, her face just inches from Rafael's, and she growled, "I'm a martial arts expert, I can take 'em down."

"You can't wrestle a bullet," he said.

"But I can take at least one of them by surprise."

"Risky."

"I have to protect my woman," she grimaced, as Virginia's face turned crimson.

Rafael, mildly surprised by Sandy's admission, gazed back and forth between the two women and, facing Virginia, asked, "You OK with that?"

"She makes her own decisions."

"So be it. Get moving."

Marvin gave Virginia a boost to enable her opening of the scuttle. She latched onto the spring loaded staircase and pulled it down. The pair scrambled up to the warm attic, dragging the staircase back to its resting position and closing the hatch from within.

George and Rafael took up positions on either side of the corridor that led to the living room, affording them minimal cover, given the thin layer of drywall that separated them from the eventual projectiles. The two bedrooms each had a small window that had been locked the night before, and that had been previously fitted with wrought iron bars. The house had a State-of-the-Art security system that they had disabled in an attempt to avoid police scrutiny, should the alarm have been tripped inadvertently.

"The Alarm," George said, "should we arm it?"

"No. They'll send the police."

"But they'll notify our next of kin," he stuttered, the pistol holding hand shaking violently.

Rafael smiled. "There are two out there that we know of, maybe a third. They'll come in shooting, because they don't know where we are. We have the upper hand and should be able to take out two from the get go, if you can calm down."

"What about the third?"

"That's an unknown, there may not be a third."

"Shit. I've never been this nervous," George admitted, drying his sweaty forehead with the back of his sleeve.

"I've trained for this," Rafael rasped, adding, "but it never gets any easier."

Virginia had slid the attic access open an inch and called out, "We're ready."

Without warning, a kaleidoscope of sparks flew from the front door handle, briefly illuminating the darkened room. And then, a muffled cry of pain from outside, followed by a burst of automatic weapon fire and the thump of the chromed door handle dropping onto the couch.

"Take aim at the center of the door," Rafael barked.

It had taken some shoving on the part of the intruders, with the couch impeding their entrance, but two men jumped through with their weapons on full auto. The unlit room was a cloud of smoke, the pungent odor of gunpowder filling every crevice, but Rafael's directive had resulted in multiple hits to the infiltrator's bodies. The two black clad individuals went down, with one draped over the arm of the couch and the other lying face forward on the carpet.

"Don't take your eyes off of them," Rafael ordered.

"They're dead," George moaned.

"Look closer, they're wearing vests."

"This one's moving," George squealed, his voice a few octaves higher than normal.

"Take their weapons, now," he shouted, as Virginia dropped from the attic access and hit the ground with a thump.

"Are we clear?" she asked, her revolver pointed toward the now shred front door.

"There's a crispy critter just outside," Rafael yelled.

"He's waking up," George shouted, "should I shoot him again?"

Rafael ran to his side and shoved the floor lying man onto his side and yanked the couch hanger to the ground, shouting, "We need them alive."

The house was still as dark as an unlit coal mine, and

the electrocuted invader on the front lawn had shorted out the aging home's fuse box, rendering the overhead high hats useless. The only light source available emanated from a small LED flashlight that Virginia had produced from a pocket, as well as an iPhone.

"Turn them over," Rafael ordered.

Marvin had made his way down from the attic, and with some effort had managed to roll one of the intruders onto his back with the use of his foot, while George accomplished the same with the second.

"Hand me that flashlight," Rafael demanded, adding, "well, well, the POF uses women."

Virginia advanced to the slowly awakening body and launched a pointy toed kick to the woman's right ribcage. She moaned, but otherwise remained silent. The second perp was male, as was the roasted individual on the lawn.

Darkness had begun to dissipate, and with Virginia left to guard the two suspected POF soldiers the three men exited to drag the barbecued body into the garage. With a handful of large, black trash bags and a roll of duct tape they'd managed to seal the body from the elements and temporarily avoid detection, vis-a-vis the odor of decomposition. They locked the garage and returned to deal with the still breathing prisoners.

Chapter Twenty-four

Saturday, 8 A.M.

The marauders had been relieved of their bulletproof vests, but had been left on their backs. With the door jamb still intact, what remained of the front door had been shut, the couch continuing to act as a barrier.

The safe house was located in an older residential neighborhood, and despite the fact that the intruder's weapons had been suppressed they had by no means been silent. Both Rafael and Virginia were concerned that someone might have borne witness to the shootout, and that their anonymity could be wearing thin. They were in need of an immediate plan of action.

"We can't stay here much longer," Virginia advised.

"Yeah," Rafael agreed.

"What about the two shits?" George asked.

"They're bait."

"And we're fishing for, what?"

"The rest of their crew."

"They could be expendables," Virginia suggested.

"Yeah, there's that."

"I'm hungry," Marvin exclaimed.

"We're all hungry," Rafael admitted, adding, "we need

to load this pair into the van."

George gazed askance at his friend and breathed, "You take one and I'll do the other."

The prisoner's hands had been secured behind their backs with Zip Ties, but their feet had been left untethered. George nudged his chosen detainee, grabbed the man by the armpits and brought him to his feet. Marvin followed his cue, doing the same with the female, and together they squeezed around the couch, out into the open air and into the rear of the borrowed van. This time, however, they Zip Tied their ankles together, slammed the door shut and returned to the house.

"It's already pretty cold inside that van?" Marvin advised.

"We're outta here in ten," Rafael said.

"Where to?" Virginia, with her right arm around Sandy's shoulder, asked.

"New York."

"I'm not gonna ride in that fucking van for twelve hundred miles," Sandy complained.

"You won't have to," Rafael advised, as he disappeared into his bedroom to make a call.

"Bina?"

"Now what?" she sneezed, answering on the first ring.

"Cold no better?"

"In this place? Lucky if I survive the night."

"I need the emergency credit card number."

"Use it, and it will set off bells in Tel Aviv," she warned.

"I have to charter a jet back to the City."

Bina laughed, a few coughs interrupting her apparent glee, and replied, "Are you nuts, that'll cost a fortune."

"I've got two tangos that need a ride, can't fly commercial."

"Yeah, guess not, but Tel Aviv should be notified."

"And tell them that I'd gone AWOL on a hunch?"

"OK, here's the number, but if it comes back to bite you did this on your own."

"Agreed."

Rafael dialed the number of a charter service that his people had used in the past, and arranged for an immediate departure to New York.

He walked back into the living room and called out, "Let's go. We're headed to Fort Lauderdale Executive Airport."

***

* * *

The chartered Cessna Citation X was wheels up thirty minutes after their arrival. Rafael had notified his FBI contact of the whereabouts of the van, and they'd settled in for the flight. The charter company had arranged for sandwiches, soft drinks and coffee, and with the prisoners securely belted into their seats, Rafael and company dined in silence, until George decided to break the ice.

"What's the plan?" he asked.

"I'm going to attempt to draw the remaining POF members out into the open," he whispered.

"And the bait's in the rear?"

"Those two, plus myself."

"And then what?"

"You must know what we do with terrorists."

"But they represent only one tentacle."

"It's about sending a message, annihilation comes later."

"Think they'll pay attention?"

Rafael shrugged and replied, "That's all we've got."

"Why not send the troops into Gaza and wipe them out?"

"They're like ant colonies. You kill one and another digs its way to the surface. But if they come to realize that you'll keep batting them down, at some point they might change course."

"Wishful thinking," George murmured.

"Probably, but world politics makes anything more a risky venture."

"That never bothered your people before," Marvin, who had been listening, offered.

"It's become more complicated."

"What happens to them when its over?" George asked, gesturing toward the rear of the plane.

"Depends."

"On what?"

"How my plan goes down."

"You might let them go?" Marvin asked incredulously.

Rafael thought for a moment, and replied, "Hmm. They're ideologues, that won't change. So I guess they're doomed."

"Where do we fit in?" George asked.

"Right now, you're along for the ride."

"And later?"

"We'll see," he said, nodding at Virginia, who had been privy to the entire discourse.

Rafael rose from his seat and headed for the flight deck. I need to think about those two, he said to himself. They've seen and heard more than I would have liked, and while I'd hate to take them out, it might become necessary at some point. On the other hand, they're citizens, and they may become useful pawns.

The Cessna touched down at ten minutes past noon, and as it taxied across the runway at New Jersey's Teterboro Airport, Rafael unlatched the prisoner's seatbelts. The pilot and copilot had been required to ignore the captives, and Rafael had produced false credentials that had identified himself as a U.S. Marshall transporting prisoners. The Israeli had taken a risk with the ruse, since the Marshall service has its own aircraft, but the black, American Express credit card number had paved the way for silence.

Bina had arranged for transportation, and a black van had been parked, awaiting their arrival. When the aircraft had come to a stop, the van pulled to a distance of fifteen feet from the aircraft's exit stairs and its rear doors flew open. The van driver identified himself with a prearranged code word that both Rafael and Bina had agreed upon, and the group scurried from the aircraft with the speed and coordination of a well planned military operation, and took their places in the truck. The still immobilized pair were relegated to the rearmost cargo area.

Since the JPA basement office was off-limits to

anyone other than a Mossad operative, they had previously leased a vacant, two story building in the South Bronx for just such an occasion. The structure had a storied past, having been a clothing factory in the fifties, an illicit drug storage facility in the seventies, and more recently, a rodent retreat. But it was about to house the inhabitants of the black van, whose driver had been discharged at a bus stop, handed a fistful of cash and told that his vehicle would be returned unharmed.

"Put them in the corner," Rafael ordered, indicating a first floor area that was devoid of windows or doorways.

As the two designated drudges—George and Marvin— pushed the prisoners to their resting place, Marvin turned to George and said, "We're not animals, we should have allowed them bathroom privileges."

"Yeah, I can see that she'd pissed her pants."

"What should we do?"

"Remember, they came in shooting."

Just then, Rafael signaled for them to return to the other side of the voluminous ground floor. And as they walked across the sometimes cracked concrete slab, George took note of the brick wall interior, the loose wiring that hung from the ceiling, and an odor suggesting that the structure had been no stranger to urine.

"They're not going anywhere," Rafael advised, "leave them be."

"How are you going to contact their people?" Marvin inquired.

Virginia entered the conversation with, "It's my turn to make things happen."

"Meaning?"

"You saw me on the phone, right?"

Marvin nodded affirmatively.

"I'd called my contact, and she'll pass them the message."

"You didn't give them this address, I hope," George droned.

"No."

"And now your contact knows that you're workin' two sides," Marvin added.

"Actually, three."

"Yeah, right, the State Department."

"What happens next?"

"She has my number—we wait for the inevitable call."

"I'm new to this game," George admitted, "but it seems to me that if they agree to meet they won't be bringing the entire crew."

"A likely scenario," Rafael agreed, "but then we ladder

up."

"Meaning?"

"Assuming that we survive the anticipated conflict, we use them to reach the others."

"So we leapfrog to the top?"

"That's the plan."

Chapter Twenty-five

Saturday, 4 P.M.

Virginia's cellphone had begun to ring and she stared at it, as if not wishing to appear too anxious. But she picked it up and snapped, "Yes?"

"We got message," an accented voice announced in broken English.

"Good," she replied, in a disinterested tone.

"What you want?"

She smiled at Rafael and said, "Come get your people."

There was a period of silence, and then, "You bring."

"Not gonna happen."

Another moment of silence, and then came the reply, "We come, where?"

"Bronx Zoo. When you get there, call me again and I'll give you the final destination."

The call had ended abruptly, but the confused expression on the faces of George and Marvin had prompted an explanation.

"The double location approach is for tactical advantage, we don't want to walk into an ambush," she'd explained.

One hour later, 5 p.m., the same fractured English speaking voice came over the phone and Virginia, belted into the front passenger seat of the black van, its engine idling in the zoo's lot, said, "Describe your vehicle."

"Brown delivery truck."

Rafael, with a pocket sized pair of binoculars pressed against his orbits, called out, "I see it."

"OK, go to..."

They had discussed various geographic options for the proposed handoff, but none of them had seemed viable due to the risk of exposure. And with that in mind, Rafael had called Bina and explained that he was about to burn their Bronx real estate. In context, the word, *burn*, was understood to mean the end of its anonymity, and was not an uncommon occurrence in the obscure world that they inhabited.

The black van parked around the corner from the South Bronx building where they'd left Marvin and Sandy to watch over the prisoners. And convinced that the POF truck had yet to arrive, they entered the building and prepared to set their trap.

Rafael handed Sandy a roll of silver duct tape and said, "Put this over their mouths."

Without hesitation, she ripped off a length and

slapped it across the lips of one and then the other POF soldier.

Rafael then took George's semiautomatic and handed it to Virginia, replacing it with her revolver, saying, "Make sure that they're fully loaded."

George didn't question the exchange, but the response to the apparent demotion was visible in his facial expression.

"The back door is bolted from within, leaving the front door as the only entry point," Rafael advised, adding, "Virginia and I will stand on either side and hit them when they enter."

"What about the rest of us?" Marvin asked.

"Sandy has some lethal skills but you, I'm afraid, are a liability. Find a place to hide."

"And me?" George said, hesitantly.

"You take the alcove on the left side of the hostages. It's deep, and they won't notice you at first. Five rounds won't go very far, so don't fire unless you have to."

"If they're smart," Virginia said, "they'll send in a few throwaways to test the water."

"That's where Sandy comes in. She'll have to use her Krav Maga training to immobilize one, while the two of us do the others."

"So no shooting," she declared.

"Not unless we have to."

There were no windows to signal the arrival of their guests, and anxiety built as they waited for the door to open. Fifteen minutes later the steel door flew against the inner brick wall with a bang, followed by the crouched entrance of three, armed marauders. Sandy jumped the first entrant, disabling the thin male in a most permanent fashion, while the remaining two terrorists opened fire at no one in particular. Bullets ricocheted off of the bricks and concrete flooring as Rafael leapt forward and grabbed the smoking muzzle of one man's automatic rifle, breaking the terrorist's wrist in the process and forcing him to the ground. But the third shooter had made his way across the room to the hostages, summarily executing them a second before George slid from the alcove and nervously peppered the man with the revolver's five rounds. The shooter collapsed like an unstrung marionette, with his stunned assassin staring into his clouding dark eyes as his life slipped away.

"Over here," Rafael shouted.

George snapped out of his trancelike state and ran to the caller. "What?" he said.

"Watch over this guy," Rafael ordered, as he

cautiously peeked out into the street.

"I'm empty," George began to say, holding the revolver above his head. And realizing that no one seemed to care, he knelt and retrieved the downed man's rifle, aiming it directly at his head.

Rafael, who was being covered by Virginia from behind, returned and exclaimed, "All clear."

"They'd left their own people," George said, with a tone of amazement.

"Correction, killed their people," Virginia said.

"Not surprising," Rafael admitted, closing the door and locking it.

They all gathered around the single survivor, where George was once again transfixed, the rifle still aimed squarely at the man's head.

"Gimme that," Rafael said, dislodging the weapon from his hands and leaning it against a wall.

Apparently feeling that she'd paid her dues, Sandy entered the conversation, to the surprise of her girlfriend, and said, "Let's waterboard this one."

Rafael grinned and replied, "Not just yet," as he nudged the man to a seated position.

The man held his broken wrist with the opposite hand and scowled, but otherwise kept silent.

"You speak English?" Rafael inquired in Arabic.

"Little," was the raspy reply.

"Your people left you behind, where did they go?"

"Zine be-ayn (Hebrew for a dick in your eye)."

"You speak Hebrew?"

"Lech tis-day-en (fuck off)."

"You've got the curse words right, now, answer my question?"

"You won't find them," he spat.

"Do you want to live?"

The man shrugged, as if he didn't care.

"Do you want your family to live?"

With that, the prisoner locked eyes with his inquisitor, and growled, "That's what you jews do, kill Palestinians."

"So do you."

"We don't."

"Really, look across the room."

"They couldn't be trusted."

"Now you're in the same boat."

"I am a believer."

"A lot of good that's going to do you."

"Allah is my savior," he said, adjusting his position on the concrete.

"Don't count on it."

"I will go to paradise before I tell you anything."

Rafael laughed and said, "Good luck with that."

"I need a bathroom," the man advised.

"You can shit in your pants, for all I care."

Rafael walked off to the opposite side of the room, where Virginia suggested, "Let me have a go at him."

"Be my guest."

But before she began her trek across to the other side, George piped in with, "What if they come back with reinforcements?"

"Good possibility, so we should prepare to depart.

"To where?"

"Away from here."

"So we just drive around forever?"

"If our guest refuses to cooperate, I will arrange for a transfer to Tel Aviv. They'll make certain that he talks."

"Maybe Sandy's suggestion is the way to go," Marvin said.

"We don't have the time or equipment," Rafael explained.

Disinterested in the conversation, Virginia had made her way across the room and was seen standing over the hostage. They watched in amazement as the man appeared to morph into a state of hysteria, which only ceased after Virginia had rendered a swift kick to the side of his head. She stood in place for a few moments and then returned to the group.

"What happened?" Rafael asked.

"He'd made a lewd comment and I told him that my people would do the same, in spades, to his wife and family."

"We don't know if he has a family," Rafael said.

"We do now."

"Why'd you kick him?" Marvin asked.

"Heat of the moment."

"OK, bring the van around," he told George, "we're outta here."

Chapter Twenty-six

Saturday, 6:30 P.M.

JPA Headquarters, Manhattan, N.Y.

Bina had just finished her frozen turkey diner when the secure traffic had come across her screen. On first glance, to the uninitiated, the encrypted message would have appeared to have been an assembly of unrelated letters, but a keyboard macro summoned the proprietary software that had been designed to render an intelligible dispatch.

She yawned, shoved the aluminum foil that had contained her dinner to one side and, expecting the usual tiresome transmission, took a cursory glance at the screen. But that brief glimpse had been enough to shock her awake.

"An inspection?" she shouted to herself. "There's never been an inspection."

And then she read further down the screen, where it demanded that both operatives be present.

Oh shit, she thought, realizing that the communique had not specified a time or date for the review. She dropped the plastic fork that she'd been toying with and reached for the encrypted cellphone.

"Not now Bina, I'm in a rush," Rafael said, realizing

that no one else had his number.

"We have an emergency," she pleaded.

"Handle it."

"Not possible."

"Listen, the warehouse is burned, I'm on the run," he said excitedly, as he made his way to the van.

"Tel Aviv is coming."

"Repeat."

"They're coming to check us out."

"Shit, for real?" he blurted, standing beside the driver's side door.

"Just got the news and it was clear that we're both to be present."

"Might not be so bad, I've got a package for them."

"And you're going to explain it, how?"

"Yeah, that could be a problem, but this tango needs the works."

"Tango in possession?"

"Yeah, and I've no place to hide."

"Why is that necessary?"

"I upset the hive, and the inhabitants are likely in pursuit."

"That wasn't our directive."

"I remember, observe only."

There was a period of silence and Rafael, still standing beside the vehicle while all others were within, said, "Bina, you still there?"

"Thinking."

"Do it quickly."

"OK. There's a shuttered restaurant near the Bronx Zoo. Use your skills and gain entry," she advised, rattling off the address.

"Knew I could count on you."

"What about the inspection?" she said.

"When are they arriving?"

"Didn't say."

"Stall them."

"With what?"

"Make up a medical explanation."

"Fine, I'll tell them that you've been Baker Acted."

"What's that?"

"A free pass to the nuthouse."

The Chinese restaurant had been closed down for a health code violation, as indicated by the large sign that had been pasted across the front door. Rafael worked his way around to the rear and found a door that had likely been used as a carry out to the dumpster that sat just five feet from its edge. Without any tools, he had only his body weight to force it open. But the metal door would not give. He returned to the idling van and commandeered George and Marvin, and together the three men managed to ram the undersized dumpster into the steel door, sufficiently denting it to the extent that it could be shoved aside. But that also meant that it could not be secured.

"Inside," Rafael ordered, as Virginia and Sandy marched the prisoner into the dark interior.

"Stinks in here," Marvin observed.

"Yeah, probably the reason for its closure."

"The odor?"

"Bugs," George advised, following the thin beam of light from Virginia's small flashlight.

Rafael surmised that the restaurant had been abandoned, as there was no electricity, water or gas. And with the tables, chairs and silverware still visible it appeared to him that the proprietor had left in a hurry.

"I hate Chinese food," Sandy exclaimed.

"They didn't leave any behind," George said.

"Now what?" Marvin inquired.

"First order of business ... dispose of our guest," Rafael indicated.

"We schlepped him here to kill 'em?" he complained.

"He needs intense interrogation."

"Here?"

"His worst nightmare," he said succinctly, with emphasis on *nightmare* for the prisoner's benefit.

"At least we're safe in this dump," George exclaimed.

"No guarantee," Rafael advised.

"We weren't followed, I watched."

"Our van was left unguarded at the warehouse during the firefight."

"So?"

"There was ample time for them to install a tracking device."

"But they couldn't have known that we'd survive," Marvin said.

"That's what I would have done," Virginia offered.

"The tracker?"

"Yes," she said.

"I'm not gonna sit in this dark shithole waiting for another attack," Sandy growled.

"What's your alternative?" Virginia asked.

"We shake the crap outta this monster, find his buddies and strike preemptively."

"Great idea, but he ain't talking," George blurted.

"Let me have a try," Sandy said.

"I need him alive," Rafael warned.

"What good is he if doesn't talk?" she asked.

"My plan is to send him to Tel Aviv," he said, loud enough for the captive to hear.

"OK, I'll try not to kill 'em," she agreed.

The shuttered restaurant was so dark that they could barely see each other without Virginia's LED flashlight, and everyone knew that its batteries would give out at some point. With that knowledge, Sandy wasted no time situating herself behind the seated and restrained POF soldier, withdrawing briefly, as the stench of urine assaulted her nostrils. Placing the fingers of both of her muscular hands about the man's throat, she began to squeeze, slowly building up pressure as she leaned toward his left ear and whispered, "Do you want to die?"

The man coughed, and replied, "Fuck you, bitch."

She continued to increase her viselike grip, repeating the same question over and over, until the man's coughing increased in frequency and then she stopped. Without missing a beat, she placed the palms of each hand on either side of his head and began to slowly twist his head to the right. When resistance denied any further movement she held it in place, and said, "This is when you tell me what I need to know, or I end your miserable life."

"Allah will receive me in paradise," he breathed.

"Not today, my friend," she advised, freeing one of her hands and reaching into a pocket for the pork jerky that she'd carried for occasional bouts of hunger. "Open your mouth," she demanded.

Apparently unaware of what was to come the man complied, and she jammed the jerky deep into his throat. With the palm of her free hand she slammed his jaw shut, forcing him to reflexively swallow the flat material. He wretched, as the sharp edged jerky made its way down his esophagus without any promise of its expulsion.

"Relax," she counseled, "you just ate a pork rind."

The man's head flew back but she held tight, resuming her grip.

"Haram, haram," he sobbed.

"C'mon, a big, strapping terrorist like yourself can surely handle a little pork," she cooed, adding, "does that mean paradise is off the table?"

"Alkaliba (Arabic for bitch)," he rasped.

"Since you won't get to see the rivers of honey, or the promised virgins, how about surviving for this world?

The man was silent for a few moments, and then hissed, "What do you want?"

"Where are the others?" she demanded.

"We are everywhere," he spat.

"The New York location will do for now."

He rattled off an address on the lower East side and was once again silent.

Rafael had been listening from less than a foot away and he whispered, "Impressive, Mossad could use you."

"Not today, thanks, but shouldn't we get moving?"

"And do what?" he asked quietly, adding, "we don't have much firepower and even less ammo."

"There must be some way we take them out."

Virginia waved her flashlight's beam for them to approach, and in the darkness Rafael tripped over a chair leg. Recovering, he ambled over to Virginia's side of the room.

"I have a contact at the DEA," she muttered.

"And?" Rafael rejoined.

"These guys have automatic weapons and I'd doubt that they're here legally. That might be enough for the DEA and ICE to move on."

"I can't be part of that."

"Why?"

"I'm not a registered foreign agent."

"Understood. But my cover is already blown, so I'll take point."

"What about shithead?" Sandy asked.

"He stays here—for now," Rafael advised.

Virginia's cellphone had less than a quarter of its battery charge remaining, and that meant that lengthy conversations and explanations would be out of the question. She stepped out beyond the broken rear door and made her call. Ten minutes later, she returned to the darkened interior, aimed the flashlight at Rafael's torso and said, "We need to talk."

"Is it on?" he asked.

"Not exactly."

"They balked?"

"My contact refused to get involved."

"Personal issues?"

"Apparently, word's out that I've gone rogue."

"So that's it, we're out in the cold."

"Not exactly. I know where to get some hardware."

"What kind of hardware?"

"MP5's."

"I don't have access to cash right now," he advised.

"Won't need any—how are your lock picking skills?"

Chapter Twenty-seven

9 P.M.

A firearms dealer on the lower East side was to be their target.

Virginia, as well as other State Department operatives, had taken past advantage of the distributor's selection of hard to find weapons. Much of the owner's inventory had been obtained for out of state shipment, or had been earmarked for law enforcement, due to the fully automatic nature of the arms and the fact that they could not be legally sold to the general public.

They'd arrived several hours after closing and found the front door sealed by a rolling steel plate that had been secured by a keyed, primary and secondary locks. The POF hostage had been left behind at the shuttered restaurant with Sandy as his guardian, while Marvin and George waited in the Van. Virginia was the first to exit the vehicle and cover her face bandido style with a kerchief. Rafael took a similar precaution by pulling his shirt over his head in order to cover his face from any overhead surveillance.

"Can you pick them?" Virginia asked, as Rafael knelt to get a better view of the mechanism.

"Maybe, but make sure you block me from the street."

A one week old newspaper had been stuffed into a narrow crevice that sat between one end of the steel plate and the brick wall. Virginia dislodged it and opened it wide, as she stood before Rafael attempting to conceal him from inquiring eyes.

"I think you're good, the street's empty for the time being," she observed.

"OK, I've overcome number one ... moving on to the second. But what about the inevitable alarm system?" he asked, his eyes glued to the keyhole.

"Leave that to me."

"You're an expert?" he chuckled.

"Been here before. And out of curiosity, with my government ID in hand, I had asked about their security system. Unless it's been updated since last year, I can defeat it."

"Get ready, because the second lock just gave way."

"The front door should be a no brainer, and then we're in," she said.

Three minutes later the front door slid open, followed by the alarm's warning chirp and Virginia's rush to the keypad.

"Shit, shit," she shouted, "we're fucked."

"What's wrong?"

"They'd substituted a fingerprint reader for the keypad," she said, anxiously.

"Can you beat it?" Rafael asked, his body half across the threshold.

She gazed at him with a terrified expression, and then proceeded to rip the half inch thick device from the wall. As the screen dangled from a handful of multicolored wires, she began detaching them one by one, until an ear piercing siren began to wail throughout the store. Virginia looked up at Rafael, and shouted, "We're done, let's go."

They ran from the store without looking back, jumped into the van and, to the surprise of its two occupants (George and Marvin), Rafael floored the accelerator and screeched around the corner at the end of the street.

"What happened?" George cried out.

"Tripped the alarm," Virginia replied.

"What about cameras?"

"Didn't see any."

"You can bet they were there."

"Too late now."

Rafael had remained silent, his fingers squeezing the steering wheel, as he brought the van to a stop beside a curb. Without turning, he removed a cellphone from his pocket and dialed the JPA basement office. The phone rang nine times without an answer and he lowered the device to his lap.

"Something's wrong," he said.

"No shit, Sherlock," Virginia exclaimed, "we've got nothing for our efforts."

"Not that. My partner isn't answering the phone."

"Since when do you have a partner?" she asked.

"Not important, but my call should have been answered on the second ring," he advised, with a concerned expression.

"Nobody's perfect."

"She is."

"Oh, you have a girlfriend," she teased.

"Everybody out, now," he shouted.

"What?" she roared, adding, "here, in the bowels of the city?"

"I can't take you where I need to go."

"What about us?"

"Find your way back to the restaurant."

"We'll never make it on foot," Marvin complained.

"Boost a car, call an Uber, I don't care, I have to go."

He left the triumvirate standing beside a shuttered coffee shop, as he rushed back to investigate. Halfway there, a series of poorly timed traffic lights playing havoc with his urgency, the cellphone rang.

"Yes?"

"It's me, lehikaness letzarot (Hebrew for, I got in trouble)," her panicked voice conveyed.

Jamming the accelerator to the floor, ignoring a red light, he yelled, "What's happened?"

"Under attack," she whispered.

"Where are you?"

"Hiding place."

"Who are the attackers?" he bellowed, swerving around a slow moving bus.

"Don't know, but they're heavily armed."

"Are you hurt?"

"Not yet."

"Stay there, on my way."

"No, they'll see you."

"I can't leave you by yourself."

Following a brief moment of silence, she asked, "Are you armed?"

"Poorly."

"Go to the grocer."

The grocer was an ex-Israeli special forces soldier who had moved to the U.S. at the conclusion of his enlistment.

A staunch supporter of Israel, he'd maintained a loose connection with the Intelligence service and had been frequently called upon to assist, hide or arm undocumented agents. He had been aware of the JPA office from its inception, although its exact whereabouts had been kept secret. And while handguns would often find their way into the U.S. via diplomatic pouch, the grocer had been the go-to supplier for automatic weapons and ammunition.

Three blocks west of the JPA basement facility was an unlikely business for an Israeli. The red neon sign seated above its entrance flashed *Bodega West* to anyone who cared to look. It was a small, neighborhood store—open until midnight six days a week—that carried cigars, cigarettes, an assortment of bad for your teeth candy, as well as a selection of delicatessen type food. And on any given day, the grocer, aka, Ezra Green, could be found behind the white marble countertop slicing through hoagie bread and filling the open gap with ham, salami, cheese, lettuce and various condiments. But the claustrophobia inducing bodega had, for many years, served as a front for a massive store of arms hidden in its basement.

Rafael, in a sweat, double parked the van just outside

of the Bodega and ran inside. Ezra, a fat, Hebrew National salami gripped in the fingers of his left hand, looked up and offered a quizzical expression. "You have a food emergency?" he chuckled, with an exaggerated yiddish accent.

Rafael had never required the Grocer's services, and he searched his memory for the code phrase, finally, leaning across the counter past an elderly customer and calling out, "Duck soup."

Ezra turned to face the shelf behind the counter and in response, replied, "Afraid I don't have any."

"Can you check in the back?"

The grocer smiled, wax paper wrapped the hoagie that he'd just finished preparing for the elderly woman, and said, "You can pay me another time."

The woman smiled and promptly left the store.

Ezra walked to the front door, flipped a sign around to inform customers that he'd return shortly, and motioned for Rafael to follow him to the rear of the establishment.

They descended a steep staircase into the darkened, mustiness of the basement. Ezra reached to his right and flicked a switch that lit the confines with the brightness of a nighttime baseball stadium. Rafael squinted and said, "I need..."

"Take what you like," Ezra suggested, as he gestured toward the collection of rifles, submachine guns, pistols, grenade launchers, plastic explosives and more.

The JPA operative wasted no time in securing a few MP5's, an MP7 and an older Uzi, along with all he could carry, fully loaded, high capacity magazines and, finally, a powerful, LED flashlight and a few grenades.

"Planning an invasion?" Ezra asked.

"A rescue."

"Good luck, my friend. Take the staircase down the other end to the street," he advised, as he handed Rafael a burlap sack to conceal the hardware.

"Thank you."

"I'm here if you need me," Ezra informed, as he headed back up to the bodega.

Rafael lugged the weaponry to the waiting van, tossed the heavy sack onto the passenger seat, and headed for his underground office. It was almost ten p.m., but city traffic was still fierce and Rafael found himself punching the horn and cursing at the drivers whose cabins were lit by the telltale bluish light of a cellphone's liquid crystal display. I don't know what I'm going to do when I get there, he thought, his right hand resting on the gun filled sack, preventing it from sliding to the floor. Bina didn't know how many were involved and I don't even know if they are still on the premises.

He hit the speed dial for her cellphone, but it rang without answer and he wondered if the battery had died or, even worse, if she'd been eliminated.

At the time of the basement facility's creation, a niche —hidden from view by a metal door and a wheeled refrigerator—had been constructed large enough to conceal two people and a tall oxygen canister, the latter to be used in the event of a prolonged interval of confinement. Bina's last call had originated from that room and, while it was unlikely that the intruders would have divined the existence of such a hideout, the sound of her terrified voice had made his blood boil.

The van came to a screeching halt fifty yards from the pawn shop's entrance. Rafael reached into the sack and withdrew a semiautomatic pistol, an MP5 with three spare magazines, and two stun grenades. He shoved the pistol into his waistband, chambered a round into the submachine gun and slid from the driver's seat, carefully closing and locking the door as silently as possible.

The street is quiet, he said to himself, as he surveyed the surroundings in search of a lookout or getaway vehicle. Either they're gone, or their transportation is staying out of sight, waiting for a pickup call, he considered. The usually lit streetlights were ominously dark, and he wondered if happenstance had played a role, or if there had been human intervention. A few glass shards crunched beneath his feet making the latter the more plausible explanation. He continued to make his way closer to the pawn shop, slithering along the walls of the attached storefronts, until he found himself a foot from the shop's entrance. A quick glance revealed that the front door had been breached, but there were no visible sentries to prevent his passage.

This could be a trap, he told himself, as he nudged the door open farther with the MP5's muzzle. The interior was unlit, and he entered with caution, his eyes panning the surrounding counters before locking on to the door leading to the basement. With no obvious evidence for hidden attackers, he lit the LED torch and rapidly swept its beam from side to side as he walked toward the back of the store.

The door to the basement had been secured with an electronic keypad that activated a series of two inch, stainless steel bolts that protruded from its top and sides in a fashion similar to a safe. But the door was ajar, and Rafael stood before it for a few moments trying to fathom how it could have been defeated. Leaving those thoughts behind, he concentrated on the object of his mission—Bina, as he began to descend the staircase.

Normally, a sensor would detect the presence of movement and the basement lights would illuminate automatically but, in the case of an emergency, the automatic feature could be overridden from below, a precaution most likely taken by his partner, he presumed.

The basement was dark and quiet, save for the undulating screensavers on three of the desk mounted computer screens. Rafael intensified his grip on the MP5 and panned the torch from left to right as he lowered his feet from the last step and froze. The basement appeared absent the intruders, but he could detect the faint odor of spent gunpowder, an observation that did not bode well for Bina. Unwilling to risk calling out, he began to investigate every crevice and potential hiding place, of which there were few, before partially rolling the still in place refrigerator to reveal their secret alcove. The entire search had taken less than two minutes, after which he'd slung the submachine gun from a shoulder and shoved the refrigerator entirely to one side of the steel door.

"Bina, don't shoot, it's me, Rafael," he called out loud enough for her to hear through the thick door.

There was no response, and since the door locked from within, a secondary, remote keypad had been installed in their bathroom. He ran to it and punched in the code, thereby producing an audible click. Bina was lying on the floor, barely breathing, the oxygen mask covering her face and mouth.

"Bina," he shouted, removing her mask and dragging her from the cubicle.

She moaned a few times and finally opened her eyes, and coughed, "Where the fuck were you?"

Chapter Twenty-eight

Saturday

Midnight

Not many cars had been observed in the vicinity of their failed arms store break-in, but after walking for thirty minutes in an uptown direction they had come across several older vehicles, one of which had been parked illegally.

"This is our ride," Virginia had indicated to George, as Marvin sulked like a disappointed child.

"You've done this before?" George asked.

"Believe it or not, it's part of our training."

"Can I help?"

"Watch for onlookers."

"The owner might call the police," he'd said, as she set about unlocking the driver's side door.

"They'll just assume that it'd been towed," she'd corrected, gesturing upward at the no parking sign.

They'd abandoned the stolen car and had made their way back into the Chinese restaurant. It was 1 a.m., and they were literally in the dark as far as Rafael's whereabouts had been concerned.

"I'm thirsty and hungry," Sandy advised.

"He give you any trouble?" Virginia asked, waving her flashlight in the direction of their captive.

"Not a word, but where's the Israeli?"

"Had some kind of emergency."

"He'd dumped us in the middle of the city," Marvin complained.

"Then how'd you get here?" Sandy asked.

"Stole a car," Virginia gloated.

"So we're on our own?"

"For the time being."

"What about the Palestinian?"

"Rafael wanted him alive, but I don't give a shit," Virginia spat.

"Let's waste him and split," Sandy suggested.

"Works for me, but I think we should wait and see if Rafael returns."

"We need food and drink," George called out.

"Nothing's open at this hour."

"Another hour and I'll go cannibal," Marvin announced.

"There's a place called Cafeteria, in Chelsea. Its open 24 hrs," Sandy suggested.

"How do you know about that?" Virginia asked.

"Been there."

"With your last BFF, I suppose," she sneered.

"Yeah," Sandy blushed, her crimson cheeks invisible in the darkness.

"Well, the four of us could fit into the stolen car."

"I'll take care of the scumbag," Sandy offered.

"No need," Virginia replied, adding, "just leave 'em, the rodents will do the job."

They were about to depart via the broken rear door, when they were thwarted by the sound of footsteps on gravel. Virginia turned and warned, "We've got visitors, go hide."

She stood by the damaged doorframe, a length of its metal structure held over her head, as she waited for the inevitable. But suddenly, a flashlight illuminated the face of the intruder apparent and she called out, "Almost hit you over the head."

"Would have telephoned, but..." Rafael grinned.

"I assume that she's your partner?" Virginia said, nodding toward Bina.

"Equal partner," Bina snarled.

"This is Bina, the Mossad's most ferocious operative," he advised.

"I'm Virginia. Nice to meet you, but we were just about to take off."

"To where?" Rafael inquired.

"Anyplace but here. Actually, we need some food."

"We have a problem," he advised, as the pair passed through the doorway into the darkness.

"And those you'd left behind, meaning us, do not?"

"We all do, but our previously secure location has been compromised."

"Explain?"

"We were attacked."

"Shit. The POF?"

"That's my best guess."

"And you were there?" she asked of Bina.

"Yes, but I'd hid."

"Live to fight another day."

"Pretty much," she agreed.

"Now what?"

"I'd signaled Tel Aviv before we'd destroyed the computers and locked up. They'll send a team, but it will take some time."

"It once took me a few hours and a hammer to totally disable a bunch of hard drives," Virginia admitted.

"A few, small, prepositioned explosives can do the job in an instant," Bina explained.

Virginia nodded knowingly, and said, "I assume that

you'd returned for a reason?"

"Two reasons," Rafael admitted, "I felt responsible for those inside and we need your help."

"Those inside?" she said, tentatively.

"I knew that you could take care of yourself, but the others—"

"What kind of help," she asked, ignoring the offhanded compliment.

"I can't allow the attack on our facility to go unanswered."

"And we're going to fight them with broken chair legs from a Chinese restaurant?"

"Not quite. I've got some hardware in my vehicle."

"Any idea where to find them?"

"Not yet, but the prisoner knows—if you haven't already killed him."

"Nope, was gonna leave him for the rodents."

"Not a bad idea, but first I need to squeeze him some."

"I'll take care of that," Bina said, authoritatively.

"Don't kill him until we've gotten what we need," Rafael insisted, as Bina made her way into the restaurant's interior.

Rafael and Virginia had remained at the rear of the

restaurant, keeping watch for potential intruders, when Bina returned twenty minutes later.

"He was a tough bird," she exhaled.

"Was?" Virginia said.

"Don't worry, I got the goods."

"Where are they?" Rafael asked.

"Not far from our place."

"OK, lets get organized and hit them hard."

"There might be one small problem," Bina announced.

George, who had been listening near the door, chimed in with, "What kind of problem?"

"They're in an old apartment building."

"Other tenants?" Virginia asked.

"Don't know and hadn't thought to ask before I'd sent him on his way."

"Aside from the risk of collateral victims, there's a noise consideration," Rafael advised.

"That's where good aim and expedience comes in," Bina said, adding, "I vote we go."

"What about the rest of us?" George asked.

"Neither you nor your friend can shoot worth squat," Virginia mentioned.

"She's right," Rafael agreed, continuing, "too big a

risk, you're the designated driver."

The insult had struck him hard, but George realized that he was out of his league. He walked off to inform Marvin of their upcoming role.

"It's time," Bina said.

"Almost 2 a.m. Maybe we'll catch them off guard," Rafael submitted.

They piled into the van with George at the wheel and Marvin riding shotgun. Rafael passed an MP5 to Virginia and another to Bina, while an MP7 sat in his lap, and Sandy toyed with a long magazine protruding from the bottom of her Uzi.

"Ever use one of these?" Rafael asked, holding up a stun grenade.

"In training," Virginia advised.

"Take one, it may be useful."

"Be careful with that, it's got a light trigger," he warned, nodding at Sandy.

"No worries," she mocked.

They'd taken the long way into the city to allow enough time for the hastily constructed plan to sink in.

The lower East Side building had been renovated, and even in the darkness of night its appearance spelled yuppieville. George double-parked several car lengths from its front entrance and turned. "This is not the abandoned building that I'd been expecting," he noted.

"Hmm, could be a problem," Rafael agreed.

Virginia exited the van and stood by its front fender, returning a few seconds later to its interior. "This place is occupied, and you can bet that there will be collateral damage," she instructed.

"It's still a go for me," Bina called out.

"Not so sure about that," Rafael replied. "If I were a terrorist, I would have chosen a place like this, where there are numerous innocents."

"Preservation of life is something we think about, while the terrorists don't give a shit," Virginia mumbled.

Rafael considered the options, leaned forward and said, "Drive on."

"You're gonna give them a free pass," Bina complained.

"No, but we need a new plan."

"My plan involves shredding their asses, right now," she growled.

"Remember the directive."

"Fuck Tel Aviv, they weren't watching my rear when the bullets began to fly."

"No, that was my job," he whispered.

Ignoring his admission of guilt, she shouted, "Stop the van and let me out."

"You're not going anywhere," Rafael ordered.

"We're equal partners, you don't control me," she seethed.

"I'm doing what I should have done earlier, I'm watching your back."

She pushed into the seat, frowned and replied, "The new plan better include annihilation."

Chapter Twenty-nine

Sunday, January 14th

5 A.M.

They'd slept in the van, having driven to battery park after stopping at the Cafeteria in Chelsea and loading up on food and drink. A police car had come by sometime during the early hours and an officer had knocked on the driver's side window to inquire about their intentions. George had explained that they were tourists and had neglected to make a hotel reservation. The police officer had insisted that they be gone by sunup and George had agreed. And he was the first to open his eyes when he'd heard something hit the windshield. One of New York's resident homeless was in the process of cleaning the glass with a squirt bottle and a wad of newspaper.

"Go away," he shouted, rolling down his window.

The man paid him no heed, so he reached into his pocket, pulled out some loose change and offered it through the window. That was all it had taken for the disheveled being to cease his useless activity and move on.

"What was that?" Rafael yawned.

"Nothing important, but we'd lucked out with the cops."

"The weapons had been under a blanket," Rafael advised.

"Good to know. Now what?"

"Hold that thought," he said, reaching for his buzzing cellphone and exiting the van.

The others had begun to awaken, and Virginia leaned forward and asked, "What's happening?"

"Phone call."

She slid past Sandy in an attempt to exit but was thwarted by Rafael's return to the vehicle.

"Problem?" she asked.

"Not for you," he hissed.

"Explain."

"We'd been expecting some visitors ... they've arrived."

"Did they bring reinforcements?" Bina called out.

"Don't know, but they came with a shitload of anger."

"We didn't do anything wrong," she protested.

"I did."

"What do they want?"

"To meet."

"When?"

"This morning."

"Where?"

"Intercontinental, Times Square."

"I'm not dressed for a meet," Bina said.

"Neither am I, but you weren't invited."

"Doesn't sound good."

Rafael shrugged, and said, "Let's get something to eat and then I'm off to face the heat."

***

8 A.M.

They'd returned to the Cafeteria where they'd dined in silence. Rafael had taken the check, paid with a credit card and they'd all headed back to the van. He'd handed the keys to George and said, "If I'm still in the game, I'll meet you back here at 2 p.m."

"What should we do?"

"You've got a full tank of fuel, make like a tourist."

As the van disappeared into the building traffic, Rafael hailed a taxi and headed for the hotel. He'd decided to arrive early to organize his thoughts in preparation for the unknown. The taxi had dropped him off at the entrance and he'd sauntered through the doors as if he'd been there before, located the lounge, as suggested by the caller, and had taken a seat. It was now 8:30 a.m., a half-hour before the scheduled meeting. Rafael had faced all manner of threats during his military life, but the specter of facing off with his Mossad superiors had him in a sweat, and he found himself taking deep breaths in an attempt to calm his nerves. But much to his surprise, the visitors from Tel Aviv had been waiting in a darkened corner. They'd allowed him a few moments to settle down and then presented themselves.

"Follow us," the taller of the pair demanded.

"Am I allowed to know your names," Rafael asked, as they walked in tandem to the elevator.

The shorter of the pair smirked, declined a reply, and nodded toward the open lift. Rafael did as told and entered. When the elevator had reached their floor, the three men exited with Rafael sandwiched between the Israeli visitors. They walked roughly twenty feet and entered what Rafael assumed to have been their room. The tall one locked the door and said, "Take a seat at the desk."

Rafael considered the request, and slowly lowered his buttocks onto the waiting chair. "What's this about?" he asked, although he already knew the answer.

"What is there about orders that you fail to understand?" the shorter male inquired.

"I saw an opportunity to gather intel," Rafael

responded.

"And it'd backfired."

He grimaced and replied, "Sort of."

"And the intel?" the tall man asked.

"A Hamas breakaway faction is in play."

"Ah yes, the alleged POF."

"They exist," Rafael insisted, "I can show you their bullet marks."

"Bullet holes, yes, but you could have done that yourself."

"Am I on trial for this?" he bristled.

"You are, as the Americans say, a person of interest."

"What reason would I have had to destroy our office?"

"We are aware of the boredom that comes with your posting."

"So I shot up the basement to create some excitement?"

"Perhaps."

"That's insane. And I did not fabricate the POF."

"We are aware of their existence," the short man admitted.

"Then why aren't we talking about a response to their assault?"

The two Mossad agents gazed at each other, and then

the taller of the two turned and said, "They'd been deactivated months ago."

Rafael frowned and spat, "Not possible—we'd dispatched three of them within the past twenty-four hours."

"And you're certain that they were POF?"

Rafael paused, as the question hung in the air like a pungent fart. What proof do I have, he asked of himself, as he ran a hand through his uncombed hair. That they were terrorists is incontrovertible, but could they have been some other faction—yes. He took a deep breath and said, "No, I'm not absolutely certain about their affiliation, but they did have murderous intent."

"Can Bina substantiate your claim?" the tall man asked.

"Only by virtue of what I'd told her."

"We understand that a rogue State Department agent is part of your cabal, correct?"

"A State Department agent, yes, but rogue, not sure."

"Can she substantiate your claim?"

"How do you know the agent's gender?"

"Are you serious?"

"Sorry, and I think so."

"Why are you hesitant?"

"She played me. I'd thought that she'd been working for me alone."

"So you don't trust her to back you up?"

He thought for a moment and replied, "Not unless it suits her purpose."

"And that would be?"

"She's a definite double agent, but there may be a third side."

"A juggler."

"Maybe."

"And the third side?" the tall man inquired.

"She'd set up two young fools, allegedly, on behalf of the POF."

The short man rubbed his bald head and took a seat on the unmade bed. "When had this so-called setup taken place?" he asked.

"A few weeks back."

The bald man turned to face his partner, frowned, and said, "Are the Americans playing games?"

"It was they who'd given us the coordinates for the attack," the tall one advised, continuing, "could they have misled us?"

"Makes no sense," the tall one admitted.

"Let's get back to your intel," the bald man suggested,

"you'd talked about retribution."

"Yes. We know where the terrorists are, POF or not."

"And they are Palestinians?"

"Without a doubt."

"And you are certain that they were the basement marauders?"

"Yes."

"Then their affiliation is of little importance, we need to respond."

"There is one small problem," Rafael indicated.

"Go on."

"They are in an occupied apartment building."

"We'll flush them out."

"I'm off the hook?"

"For now."

"What about the double agent?"

"We'll get back to you on that."

"And the others?"

"Tell me about them."

"The double has a girlfriend that has been useful, and then there are the two young men."

"Are you willing to vouch for them?"

"I don't think that the girlfriend is involved with the agent's intrigue, and the other two are clueless innocents, so, yes."

The two Mossad representatives disappeared to the bathroom and returned moments later. The tall man, the apparent spokesperson, cleared his throat and said, "Go back to your group. Other than Bina, tell them nothing of our conversation and wait for my call."

"We have no place to convene, we're basically living out of a van."

"That's on you."

Chapter Thirty

2 P.M.

The van sat waiting, double-parked, when he'd arrived at the appointed location. Rafael knocked on the driver's side window and George unlocked the doors.

"What happened?" Bina asked.

"Not now," Rafael whispered, as he sat beside her in the rear of the van.

"The girls have gone for food," George informed.

And just as he'd disgorged the last syllable of his sentence, Virginia and Sandy returned carrying two plastic shopping bags. They forced their way into the back seat and began handing out the wrapped sandwiches and soft drinks.

"What's the plan?" Virginia inquired, taking a bite from an egg salad sandwich.

Rafael procrastinated, pretending to chew longer than necessary on his lunch, and replied, "Working on it."

"We can't sit here all day," George complained.

"So drive."

"Where to?"

"Anywhere."

They drove northward, eventually finding themselves

just outside of the Bronx Botanical Gardens, where George came to a stop and announced, "We're running out of fuel, and there's no free parking around here."

"Find a gas station," Rafael ordered, checking the time on his phone.

The two inquisitors from earlier that day had indicated that they would be in touch towards the latter part of the afternoon, but Rafael was getting antsy. It was close to 4 p.m., and they had not called. If this is their idea of punishment, he thought, it's working.

With the van's fuel tank filled, they'd driven until street parking had become available. The space had just been vacated by a midsize sedan and it had taken some effort and a minor front fender dent before the van had come to rest beside an apartment building, its dirty beige bricks attesting to years of neglect. Rafael finished the last of his soft drink, lowered the paper cup to the floorboard, and was about to suggest a place for them to spend the night, when his cellphone began to ring.

"Yes?"

"Are you secure?" the voice asked.

"With my group," he said.

"You are to stand down."

"What?" he shouted.

"Are you questioning orders, yet again?"

"No but..."

"We will deal with them from the other side," the voice cut in.

"Them? You've established their origin?"

"Yes."

"And?"

"It's need to know."

"I need to know," Rafael said, but the call had been terminated.

"What's going on?" Bina insisted.

Rafael hung his head, exhaled and hissed, "They want us to stand down."

"That's not SOP (standard operating procedure)," she seethed.

"Tell them that."

Virginia, Sandy's sleepy head resting upon her shoulder, said, "So we're out in the cold?"

"Appears so," Rafael groaned.

"Well," she exclaimed, "This is where we part ways."

"That's your decision, but it appears that you're a wanted woman," Rafael advised.

"Seems so," she agreed.

"You know that they'll find you."

"I may have crossed a few lines, but I've never been disloyal."

"Might be a tough sale when treason's on the table."

"And if I stay?"

"We might be able to negotiate on your behalf," he said, realizing that he was dancing on thin ice.

Sandy had awakened and the two women conferred.

"We have no place to run," Sandy said.

"There are countries without extradition," Virginia advised.

"That won't stop your people from taking us out," Sandy reminded.

Virginia toyed with a length of blond hair and replied, "OK, we're in for—whatever."

"If we go after them, we may be pursued from three sides," he suggested.

"Three?" Sandy repeated.

"Local police, the Israeli and US governments."

George twisted in the driver's seat, faced rearward and said, "The police don't care about gang related shit."

"Interesting," Rafael returned.

"We waste them, throw some drugs around and take off," George continued.

"That's assuming that we're the victors."

"True."

"And where do we get the drugs?" Virginia said.

"Leave that to me," Sandy cut in.

"You're not a user," Virginia scoffed.

"But I know where to get the shit."

"Oh, we're back to your last BFF."

"You want it or not?" she sneered.

The van was a cocoon of silence, as they all considered the risks and limited potential gain from the planned act of revenge. Rafael was the first to speak, when he said, "I like George's idea, it gives us a possible out."

"Have a gang in mind?" Virginia asked.

"MS13 sounds like a good candidate," Marvin proposed.

"And how do we accomplish that ruse?"

"Leave behind some written nonsense with their logo."

"Not sure it'll be convincing."

"As long as it appears gang related, it won't matter which one," George suggested.

"OK, let's go with it."

"When?" Virginia asked.

"Wait a minute," Bina interrupted, "It appears that I'm not on the Mossad's shit list, and I'd like to stay off."

"What are you suggesting?" Rafael inquired.

"I don't want to be involved."

"You were the one who couldn't wait to get at them."

"That was then."

"What's changed?"

"I want to live to fight another day."

"That day is now."

"If your gang thing doesn't work, the Mossad will hang us," she said.

"Can't worry about that now," Rafael breathed, adding, "I'm more concerned about cheap construction and stray bullets."

"OK, if we're gonna do this, we need to go back to the grocer and get some suppressors," Bina submitted.

Rafael took command of the driver's seat and drove to a location several blocks from the Bodega. All but Bina exited and awaited the van's return. It would have been a major violation of protocol for them to have shown the others where their weapons had come from, so they'd ventured off on their own. The Bodega was still open when they'd arrived and parked fifty or so feet from its entrance. Rafael left Bina at the wheel, as he entered the store, mouthed the code phrase and was ushered back down to the basement. It had taken no more than five minutes to locate the correct suppressors for their weapons. The pistol had, however, presented a dilemma, and he'd left without acquiring the matching tubular device.

"Got 'em?" she asked.

"All but the handgun."

"Good enough."

"You're back with the program?" he said, as she drove toward the pickup location.

"More or less."

"I need you to be more."

"Trying," she said, as she pulled to the curb for the others to get in.

With the stand down order hanging over his head, Rafael had decided to disregard the likelihood of collateral damage. A lightening strike was to be their plan of action. Both he and Bina would burst through the apartment's front door firing at anything that moved. Virginia and Sandy would come up from behind and take out anybody they'd missed. It wasn't the best plan of action, but they had only this singular chance for revenge. There was, however, at least one caveat. The number of terrorists occupying the dwelling was an unknown, as was their potential for success. Each participant knew that the risk of being killed was high, but with the exception of Sandy, who'd had little skin in the game, the gamble had been considered acceptable.

They parked the van several hundred feet from the building's entrance. It had been decided that a daytime approach would limit the number of innocent casualties, as some would be at work, out shopping or doing whatever. It was almost 4 p.m. when they'd pushed through the heavy, locked entry door and made their way up the stairs to the third floor. The prisoner had provided an apartment number, but they had no advance confirmation of its veracity, so they'd each put an ear to the various doors, listening for a foreign tongue or anything that would flag their target. After a few seconds of listening, Rafael smiled and signaled for the others to come forth.

"They're in here," he whispered, his index finger touching the offending door.

Bina picked up the truncheon that she'd taken from the van and had leaned against the wall near the elevator. Holding it with both hands, she prepared to use her body weight to break down the apartment door.

"Let me do that?" Rafael offered.

"A woman isn't strong enough?" she hissed.

"OK, but make it count."

She backed up against the wall opposite the door and

came at it with all she had. The flimsy hinges gave and the door fell flat on the apartment's linoleum floor. The two men that Rafael had heard through the door had been seated on a couch backed up to a window. They'd jumped at the sound of the door crashing down and had run to the solitary bedroom. Only a few seconds had passed, but by the time Rafael and Bina had reached the bedroom it had become clear that the inhabitants had fled via the fire escape and had been observed running down the street in different directions. Virginia and Sandy had cleared the few remaining rooms and joined Rafael and Bina in the living room.

"We blew it," Bina admitted.

"Well, no shots fired," Rafael smiled.

"And no terrorists," Virginia moaned.

"Is that it, we're done?" Sandy asked.

"We live to fight another day," Bina said, leading the way out of the apartment.

Chapter Thirty-one

Sunday, January 14th

11 P.M.

Tel Aviv

Following their meeting with Rafael, the two Mossad agents had contacted their home office. Their superiors had been well aware of the POF's existence and the standing animosity between the splinter group and Hamas. They had hoped to use the POF's hostility as a wedge against the parent group, but the New York attack had altered the dynamic and they were no longer considered useful.

Ariel Bruck, the Mossad's acting director, had been spending the evening with his wife when the call had come from New York. Ordinarily, any one of his subordinates would have been on the receiving end of the communication, but after having learned about the loss of their New York location he'd asked to be the first contact.

"It's late, do you have to go?" Mrs. Bruck had asked, as her husband of twenty-five years pulled a pair of freshly pressed slacks over his boxer shorts.

"Trouble at the office," he'd replied.

"Let the others take care of it," she'd whined.

He'd smiled and said, "Sorry motek (sweety) I have to go."

An hour had passed, and he was in the process of reviewing the latest intelligence related to the POF, when his second in command sauntered in, yawned and took a seat before his desk.

"I woke you?" Ariel said, without taking his eyes from a red folder.

"Was getting laid."

"Good for you, Moishe."

"What have you got?"

"The POF, we must teach them a lesson," Ariel said, lowering his half glasses to the blotter.

"Tonight?"

"You can think of a better time?"

"I'll assemble a team."

"Already been alerted."

"Punishment or elimination?"

"The latter, if possible."

"There will be consequences."

Ariel shrugged, and replied, "What else is new."

"Intel?"

Ariel slid the folder across the desk, and breathed, "It's all there."

Moishe speed read the documents and asked, "Ground only?"

"Jets make noise."

"So this is a stealth op," he mumbled.

"Aside from the drone, yes, stealth."

"What do you wish of me?"

"Watch the drone camera, make certain our people make it back safely."

"And if I suspect trouble?"

"The drone is armed, have the pilot release a missile."

"So much for stealth," Moishe breathed.

"We protect our own."

Moishe gazed at his black, plastic encased wristwatch, and said, "Better tell my girlfriend I'll be late."

"The team has already entered Gaza, you'd better get going."

Without another word, Moishe rose and headed for the drone shack, the high-tech facility that housed the pilots and their huge screens.

Moishe announced his presence to the security guards at the door and entered. A pair of female drone drivers were seated at their monitors, their hands grasping the joysticks before them.

"I was told to watch a penetration team," he

proclaimed.

"On me," one driver called out.

"Where's the other drone going?" he asked, as he stood over the designated pilot's shoulder.

"Classified," she said.

Moishe shrugged. His security level was at rooftop level, but he was tired, horny and did not feel the need to flaunt his superiority, so he concentrated on the ground passing beneath the drone's camera. From time to time he glanced over at the classified screen, but he grew weary of the empty, greenish image presented by the night vision equipment. His drone driver's screen wasn't any prettier, but his eyes locked onto the six, heavily armed Israeli special forces soldiers whose images were filling the monitor.

"Can we get a panoramic view?" he asked.

Without responding, the pilot flicked a switch and the screen split into three sections showing the terrain to the left and right of the soldiers.

"See any movement out there?" he asked.

"Negative," she responded.

"There will be."

He watched, as the men stopped every now and then, appeared to scan the surrounding area with night vision goggles, and then moved on. Suddenly, the team came to a complete halt. Two men dropped to a prone position, their rifles aimed directly behind the team. The remaining four pointed their TAR-21 Tavor automatic rifles in different directions, like the spokes of a wheel. The side view cameras had continued to be devoid of movement, but the men had obviously detected a threat and Moishe watched intently. Suddenly, a barely visible muzzle flash was seen from a rearward pointing Tavor, and Moshe's hands tensed on the pilot's seat back. "They've made contact," he said.

"Not clear," the pilot replied, her eyes glued to the screen.

"A round was fired," he countered, angrily.

"But just one."

"There's another, from a forward position," he said with alarm.

The pilot zoomed in on the team and then panned around their position. "I don't see any bogeys," she exclaimed.

"They're not shooting at rabbits," he derided.

She zoomed out, the screen's image displaying a wider field of view, and then the source of the teams concern became apparent.

"To the left," she said, "six tangos."

"I see 'em."

"They're not moving, but the team is stuck in place."

"Can you launch?"

"The explosion will blow the mission," she noted.

"Kinda looks like it's already a no go."

"OK, acquiring target," she advised.

"Hurry," he urged.

"Fox one," she cried out.

With their eyes focused on the screen, a bright flash momentarily obliterated their view. The enemy targets were no longer visible, but neither were their own team members.

"What happened?" Moishe cried out.

"Hellfire lit up the screen," the pilot advised.

"And our people?" he asked, urgently.

"They were out of the weapon's range."

"But I can't see them."

"I'm coming around, keep watching."

The drone returned over station and the image now revealed the Israeli team moving forward, toward the original objective.

"I see them, we should call them back," he said.

"Do we have confirmation?"

"I'm in command right now."

"But they're only fifty meters from destination."

"Abort, they've been compromised," he shouted.

The pilot hit her microphone's talk button and relayed the order. The team could be seen reversing position and heading back to the border.

"Keep an eye on them until they cross over," he ordered, as he left the shack.

Ten minutes later he found himself seated across from the acting director.

"The mission went south," he advised.

Ariel Bruck's complexion turned from marginally sunburned to a ugly shade of purple, and he said in a soft, but angry tone, "How?"

"Their movement had been blocked and we'd released a missile."

"So you blew the mission."

"To save our people."

"Did the team call for air support?"

"Well, no, but..."

Ariel raised his right hand, as if to say, enough, and hissed, "You've fucked up, admit it and go home."

Moishe lowered his head, rose and silently left the office.

Chapter Thirty-two

Sunday, 6 P.M.

New York City

Considering the seven hour time difference, the two Mossad representatives had received notice of the failed Gaza attempt at 5 p.m., local time.

Mission failures had never been an acceptable option, but it had remained a recognized possibility. And while campaigns involving distant targets had been largely successful in the past, the Gaza neighborhoods had often presented formidable obstacles of demographic and geographic nature, heightened by the existence of the ever present sentinels. And while the POF fiasco had begun with the appearance of several hostiles, it had ended with the egregious error perpetrated by one of their own— Moishe Levin. Nobody was happy, not the acting director, nor the special forces troops who'd risked their lives, nor the recent New York Mossad arrivals. They had tossed around the idea of returning to Tel Aviv without informing Rafael and Bina of the POF debacle, but in the end they'd made the call.

Rafael and company had been searching for a place to spend the night when the call had come through. He slipped the phone from a pocket and put it to his ear. "Yes?" he said.

"The raid did not go as planned," the voice revealed.

Rafael did not ask for clarification, he knew from their past conversation that a mission had been in the offing, so he sighed heavily and replied, "Where do we stand?"

"You have a green light to deal with the locals."

"By any means?"

"Yes, but we cannot afford a diplomatic confrontation."

"It could get messy."

"Keep it to a minimum."

"I'll do my best, but we need a place to roost."

An uncomfortable pause followed, and then the voice came back with, "There is a house..."

The address provided belonged to a single family home in a Westchester suburb of New York. It had been purchased for an Israeli ambassador who had preferred a Manhattan hotel as his place of occasional residence. With the exception of it original owner, the single story home had never been occupied.

"What was that about?" Bina inquired.

"We sleep indoors tonight."

"And then?"

"We track down the animals."

"What happened to stand down?"

Rafael shrugged.

George was back at the wheel, and Rafael provided directions to their destination as they drove northward.

***

8 P.M.

Pelham, Westchester County

New York

The house, a four bedroom, fully furnished affair on a large lot was located in an upscale neighborhood. The remnants of a recent snow storm covered what would have been a lush sheet of green during the warmer months. But darkness served as an effective camouflage for winter's somberness, and the group of five lugged their firepower and took refuge in the home's frigid interior.

"It's freezing in here," Sandy complained.

"Must be an oil or gas heater in the basement, I'll take a look," George said, as he disappeared to search for the access door.

"How long have we got?" Virginia inquired.

"As long as we need," Rafael replied, making certain

that the windows facing the street were completely obscured.

"I think we should ditch the van," she suggested.

"Been on my mind ... I'll dispose of it later tonight."

"And its replacement?"

Rafael held up a credit card that had been provided by his superiors and said, "Hertz delivers."

"And food?"

"Looks like pizza is our best bet for tonight."

"Delivery?" she said, quizzically.

"Sure. We're just one happy, hungry family."

"I don't think the terrorists will be returning to the apartment," Virginia advised.

"Me neither, so my contact is trolling for intel."

"My clothes are beginning to stink, we'll all need some new things."

"OK. First order of business is pizza, then van disposal. I'll have a vehicle delivered to us in the morning and we'll find a place to buy some clothes, courtesy of the Israeli government."

The two, meat laden pizzas had arrived and they'd gathered around the oval kitchen table and dined in silence. When the last slice had been consumed, Rafael rose and announced, "Anyone for a walk?"

"At this hour?" Marvin questioned.

"Need to hide the van and walk back."

"I'll go," Bina suggested.

"No, you stay and guard the troops."

Rafael had yet to raise the issue of trust, where it pertained to Virginia and her apparent, multiple allegiances. And since George, Marvin and Sandy were essentially recent, unvetted acquaintances, Bina was the only person he felt comfortable leaving in charge. So he locked gaze with Marvin and said, "You're elected."

Marvin feigned a pained expression and followed Rafael through the front door. The night air was glacial, and puffs of smoke exited their lips as they walked to the van and entered. Bina stood watch at the partially opened front door, which she held ajar until she'd been convinced that all was in order. She then turned and addressed the remaining inhabitants.

"In Rafael's absence, I am in charge," she declared.

"Shouldn't we share that responsibility?" Virginia chimed in.

"Not a negotiation," she barked.

"OK, chief, orders?"

"Check the weapons for operability and inventory the ammo."

"And after?" Virginia asked.

"We sleep."

An hour had passed by the time Rafael and Marvin had returned and locked the front door for the night. Marvin had walked off to use the restroom, while Rafael and Bina sealed themselves in a bedroom.

"Any problems?" he asked.

"No. And all weapons have been checked," she advised.

"Not sure how much confidence should be placed in Virginia," he said.

"Something you haven't told me?"

"Her uncertain alliances trouble me."

"She's been pretty solid so far."

"But who is she really working for, that's the question."

"You think she might turn under pressure?"

"Possibly, and especially since she's been declared rogue by the State Department."

"I could take her out while she sleeps."

"But if we're wrong, we could lose a needed asset."

"And that would leave only the two jerks, since Sandy would likely bolt with her friend gone."

"Yeah, there are risks either way."

"So we keep her in the loop?"

"On a short leash."

"OK. Any further intel?"

"Not yet, but we can't spend too much time here without the neighbors getting curious."

"Where'd you dump the van?"

"Shopping mall parking lot."

"Cameras?"

"None that I could see, but I'd slid it between two eighteen wheelers that were spending the night."

"OK, time for bed," she said, thumping the mattress with her right hand."

"Are you suggesting...?" he smirked.

"Not on your life, go to your own room."

"But these are desperate times," he argued.

"Not that desperate," she chuckled, rising to open the door for his departure.

Chapter Thirty-three

Monday, January 15th

6 A.M.

Pelham, N.Y.

George awakened early, the clothes that he'd slept in clinging to his body like a wrinkled pile of malodorous fabric. He yawned, took care of his morning bathroom necessities and found his way to the kitchen. Rafael was already seated at the table, spooning chicken soup from a can.

"Is that all there is?" George yawned.

"They weren't expecting guests," he replied, his gaze focused on the pockmarked, dark, wooden table.

"Coffee?"

"None that I could find."

"I can't function without it," George complained.

"The IDF taught us how to cope," Rafael grinned, with the spoon protruding from his lips.

"How does that help me?"

Rafael ignored his remark and tipped the can in the air to drain the remaining liquid. And as he lowered it to the table, Bina entered with Virginia and her girlfriend in tow.

"If you're looking for breakfast, forget it," George sneered.

"Where's your friend," she asked.

"Marvin is a late sleeper."

"This isn't a friggin' hotel," Sandy quipped.

"We're making the best of a shitty situation," he replied.

"It's likely to go downhill from here," Rafael suggested.

"Meaning?" George asked.

"I'd received a call at 5 a.m., I know where they are."

"Where?" Virginia asked excitedly.

"In a minute but, first, we need to all be on the same page."

"What page is that," Marvin inquired, as he padded, barefoot, into the kitchen and plopped onto the only empty chair.

"In order to pull off an effective raid, we have to be singleminded."

"Huh?" George mumbled.

"One goal, multiple targets, all to be dealt with simultaneously."

"I'm on board with that," Sandy called out.

"And you two?" Rafael asked, glaring at George and

Marvin.

"I'm OK with it," George said.

Marvin, on the other hand, hesitated, but when George speared his flank with an elbow he said, "Yeah, I'll whack a few."

"We don't have enough firepower for everyone, but there are some pretty decent carving knives on the counter, and I saw an axe in the garage," he advised.

Sandy leaned to her left and hefted a few of the knives, finally, balancing one across two fingers. "With the right knife I can hit a bullseye at twenty feet," she announced.

"And?" Rafael inquired.

"This pair will do just fine," she said, revealing her choice.

"Where and when are we going?" Virginia asked.

"A warehouse on 12th street, Brooklyn, tonight."

"Shouldn't we practice for a day or so?" Marvin asked, his voice quivering nervously.

"No time to waste," Rafael advised.

George had been listening intently. The entire situation had mushroomed in ways that he could never have imagined. There was a sense of helplessness enveloping him and he asked, "Is there an upside for us?"

gesturing at Marvin and himself.

"Sure. We kill the bad guys," Rafael said.

"But what happens to us afterwards?"

"There won't be any medals, if that's what you mean."

"I'd settle for survival and freedom from the authorities."

"Let's wait until the dust settles."

"Not good enough," Marvin cut in.

"What do you want?"

"A guarantee."

"I can't provide that here, but if you're both willing to go *Law of return*, I'll make it work."

"Leave everything behind?" Marvin whined.

"Right now we have more immediate concerns," Rafael advised, shifting the conversation.

He left the room to allow his proclamation to sink in, and to arrange for a new vehicle.

***

9:15 A.M.

The dark gray Chevy Suburban had arrived, and after taking care of the paperwork, Rafael wasted no time in organizing his team.

"Here's how it has to go down," he explained, as the group gathered around the kitchen table, continuing, "the targets are occupying an empty warehouse. We don't have enough time to obtain the building's blueprints, so a two pronged attack will have to work."

"Are you certain about there being two entries?" Bina asked.

"Drone intel has confirmed it."

"Who's UAV (unmanned aerial vehicle)?" she asked.

"OK, it was a store-bought drone that one of our people used to take photos."

"Better hope it hadn't been seen," Victoria advised.

"There was no sign of scatter, of the occupants, that is."

"The drone driver, was he one of the Tel Aviv visitors, or a paid pilot?" Bina inquired.

"The former," Rafael replied, adding, sarcastically, "are we finished with twenty questions?"

The group nodded in the affirmative.

"If there are no signs of their departure, we go in at midnight tonight."

"Do we know if they have more than one location?" Virginia inquired.

"Negative."

"So we risk slicing a single tentacle, while the host survives," Bina interjected.

"That's all we've got," Rafael admitted, adding, "but it's the message that counts."

"OK, let's say we whack everyone in that building and we make it out," Marvin posed, "then what?"

"We crack a bottle of champagne and prepare for the next battle."

"Uh uh, that wasn't the deal," Marvin groaned, "you have to get us out of here."

"You didn't appear too happy about moving to Israel."

"Would you, if the table had been turned?"

"I'm here, aren't I?"

Marvin grimaced and replied, "Point taken, and if that's all there is, I guess I'm in."

George nodded his agreement with the proposal.

"Then it's settled, if we prevail, the four of us will fly to Tel Aviv."

Virginia grasped Sandy's hand and offered, "That leaves us out in the cold."

"You're an agent of a foreign government, what would you have me do?"

"We've been supportive of your government's affairs, to the extent that we have, and are about to risk our lives.

That should be worth something."

"Let's get through tonight, and if all goes well I'll query my superiors."

"Now that we've gotten the bullshit out of the way, where are the doors?" Bina growled.

Rafael removed a small pad from his pocket and drew what had been described to him during the early morning call and advised, "There are actually three doors, but one of them is on a loading platform and is too large, heavy and I assume noisy to be used. The second metal door is up front and to the left of the loading dock and the third is around the left side of the building."

"Is this a single story structure?" Virginia asked.

"Yes," Rafael responded.

"What about the roof?"

"Intel claims that it's flat, tar based and impenetrable."

"Shit."

"Were you hoping for a Spiderman moment?" he ridiculed.

She narrowed her brows and shot a deadly glance at her inquisitor.

"OK, myself, Bina and Sandy will take the door near the platform, while Virginia, Marvin and George will infiltrate the side door."

"Wait a minute," George called out, "they're metal doors, with locks, I assume. How are we going to get through them?"

"Duct tape and this," he said, holding up a fragmentation grenade.

"Holy shit," George breathed, "that could kill us all."

"Not if you give it about fifty feet."

"Sure of that?" Marvin asked, nervously.

"Those are the specs," Rafael grinned.

"So we blow the door and rush in?" George said.

"No, since we'll have the exits covered, we wait for them to get curious."

"And?"

"Like shooting fish in a barrel," Bina giggled.

"You're presuming that they'll run for the exits, but what if they take up positions inside?" Virginia asked.

"We go commando," Rafael came back.

"I'm not running in there naked," Marvin announced.

Everyone, except for Marvin, burst out laughing.

"What?" he said.

"You can keep your clothes on," Rafael snickered.

George shook his head, an expression of disbelief.

"This is an on the fly mission," Bina advised, "we'll

recalibrate as the situation dictates."

"I'm still not on board with the grenade thing," George complained.

"I'll admit, there's risk," Rafael said, "and Primacord would have been a better choice, but we don't have any."

"How long do we have to run back the fifty feet?"

Rafael grimaced and replied, "About three to four seconds."

"I can't run that fast," Marvin complained.

"But I can," Virginia piped up, adding,"just leave me a clear escape path."

"What about the front door?" Sandy asked.

"I'll pick the lock," Rafael informed.

"Won't that take time?" Marvin questioned.

"A bit, but the explosion should draw their attention."

With the game plan set, Bina drove off in the Suburban in search of food, while the others engaged in small talk, or, as in the case of the two male, South Floridians, nail biting.

Chapter Thirty-four

Midnight

The continued drone surveillance had not detected any exterior movement, which had suggested that the POF members had not left the building. With George behind the wheel, the Suburban rolled to a stop less than one hundred feet from the target structure's loading dock.

During her grocery outing, Bina had purchased several cans of black and brown shoe polish. It wasn't the typical camouflage material, but it was the best she'd been able manage on short notice. And as they sat in the parked vehicle, its exterior lights extinguished, she passed the cans around.

"You want me to put this shit on my skin?" Marvin complained.

"The moon's out, your pasty white face will reflect its light," Bina grumbled.

Rafael handed the MP7 to Virginia, an MP5 to Bina—the extra MP5 having been rendered inoperative during their prior operation—and kept the Uzi for himself. The leftover pistols were awarded to George and Marvin with the warning, *"Don't fire unless you have a clear shot."*

They'd exited the vehicle at ten minutes past

midnight, and with their backs against the brick wall they'd inched their way toward the loading dock. Rafael had tried to use hand signals to convey his directional orders, but George and Marvin had proven clueless, so he'd whispered his orders in their ears as he'd offered up a roll of black duct tape and the grenade. Marvin reached for the tape, but Rafael grew angry as neither man appeared ready for the explosive. Finally, George took hold of it and said, "I hold this spring thing closed while I pull the ring?"

"No, you hand the grenade to Virginia and she'll place it."

"Thank God," he breathed.

"She's already on station, get your asses over there."

The two men scurried in a crouch to where Virginia knelt waiting. George handed her the M67 fragmentation grenade and Marvin passed the tape. That accomplished, the pair ran for safety. They took refuge behind a steel dumpster, full of rotting food and auto parts, and watched as she prepared to blow the door. But just as she'd turned to signal *fire in the hole*, Marvin's attention was diverted by a flash of light emanating from an elevated corner of the building, and he called out in a loud whisper, "Wait, camera."

Virginia, in a fit of exasperation, left the M67 attached

to the door and quickstepped the roughly fifty foot distance.

"What the fuck is wrong with you?" she growled.

Without saying a word, he gestured upwards.

"Did you see an artificial light source, or a reflection?" she demanded.

"Reflection ... I think."

"Move around and see if you can reproduce it."

He shifted his position, and there it was again. "Reflection," he said.

"OK, not another word, and stay out of my way," she ordered, as she returned to the door.

Less than a minute later she came running back, sliding behind the dumpster like a baseball player arriving at home plate, her arrival accompanied by a ferocious explosion. The door flew open with a puff of smoke and they waited with their gun barrels aimed at the opening.

"Wasn't sure I could run fast enough," she breathed.

"Me neither," George muttered.

"See anything?" Marvin wheezed.

"Not yet."

"How will we know if Rafael made it in?" George asked.

"In a perfect world we would have had radios, but I

think the answer will be gunfire."

Save for the occasional racket perpetrated by the dumpster's scavenging rodents, it remained quiet for almost seven minutes, and then, several bursts of automatic weapons fire broke the silence.

"They're in," Marvin acknowledged.

But just then, a loud ping was heard, followed immediately by a chunk of brick striking Virginia on the back of her head. "They're shooting at us," she screeched.

"Oh shit, look up, they're on the roof," Marvin choked.

"What the fuck," Virginia cried out, "Rafael said the rooftop was impenetrable."

"They know we're here, I'm gonna return fire," Marvin squawked, as he raised his pistol.

"Wait," Virginia said, "you'll just put us in further danger, and you won't hit anything."

"So we just sit here like ducks in a shooting gallery?"

"We're safe behind this garbage can."

"Rafael may not know about the roof?" George said anxiously.

"He'll figure it out."

As they alternately scanned the rooftop and open doorway, an occasional muzzle flash was observed departing from weapons apparently aimed at targets other than themselves.

"They're shooting high and to our left," George observed.

"Rafael may have found his way to the roof," Virginia mumbled.

"Should we help?"

She hesitated and then replied, "You two say here, I'll see if I can even the odds."

"But we're armed," Marvin complained.

"You'll just get yourselves killed, and I have an automatic weapon."

"What if you don't make it back?" George's voice quivered.

"Run like hell," she said, just before racing across to the blown doorway.

Suddenly, sustained bursts of the now familiar sound of suppressed, automatic weapons fire increased in frequency, and the two South Floridians prepared to follow Virginia's directive.

"That doesn't sound good," Marvin warned.

"But we don't know who's doing the shooting," George countered.

"Shit, I've got a bad feeling."

"Maybe it's the giant bag of Cheetos you ate."

"Not that kind of feeling."

"I say we wait."

"OK, but not too long."

"Define, too long."

"I wanna go home, to my boring life on the beach," Marvin whined.

"Me too, but that train's left the station."

"What will happen to my condo?"

"You'll figure it out."

"From Israel?"

"Not the worst of all possibilities."

"I don't speak Hebrew."

"Doesn't matter."

"But..."

"Shut up already," George cut in, "you want them to start shooting again?"

Marvin lowered his head and began to sob. George gazed down at his friend and for one brief instant considered abandoning his watch to offer comfort, but his attention was abruptly drawn to the doorway.

"Someone's exiting," George advised, excitedly.

"Coming for us?" Marvin howled, each syllable drenched with the tone of fear.

"It's Rafael, Bina and Sandy," George chuckled

nervously.

The returning warriors slipped behind the trash bin and dropped to a crouch. Rafael's shirt was covered with blood, as was one side of Sandy's face and hands. Bina appeared unharmed.

"Were you shot?" George asked, with genuine concern.

"A few scratches ... flesh wounds," Rafael breathed.

"And you?" he asked, addressing Sandy.

"Not my blood," she said, with sadness.

"Where's Virginia?" George asked, excitedly.

Rafael shook his head slowly, from side to side, while Sandy began to weep.

"She's dead?" Marvin said, incredulously.

"We think so."

"You think?" George growled.

"We didn't neutralize them all," Rafael explained, "we had to leave her."

"Alive?"

"Don't think so."

"But you don't know for sure."

Rafael shook his head negatively.

"What happened to *leave no one behind*?" Marvin cried out, wiping his tearful eyes with the back of a sleeve.

"That's your Marines."

"And you guys don't give a crap?" he said, angrily.

"I'd sacrificed one for the benefit of three. It was a command decision."

"I'm gonna find her," Marvin seethed, as he rose, preparing to run for the door. But a burst from a non suppressed weapon stopped him in his tracks, and he dropped to the ground.

"They're still on the roof," Rafael said.

"I can sneak up there."

"We took out four, possibly five of them, but there are at least three survivors. And our weapons were no match for theirs."

Marvin gazed at his pistol, its stainless steel frame illuminated by the moonlight, and said, "We have to help her."

"We'd have to get them to abandon their rooftop position."

"I get it, they're not gonna give up their advantage," Marvin agreed.

"Unless..."

"What?" George asked.

Rafael reached into his pocket and withdrew his cellphone. He punched in a few numbers and waited.

Someone had apparently responded, but the entire conversation had taken place in Hebrew. Rafael terminated the call and said, "Keep your eyes on the roof."

Ten minutes passed, and then a faint buzzing was heard from above, followed by smoke and a few visible flames.

"What's going on?" Sandy, who had harnessed her emotions asked.

"Trying to smoke them out," Rafael whispered.

"How?" she said.

"A drone dropped a few small, impact ignited incendiaries."

"Toy drones can do that?" she said.

"Not a toy, a commercial drone. And, yes, it can carry all kinds of things."

"So we can go now?" Marvin asked, half off the ground.

"Not yet."

"What are we waiting for?"

Rafael ran a sweaty hand through his greying, black hair, a sign of exasperation, and replied, "To thin the herd."

"They may have left the roof, but they're still in the building," Bina instructed.

"So we go in and take 'em out," Marvin urged.

"And get yourself killed," Rafael offered.

"We have to get to her if she's still alive."

"A noble sentiment, but not…"

Before Rafael could complete his sentence, a head appeared through the open doorway. He dropped below the upper lip of the dumpster and edged around to one side for a better view. "They're looking for a way out," he whispered.

"Let's wait until the three remaining are visible, and then give them everything we've got," Bina suggested.

"I've got a clear shot from this angle, you take the other side,"

"What about us?" Marvin muttered.

"Don't fire until they get close, or you'll miss."

Three minutes later, two men appeared at the open doorway. They stood by the frame with their weapons shifting from side to side, as they inched their way out into the open. But the third terrorist was nowhere to be seen. Using hand signals, Rafael gestured for Bina to take the shot, as he prepared to do the same. They took careful aim and let loose with a long burst of automatic fire. The two men dropped to the ground like sacks of potatoes.

"Are we clear?" Marvin asked, nervously.

"Not sure. There should be a third."

"Maybe you wounded him," George said.

"And maybe he's waiting inside."

"Got anymore of those explosives?" George inquired.

"No, just had the one," Rafael replied, as he examined the base of the dumpster with his right hand, adding, "this thing has wheels."

"Think we can push it?" Bina asked.

"It'd make a hell of a shield," Rafael replied.

"A magen," Bina smiled.

All five pushed from the same side of the wheeled cart and it began to creak across to the other side. The noise was, however, unavoidable and it had caught the attention of the third gunman, who stood just inside the doorway firing his weapon on full automatic. The rounds struck the steel cart like a hailstorm on steroids, but his thwarting attempt had been hopeless from the onset. And when he'd stopped to insert a fresh magazine, Rafael jumped out in the open and shred his body with ten well aimed, 9mm rounds.

Chapter Thirty-five

6 A.M.

Tuesday, January 16th

Tel Aviv

Mossad, Office of the Acting Director

Ariel Bruck had just arrived at his office. He'd spent a sleepless night caring for his wife who had contracted a nasty case of the flu, and he was in a pissy mood. Intelligence traffic had come through hours earlier and an eyes only envelop greeted him as he plopped onto his creaky desk chair. He stared at it, wishing that it had been he who had contracted the illness, a reasonable excuse to have remained at home. But he rose, filled his mug with steaming, black coffee and returned to the desk and the waiting communique.

"Find Seren (Captain) Levin," he barked into the intercom connected to his secretary.

"Yes sir," a sleepy voice replied.

While he waited, he broke the seal and sliced open the envelop. Inside was a single sheet of paper that, unlike days gone by, had actually been spit out of a computer's attached printer, rather than a typewriter. The message had originated from the two New York emissaries who had been dispatched to check up on the office operating under the alias of the JPA. He read the message, gulped down a few mouthfuls of cooling coffee, as he crunched on a strip of his wife's mandel bread, and re-read the dispatch.

Green light for New York thugs executed. Intel faulty. Elimination incomplete.

What the hell does that mean, he wondered. I'm fucking tired of this cryptic bullshit. They had a full sheet of paper, why so stingy with words.

And as he sat staring at the single line of text, Seren Moishe Levin entered the office carrying a plastic cup full of his favorite Turkish brew.

"Sit," Bruck droned.

"Problem?" Moishe asked, sipping the tarry, sugar infused liquid.

"Maybe."

"Explain."

"The two assholes you sent to New York, are they also morons?"

Moishe almost choked on the coffee, stifled a chuckle and said, "Why do you ask?"

Bruck slid the sheet of paper across his desk and said, "This their idea of joke?"

"This can't be good," he mumbled.

"In fact, it isn't."

"Shall I respond?"

"Recall them, immediately."

"But we know nothing of our JPA people's status."

"And that's all you've concluded?"

"Well, there is the incomplete thing."

Bruck pushed his chair back angrily, stood and leaned across the desk, growling, "Whom do you think had provided the fucking faulty intel?"

Moishe hesitated, and stuttered, "The morons."

"Find a way to contact Rafael, aka Andrew Cosgrove, if he's still alive. He can be trusted."

"I'll do my best," Moishe said, rising to leave.

"And ask about his partner."

And as Moishe reached for the door, Bruck called out, "Send a cleanup team."

"To do what?"

"To clean up the fucking mess that the morons created."

Idiots, that's all I have to work with, Bruck told himself, as he reached for the mug of cooled coffee, grimaced, and poured the contents into a trash bin.

He spent the next twenty minutes on the phone with his wife, trying to decide whether or not she needed medical attention, finally deciding that she'd tough it out with her home remedies. His secretary had provided a freshly brewed carafe of coffee, and he filled a mug and sat back hoping for a period of relaxation. But two sips later the phone rang and he glared at it, willing it to stop.

"Yes?" he breathed.

"I found Rafael," Moishe gloated.

"And?"

"Bina is OK."

"Glad to hear, but what happened?"

"There was a firefight, and a State Department agent was killed."

Bruck's eyes widened in concert with his rapidly increasing pulse, "State Department?" he shouted.

"I don't have all the details, but she was assisting our team."

"Holy fucking shit. A simple takedown has turned into an international incident."

"Maybe not."

"How is that possible?" he barked.

"She'd been thought to have gone rogue."

"But we weren't supposed to be there in the first place."

"Maybe we can pin the affair on the rogue agent."

Bruck removed the phone from his ear, took a deep breath, and ordered, "Get in here, right now."

The recently consumed coffee was now a bilious accretion lining the back of his throat, and he poured himself a glass of water. But the vile taste refused to depart, as a cold sweat began to build on his forehead, accompanied by a subtle discomfort on the left side of his chest. I don't need another heart attack, he said to himself, as he tried to conjure the calming technique that he'd been taught at the medical center. He closed his eyes, slowed his breathing to a constant rhythm and focused on a favorite vacation spot. The chest pain began to recede, as did the cold sweaty sensation, and he thought, maybe it's time to retire. But just then, Moishe knocked and entered.

"You don't look well," he observed.

"Thank you Dr. Levin," he said, sarcastically.

"Sorry."

"I need to know exactly what happened in New York," Bruck snapped.

"Our people, the morons, had given Rafael the green light to go after the POF faction."

"Did they succeed?"

"As far as Rafael could tell."

"Meaning?"

"There might have been others that hadn't been holed up in the warehouse."

"And someone was killed for this?"

Moishe nodded affirmatively.

"If word gets out that we, I mean you, screwed up the Gaza attack and now this ... it won't help the Mossad's reputation."

"What would you have me do?" he said, apologetically.

"Find out what the American State Department knows about this, without claiming any responsibility."

"And how do I explain knowledge of the event?"

"We're an intelligence agency, we gather information," he said, refraining from calling his subordinate an idiot.

"And Rafael and Bina, do I recall them?"

"Not yet. Transfer adequate funds to our New York account and have them find a place to stay until I figure out our next move."

"There is one other issue."

"I can't deal with anymore fuckups today," Bruck groaned.

"Three young Americans had been working with our people."

"They're alive or dead?"

"Alive."

"So?"

"Our operation has put them in a precarious position."

"Did we ask them for assistance?"

"Yes and no."

"Can we dispense with the riddles?"

"They were involved with the firefight."

"Ok, so they're a liability … deal with it."

"Not that simple."

"One bullet for each, it really is quite simple."

"Rafael had promised them a free ride."

"They're Jews?"

"Two for sure, the third is unknown."

"OK," he hissed, "have Rafael find a place for all of them until we figure out the endgame."

Moishe remained seated a few seconds too long, but Bruck's angry facial expression convinced him to leave.

This is becoming more complicated by the minute, Bruck said to himself. They don't want peace, those Gaza jackals, they want us gone, and I'm not sure how much more of this bullshit I can take. I took this job two years ago, as acting Director. Isn't it time for a real Director to

show up, he wondered. But who am I kidding, the agency
has grown to depend upon me, and retirement isn't my
thing.

It was now 8 a.m. in Tel Aviv and 2 a.m., New York
time. Bruck was just about to visit the restroom, when his
secure line began to buzz. He groaned, exhaled and
returned to his desk hoping that he wouldn't wet his pants,
as age had begun to weaken his sphincter muscles.

"Bruck here," he said, in a monotone voice.

"This is Vasily," the voice announced.

Vasily Romanov, the fifty-one year old son of a
Russian immigrant family, had been born in Volgograd. At
the age of five, his parents had sold their ancestral home
and belongings, and had emigrated to Israel under the Law
of Return. Vasily had been an outcast at first, but had
quickly learned to read, write and speak Hebrew. As a
handsome young man, with a full head of black hair, he
had been a sought after member of the young social set, a
distinction that had followed him through his many years
of higher education. Following a necessary stint in the IDF
he'd been offered a position as a analyst in the Mossad, but
he'd quickly grown restless behind a computer screen and
had requested a field position. The New York visit had

been his first physical venture into the murky, clandestine world of international intelligence. His partner, on the other hand, had been no stranger to spy craft and had done his best to indoctrinate his student.

"Speak. I don't have much time," Bruck said, squeezing his thighs together and hoping to stay dry.

"We'd questioned the POF's presence in New York..."

"Get to the point," Bruck urged.

"They're planning an attack."

An attack, Bruck thought. Maybe they're not such morons. "On what?" he asked.

"We don't know yet, but we suspect a high value target."

"And you've vetted your source?"

"As best we can."

"I hope that this is not the same source you'd used recently," Bruck said forcefully.

"No, it is someone close to them."

"So the warehouse location was just a diversion."

"It appears so, but should we notify the locals?"

"Remember, you're in country as a tourist."

"But there could be casualties."

"Do nothing until we speak again."

"When?"

"Call me back in one hour."

He lowered the phone and ran to the bathroom. With his bladder no longer crying for evacuation, he buzzed his secretary.

"I need Seren Levin, tell him it's an emergency," he advised.

Moishe came running from his office down the corridor and without knocking entered and, out of breath, huffed, "What's the emergency?"

"Calm down, Moishe."

"OK, I'm relaxed. What's happened?"

"It turns out that the morons may not be so stupid after all."

"I don't understand."

"Vasily called and claims that the POF is planning to strike."

"Here?"

"Oy vey, Moishe, Vasily is in New York, you sent him there."

"Sorry, you caught me off guard."

"We have a problem. Our people cannot go to the police, or the Federal Government without making it known that they are not there in the capacity of tourists.

But I cannot, in good conscience, allow those POF animals to harm innocent human beings."

"We could pass on an anonymous tip."

"Which they may not accept as being credible."

"Do we know where they plan to strike?"

"Not yet."

"What about timeframe?"

"Currently unknown, but apparently imminent."

Moishe starred blankly off into space.

"Are you hypoglycemic?" Bruck asked.

"No, why?"

"You seemed out of touch."

"I was trying to arrive at a solution, but I've got nothing."

"There is one possibility, and that involves the dead agent."

"The rogue?"

"We don't know that she was a rogue, but the State Department is probably not aware of her demise or the circumstances."

"So?"

"We cut a deal, a quid pro quo."

"Explain."

"We keep her multiple alliances under wraps, tell

them where to find the body, and their problem gets swept under the rug. In exchange, we give them our POF intel and they forgive our illegal presence and activity in their country."

"Will they go for it?"

"Think about it. There are more pluses on their side of the deal, since they'll have a chance to thwart an attack that they might not have otherwise had knowledge of, and they get to avoid the scrutiny that a rogue agent can precipitate."

"You want me to make the call?"

"It's not that simple. They will want to know how we acquired the intelligence, when and where the attack will occur, etc."

"Why not simply say that we do not have all the facts?"

"The terrorists have come from our side of the world, the Americans will expect more from us."

"What do you suggest?"

"Vasily is to call back shortly, I will insist that he pressure his source for details."

"We'll have to move quickly, before the agent's body decomposes."

Chapter Thirty-six

Tuesday, January 16th

New York City

1 A.M.

Rafael had had barely enough time to relocate his crew, and given the hasty call from Tel Aviv he'd zeroed in on a hotel. A last minute decision had brought them to the Bronx Comfort Inn and Suites, where they'd taken a room with a double bed and pullout for Rafael and the two male Floridians, and an adjoining room for Bina and Sandy. Before arriving at the hotel there had been a brief discussion regarding Virginia, but Rafael had silenced the cacophony. And now that they'd been temporarily sequestered in their rooms Rafael called them together to discuss what little he knew of their futures.

"When are we leaving for Israel," Marvin inquired.

"It's in the works," Rafael said, knowing that their acceptance had yet to have been finalized.

"What about me?" Sandy asked.

"Are you a Jew?" Bina inquired.

Sandy shook her head in the negative.

"We'll figure it out," Bina replied.

"What about the elephant in the room?" George said,

his voice tinged with anger.

"Meaning?" Rafael replied.

"Virginia."

"Nothing we can do."

"We can't leave her body for the buzzards," George whined.

"We have no choice."

"She has no family," Sandy offered, "I'm her closest friend."

"What do you propose?" Rafael asked.

"She deserves a good burial."

"Agreed, but we can't go back. And how would we explain her demise?"

"Innocent victim of a gang shootout," Marvin suggested.

Rafael considered the proposal and replied, "It would still provoke unanswerable questions."

"So we just forget about her?" Sandy protested.

"Unfortunately, yes."

With tears running down her cheeks, Sandy walked off to her room.

"That was cruel," George said.

"As is the world we live in," Rafael breathed.

"And if it had been me?"

Rafael tilted his head and grimaced.

The expression had not been lost on George, and he realized that either he or Marvin could have been stretched out on that rooftop waiting for a sharp beak to tear into his flesh. But I'm knee deep in alligators, he reminded himself, and my only option is to move forward. And I have no one to blame but myself. I could have thanked my lucky stars that I'd survived the Synagogue attack and moved on, but no, I had to seek revenge. Well, once an asshole always an asshole, he thought, as he plopped down on his bed to take a nap.

He had no idea how much time had passed, but the room was still dark and Marvin was shaking him, when he heard, "Wake up, wake up."

"What? What's happened?" he asked, yawning and tossing his still shoe clad feet over the edge of the bed.

"Rafael want's us all in the women's room."

"Now?"

"Immediately."

They walked next door and what they saw stopped them cold. Bina was standing over a very pale Sandy, just outside of the bathroom.

"Holy shit," George called out.

"Keep your voice down," Bina ordered.

"What happened?"

"She hung herself from the shower rod."

"Where the hell were you?" Marvin growled.

"Down the hall at the ice machine, but I don't answer to you," she snapped.

Rafael stepped in, and as calmly as one could, advised, "She was despondent, but I hadn't contemplated this," he said, gesturing toward the body laid out on the carpet.

"Its your fault," Marvin decried.

"Get over it, like it or not, this is how war proceeds."

"We should have gone back for Virginia," he insisted.

"She still would have been dead, and maybe some of us along with her."

"Are we gonna leave her to rot as well?" Marvin hissed.

"Does she have any family?" Rafael inquired.

Both Marvin and George shrugged, indicating lack of knowledge.

Rafael disappeared and returned moments later, pocketing his cellphone as he approached, and advised, "Someone will be along to dispose of the body, we have to make ourselves invisible."

"How do we do that?" George asked.

"In about thirty minutes we'll all go out for a walk and return twenty minutes later."

"That's it?" Marvin sniffled, as he wiped his eyes with a hotel supplied tissue.

"She's gone, Marvin. It was her decision, and now we have to think of ourselves," Bina counseled.

"That sucks," Marvin moaned.

"Did they say anything else?" Bina asked.

Rafael motioned for her to follow him into the corridor.

"There's a wet team en route from Tel Aviv."

"To do what?" she whispered.

"Not sure, but I was told that we're to hang in."

"And twiddle our thumbs while our people are dying?" she said.

"Apparently, the POF are planning something big."

"Where did you get that from?"

"One of the Mossad investigators."

"They've fucked up before."

"I know, but the Director feels that their intel is credible."

"You've spoken with Ariel?"

"Didn't realize that you two were on a first name basis," he chuckled.

"Long story."

"I don't need to know. And, no, I have not communicated with him."

"So how do we fit in?"

"Not entirely clear, but the investigators are trying to vet their intel and squeeze their informant for details."

"And the wet team?"

"Reinforcements, I hope."

"Do the investigators have a bead on the POF's base of OP?"

"They're checking into it."

"If they're planning an assault, our basement facility was probably just a target of opportunity," she said.

"Or a diversion. Anyway, the cleanup person should be here shortly, let's get moving."

***

6 A.M.

A restless night had been had by all, and after devouring the hotel's free hot breakfast, Rafael gathered the remaining team in his shared room.

"Normally, what I'm about to tell you," he advised, aiming his gaze at George and Marvin, "would be classified and unavailable to you two. But we've become a team of sorts."

"Are you certain?" Bina interrupted.

He nodded, yes, and continued, "Shortly before breakfast, I'd received a phone call. The alleged target is a subway station."

"Which one?" George asked.

"Still waiting on that, but they've chosen an unlikely hideout."

"Where?" Bina urged.

"They're on a large boat mored at Chelsea Piers, specifically, pier 59."

"Got the boat's name?"

"Little Milly," he sniggered.

"So we take 'em out before they do damage," Bina said.

"Not that simple."

"It is for me," she snapped.

"Remember, we're not supposed to be here."

"So we let them kill hundreds?" she growled.

"When the Director has all of the details he will decide."

"What's there to decide?"

"Who takes them down."

"I definitely want a piece of them," she declared.

"We may end up in a stand down posture."

"So the locals can get the credit," she mumbled to herself.

"No, so we don't create an international debacle."

"I'm fuckin' tired of politics," she rasped.

"Then quit the intelligence business."

"Any news about us?" George asked, nodding toward Marvin.

"Not yet, but with Sandy out of the picture there shouldn't be a problem."

"We don't have our passports," Marvin advised.

"When the time comes, we'll fly chartered and when we get to Israel I'll take care of entry."

Bina was uncharacteristically sulking in the corner of the room, as she sat on one edge of a bed. But with a lull in the conversation she spoke up and suggested, "I guess we can send the wet team home when they arrive."

"They're already in country."

"Where are you getting this info from?"

"The two investigators."

"Is one of them that arrogant fool, Vasily?" she snapped.

"Yeah, afraid so."

"I don't trust his judgement."

"We don't have a choice."

"His intel got Virginia killed and, by extension, Sandy."

"Faulty intelligence is an occupational hazard."

"I say we go for the boat."

"Not our decision."

"Then we may as well go home," she said, her voice trailing off as she walked into the corridor.

George, who had been quietly taking in the verbal sparring between Bina and Rafael, cleared his throat and offered, "If you change your mind, I'm in."

"Look, I want them as much as anyone else, but it could mean the end of my career, or life."

"And if we wait too long, a subway station might go boom."

"Yeah, there's that."

The bedside phone began to ring, and Rafael starred at it, hesitant to respond. But after six jingles he picked up the receiver and said, "Yes?"

"You have a visitor in the lobby, sir," the desk clerk advised.

"Name?"

"Refused to supply one."

"OK, thank you."

"Will you be coming down?"

"Yes."

In the absence of Bina, he turned to George and said, "I need backup, you up for it?"

"Backup?"

"Someone at the front desk is asking for me. Could be friend or foe."

George reached into a canvass bag and withdrew a loaded pistol that he slid between the wasteland of his khakis and his bare skin, as Rafael did the same.

They took the stairs down to the lobby, and as Rafael made his way to the desk, George hung behind with his right hand gripping his pistol's butt. Curious, he inched his way forward until he had a partial view of Rafael and the visitor. Nothing threatening appeared to be in play, so he relaxed his grip and waited. It was seven-twenty a.m., and aside from the desk clerk and the two apparently congenial men, no one else was about. Another ten minutes had passed, and the two men began walking in his direction. George tensed and reached for his waistband but Rafael waived an all clear.

"He's one of us or, rather, my people," Rafael said, of the nameless man.

George did a quick assessment of the newcomer, whose biceps protruded from a white cable sweater over a pair of green corduroy slacks, and whose square jaw barely moved when he said, "Shalom."

At a loss for words, George simply nodded in reply.

"He's here to help with our problem," Rafael advised.

"Just you?" George said, addressing square jaw.

"No, there are three of us."

"But three of them equals six of any others," Rafael chortled.

They started up the staircase, when George stopped and said, "I thought that we were in stand down mode?"

Rafael and the newcomer smiled at each other and declined an explanation.

"C'mon guys, my skin's in the game too," George complained.

Now at the top of the stairs and on a landing, Rafael turned and replied, "When we're all together, then we'll explain."

Marvin and Bina were sitting on the pullout cot in Rafael's room, glaring at each other, when the men entered. They looked up with surprise, as Rafael locked the door and introduced the visitor as a no name, Mossad operative.

"No questions until he's finished," Rafael ordered, his right index finger pointing at the man in the cable sweater.

Bina and Marvin directed their gaze to the newcomer and waited, as the man assessed the inhabitants and advised, in accented English, "There will be seven of us, myself and two of my people and you four."

"Doing what?" Marvin said, adding, "Sorry, you said no questions."

The man ignored him and continued, "We're going off the books, asymmetric, if you will. Available intelligence is thin and time is of the essence. If we wait for diplomatic channels to decide upon a course of action it may be too late. This will be a pre-emptive strike."

There was silence in the room. Both George and Marvin sat with their mouths agape, as it was about to become very real, even more so than what they'd already been through.

This guy's a commando, or special Operations, George said to himself, as he drew in a tremulous breath.

"Questions?" the man asked.

"The Director is out of the loop?" Bina posed.

"Officially, but we've had a back channel conversation."

"So we won't be dead meat if we get home again?"

"I'm glad you said, if. There are a lot of unknown variables with this operation, it could go south really fast. But, no, it won't make the news."

"And that's the logic behind the decision," Rafael commented, adding, "if we can get this done with a stealth operation, the Director will take the diplomatic heat."

"And if it doesn't go as planned?" Bina asked.

"They'll light Yahrzeit candles."

Chapter Thirty-seven

Tuesday, January 16th

Tel Aviv

1 P.M.

Ariel Bruck had just finished lunch, which had consisted of Sabih—pita bread filled with fried eggplant, hard boiled egg, tahini sauce, hummus, salad and a mango dressing— washed down with a Diet Coke. He'd belched, reached for a bottle of chewable antacids, consumed two and shouted into the intercom, "What time is it in New York?"

"They're seven hours behind," his secretary advised.

Should've heard something by now, he said to himself, wiping a dollop of dressing from the face of his wristwatch. But as he was about to consider a trip to the loo, Seren Levin knocked and entered without waiting for permission. "Any news?" he asked.

"Not yet," Bruck replied.

"You sure about the mission?"

"I have my doubts, but there are lives and our reputation at stake."

"If word gets out, the Knesset will take our heads."

"And if the attack goes down while we're trying to convince the Americans?"

"Yeah. It's the proverbial rock and a hard place."

Bruck shook his head in agreement.

"We have to try, there is no other choice."

"I'll make the call."

"Does the wet team have access to explosives?"

"They took some with them on the charter flight."

"Have them blow Little Milly out of the water."

"There's the issue of collateral damage."

"Make it a discretionary decision. But if possible, it would bring the matter to a close in a most decisive fashion."

"I agree, it would be preferable to a firefight."

Moishe loitered in his chair, and Bruck stared at him and said, "What's on your mind, Moishe?"

"I should be with them."

"You're thinking about the Gaza screwup, I understand."

"I need redemption."

"There isn't time and I need you here."

"Face it, Ariel, I'm just your sounding board."

"And a very good one, at that," he grinned.

"No, seriously, what do I really offer?"

"Objectivity."

"Artificial intelligence could provide that."

Bruck removed the pair of bifocals that he'd recently begun to require, rubbed his eyes and said, "You are my right hand, I cannot and will not remain in this office without you. Understood?"

Seren Levin smiled, shook his head in acquiescence, and left the room.

That one is a piece of work, Bruck thought. Known him forever and, truthfully, I could probably get along without him, but it's nice to have someone to lean on at times. The Gaza mess has gotten me thinking, however, and I'll make certain that I do not put him in such a position again. And he thinks that he's my sounding board, he laughed to himself. Well, no more tactical decisions for Moishe, he's just achieved errand boy status.

The encrypted desk phone began to buzz, and he reached for it.

"Bruck here?" he droned.

"This is Vasily. We have not been able to predetermine the exact coordinates of the target."

"You'd said that your source is on the inside," Bruck urged.

"Not inside enough for the required intel."

"Do you have a time frame?"

"Soon."

Bruck shook his head, took a deep breath, and growled, "That's about as useless as tits on a bull."

"Sorry, sir, but that's all we've got."

"What time is it there?"

"Almost 7 a.m."

There was a pause in the conversation, and Bruck finally barked, "Call Rafael and tell him to get ready."

"Sir?"

"He'll know what that means."

"What of us?"

"You and your partner catch the first flight home."

"And the POF attack?"

"No longer your problem."

"But..."

"That's an order, get your ass moving."

He slammed the receiver back onto its base and did something entirely out of character. He slid open a bottom desk drawer and removed an unopened, eighty-five dollar bottle of Jameson Gold Reserve. After pouring two fingers into a coffee mug, he stared at it and wondered what his wife would say if she were to witness his digression. I was never a true alcoholic, he said to himself, but there were times when I could have been a danger to others. But I really need this to soften the blow of what's about to come.

When the PM hears about what I've decided to do in New York, he's gonna have kittens and probably my head. I've got enough shekels put away to cover expenses ... if and when I get the boot. And it'll likely be sooner rather than later.

There was a knock at the door, and Seren Levin entered, as usual, without announcing his intention.

"I just heard," he said, sliding onto the chair before Bruck's desk.

"Are there no secrets in this place?" he said, staring once again at the whiskey filled mug and pushing it off to one side.

"Vasily called. He whined like a spoiled child."

"I told him to come home."

"So the New York affair is finished?"

Bruck suppressed a grin and wondered if, given his subordinate's new designation of errand boy, he should share the decision. In the end he replied, "Not exactly."

"Meaning?"

"That's all you need to know," he advised, reaching for the mug and taking a pensive sip.

"Have I been demoted?" Moishe asked, angrily.

How perceptive of him, Bruck thought, responding with, "It could only cause you pain."

"Pain?"

"I am responsible for the fruits of my decisions, rotten or otherwise."

"So it's not over," he mumbled.

Bruck shrugged, a noncommittal response to Moishe's question.

"When you'd been appointed as acting director, I'd agreed to stick with you through thick and thin. I'd assumed that the sentiment would work both ways."

"I'm protecting you," Bruck said, his face half hidden by the mug.

"I don't need protecting, I need to be in the loop."

"Listen carefully. If what I have planned falls apart, they'll be looking for my replacement. And who better to carry on than someone who's been privy to the inner workings of this office."

"Me?"

"Yes. So it's better that you can honestly claim ignorance of my plan."

"I don't want your job. If you go, I go."

"I appreciate your loyalty, but if I get canned someone has to steer the ship. And that someone is you, even if only on a temporary basis."

Moishe exhaled noisily and breathed, "I understand,"

adding, "so you're gonna blow the boat," more a statement than a question.

"Forget our earlier conversation and you'll come out of this in one piece."

Chapter Thirty-eight

Tuesday, 7:30 A.M.

New York

Rafael had just received Vasily's call. The conversation had been brief, and while the caller had said little else other then "Get ready," the message had been clear.

The wet team members had been waiting in a parked step van, and Rafael had made his way down to the lobby and out onto the street. He knocked on the side of the vehicle and a few seconds later the door slid back.

"Get in," a nameless team member ordered.

The door glided closed and he entered the darkened confines of the rear compartment. The walls of the van had been outfitted with ropes and hangers, from which dangled several backpacks and canvas cases containing automatic rifles. He took a seat on the bare floor and advised, "We're go for the raid."

"Dark or light?" the driver called out.

"Our decision."

"An hour after sundown," the leader apparent instructed, continuing, "but that could change if we monitor activity."

"Drone?" Rafael asked.

"We've got a team member at the marina with eyes on."

"I thought you were only three?"

The man grinned, and said, "I'd lied."

"What's the plan?" Rafael asked.

"We're on point, and you and your people will follow our lead."

"Some advance knowledge would be helpful."

"The marina has other inhabitants, an exact plan of action isn't possible."

"So stealth is out the door?"

"Possibly."

"I was hoping for a surgical attack, but that sounds unlikely."

"There will be casualties, and we'll try to make certain that they're all tangos (terrorists)."

"Have you considered the potential for collateral damage?"

"Unavoidable."

"Seriously?"

"It's either a couple of innocents at the marina, or a shitload on their way to or from work. Your choice."

"OK. It's your ballgame."

"Go back to your people and we'll call your cell when

its go time."

As he was about to exit the van, he was handed a cloth bag containing four bulletproof vests. He tossed the sack over one shoulder and headed back to the hotel.

He found Bina, George and Marvin lounging in his room, and he tossed the sack onto a bed and frowned. "Looks like we've been designated as followers, not leaders," he lamented.

"We're going in?" Bina asked.

Rafael's head bobbed affirmatively.

"When?" she inquired.

"We're on call," he replied.

"What's in the bag?" George asked.

"Vests."

"That's thoughtful."

"They don't always work," Rafael instructed.

"They do in the movies," Marvin interjected.

"There is ammunition that can pierce the vest," Bina explained.

"Shit," George mumbled, his hand inside of the sack, fingering a vest's fabric.

"I suggest that we get some rest, since my guess is that we'll be on the move after dark," Rafael advised.

* * *

***

9:30 P.M.

They'd passed the hours munching on delivered pizza, soft drinks and a box of assorted Dunkin Donuts. The call had come at nine o'clock, with instructions to be ready for pickup at the end of the street at ten p.m., sharp. Under Bina's direction, they'd already cleaned the weapons, loaded their magazines and secured them in two burlap packs. Marvin's attempt at modeling one of the vests had resulted in some laughter, as he'd donned it shirtless, across his bony chest, Rambo style.

At nine forty-five they made their way down to the street and, although seized by a building adrenaline high, nonchalantly walked toward the waiting, oversized, windowless step van and entered. Three men, their faces streaked with green and black camouflage material sat in the rear, while the driver, sans face paint, put the vehicle in gear and rolled away from the curb.

"Got some of that face stuff for us?" George asked.

One of the rear seated commandos gazed at him askance and replied, "Not for you."

Rafael leaned forward from a third row seat and addressed the man with whom he'd been in contact, and said, "What's our intended role?"

"You're backup," the man said.

"Did that come from the Director?"

"My decision."

"So we babysit the van," Bina growled.

The man did not reply, but his silence had been confirmatory.

She nudged her partner and whispered, "I'm not good with that."

"Me neither, but we're already at the cliff's edge and I'm not going to jump."

"I don't follow," she said.

"We've been off book for this entire fiasco, and we'll be lucky to keep our jobs."

"I don't take orders from them," she murmured, nodding toward the commandos.

"Let's see where this goes," Rafael suggested.

It was a quarter past ten when they'd come to a stop just outside of the marina. And it was dead quiet inside of the van, as they surveyed the surroundings with their eyes focused on Little Milly and the nearby vessels.

Rafael broke the silence when he asked, "You gonna walk or drive in?"

The man that he'd been speaking with, the leader

apparent, replied, "We're commandos, not cowboys—we walk."

"And we stay behind and watch?"

"Pretty much," he replied, pressing a small communications device into Rafael's outstretched hand, adding, "if I call, you drive right up to the front door and start shooting."

"Do we know if any of the boats are inhabited?"

"Irrelevant."

"Collateral damage is relevant?"

"We've had this discussion, collateral damage is unavoidable."

"That should help my sleepless nights."

"Not my problem," the man said, as he and his three team members exited the van and took off into the night.

Rafael slid into the driver's seat and watched, as the team made their way toward the boat using any and all available structures to conceal their advance.

"See anything?" Bina asked.

"Looks like an electric security cart rolling down the dock."

"Can they avoid it?"

"If they can't, they'll probably take him out."

"Shit," George hissed.

"What's your problem?" Rafael inquired, keeping his eyes aimed straight ahead.

"Will the killing ever stop?"

"When we're dead."

"Muzzle flash," Bina called out.

"Where?"

"Little Milly's aft-deck."

All eyes locked onto Little Milly's transom, from where a brief volley of flashes could be observed. Rafael raised the small walkie-talkie, waiting for a signal to gun the engine and race toward the boat, but the small, black box remained silent. He rolled down the driver's side window, allowing a rush of salty air to penetrate the vehicle's interior.

"Reminds me of home," Marvin noted.

"Forget about Miami," George advised, "we're not going back."

"Well, at least the sea air covers up your stink—when was the last time you'd taken a shower?"

"You don't smell like a flower shop either," George snarled.

"Both of you, shut the hell up," Bina roared.

"The flashes have stopped," Rafael informed.

"The ones that we can see," Bina said.

"I think we should go in," Rafael suggested, fiddling with the communication device's power switch, making certain that it had been engaged.

"And get shot by our own people ... not a good idea."

"Waiting is making me very nervous."

"Chew your fingernails."

And then came a chirp from the radio, followed by the order, "Move in."

Without hesitation, Rafael released the parking brake and hit the accelerator. The rear seat passengers where thrown backward, but they'd held on tight, each gripping their assigned weapon. It had taken less than a minute to reach Little Milly's boarding ramp, and a sudden crack in the windshield revealed that the firefight was still in progress.

"Keep your heads down," Rafael ordered, as they slithered from the van in a crouch.

"They know we're here," George stuttered from the foot of the ramp.

"One round to the windshield, probably a stray," Rafael whispered in assurance, as he ascended the ramp to the boat's gunwale with the others in tow.

With hand signals, Rafael gestured for Bina to head toward the afterdeck, while he motioned for Marvin to take a position over a deck hatch, as he and George carefully entered the main upper deck cabin.

"Tell your guys not to shoot us," George breathed.

Rafael removed the small radio from his pocket and clicked the talk button three times, an indication that he was on scene, but the sound of suppressed weapons fire made it unlikely that his signal would be heard, and he mumbled, "Keep your eyes open for camouflaged faces."

"What if the terrorists are wearing the shit?"

"Then we're fucked," Rafael whispered, moving deeper into the dimly lit cabin.

And then it happened. All at once, rounds whizzed by from two sides of the cabin, less than twenty feet from their position. The muzzle flashes had clearly revealed the shooter's location, and both Rafael and George opened fire with their automatic weapons. The exchange had lasted only seconds, the thud of a body hitting the deck a moment before the thumping of weighty feet running from the cabin was heard.

"Keep moving," Rafael ordered.

"Where to?"

"Follow the shooter."

"Think there are more?" George asked anxiously, as they made their way through a companionway into a dinning area.

"Shut up and keep your eyes open for Bina," Rafael said, as he reached for the radio.

"The gunfire is coming from below."

The sound of an unsuppressed weapon caught their attention, and they froze. At the same moment, Rafael moaned, "I'm hit."

"Where?"

"Shoulder," he cried out.

An instant later, Bina appeared before them, her weapon aimed directly at George's head.

"Don't shoot, we're on the same side," George called out in the semidarkness.

"Rafael?" she screeched.

"Yeah. Nice shot," he groaned.

"I hit you?"

"Afraid so, but I'll live."

"Where are the commandos?" she asked.

"Below deck."

"You stay here, we'll go and assist," she advised, nudging George with her free hand.

"Not gonna happen."

Chapter Thirty-nine

Wednesday, January 17th

Tel Aviv, 6 A.M.

Acting Director Bruck had awakened at 4 a..m., set the coffee machine for his still sleeping wife, and dressed without his usual morning shower. Thirty minutes later he trotted into his office and began to read through the intelligence traffic that had arrived during the evening and early morning hours. Sleep had been an unavailable commodity that night, the New York operation having consumed his thoughts. And as he sat behind his desk, waiting for the coffee to cease brewing, he could feel his pulse quickening.

I've been down this road before, so why am I so anxious, he wondered. The shit is going to hit the fan no matter the outcome, since I had not discussed my plan with the PM, or my American counterpart. But will they thank me if all goes well, he asked himself. I guess the best that I can hope for is a backchannel commendation. But if we fail, well ... they're gonna come at me from all sides, and it won't be pretty.

The noisy machine had stopped gurgling, and he rose, grabbed the oversized mug with the silly, comic book character that his wife had gifted him with, and filled it with the steaming, black liquid. It was now 7 a.m., and he reached for the intercom button but was interrupted by the buzz of the encrypted telephone.

"Yes?" he said, tentatively, the coffee mug still held by the finger of his right hand.

"Vasily here, sir. The team has yet to check in."

"Is that supposed to cheer me up, durak (Russian for idiot). And didn't I tell you to come home?"

"I'd thought that I could help, and sorry, but I'd figured that you'd want to know."

"Do you have eyes on?" Bruck asked, taking a sip from the mug and wincing.

There was a brief pause and then, "No."

"So you're relaxing with a cup of tea while our people are being shot at?" he said, with dripping sarcasm.

"I've switched to coffee, sir."

"We're going to have a long conversation when you get back."

"Sir?"

"You and your partner go over to that boat and get me some credible intel, understood?"

"Now?"

"Hell yes."

"But it's midnight here."

Bruck pinched the skin of his left forearm, making certain that he wasn't dreaming, and shouted, "There is no time clock for Mossad, Vasily. If you value your job, get your butt on scene immediately."

"Am I to engage, sir?"

"I need intel, get it by whatever means necessary," he growled, and terminated the call.

That idiot. If his father hadn't been a war hero and friend of the PM, he'd be digging holes on a kibbutz.

Recalling his intent to speak with his secretary, he pressed the intercom's buzzer and called out, "Have you see Seren Levin this morning?"

"I've just arrived, sir," she said, apologetically.

"I need to speak with him."

His coffee had turned into an undrinkable, cold, murky liquid and he shoved the mug off to the side of the desk. The intercom came to life sooner than expected and the message that had been conveyed had done nothing to brighten his already dismal morning.

"There is a communique on my desk from Tat Aluf Wexler (Brigadier General), sir."

"From when?" Bruck inquired.

"No timestamp, but must have come through during

the early hours."

"Bring it to me."

She handed the sealed envelop to Bruck and left the office. He examined it carefully, taking note of the General's signature on its face, and abruptly slit it open.

Once again, problems on the Golan (Golan Heights). We (the army) can handle it, but thought you should be aware.

He lowered the message to the desk blotter and grumbled to himself, we'd offered them a path to prosperity, but they'd rather cause mayhem. And for what, he asked himself. They don't have a chance in hell to best us. Well, the army has the will, technology and firepower to beat them back, he thought, as he lowered the dispatch into a shredder behind his desk.

The office door opened and Moishe Levin appeared without entering.

"Since when do you wait for an invitation?" Bruck said.

"Your secretary said that you weren't in a good mood."

"What else is new, have a seat."

Moishe carefully lowered his buttocks onto the thinly upholstered chair and grimaced.

"Problem?" Bruck asked.

"Slipped on a wet floor."

"Don't expect hazard pay," Bruck chuckled.

"I've heard that there is some action on the Golan?"

Bruck gazed back at the shredder, wondering where he would have obtained the intel so quickly, and said, "What kind of action?"

"Missiles and RPG's (rocket propelled grenades)."

"Coming from where?"

"Hamas, the Syrian rebels ... who knows."

"Casualties?"

"Some, but so far, not ours."

"And why does this interest you?"

"I need some way to redeem myself."

"As the Americans say, that train has already left the station."

"It's eating me up."

"See a psychiatrist."

"You're supposed to be a friend."

"You want me to manufacture a conflict so you can play hero?"

"What about the Golan?"

"That's the army's purview."

Moishe released a blast of air, effectively deflating his

lungs in desperation, and said, "Any news from New York?"

"I'm waiting for a call from the Russian."

"Vasily is a buffoon."

"On that we can agree, but we're stuck with him right now."

Moishe nodded his agreement.

While Bruck was conjuring a way to rid himself of Moishe and his gloomy attitude, the encrypted phone came to life. He raised a hand, as if to say keep quiet, and reached for the device.

"Yes?"

"It is Vasily. I am on the dock and I see no activity."

"Are you armed?"

"Yes."

"I need a damage report."

There was a brief period of silence and then, "Yes, sir."

"Call me back with your assessment," he said, and terminated the call.

"Vasily?" Moishe asked.

"Yes, I have to deal with him like a child."

"I'll find him a desk job when he returns."

Bruck grinned with approval and offered, "How about a vacation?"

"For me?"

"You could use some time to recharge, regain your sense of worth."

"But work is all I have."

"Take your significant other, if she'll put up with you, and go someplace quiet."

"You're trying to get rid of me," Moishe mumbled.

"No, my friend, I'm trying to help you to regain focus."

"Well, maybe, when things calm down."

"I don't expect that to happen anytime soon."

"I'll think about it," he said, and left the room.

Chapter Forty

Midnight

Little Milly, New York

The terrorist's floating sanctuary had turned out to be larger, and with more hiding places than anticipated. As a result, the firefight and cat and mouse game had continued for several hours, but in the end, the Mossad had experienced only two, nonfatal casualties, with one from friendly fire. All but a single POF fighter had been neutralized, the remaining individual having sustained a head wound of nonlethal nature. At a little past midnight, the four commandos and Rafael's group convened in the boat's dining area, while Vasily and his partner stood off to one corner of the room as bystanders.

"Everyone is accounted for," the commando leader announced.

"What about him?" Rafael asked, pressing a gauze against his shoulder wound and gesturing toward the wounded POF.

"He comes with us."

"Ask him if there are others in the city," Rafael said.

"Would you believe his word?"

"Hmm, guess not."

"What about this boat?" Bina asked.

"Aside from all the bullet holes, it's still afloat."

"I meant, we should scuttle it."

"Seriously, in a marina?"

"OK, bad idea. I'm just angry."

Vasily stepped forward and said, "Excuse me, but I have to report back to the Director."

"Don't let us stop you," Rafael frowned.

"What should I tell him?"

"Are you, or are you not an intelligence officer?" Rafael hissed, through clenched teeth.

"I'm simply asking for guidance."

"Tell him, mission completed."

"How many?"

"Eleven tangos down," the commando leader advised.

"What about clean up?" Vasily asked.

"Not my problem," the leader replied.

"Nor mine," Rafael chimed in.

"Someone will be alerted by the odor."

"That's the first intelligent thing you've said," the leader observed, adding, "ever captain a boat?"

Vasily was dumbfounded, and replied, "No, why do you ask?"

The leader glared at him for a long moment, and

countered, "Never mind, I'll think of something."

While Vasily exited the vessel with his partner, the commando leader turned to Rafael with a proposal, and said, "He was correct in his assessment. Someone will eventually take note of a terrible odor and report to the authorities."

"But we'll be long gone by then."

"If the LEO's (Law enforcement officers) don't get here first."

"The adjacent boats are unoccupied," Rafael said.

"Are you certain that the gunfire, suppressed or not, has gone unnoticed?"

"No."

"Then we need an immediate decision, and we have to vacate this marina with or without this vessel."

"So you agree, we scuttle her," Bina offered.

The commando turned toward her and instructed, "We take her out to sea."

"We don't even know if the boat is seaworthy, or if it has sufficient fuel," Rafael advised.

George had taken note of Bina's initial scuttle suggestion, and had made his way to the wheelhouse. He'd returned just as the discussion veered in the direction of a sea voyage, and suggested, "I've checked the boat's logs, and it's most recent voyage had been to Montauk. So we can assume that she's seaworthy. Furthermore, she's got a three quarter load of diesel fuel that should easily get us to scuttleville, assuming you have a way for us to get back to dry land."

"Impressive," the commando admitted, adding, "can you handle the trip?"

"I'm not familiar with New York harbor, but I can read a nautical map, and there are several on the bridge."

"There's a small tender on the port side. One of my men will follow and pick you up."

"Wait a minute, I said that this boat can probably survive the trip, but a tender?"

"Take a look, it's at least a thirty foot inboard. Might not be a comfortable ride, but it should do the trick."

"I'll need some help."

"I guess that's me," Marvin groaned.

"Where did you get all this nautical knowledge from?" Rafael asked.

"I'd worked part-time on a charter fishing boat."

"Enough small talk. Once you've arrived at your chosen location, torch it and don't look back," the commando instructed.

"What happens if I get stopped by harbor police on

my way out to sea?"

The commando locked eyes with George, his dull gray eyes resembling those of a great white shark, and shoved his Tavor assault rifle against George's chest. "Take them out and keep going," he barked.

George walked out to Little Milly's port side, eyeballed the tender, and returned to the main cabin, as the two chosen commandos climbed down a ladder to the small craft and waited. Rafael, Bina and the remaining commandos returned dockside, as Vasily and his partner had already left the scene. It had been decided that, if all were to go as planned, the tender would not return to the marina. It would instead head to Port Jefferson Marina where they would quickly abandon the vessel. The step van would be awaiting their arrival and would whisk them all to Long Island's MacArthur Airport, where a long range chartered jet would be waiting.

The Tender had already departed to allow Little Milly enough room to leave the pier, and they would meet up just outside the Marina, where the small powerboat would follow off to one side. The lines had already been removed and the big boat was free to go. A few puffs of black smoke belched from beneath Milly's transom, as George engaged the diesel engines, keeping his fingers crossed that no other security personnel were about to question the late night exodus.

"Aren't you just a little bit nervous right now?" Marvin asked, seated beside his friend on the bridge.

"Let's see. Guiding a big boat that I have no familiarity with through unfamiliar water in the pitch dark … shit yeah, I'm so nervous that I could pee my pants."

"Do we really need to have those red and green lights blaring in the dark?"

"No Marvin, we can turn them off so every ship in the area can ram the hell out of us."

"Sorry."

"What's that thing?" Marvin asked, his index finger tapping the screen of a computer like device mounted on the bridge.

"It's an automated, GPS guided map, and it's the only way for us to get to our destination."

"Cool."

"You can program that thing?"

"Already done."

"What am I here for?"

"You can get off anytime you want," George chuckled, his eyes dancing between the screen and the open water.

"Funny. Hey, I've heard about boats sinking in the

dark, after hitting submerged logs and crap."

"That's what you're here for, to keep watch."

"Don't you have sonar for that?"

"Doesn't seem to be working."

"Shit. Can I watch from here?"

"No, get your keister to the bow."

"What if you need me for something?"

"Then I'm SOL (shit out of luck)."

Until leaving the Marina and arriving in open water, Little Milly had been tooling along at idle speed, but with the horizon beckoning, George pushed the throttles up a few notches, checking every now and then to make certain that the tender was keeping up and out of the big boat's wake. Marvin, his hair blowing in the wind, held tight to whatever he'd found to keep him aloft, as he kept a pair of night vision binoculars close to his eyeballs. A raised right arm was the signal that a potential obstruction was in their path, and George kept a close watch on his friends arms.

They had estimated the distance from Manhattan to Montauk to be approximately 189 kilometers, or 117 miles. Although George had no prior knowledge of Little Milly's abilities, her log books had suggested that she could propel herself at upwards of 18 knots, roughly 20.7 miles per hour, a good clip for a vessel of her size. And at that speed she would require about six and one half hours to reach Montauk. The tender's inboard engines could exceed the big boat's top speed by a wide margin, so George did not fear losing the commandos. With Marvin's arms giving no sign of danger, he pushed the throttles to their stops, set the computerized GPS to automatic guidance and sat back for the ride. The GPS device would take control of the rudder and, if nothing got in their way, steer them to the desired waypoint, several miles off of Montauk's coast.

It had been a long, stressful night, and George found himself drifting off, the constant drone of the big diesels lulling him to sleep. But he would awaken every now and then as his body began to slip from the elevated Captain's chair. About an hour into the voyage he was awakened by something other than his own body's movement. A strange odor had permeated the bridge, and as he rose to investigate he was thwarted by someone pressing a knife to his throat.

"What the fuck?" he cried out, caught off guard.

"I kill you," the foreign accented voice informed.

"What are you waiting for?" George screeched, his heart racing as he considered his nonexistent options.

"You drive boat."

"Who the fuck are you?"

"Drive boat."

And then it dawned upon him, we hadn't killed them all, he said to himself. "Where were you hiding?"

"No talk."

"Where am I to drive to?"

The terrorist did not reply, but the knife remained pressed against his skin. I have no way to call Marvin, and no way to contact the commandos ... I'm fucked, he thought. And like a halfwit, I'd stored the Tavor in a cubby.

The malodorous militant's body was pressing against his own, and a thought came to mind and he said, "I have to lean forward to program guidance, can you move the knife?"

The man hesitated, but lowered the blade just far enough to reduce the risk of a slit throat, and for George to insinuate his right foot between the man's legs, quickly destabilizing the terrorist's stance. The fighter faltered and side stepped, as George quickly released the autopilot and shifted the rudder to a hard turn to port (left). The big boat took a few seconds to respond, but it had been enough to toss the militant against a bulkhead and allow George to kick the knife from his clutches. Little Milly was now making a wide circle, and George had not witnessed Marvin's body careening to the salt water soaked deck.

Moments later, Marvin came running onto the bridge, his face having assumed an angry scowl.

"What the fuck, George, you almost—where'd he come from?" Marvin shouted, finally noticing the POF member stretched out on the wheelhouse floor.

George reserved his reply until he had reengaged the autopilot, and said, "Hidden below."

"Are there more?" he asked with a tremulous voice.

George shrugged.

"Let's get the commandos on board to search," Marvin screeched.

"Can't."

"Why not?"

"We'll lose the tender."

"I'm not gonna wait for the next one."

"Take the rifle from that cubby," George advised, gesturing to his left, "and search the boat, including the engine room."

Marvin stood motionless, as if fearful of the suggestion, but ultimately grabbed the Tavor and disappeared.

Chapter Forty-one

Tel Aviv

Wednesday, January 17th

10 A.M.

Ariel Bruck had been handling calls from his field agents. The Golan Heights issue had been escalating and the rockets had been traced to have been coming from both the Syrian and Hamas led forces. Calls had been made to the Hamas office of operations and, as usual, they'd denied involvement. Accordingly, an air strike had been mounted against the presumed Hamas launch site, but a more cautious approach had been employed for the Syrians, consisting of the Iron Dome's deployment (Israeli missile defense system). And he'd just terminated a conversation with an army officer, when the encrypted phone began to signal an incoming call.

"This is Vasily, the operation is complete."

"Meaning?" Bruck asked.

"The terrorists have been neutralized."

"Casualties?"

"Two of ours shot, none fatal."

"The team is on its way home?"

"Not sure."

"What is wrong with you, Vasily. You are my eyes and ears in country, but you're failing."

"We'd left as they were deciding what to do with the bodies, sir."

Bruck lowered the phone, removed a bottle of antacids from his top drawer and popped two into his mouth. "Call Rafael and get back to me," he ordered, terminating the call.

He sat back in his chair and sighed. It was time to have the conversation that he'd been dreading, but it had to be done. And rather than have his secretary do the dialing, he removed a small black notebook from his lower desk drawer, lifted the receiver and punched in the private number for a U.S. State Department official with whom he'd established a relationship in the past.

"Marcus? Ariel Bruck."

"How's the weather?"

Bruck recognized the code word for Middle East conditions and replied, "Could be better."

"Sorry about that, what can I do for you?"

"It's about what we can do for each other."

"I'm listening."

"One of yours is out of business and I can give you her vector."

There was a pause and then, "We've been afraid of that, we'd lost contact."

Bruck rattled off the address of the building in question, but Marcus came back with, "From whom have you acquired the intel?"

That was the question that Bruck had been waiting for and he replied, "A terrorist group, known to us as the POF, had established a foothold in New York and had been planning a subway attack. Some of my people happened to be on scene and took the opportunity to preempt, she'd offered her assistance," he advised, with a partial truism.

"Are the local authorities aware of this?"

"Not to my knowledge."

"Let's keep it that way."

"Are we good?"

"We'll take care of the agent. What I assume had been a firefight hadn't happened, and your people were simply tourists."

"Appreciated."

"No, thank *you*. Anything else?"

Bruck had considered discussing the Little Milly operation, but decided to leave that to chance. "No, that's all."

"See you when I see you," Marcus said, and hung up.

Whew, Bruck said to himself, that was easier than anticipated. There was a lot more to the story, but he didn't ask for details and I'm thankful for that. But if those POF bodies begin to surface the shit will surely hit the fan.

Chapter Forty-Two

Little Milly

4 A.M.

Marvin had searched every visible inch of the boat and had come back with a smile. He had not found any other stowaways, but had located their prisoner's engine room hiding place—the giveaway having been represented by the presence of several slices of Pita bread lying beneath an exhaust manifold. The POF man had been hogtied in one corner of the wheelhouse, his lips sealed by a length of duct tape.

"We're clear," Marvin announced, leaning the Tavor against the bulkhead opposite the prisoner.

"Great."

"The engines looked good, no oil leaks and not much water entering the bilge."

"So now you're an expert?" George laughed, keeping his eyes on the water ahead.

"I know some things."

"We've got another two or so hours before reaching our destination."

"I'm gettin' hungry."

"Go check the galley."

Marvin returned ten minutes later with a jar of hummus and an opened package of Pita bread.

"That's all you'd found?" George groaned.

"Guess they hadn't been planning a lengthy stay."

They'd just finished the package of bread when the prisoner had begun to writhe about. Marvin guessed that the man needed a bathroom, but George ignored the apparent request and called out, "Just piss in your pants."

The writhing had ceased, but the man's khaki colored chinos displayed a monumental wet spot and Marvin advised, "That's gonna stink."

"Yeah, probably. Drag him out to the bow and secure him to a stanchion so I can keep an eye on him from here."

Marvin scrunched his nose, grabbed the man by his ankles and began sliding his body along the wooden deck. But just before he'd closed the wheelhouse door, he suggested, "Maybe I should feed him to the sharks?"

The prisoner apparently understood that sharks were not in his best interest, and began squirming about, presumably to prevent his removal. And while he'd given the initial impression of not speaking much English, he'd managed to chew a portion of the tape, to the extent that he was able to make audible, "I have information."

George, having heard the man's words, called out to

Marvin, "Hold it, bring him back inside."

Marvin complied, but kept his distance from the smelly fighter and waited with a quizzical expression.

"Didn't you hear him?" George asked.

"No, his head was inside, while I had his feet on the outside."

George took one last gaze out of the windshield, making certain that nothing large was in their path, and knelt before the man, ripping the tape to one side of his face. "Let's have it?" he demanded.

"No sharks," the man shuddered.

"Depends upon your information," George advised, knowing that he had no intention of tossing the guy overboard.

"You Director is target," the man admitted.

"I don't have a director," George said, but pressed onward, and added, "Director of what?"

The man shook, as if chilled, and said, "Mossad."

"When?"

"Don't know."

George replaced the tape and locked eyes with Marvin. "We have to tell them, ASAP."

"How?"

"Radio."

"We're not supposed to be out here, you hit the talk button and that show's over," Marvin said.

"Go out and see if you can flag down the commandos."

"They'll never hear me, and waving my arms in the dark?"

"See if there's a flare gun up here."

"And that won't give away our position?"

"Shit. We have to find a way."

"It's gonna have to wait two hours," Marvin suggested, adding, "what are you doing?"

"Slowing down. If the commandos see us cutting back to idle speed they might suspect trouble and investigate."

"We'll be late to arrive."

"Not by much," George instructed, as the boat began to bob over the waves.

Sure enough, the commandos had slowed as well and had turned amidships, coming within twenty feet of Little Milly's port side. Marvin ran out and shouted, "We have a problem."

"Engine failure?" one of the men shouted.

"No, something more important—can one of you come aboard?"

Marvin watched as the two commandos apparently conferred. Boarding a bouncing vessel in open waters was never a safe undertaking, but the choice had been made and the tender dropped behind Little Milly, coming within feet of her transom ladder. Several minutes later, a very wet military man approached and growled, "What's the problem?"

Marvin led him to the bridge, where he frowned at the trussed up terrorist and said, "Guess we'd missed one."

"Is that it?"

"No," George advised, continuing with, "under threat of making him shark bait, he told us that your Director is a target."

The commando had been taken by surprise, but without hesitation he removed the prisoner's silver tape and repeated the questioning. Satisfied that the intel was at least marginally credible, he said, "Show me your radio."

"It'll give away our position," Marvin complained.

Ignoring Marvin's warning, he reached for the microphone, punched in the frequency that his unit commander monitored on a twenty-four hour basis, and called out, "Foxtrot, Whiskey, Romeo fifteen (his code name) condor, red alert, condor (Ariel Bruck's code name) ... I repeat, red alert, condor."

"Acknowledged," came the barely audible reply.

"That's it?" George asked.

"They don't need the details, only that he is in danger. They will cordon off his office and residence and post surveillance."

"What about him?" Marvin asked, facing the POF man.

"Burn him with the others," he said, as he left the wheelhouse and headed back to the tender.

They were back underway ten minutes later, and Marvin had returned to his post at the bow.

At 5:45 a.m., the GPS signaled that they'd arrived at the last programmed waypoint, thirty minutes earlier than George had predicted. He gradually eased back on the Glendinning synchronizer, a single lever that served to control the speed of both engines simultaneously, and brought the boat's progress to a halt. The seas were four to six feet and choppy, and whitecaps were causing the now stationary boat to bob from side to side. The commandos had taken the cue to throw a line over Little Milly's transom, and Marvin had rushed to the rear to tie it off to an available cleat, as a salty mist of sea water shrouded his body, causing him to slip several times.

One commando remained with the tender, while the

other boarded the big boat to help set it aflame.

George exited the wheelhouse with the Tavor in one hand and called out to the approaching Israeli, "Got a match?"

The man grinned, ever so slightly, and produced a fragmentation grenade, saying, "Toss this in the engine room and run."

Recognizing the explosive from the Brooklyn fiasco, he cried out, "I can't run that fast."

"Got a better idea?"

"What about a fuel tank?"

"Takes a lot to ignite diesel," the man instructed.

"What if I start the engines, leave 'em in neutral and drop the grenade down a fuel fill access?"

The commando considered the suggestion and replied, "A weak option, but the blown tank should fill the engine room and it might ignite from there. How far is the engine room?"

"Two decks down."

"Too far to run from, where's the filler?"

George directed the man to the nearest fill cap, which they quickly unsecured. Fortunately for the pair, the boat's builder had located the fill stations within running distance from the rear of the boat. Still holding the inactive grenade, the commando gently eased it part way into the pipe, making certain that the fuel filler's diameter could accommodate it girth, and convinced that it would fit, he pulled the pin, dropped it, and shouted, "Run like hell."

They'd made it onto the tender just as the explosive detonated, the blast causing the boat's fiberglass and wood rear end to break away and launch the tender forty feet into the crashing waves.

"Shit," Marvin said, "what the hell was that?"

In response, the grenade tossing Israeli offered a toothy gun, as they engaged the inboard engines and began to back even farther away, in the direction of Port Jefferson. Seated in the rear of the open vessel, George watched as plumes of black smoke rose from the bright orange flames shooting from the big boat, while the dark sea began to rise against its hull. She's sinking, he thought, and with it, all evidence of our battle with the POF.

Chapter Forty-three

Tel Aviv

Wednesday, 1 P.M.

Security agents had arrived with armored vehicles, swarming Ariel Bruck's office and home. Both Bruck and his wife had been taken to different safe houses that had been surrounded by a dense perimeter of soldiers. Seren Levin had been left in control, infuriated by the fact that his presence might be misconstrued as the potential target.

The Mossad had anticipated such a scenario, and an existing plan of action had been rapidly executed. What they had not known, however, was the veracity of the warning or its intended timeframe. And for that reason, the safe houses had been outfitted with provisions to accommodate a lengthy stay. The houses themselves were not one's typical domicile. Outwardly, they had been constructed to give the appearance of a normal, middle class residence. But despite the facade, solid, ten foot concrete walls supported a steel and concrete ceiling that itself was six feet thick. And the entire living quarters were underground, served by a staircase whose entrance had been camouflaged with a hinged wall, to which had been attached a faux toilet and associated plumbing pipes. A causal, or a more discerning observer would rightly assume that it was a functional commode, complete with running, albeit recirculated, water. The wall could be operated both electrically and, in the event of a power or generator failure, manually. The interior air was recirculated and filtered, drawing from an intake located fifty feet from the structure, and whose appearance had been altered to give the impression of a large, stationary flowerpot. Assuming that one were to divine the true nature of the structure, penetration would be extremely difficult.

"Where is my wife?" Bruck insisted.

"She is at the secondary site," an agent advised.

"She should be here, with me," he snarled.

"The protocol had been established years before your arrival, sir."

"My fault, I should have reviewed the plan when I'd taken office."

"I assure you, she will be fine."

"Can we communicate?"

"Yes, the green phone is a direct connection."

Bruck rose from the black leather couch, gazed about the windowless room, and strode over to a credenza containing the phone.

"Motek, are you OK?"

"No, I'm not OK. Your people dragged me out of my home with no explanation and deposited me in this concrete tomb."

"I'm sorry, motek, but it was necessary."

"Are you in danger?"

"We are each safe in our, *tombs*, as you've called them."

"What is this about?"

"Trust me, it will all be over shortly," he said, ignoring her question.

"Well, at least they had the presence of mind to bring shorty."

"Did they bring the cat food?"

"Two bags."

"Good. He'll keep you company."

"Why can't we be together?" she whined.

"Protocol."

"I should have married the electrician," she said, and hung up.

The surrounding military presence had been cautioned about making themselves obvious and, to that end, the twenty odd, seasoned soldiers were either dressed in casual attire, or had assumed the personas of various utility personnel. Two heavily armed Mossad agents had been posted inside each of the safe houses, and they'd been instructed to make themselves as unobtrusive as possible. But Mrs. Bruck, true to her nature, was making her watchers uncomfortable, while Shorty howled up a storm and triggered paroxysms of sneezing from an unsuspecting agent. And despite her controlling personality, she'd been ordered to sequester the cat behind the closed bedroom door, a demand that neither Shorty nor Mrs. Bruck had found appealing.

A bank of secure computers had been installed in the Director/Acting Director's dwelling, and Ariel Bruck found himself glued to the screen depicting a realtime view from a surveillance drone that was hovering over the Gaza neighborhood common to the POF. Aware that Seren Levin was now warming his personal desk chair, he lifted the receiver that provided a direct connection to his office.

"Moishe?" he said.

"Moishe the sitting duck at your service," he replied.

"Very funny. I'm no more amused by these circumstance than you are."

"I have not heard from New York," he advised.

"Give it time."

"If the threat is real, I may not have time."

"I'm watching a drone feed from over their

neighborhood. It's quiet."

"That could mean that they've already crossed the border."

"The known tunnels and entry points have been blocked."

"We've been fooled before."

"You know, in the past your pessimistic attitude had proven useful, but today, not so much."

"I'm still down in the dumps."

"This may be your chance to shine, the redemption that you've sought."

"Perhaps, but I have things to do before I die."

"Nobody can get to you in that office."

"A missile could."

With the conversation going sideways, Bruck exhaled and said, "Call me when you hear something," and hung up.

Chapter Forty-four

Port Jefferson, New York

8 A.M.

They'd watched Little Milly's transom disappear beneath the waves, her bow following minutes later, as the tender made its way to Port Jefferson and their waiting transportation. With sunrise had come a calming of the sea, and the waves had dropped down to one to three feet in height, allowing the small boat to pick up speed. The constant pounding had proven hypnotic, and Marvin had curled up in the rear of the vessel, his snoring competing with the boat's roaring twin engines.

"How much longer?" George inquired, not having a nautical map to refer to.

The two commandos were occupying the front bench seat and, without turning, the driver shouted, "Just up ahead, about five minutes."

"Been here before?"

"Once."

"Vacation?"

The two Israelis burst into raucous laughter and the man in the passenger's seat replied, "You might call it that."

"What's so funny?"

"It's classified," the driver chortled.

George had been put off by the response but had decided to let it pass, and asked, "Are we going straight to the airport?"

"You'll have to discuss that with Rafael."

"There's been a change of plans?" he bristled.

There was no reply, as the driver directed the boat toward a wooden pier whose pilings had the appearance of severely decayed toothpicks. The Commando passenger hoisted himself onto the wooden platform, as the driver tossed the bow line up to his outstretched hands. George and Marvin required some assistance to make the transition from boat to dock, but following some unmanly moves they'd achieved their goal, and the four cautiously approached the waiting vehicle.

"Hold it," the lead commando ordered, when they were within forty feet from their ride.

"What is it?" Marvin whispered.

"Something's not right."

"Looks OK to me," George said.

"Engine compartment is open," the leader observed.

With hand signals, the leader directed his partner to the unseen side of the van and, with weapons at the ready, the leader knocked on the side door. No response. He turned and motioned for George and Marvin to take cover behind a rusting dumpster. When they were out of sight, he ripped the door back and poked the muzzle of his rifle into the interior. "Clear," he called out.

The second commando returned to his partner and said, "There's a blood trail leading inland."

"One or more?"

"Looks like one, but I'd need to follow it to be certain."

"We're not leaving until we find out what's happened."

"And transportation?"

"The van's been disabled, we'll have to improvise."

They called for Marvin and George to leave their hiding place and explained their findings, omitting the blood trail.

"Where could they have gone?" Marvin asked.

"Not for breakfast, that's for sure," the second commando suggested.

"So we wait?"

"No, we keep moving."

"To the airport?" George asked, hopefully.

"That's on hold," the leader advised.

The two Floridians were following the commandos through a patch of scrub brush, when the second commando held up his right fist, and called out, "Stop."

"What is it?" the leader inquired.

"Tire tracks ... looks like off-road vehicles, two of them."

"Fresh?"

"Affirmative."

"Could be the abductors."

"There's been a kidnapping?" George screeched.

"At best."

"What does that mean?" Marvin chimed in.

"Didn't want to alarm you, but we saw some blood back by the van."

"Your people were heavily armed," George said, "maybe it's not their blood."

"If that were the case, they'd have been here to greet us."

"Shit."

"Now what?" Marvin stuttered.

"We follow the tracks."

"You thinking POF?" George inquired, as his feet crunched on pebbles and assorted detritus.

"They're on the top of the list."

"How could they have known our destination?"

"If I had to guess," the leader said pensively, "I'd say we have a mole."

"Holy fucking shit," George cried out.

"Keep your voice down, there could be listeners."

"Think it's Rafael?" Marvin asked.

"Could be anyone."

"Then they'd know about us," George said.

"Keep moving."

"The POF were supposed to be a small, inept group," Marvin whined.

"Apparently not," the second commando advised.

"Maybe they have help."

"I guess they could have patched things up with Hamas," the leader suggested, "but right now that's irrelevant."

"What do we do if we find them?"

"Shoot first, ask questions later.

"But you only have two weapons?" George noted.

The two Israelis exchanged glances, ripped open hidden pouches on their fatigues and produced a pair of semiautomatic sidearms. "Now we have four," the leader said, passing a handgun to Marvin and George.

"You think it's wise to follow these tracks?" Marvin

asked, sliding the pistol into his waistband.

"That's all we've got?" the leader barked.

"If there's a mole, and they know about us, this could lead to a trap."

The two Israelis considered Marvin's concern and the leader replied, "Guess you're not as useless as you appear."

"Gee, thanks."

"I agree, it could be a trap, but we have no choice. We'll proceed with caution."

They walked for another thirty minutes, and at 10 a.m., the trail stopped cold.

"No more tracks," one commando observed.

"There's a patch of fresh kicked up dirt twenty feet to your right," the leader noted.

"Damn, looks like a truck tire. They'd loaded the AWD's (all wheel drive) onto a truck."

The leader produced a pair of compact binoculars and performed a 360 degree scan. "There's a road up ahead," he announced, "and I can see a canvas topped, military style vehicle just sitting idle."

"Think they'd be dumb enough to sit out in the open?" the second commando asked.

"No, but they might think that we'd assume so."

"So they're waiting for us to approach," Marvin mumbled.

"We're not gonna play that game," the leader said.

"Whac-A-Mole?" the second commando grinned.

The leader nodded his approval.

"What's that?" George asked.

"There are four of us, and we each show ourselves, one at a time, at different locations."

"That'll get us killed," Marvin grumbled.

"Guess you've never played the game."

"Nope."

"It's head up, head down, and shift position, real fast."

"Done that before?" George asked.

"Yeah, confuses the hell outta the opposition."

"So we don't shoot?" Marvin said.

"Not unless you have to. But remember, as you shift position you keep moving closer to the truck, forming a loose perimeter."

"Sounds complicated," George protested.

"It's easy, as long as you don't get shot."

"How do we know who goes first?"

"Simple, I'm first, my partner is next and so on. We pop up five seconds apart."

"What if we mess up the sequence?"

"The audience will ask for a refund," the leader snarled sarcastically, adding, "don't worry about it."

"Ready? We'll move to within thirty meters of the truck..." the second man advised.

"Wait a minute," Marvin interrupted, adding, "we don't know where they're hiding."

"You will when the shooting begins."

"Great," George whined, as they began the trek.

Chapter Forty-five

Wednesday, January 17th

6 P.M.

Tel Aviv

Seren, aka, Moishe Levin, sat in Bruck's office nervously fidgeting with a non official cellphone. He'd been waiting for a call that had been late in arrival, and the entire pot of dark tea that he'd consumed hadn't helped his state of mind.

For security purposes, the connection to the safe house had been accomplished via the single direct connect telephone, where contact could only be initiated from the secure location. During Bruck's last conversation with his subordinate, he'd asked to be advised of any developing news, not realizing that he would personally have to be the initiator of such contact. He'd spent the better part of the day waiting for the call that never came and, with his eyes glued to the screen depicting the drone feed, he could no longer focus adequately.

"Is there something wrong with this monitor?" he asked of a seated Mossad agent.

"Looks good to me, sir."

"It's blurry."

"Maybe you need a rest."

"Excuse me?"

"I meant that your eyes may be fatigued, sir."

Bruck shot a few daggers at the man, but took his advice and closed his eyes without leaving the chair.

The monitor had been programmed to chime when the drone forwarded event alerts. Bruck nearly jumped a few inches in the air when the computer began to report. He reached for the trackball that served to control the pointer and moved in close to the screen. The Drone is recording some activity, he said to himself, as he watched—in realtime—as six or so people exited the presumed POF office/warehouse. The open line telephone to the drone driver was in his right hand in a flash, and he said, "This is Director Bruck, can you zoom in?"

Without replying, the computer image rapidly changed to a close up view of the individuals in question. There was no doubt about their intent, as they were all dressed in fatigues with AK47's dangling from their shoulders, but they did not appear to be dispersing.

Should I call in a strike, he wondered, as he considered the potential consequences. If they're coming for me, why not hit them preemptively, he mused. On the other hand, what if the warning had been a hoax designed to rattle my chains? Well, a missile could take them out in a blink, but there are undoubtedly others, better wait and see what they're up to.

"Circle that building as long as possible," he said to the driver.

"She'll be bingo (low or empty) fuel in another hour, sir."

"Give it thirty minutes, RTB (return to base), refuel and get back on station."

"Affirmative."

I should have heard from Moishe by now, he said to himself, and the team should be on their way back home. I'd promised Marcus (U.S. State Dept official) that I'd get them out of country immediately but, strangely, he didn't sound concerned. Wonder what that was all about.

The drone feed had been cut and he'd assumed that it had gone back for fuel, so rather than wait for Moishe to call he pressed the buzzer that would alert him to answer the direct line.

"Ariel?"

"Yes, and I'd told you to never use my first name in the office."

"I'm alone."

"Any news from New York?"

"Just hung up with Vasily. He said that Rafael and the commandos had been planning to scuttle the boat with the POF bodies onboard."

"That should have happened hours ago—recall that asshole, and make sure he complies."

"But he is our only contact?"

"He's worthless."

"I think you should reconsider."

Bruck scratched his scalp, removed the receiver from his ear and thought, maybe your time has come as well, Moishe. "OK. One last chance to redeem himself. If he can't supply accurate and timely intel, tell him to wait at the airport with his partner."

"Wait for what?"

"Have you been drinking?" he asked, his words dripping with sarcasm.

"No," he hissed.

"They are to accompany the team back to Tel Aviv."

"I'll make the call."

Bruck slammed the phone back into its cradle. He never used to be so stupid, he told himself. Maybe he's going senile, or, perhaps he is preoccupied with something. I should have asked about his personal life but, truthfully, I don't give a crap. I'm the fucking Mossad, I'm supposed to be protecting Israel, not coddling an aging fool.

He was staring at the telephone, waiting for a response from Moishe, when one of his Mossad protectors took note and said, "I'm certain that you're aware, sir, but contact can only be initiated from your device."

"Actually, I'd missed orientation, thank you," he chuckled.

It was now 7:30 p.m., and the drone was back on station with a night vision feed. Bruck, with a plate full of Falafel in one hand and a slab of Pita bread in the other, locked onto the green tinged image and chewed, an occasional crumb tumbling to his lap. Stuffing the last of the Pita into his mouth, he reached for the link to the drone driver and said, "Can you clear up the image?"

"It's night vision, sir. Your eyes will adapt."

"Will that happen while I'm still alive?"

The drone driver giggled, and it was at that moment that it had struck him that the pilot was a female. Well, he thought, man, woman, makes no difference, but she'll get a commendation when this is over. And as he continued to chew on the Falafel and gaze at the screen, he was interrupted by his protector.

"Sir, the office has been hit by a missile."

"What?" he shouted, a half eaten morsel of Falafel

falling from his lips.

"A missile, sir."

"How do you know about this?"

The man held up his cellphone.

"And I'm the last to hear," he protested.

"Orders?"

"Casualties?"

"Waiting on that."

"Do we know its origin?"

"It appears to have been a shoulder mounted device."

"And we know this…?"

"Our people found the spent tube."

"So, an RPG," he mumbled.

"They think it was an M72 LAW rocket, sir."

"An antitank rocket?"

"Yes."

"How did the shooter penetrate our perimeter?"

"We're investigating."

It appears that the inmates are running the prison, and the Acting Director gets second hand information. That will have to change, but not now. On the other hand, it seems that the warning had been valid and I've underestimated those devils.

He turned back to the screen and wondered what had

happened to the terrorists that he'd seen earlier, when it occurred to him that not having a place to return to might ruffle their feathers, and he called to the drone pilot, "Your bird is armed?"

"Of course, sir."

"Hellfire?"

"Yes, AGM-114's, sir."

"Send one into that building."

"On its way."

The screen turned white, the greenish image returning as a slowly resolving fog.

"Can we get a clearer image of the damage?" he asked.

"What you're witnessing are flames, sir."

"From the missile?"

"Probably struck one of the large propane tanks that they use for cooking and heating."

"So, not the missile?"

"Not directly, sir."

"Why do they call it a Hellfire if it doesn't cause fire," he said, not intending to be heard.

But the pilot had indeed heard his mumbling and replied, "It's really called a Heliborne, Laser, fire and forget missile, sir. But I guess Hellfire is easier to remember."

"Thank you. Your name?"

"Segen (Lieutenant) Eden Miller, sir."

"Good job, Segen."

At that same moment in time, Moishe Levin's right hand had begun to shake, as he'd emerged from the basement storeroom that he'd allegedly visited to search for an illusive file folder. But only moments earlier he'd been cringing on the concrete floor, shielding his ears from the explosive sound of the incoming missile. The call that he'd been awaiting earlier that day had arrived with only ten minutes to spare. And now, he took the stairs to his office level to assess the damage. Just outside of the stairwell, a smokey haze obscured his view and the scent of scorched wood attacked his nostrils, but he could hear loud voices and a few calls for help. An instant pang of guilt struck him, since the carnage could have been prevented, he thought, but then rationalized that the ten minute warning would not have been sufficient to move everyone to safety. Still, he had crossed over to the dark side and there was no turning back.

Chapter Forty-six

Port Jefferson, N.Y.

11 A.M.

George sat amongst a pile of rocks, manure droppings and weeds, as he positioned himself a distance from the targeted truck. A sharp stone had lodged between his buttocks, but he resisted movement, lest he be spotted. Marvin and the commandos were to locate themselves along the axis of a four spoked wheel, but he could neither see them, nor be certain that they were in position. Suddenly, he heard the loud report of a non-suppressed weapon, the likely indication that the lead commando had popped up from his hiding place, and he counted, awaiting his turn in their treacherous game of Whac-A-Mole. Two more gunshots and he jumped up and moved in sideways toward the vehicle. Although he had not seen a telltale muzzle flash, the weapon's sharp crack had provided the shooter's approximate location—clearly out of range for his handgun—and he waited for the next round of popups. There had been no way to tell if any of his team had been hit, so he continued with the game until he was within ten feet of the truck bed. As he crouched within reach of the vehicle, a gentle breeze carried the odor of spent gunpowder and his nostrils twitched. I don't see anyone else, he said to himself and wondered, where the hell are Marvin and the commandos. Suddenly, the lead Israeli was by his side.

"You OK?" the man whispered.

"Yeah," George replied, adding "where are the others?"

"Should be here soon."

"Do we wait, or check out the truck?"

"There are at least three shooters," he advised.

"So?"

"If they'd wanted to hit us, they could have."

"Maybe their aim sucks."

"No. You can bet their rifles are scoped and the misses were intentional."

"You think they lured us to this point?"

"Whatever their motive, we're here, aren't we," he said, more a statement than a question.

"Now what?"

"We have several options. We can wait for my partner and your friend and bug out, we can look into the truck, or we wait for the others and try to counter attack."

"I don't hear any noise coming from the truck," George said.

"Yeah, our people are probably not inside."

"Then where?"

"We'll have to catch one of the devil's alive to find out."

"I like the attack option."

"I'd have to agree."

"What's the plan?"

"Don't really have one."

George launched a look of disbelief and suggested, "Let's piss them off and draw them out of the bushes."

The commando grinned and replied, "What do you have in mind."

"We boost the truck."

"Boost?"

"Take it, steal it."

"Could be wired to blow."

"I could cover you while you have a look."

The commando considered his proposal and came back with, "You know how to use this?" he said, sliding his automatic rifle into George's hand.

"Just show me the safety and I'm good to go."

The commando crawled under the truck to begin his investigation, while George kept scanning the horizon for militants. Several minutes later, Marvin and the second

Israeli came crawling out of the brush and, to his surprise, there was no accompanying rifle fire.

"Where's my partner?" the Israeli asked.

"Under the truck, looking for explosives."

"We gonna take it," Marvin huffed, apparently out of breath from the strenuous crawl.

"The idea is to get the POF to show themselves," George explained.

"Good luck with that," he mumbled.

The sound of shifting gravel signaled the return of the commando from beneath the vehicle. He exited feet first from the rear, his right hand dragging an indistinguishable block of material from which dangled a handful of colored wires.

"Semtex," he said, carefully lowering the device to the ground.

"It was wired?" George said, with excitement.

"This shit would have launched the truck airborne."

"Just gonna leave it on the ground?"

The leader grinned at his partner, and asked, "Fireworks?"

"Love it," the man replied.

"What are you gonna do?" Marvin asked.

"Use it to get them moving."

The two Floridians crawled back into the near brush and watched for unexpected arrivals, while the commandos set about dividing the block of Semtex into several smaller chunks. Their plan was to crawl behind the POF's presumed perimeter and set off the explosives in order to get them to show themselves and move forward. The only fly in the ointment was the absence of detonating caps, but they'd decided to take the risk of employing their sniper skills to set them off with a rifle shot.

The leader crawled ahead, tapped George on the shoulder and asked, "Ready?"

"Not sure."

"You'd better be. I'll leave you with the handgun. If they come close, start shooting, changing your position with each round."

George shook his head with disbelief, and replied, "Yeah, whatever," a sentiment that was seconded by his friend.

The Israelis disappeared into the brush and George gazed over at Marvin, who was lying prone twenty feet to his right side, and made a slashing gesture across his throat, as if to say, we're dead.

Fifteen minutes later they heard several pops followed immediately by the sound of loud explosions and yellow flames erupting in the distance.

"They're coming," George called out in a loud whisper.

"We need to save one," Marvin replied.

"Fuck them, save us."

Although the two friends could not see them, the commandos had been firing from behind the retreating terrorists, pushing them closer to the truck and the frightened Floridians.

"I can see them coming at us," George's terror tinged words advised.

"Should we hide?" Marvin screeched.

"The truck, get behind it," he shouted, as he rose and ran to the blind side of the vehicle with Marvin in tow.

"Shoot," he called out, blasting off a few rounds at the approaching marauders.

"I hit one," Marvin said.

"He's still coming this way."

And then the bullets began to fly in their direction, the automatic weapons sending an intermittent spray of hot metal.

From behind the truck, George shouted, "They're aiming for the undercarriage."

"They don't know that the explosive is gone."

The commandos had caught up with the POF, and were fifteen feet behind when they shouted for them to drop their weapons. At that point, George and Marvin rose from behind the truck and aimed their pistols at the four targets. The terrorists had been caught in a classic pincer between the commandos, George and Marvin. But they'd continued to approach, firing wildly for a few more seconds, and then, likely recognizing the futility of their quest, stopped, and dropped their weapons.

"On the ground, face down," the lead commando said in Arabic.

The men complied without a word.

"Just these four?" Marvin asked, his weapon aimed at the back of one of their heads.

"Roger that," the leader rumbled, continuing with, "find something to immobilize their limbs."

A two hundred foot spool of nylon fishing line was found under the truck's passenger side seat. One by one, George wrapped lengths of it around their wrists, ankles and thighs, cutting the loose end with a Ka Bar tactical knife supplied by one of the Israelis.

"We gonna leave them here on the ground?" Marvin inquired.

"Give us a hand heaving them into the truck bed," the

leader said, his facial expression suggesting that he'd considered Marvin an idiot.

The tailgate was at least four feet off of the ground, and it had taken some effort to shove the four POF into the truck. But once inside, and still face down, the lead Israeli approached the one closest to the exterior, rolled him over onto his back and promptly received a wad of spittle that missed his face by less than an inch.

"I could have shot you in the head," he said in Arabic, "but we Israelis don't do that."

"Fuck you," the man said, in clear English.

"From where I stand, you're the one who's fucked."

He nodded to his partner to roll the second nearest onto his back. Kneeling before the man, he said, "I'm going to ask you a question. Give me the wrong answer and I put a bullet in your friend's head and then yours, understood?" he said in Arabic.

The man nodded his understanding.

"Where are the people you took from the van?"

"I don't know," he replied, in Arabic.

"Wrong answer," the leader said, and promptly placed the muzzle of his Tavor against the first man's skull and pulled the trigger. Blood and brain matter splattered across the truck's interior, and Marvin began to puke his guts out, the horrendous spectacle totally unexpected.

"I keep my word," the leader advised, pressing the Tavor against the second man's head.

"Wait, wait," the man called out.

"You've got three seconds."

"My superior took them away."

"To where?" he shouted.

"I don't know."

The still warm muzzle was now against the man's left ear, and the Israeli growled, "Two seconds left."

"Airport, he took them to the airport."

"Which one."

"MacArthur."

"That's about 10 miles from here," the commando advised, to no one in particular.

"Destination?" he barked.

"Lebanon."

He pressed the rifle more securely against the terrorist's ear and shouted, still in Arabic, "There are no flights from MacArthur to Lebanon."

"Charter," the man stuttered, "we were to meet him after our mission."

The commando stood, scratched his growing, dark brown stubble, and said, "Dump them and let's get moving."

"I don't know if this truck is serviceable," his partner said.

"You're a mechanic, make it work."

Without delay, the military styled vehicle's vertical exhaust belched a cloud of black smoke, and the leader gazed over at the two Floridians and ordered, "Push those animals out onto the road."

Marvin, vomitus still clinging to his clothing, suggested, "Maybe we can use them for a trade."

The commando stopped to consider and said, "Once again, you've proven that appearances can deceive. Hide Mr. headless in the bushes ... we'll hold onto the others."

Chapter Forty-seven

Tel Aviv

8 P.M.

Safe House

The drone had continued to circle the POF headquarters, and when the dust had settled and the flames were no longer visible, there had been little doubt that the building had been demolished. Even the darkness of night could not hide the missile's devastating outcome. Satisfied by the result, Bruck ordered the pilot to resume her normal grid pattern, and accepted an offered plate of steaming ketzitzot (meatballs) and pasta, a dish that rarely graced his kitchen table. But halfway through his dinner he'd realized that he had yet to receive a casualty report from the missile attack and, more importantly, he had not been able to contact Seren Levin due to the explosion's effect on the communication system. He took note of the Mossad agent seated on the opposite side of the room reading a magazine, and called out, "Has there been an accounting of injuries?"

"I'd checked a few minutes ago, they're still sifting through the rubble, sir," he smiled.

"With whom had you spoken?"

"My partner, David, sir."

"Any word of Seren Levin?"

"I believe he'd survived."

"You believe, or you know?" he growled.

"I'll call back..."

"Give me your phone," he interrupted.

The agent lowered his magazine and walked to where Bruck had remained seated. Bruck reached out and tore the phone from his agent's hand, and said, "Go back to your magazine."

The agent blushed ever so slightly, and walked off.

He dialed Moishe's unlisted cellphone, a private set of digits known only to himself and his friend.

"Moishe?"

"Thanks," he stuttered, followed by a seemingly surprised exclamation of, "Ariel?"

Bruck's gaze turned suspicious, and he said, "What are you thanking me for?"

"Just thankful that I'm alive," he lied.

And after a moment's thought, he replied, "Were you expecting a call from someone else?"

"Who else would know this number?"

"You tell me," Bruck snapped.

He hesitated a second too long, and answered, "No

one has this number."

Bruck began to fume. "Where were you when the missile struck?"

"Searching for some documents."

"Where?"

"Basement storage."

How convenient, Bruck thought. "And where did the projectile land?"

"Not sure, I haven't been able to get into what's left of your office."

"OK, we'll speak again soon," Bruck said, and hit the end button.

Unless Moishe is extremely lucky, he pondered, the alleged records search is all too coincidental. I've been accused of paranoia in the past, but my gut is sending a clear message. Something's not right, and my friend may not be the friend I'd thought he was. I'd considered Vasily's message about a possible mole to be nonsensical, but...

His thoughts had been interrupted by urgent traffic coming via computer. He stared at the screen in disbelief, the large, red letters jolting his senses like a block of ice. The lead commando had managed to gain control of a computer at a New York airport and, despite explicit orders requiring him to avoid the use of unencrypted devices, had sent notice of Rafael and Bina's kidnapping, as well as confirmation of the existence of a mole within the Mossad. Rather than risk having the origin of his acknowledgment traced, Bruck simply deleted the message and sat back, trying to calm his rising blood pressure and racing pulse.

I'm alone with this information, he said to himself. With Moishe's loyalty now suspect, there is no one I can trust, and I must deal with the prospect of a double agent without delay.

He turned to the man who's cellphone he still possessed, and said, "The attack is over, take me back to headquarters."

"The building hasn't been cleared, sir."

"I must return," he ordered.

"And your wife?" the agent inquired.

"Leave her be."

They'd exited from the safe house in a huddle, with Bruck sandwiched between three, husky bodyguards. He was ushered into a waiting Range Rover seconds before the tires screeched against the pavement as they rapidly departed. And as they approached Mossad headquarters, Bruck gasped at the yawning hole where his and surrounding offices once sat. While he had already orchestrated the destruction the POF's main structure, he longed for a more meaningful response, something that would send a message to Hamas and POF wannabes that screamed, *hit us and we'll shatter your world*, but his personal anger had to be put aside in favor of international politics. He shook his head and thought, they can get away with terrorist acts, but we face the judgement of those who wish us gone.

The car came to a stop and he waited for the escorts to open his door, but they just sat in their seats gawking at the damage.

"We'll do what we always do," he said to the men, "we'll rebuild."

"Yes, sir," the driver acknowledged.

"I'm going in," he advised, and was promptly thrust between the now waiting bodyguards.

Security protocol had dictated that his arrival be unannounced, and the quartet strode though the intact entrance. Personnel were mulling about, their faces waxen with an expression of disgust, anger and determination, as they pushed rolling carts full of plastic file boxes from one side of the building to another. Bruck stopped and watched, as a wave of despair momentarily overtook him, but he pressed onward and said, "I need to assess the damage."

With all of the activity in the area of his destroyed office, Bruck decided to commandeer that of a subordinate who had been busy assisting cleanup and assessment. And as he gazed about the austere cubicle, he called out to one of his now ever present bodyguards, "Find Seren Levin and bring him to me."

Moishe Levin appeared at his open door fifteen minutes later and stood at attention, while two of Bruck's bodyguards stood behind him.

"So?" Bruck said, drawing out the two letters.

"Terrible, it was terrible," Moishe said, still standing just outside of the office.

"But you'd survived."

He nodded affirmatively.

"And all these years you'd felt to be unlucky."

He did not respond.

"And your records search?"

Moishe hesitated and then stuttered, "I'd stopped my search when I'd heard the explosion."

"You know, my friend, I've never visited the storage room."

Moishe glared back at Bruck, glassy eyed.

"Doesn't it seem odd that you would perform a task

that others are designated to carry out?"

"I didn't..."

"Cut the bullshit, Moishe. You'd been forewarned about the attack," he roared.

"Warned?"

"You couldn't be a hero for Israel, so you'd decided to become one for the enemy."

"No, that's not true," he shouted.

"I've come to understand that we have a mole, a turncoat, and I am sorely disappointed to learn that it's been you, my friend," he said, nodding to the bodyguards to seize him.

"Wait, wait," Moishe pleaded, to deaf ears, as he was dragged off to a cell.

How could I have been such a poor judge of character, Bruck asked of himself. I've known him for many years and had never suspected that he'd be capable of such a heinous act. God only knows what information he's leaked to those monsters.

Chapter Forty-eight

MacArthur Airport

Long Island, New York

1 P.M.

The surviving POF prisoners had been secured to the truck bed with heavy test fishing line and duct tape. And while the nylon line had not been the preferred method of immobilization, forceful attempts at freeing themselves would have most likely resulted in severe lacerations, a fact that had obviously been noted by the captives and confirmed by their lack of resistance.

George and Marvin had remained in the back with the hostages, their pistols aimed at their torsos, when the vehicle began to slow as it approached the airport. The terrorist had not provided the name of the charter company but, as they'd pulled to a stop, off in the distance the front seat passengers took note of a corporate jet sitting just off of the runway.

"That's it," the leader observed, pointing his right index finger in the direction of the waiting aircraft.

"Can you identify?" his partner inquired.

"Pretty sure it's a Falcon 50."

"Can it make the distance?"

"If I recall, it has about a four thousand mile range."

"And it's about fifty-seven hundred miles to Beirut, Lebanon."

"The'll have to refuel somewhere along the way."

"Yeah, wasn't a good choice. But a charter takes them out of the TSA loop."

"So we storm it?"

The leader drummed the fingers of his right hand on the dash as he considered the options, and replied, "The idea of a trade had initially seemed viable, but I don't want to negotiate with those turds. Let's drive the truck right up to the aircraft."

"What about airport security?"

"The plane's far enough away, that if bullets begin to fly it shouldn't harm any innocents."

"I mean't, they'll be alerted when they see this truck speeding down the runway."

"Yeah, well, a stealthy approach is out of the question."

"The Director will be royally pissed when this hits the newspapers, and you know it will."

"Let's get moving," he snarled.

They alerted the two men in the rear and took off. Given the nature of the vehicle there was no burning rubber, no giant lurch forward, but with the pedal to the metal the truck began to pick up speed and was within a hundred feet of the aircraft when they'd noticed a security SUV heading their way with its colorful lights flashing.

The leader groaned and said, "Don't stop, keep moving."

"You gonna take 'em out?" the driver asked.

And with that, the leader extended his body through the passenger side window, leaned his Tavor on the cab's roof, and aimed for the front tires of the rapidly approaching vehicle. A continuous volley followed, and a few seconds later the pursuing security car began to tip, eventually spinning out of control and off to one side of the road. The gunfire had not been missed by the plane's occupants, and a pair of rifle totting bodies scurried down the stairs to the tarmac and began firing at the oncoming truck. Several rounds pierced the windshield between the driver and lead commando, causing spider like fissures to extend in all directions, but no one had been struck. Once again, the leader began to fire from the passenger side window, causing the shooters to take refuge beneath the plane's fuselage.

"We're gonna have to ram it," the leader said.

"The plane?"

"I can't acquire the targets, so we have to take it out."

"It could explode around us," the driver advised, the truck now less than thirty feet from the aircraft's midsection.

"Aim for the nose," he shouted, as the truck swerved.

Bullets began to fly from beneath the aircraft, as the truck slammed into the front of the Falcon. Just before impact, the two front seat commandos had ducked to avoid being struck by penetrating portions of the aircraft's nose section, and with practiced precision they'd slid from their seats and began returning fire. The rear passengers—George and Marvin—had been tossed about the truck bed as the result of the collision, and jumped to the tarmac with their pistols at the ready. One of the terrorists had taken several hits and his bloody body was stretched out beside a landing gear's rubber tire, the second man, faced with two oncoming commandos, lowered his AK-47 and dropped to his knees.

"How many inside?" the leader demanded, gesturing upward toward the aircraft with his rifle .

The man paused, apparently searching for the word, and held up six fingers.

"Your people?"

He extended four fingers.

The two Floridians had now joined the Israelis beneath the fuselage, and George asked, "Aren't we going to rescue Rafael and Bina?"

"Yes."

"What are we waiting for?" Marvin cried out.

"For the occupants to make the first move."

"Like killing our friends?" George seethed.

"They may already be dead. On the other hand, if we storm the plane they might execute them."

"So we just stand here like dummies?"

The two commandos gazed at each other with a grin and said, "Speak for yourselves."

"Not cool," George mumbled, elbowing Marvin.

"This plane isn't going anywhere—they'll have to come out eventually," Marvin agreed.

"And so will the local police. I'll give them five minutes, if they don't make a move, I'll toss one of these," the leader informed, holding up a teargas canister.

Five minutes had come and gone, and sirens were heard off in the distance. The grenade had been thrown into the cabin and moments later, a single, rail thin, Palestinian emerged, coughing violently with his hands in the air. "No shoot," the man rasped.

The commandos watched as the man slowly

descended the stairs, grabbing the rail to steady himself from time to time. When he had reached the asphalt, he said, "We talk."

The lead Israeli, with his rifle aimed at the man's head, approached and said, "No, I'll talk and you listen."

The man nodded his approval.

"You're on foreign soil and you've taken hostages. You have three options. One, you and your friends can die right here, right now. Two, I can turn you over to the approaching police. And three, I can take you and your friends back to Israel."

The man's face took on an angered expression, and he replied, "We kill hostages."

"You do that and I'll blow the plane, you'll all die."

"We become martyrs."

"You really believe that paradise crap?"

The terrorist negotiator gazed about, as if looking for support from no one in particular, and spat, "I talk to my people," as he turned and began to ascend the stairs. But the second commando, who had been standing alongside the stairs, grabbed him by the arm and thwarted his departure.

"We kill your friends," the man seethed, loud enough for the plane's occupants to hear.

"Call your second in command," the leader ordered.

The man took a moment too long to respond and the Israeli put his lips close to the man's left ear and shouted his demand.

Less than a minute later, an AK47 toting male, wearing a white, embroidered cowboy shirt and jeans belted with an oversized, silver toned Western rodeo buckle, made his way out of the aircraft and stood on the top step. "We outnumber you," he advised, in perfect English.

"You're holed up in a metal tube with only one way out, I hold the ace of spades," the Israeli growled.

"What do you want?" the man hissed.

"Let our people leave the aircraft and you can have this piece of shit," he said, tapping the POF soldier on the head with the palm of his hand.

"And then you turn us over to police that I can hear coming closer?"

"Leave your weapons in the plane and you can take the truck, it still runs. But you'd better decide now."

The man returned to the interior of the Falcon, while Marvin walked up to the leader and asked, "You really gonna let them go?"

"They won't get far."

"But they should pay a price for what they've done."

The repartee had been cut short by the cowboy's unarmed return, along with two other terrorists. They slid down the stairs like running water and ran to the truck, engaged the engine and backed away from the Falcon's nose, the remains of the vehicle's windshield sliding from the engine hood as they drove off down the runway.

The two commandos ascended the stairs in a flash and escorted their ruffled but unharmed countrymen—Rafael and Bina—to the tarmac. But as the truck disappeared from view, three police cruisers and a SWAT vehicle rapidly approached. The commandos signaled for George and Marvin to lower their pistols to the ground, as they did the same with their weapons. Suddenly, they were surrounded by armored police toting high powered rifles, and the four men raised their arms in submission.

"Diplomatic passport," the leader shouted, waving the booklet in the air above his head.

"On the ground," an electronically enhanced voice shouted, as a uniformed officer approached.

Chapter Forty-nine

Tel Aviv

9 P.M.

Seren Moishe Levin sat on the damp concrete floor of a four by six foot barred cubicle. His clothing had been removed, the only remaining apparel consisting of a tattered undershirt and a pair of brown briefs. Acting director Bruck watched from a distance, as tears streamed down the face of his onetime friend, and cautiously approached.

"Moishe, Moishe," he cooed, "what were you thinking?"

Moishe raised his head, wiped a few tears from his cheeks with the back of one hand and whispered, "I'm a nobody, a nothing, a worthless piece of garbage."

Bruck glared back at him, not knowing how to reply appropriately to a traitor, one who had been his confident, his supposed friend, but he simply said, "After what you've done, there are many who would agree."

"May as well hang me, or whatever you plan on doing —just get it over with."

Bruck considered his request and replied, "What have you revealed?"

"Nothing useful," he moaned.

"And yet they'd forewarned you about the attack."

Moishe lifted his head and made eye contact for the first time during the interview and replied, "I'd provided the coordinates of your office."

"You hate me that much?"

"Not you, the institution."

"But you'd been prepared to assassinate me."

"You've said so yourself, we're at war."

"And you'd chosen the enemy's side."

"They'd made me feel important."

"And now, how do you feel?"

He paused and mumbled, "Stupid."

Bruck nodded in agreement and urged, "What else had you given them?"

"I may have mentioned your home address."

"And that's all?" he asked, suspecting that there had been more, much more that he'd leaked to the monsters.

"Yes," he breathed.

Bruck stood by the cell several moments longer, gathering his thoughts and trying to erase the elements of friendship from his memory, then walked down the corridor to where a pair of Mossad interrogators had been waiting. "He's all yours," he advised to the male and female.

"How far?" the woman inquired.

"As far as you have to go to get what we need," Bruck said, knowing that what they had in store for Moishe was not going to be the least bit pleasant.

He turned and watched them head towards the cell, took a deep breath, and headed back to his makeshift office.

Bruck's secretary had been out retrieving her car from service at the time of the missile attack, and she was waiting when he'd arrived at the office door.

"There's been an urgent call from the American State Department, sir," she advised.

"Message?" he asked.

"Said it was for your ears only."

He nodded his understanding and replied, "Get them back on the line."

"Yes, sir," she responded, walking back to a portable desk and telephone that had been set up just outside of the office.

The intercom system had yet to be connected, and there was a shout from outside of the room that informed, "Line one, sir."

"Acting Director Ariel Bruck, how may I assist you?"

"Cut the shit, Ariel, it's Marcus. I thought that we'd had an understanding," he said, sternly.

"Not sure I follow."

"C'mon, you crafty old fool, you know what I'm talking about."

"No, really, I do not."

Bruck could hear a loud sigh from the other end of the line and waited.

"There's been an incident at a New York airport."

"What kind of incident?"

"Some of your people smashed a truck into a corporate jet and one of them is claiming diplomatic immunity."

Bruck swallowed an uncontrollable desire to laugh, and said, "This is news to me."

"There's more. The claimant insists that the truck had been driven by four Middle Eastern terrorists whom we now have in custody."

"So?"

"The terrorists say that they didn't do it."

"And you believe them?"

"Ariel, we go back a number of years and I know that with you, things aren't always what they appear to be."

"And your point is?"

"Oh what the fuck, I'm putting your people on a flight back to Tel Aviv, today."

"How many?"

"Seven, three of whom appear to be special OPs soldiers."

"There should be eight," Bruck said, recalling that the wet team had consisted of four men.

"But you got seven," Marcus barked, and terminated the call.

He sat in his creaky swivel chair and grinned, thinking, I can't wait to hear the real story. But Marcus got some terrorists, that should make him feel good. However, what'd happened to the fourth team member, he wondered. And then he had a thought and called out to his secretary, "Check with the IDF and find out if there have been any recent arrivals."

"Arrivals, sir?"

"Never mind, I'll do it myself," he called out, dialing the base commander's private number.

The conversation had revealed that one man had returned to his quarters forty-eight hours prior, and that he'd been part of a four member team that had previously received travel orders. Bruck understood the code language, the missing commando had RTB (returned to base) by himself. I'll have to look into that, he thought, as he sat back and reviewed the complicated events that had recently taken place, realizing that he'd been neglecting his wife. Furthermore, Moishe's admission had revealed that their home was no longer safe to return to and he would have to find an alternative. And since he'd grown weary of the safe house, he had no place to return to.

He checked his wristwatch and discovered that it was almost eleven p.m., and he stared at the weary agent who'd been drowsing in a chair just outside of his office. "I need to speak with my wife," he called out.

"Not possible," the man said.

"Unacceptable," he shouted.

"The communication link is down, sir."

"Another attack?" he asked, jumping from his chair, fearing for his wife's safety.

"No, technical issue on our side."

"Then take me there."

"Not advisable."

"I make those decisions, now, summon a vehicle."

But while he awaited his ride, he received an unencrypted telephone call that, since his secretary had left hours earlier to tend to an ill parent, he'd answered himself.

"Yes?" he said cautiously, not knowing whether the call was for the office's prior occupant.

"We're in the air, sir—all seven of us," the commando leader advised.

"You're using an in-flight telephone?" Bruck asked, incredulously.

"Can't use my sat-phone, sir, the stewardess is watching me like a hawk."

"OK, call me when you touch down."

"Sir."

"Yes?"

"You're aware of the rodent?"

"Already secure."

"I'd tried Seren..."

"Terminate this call," Bruck said with abruptness, not wishing to discuss classified topics over what might be an open line, and with Moishe's treasonous act having been deemed classified.

He lowered the receiver to its cradle and thought, he doesn't know about Seren Levin, and for the time being I'll keep it that way. No way to tell if he'd been a lone wolf.

Chapter Fifty

Thursday, January 18th

Mossad Headquarters, Tel Aviv

9 A.M.

Bruck had arrived at his wife's safe house at one a.m. in the morning. She'd been asleep, but had greeted him with an angry scowl, while prancing around the room in her flowing, wrinkled nightgown.

"What was this all about?" she'd hissed.

Bruck had waited until she'd appeared ready to listen, and explained, "There'd been an explosion."

"Bombs go off all of the time, what'd made this one different?" she'd pouted.

He'd rubbed his forehead and wondered how much he should reveal, but concluding that only something close to the truth would work, he'd said, "Headquarters had been hit."

"Oh my God," she'd exclaimed, "that close?"

He shook his head affirmatively.

"How many?"

He'd hesitated and replied, "At least eight, but we're still counting."

"Hamas?" she'd growled.

"Or a proxy," he'd admitted, avoiding mention of the POF.

The conversation had gone on to include the requirement for the relocation of their home, which had led to a heated argument about being uprooted from her comfort zone. It hadn't been pleasant, and Bruck had departed with a headache and a promise that their new home would be larger and more attractive than the one they were being forced to leave behind.

He'd spent the darkest hours of the night alternating between the coffee urn and dozing in his office chair.

At 9 a.m., after having stared glassy eyed at a red jacketed report for longer than necessary, his secretary appeared at the doorway. "There's a solider waiting to speak with you, sir."

"Soldier?" he questioned, then recalling his conversation with the lead commando from the New York operation, he added, "send him in."

The Commando entered, saluted and stood at attention just inside the office.

"Have a seat," Bruck's weary voice suggested.

"We'd landed early this morning, sir, I'd thought it best to wait until now."

"Yes, yes. Tell me about the airport event."

He described the circumstances of the abduction that had led up to their arrival at the MacArthur airport, as well as the POF's involvement. And when he had finished, he sat back in the metal chair and waited.

"You've done well, son," he said, chuckling to himself about having put one over on the State Department.

"The two Americans are still being held at entry, sir."

"Hmm. They are jews?"

"So they say."

"Give their names to my secretary and we'll take care of them."

"They were very helpful, sir."

"I'll keep that in mind," he replied, spinning a pencil between his fingers, as if preparing to ask a question.

"I will submit a full, written report, sir."

"Are you aware of the recent missile attack on this building?"

"Hard to miss the big hole, sir."

"Had your terrorists made any mention of it?"

"No, sir," he said with conviction.

"You may go," Bruck said, releasing the pencil and retrieving the red folder.

Standing at the doorframe, the commando turned and asked, "My men, sir, we are short one."

"You'll find him confined to quarters."

"Sir?"

"I thought that you might have known about his early return?"

"No, sir. We'd been out of contact, but since the operation had taken precedence I did not expend any effort to locate him."

"But he had been with you in New York from the beginning?"

"Yes, sir."

"How long have you known him?" he asked, suspiciously.

"He'd joined us back in November, following the loss of a team member during a firefight."

"That's all, soldier," he said.

With the commando out of sight, Bruck lowered the folder that he'd held before his eyes for effect, and thought about the sequestered team member. There's something that's not right about that man's actions, he told himself. I'm going to have him debriefed downstairs, away from his colleagues. And as he made a note to himself to arrange for the interrogation before the day's end, he called out to his secretary, "There are two Americans on hold at the airport, I must speak with them."

"Unlawful entry, sir?"

"Something else, just have them brought here, today."

"Their names?"

He was suddenly aware of the fact that their names had never entered the conversation, and he replied, "Find Andrew Cosgrove (aka Rafael) and have him accompany them."

"Yes, sir."

Several hours had passed, and it was now almost eleven a.m. He had requested that a new, secure residence be located on an immediate basis, and he had done so without input from his wife. He knew that she would go ballistic upon hearing that she was to live in a place that she had not chosen, and to his good fortune, the agent charged with the task had come up empty handed. That meant that a hotel would have to suffice on a temporary basis. The Norman Tel Aviv had been their choice, based upon location and ease of establishing a secure perimeter. And to this end, several rooms had been blocked off at the end of a corridor with a barrier obstructing unwanted entry. Three heavily armed agents were to be on site at all times.

Bruck had left his wife with a secure cellphone and, dreading the conversation, dialed her number. She answered on the second ring.

"Motek?"

"More misery for me?" she snarled.

"I know that you're upset about leaving our home, but it's no longer safe."

"Is anyplace safe?" she said, sarcastically.

He took a deep breath to calm himself, ignored her taunt and replied, "Until we can agree on a new location we will be staying in a five star hotel."

"Oh goody."

"My people will gather whatever you want from the house, so make a clear list."

"When have I not been clear?" she snapped.

Oy vey, he said to himself, she's on the warpath. "You'll like the hotel Norman, it's not the crazy modern that you don't like."

"How long?" she grumbled.

"Until we can find something suitable."

"You mean a concrete fortress surrounded by a medieval moat."

Actually, not a bad idea, he thought, returning with, "No, a place that we can both agree upon."

"When can I leave this damp box?"

"Within the hour, I'm told. But there will be security,

and you must obey their commands."

"So now I'm an Israeli prisoner?"

"It's for your protection."

"And the cat?"

"He goes wherever you go."

He stared at the phone's LCD, she had terminated the call. He groaned, as a case of heartburn gradually began to escalate in intensity and he had yet to order lunch.

***

1 P.M.

During his tenure as Acting Director, Bruck had been plagued by an unhealthy weight gain, at least according to his family physician, and he had voluntarily placed himself on a modified diet. And for this reason, his typical lunch had consisted of an Israeli salad and a small package of crackers. But aside from the gastrointestinal side effects, the salad had become boring, and despite his lingering heartburn he'd requested a salami sandwich with Galil—a blue cheese variety—along with a soft drink. It had gone down just fine, but by one o'clock it had begun to beg for release.

"Sir," the secretary shouted.

"Yes," he grimaced.

"Andrew is here with the Americans."

"Give me a minute," he called out, hoping that the noxious, odor bearing cloud surrounding his desk would dissipate, continuing a few moments later with, "send them in."

Andrew Cosgrove (Rafael), with George and Marvin in tow, stood just beyond the entrance and waited.

Bruck, realizing that there were only two chairs before his desk, motioned for the pair of Americans to take a seat and said, to the confusion of the young men, "Andrew doesn't mind standing."

"These two had been essential for the completion of our mission," Andrew advised.

"Yes, yes, I've heard all about it," Bruck droned, disinterested in the details of their service.

"They are requesting Law of return."

Bruck smiled at the two Floridians and asked, "You are jews?"

"Yes, sir," they said in concert.

"Can you prove it?"

They glanced at each other, and George replied, "We'd left in such a hurry that we don't even have our passports, sir."

Bruck rose from behind his desk, turned to gaze out of a small window, and spun back to face the men, saying, "Your request is not the business of the Mossad, but in view of the circumstances, if you will fill out the forms that my secretary will provide I will do what I can to expedite the process."

"Thank you, sir," George, assuming the position of spokesperson, said, adding, "how long might it take?"

Bruck shrugged, as if to say, who knows.

"Do we remain at the airport until it is decided?" Marvin chimed in.

Bruck eased back into his chair, not having an answer to a question that had never before been posed, and said, "Without proper documents you cannot legally enter this country but, by being brought to my office by a government agent you have, in essence, already done so. I think that an exception can be made and hotel accommodations can be arranged."

"We're free to go?" George said, gleefully.

"Not exactly."

George released an audible sigh, and asked, "What does that mean?"

"You will remain at the hotel of our choice until such time as your status has been verified and your entry has been sanctioned."

"We're prisoners?" he whined.

Bruck grimaced and said, "I'm afraid so, but Andrew..."

"Who's Andrew?" Marvin interrupted.

"The man behind you, known to you as Rafael. But, as I was about to say, Andrew will keep an eye on you two and arrange for your needs."

They'd left the office with a hangdog expression, took hold of the previously mentioned forms from the waiting secretary, and were led off to a table to complete their task.

Chapter Fifty-one

Thursday, January 18th

7 P.M.

Andrew and his partner, Bina, had escorted the Floridians to the Hotel Saul, a small establishment located in a several story, white washed building. Much to the dismay of the two young men, only one room with a Queen sized bed had been available.

"You expect us to sleep together?" George complained, as he took in the narrow, white bricked interior.

"I can take you back to the airport," Andrew suggested.

"No, we'll manage," Marvin said.

"What about clothes, toiletries, food?"

"We'll have everything brought to you in the morning," Andrew replied.

"There are toothbrushes in the bathroom," Bina called out, as she examined her face in a mirror.

"And breakfast is available in the hotel," Andrew added.

"What about lunch and dinner?" Marvin asked.

"One of us, or our people, will be outside of your

room. Give them your order and it will be brought to you."

"So we really are prisoners," George mumbled.

"I know that it's not what you'd expected, but you'd wanted out and here you are."

"Is there a chance that we'll be sent back?" Marvin asked.

"I doubt it," Andrew said.

George took a seat at the edge of the bed, sighed, and said, "At least we have a window."

"There's a rooftop area from which you can get a decent view," Bina suggested.

"And the hotel offers room service for..." Andrew began to say.

"What," George cut in.

Andrew grimaced and replied, "Ice cream and popcorn."

"Great, junk food."

"Sorry. But it shouldn't take long to verify the information that you'd provided. And then you can begin the adventure."

"I've had enough adventures to last me a lifetime," Marvin grumbled.

"OK, well, we'll leave you now," Bina advised, as she and Andrew left the room, the sound of the lock clicking shut clearly audible.

"Are you OK with this?" Marvin asked, as George checked to see if the window would open.

"It's either this, or we face the mess that we'd left behind."

"It wasn't all our doing."

"Maybe, but it's gonna look that way."

"How so?"

"Virginia's people…"

"The State Department?" Marvin cut in.

"Yeah. They won't admit to any involvement, and the Israelis won't either."

"I guess that leaves the two of us right in the middle."

George nodded, yes.

"Fuck it, I'm going to sleep," Marvin advised, kicking off his shoes and pulling back the bedspread.

"What about dinner?"

"Fuck that as well, I'm tired."

With little else to do in the small room, George took the cue from his friend and stretched out on his chosen side of the bed.

At eleven p.m., George awakened to visit the bathroom, but what he'd encountered caused him to wet his trousers. Standing before him, and blocking the door to the corridor, were two masked, dark clothed males pointing suppressed pistols at his midsection. In the blackness, he could make out their six foot tall frames, the guns and not much else, as he froze like a deer caught in an auto's headlights.

"Wake him up?" one wraith ordered, waving his pistol at Marvin's sleeping form.

"Who the hell are you?"

No response.

George leaned over his friend and gently shook him, "Wake up, we've got a problem," he said.

"Huh?" Marvin groaned, rubbing his eyes with the back of each hand.

"Get up," the speaking wraith demanded.

Shoeless, Marvin jumped to attention and stood by the edge of the bed and croaked, "What's going on?"

"We're going for ride," the black clad man informed.

The two young men donned their shoes and watched as the second dark clothed man carefully opened the door, checked the hallway for interlopers and exited, motioning for them to follow.

Where are the guards, George wondered, not seeing any evidence of their existence, past or present.

"Did Rafael, I mean, Andrew send you?" George

asked, as he followed the men down a staircase.

Neither of the men replied, and George nudged Marvin as they quickstepped away from their room. "Something's not right," he whispered.

A white utility vehicle sat idle, it engine chugging. One of the black clad men shoved the two Floridians in the direction of a rapidly opening side panel, but Marvin balked, stood his ground and cried out, "Where are you taking us?"

Suddenly, the rearmost wraith produced a badge and growled, "FBI, you're under arrest, now get in the truck."

"Arrest, what the hell for?" George shouted.

And at that moment, Bina came running with a Tavor, TAR-21 automatic rifle aimed directly at the head of man closest to the truck. "On your knees," she screamed.

"FBI," the man roared, his barely visible badge held high.

Bina was now no less than five feet from the group when she barked, "On your knees, both of you, or I'll splash your brains all over the pavement."

The two men complied, but the second man attempted to lower the threat level with, "We're U.S. Federal agents, here to take these two into custody."

"Not today, Rambo," she said, through gritted teeth,"

adding, "in case you haven't noticed, you're in Israeli territory and you have no jurisdiction here."

With his badge still in hand, the negotiator pleaded, "U.S.C. 533(1) and 18 along with U.S.C. 3052 give us the right to arrest these two."

"Since when does that crap apply to Israeli citizens on Israeli soil?"

The mediator apparent flashed a confused expression at his partner, and asked, "Are you sure?"

"I'm Israeli Intelligence," she said, holding up her ID, adding, "damn straight I'm sure. Now get the hell out of my country."

The two FBI agents cautiously rose from the ground, the Tavor still pointed in their direction, and with their tails between their legs entered the truck and drove off.

As they disappeared down the road, the two frightened refugees took a deep breath and smiled. George was the first to speak, and asked, "Have we been admitted?"

"Not yet, but they don't know that," Bina said.

"I thought there were supposed to be guards outside of our room," Marvin grumbled.

"Personnel snafu," she replied.

"Why would the FBI want us?" Marvin questioned.

"Don't know, but I'll put out some feelers."

"Could they really have arrested us?"

"The U.S. Code gave them the right, if they could have gotten away with it."

"Meaning?"

"They might need our cooperation."

"But what if you hadn't been around?" George asked.

"You'd probably be on a flight back to America."

"Great, everyone wants a piece of us," Marvin moaned.

"Anyway, this place is no longer safe," Bina advised, "we'll have to move you."

"Another hotel?"

"I was thinking, a kibbutz."

"You're kidding," George groaned.

"Don't worry, it has a hotel, a pretty nice one."

Since there were no bags or personal items to cause concern, Bina loaded the two men into her Rover SUV and, taking a circuitous route to avoid being followed, drove them to the Shefayim kibbutz hotel. She had called en route and, although it had been fairly well booked, accommodations had been made for the Intelligence Service.

The Shefayim had turned out to be more modern and

accommodating than their previous location, and George grinned when they'd been shown to their room.

"Ah, two beds, great," he'd said, dropping onto the nearest mattress.

Marvin had kicked off his shoes, stretched out on his chosen bed, and drifted off to sleep.

Chapter Fifty-two

Friday, January 19th

Tel Aviv, Mossad Headquarters

6 A.M.

Following her deposit of the two Floridians at the kibbutz hotel, Bina had awakened her partner and had discussed the evening's details. They had agreed to wait until morning before presenting the information to the Acting Director, and at 6:05 a.m. they were standing just outside of his closed office door. The secretary had yet to arrive, but it had been clear from the loud voices emanating from his cubicle that Ariel Bruck was within. Suddenly, the door flew open and a uniformed officer departed in a huff. Bruck gazed up from his desk, his face twisted into a scowl and, noticing the agents waiting outside, called out, "Come."

"Sir," Andrew said, taking the lead for the partnership.

"I'm too tired for the formality crap, sit down and say your piece," Bruck breathed.

"There was an attempted kidnapping of the two Americans," Andrew announced.

Bruck's eyebrows shot upward, and he asked, "When

and by whom?"

"Early this morning two alleged FBI agents attempted to spirit them off in a van."

"For what reason?"

"Didn't say," Bina replied.

"And your response?"

"I'd lied and said that they were Israeli citizens."

Bruck rubbed his chin, took a sip from a coffee mug, and said, "If they were really Feds, they'll be back."

Bina nodded her agreement.

"The bigger question is, how did they get to them? Where were the sentries?" he growled.

"My fault," Andrew uttered, "I'd given confusing orders."

Bruck launched a steely glance at his agent and softened with, "Well, shit happens, just not at the Mossad. That must never happen again."

"They're at the Shefayim, and two of our people are glued to their door," Bina announced.

"Good, but why are the Americans interested in those two?" he asked again.

"I don't know," she replied.

"I was thinking out loud," Bruck said, "I'll do some digging," and continuing with a wave of his right hand, he added, "you can go."

When the two agents had been out of earshot, Bruck checked his wristwatch and noted that it was now 7:15 a.m. locally and seven hours earlier, 12:15 a.m., in Washington. Those young idiots are not criminals, he thought. So what would the FBI want with them, unless the Feds are acting as some other agency's proxy. And the only thing that comes to mind is that snake, Marcus. But what reason would the State Department have to go after them, he wondered. He took another pensive sip of the now cooling black liquid and a thought popped into his head. They're cleaning house, he said to himself. They can't go after my people, so the only accessible loose ends are the two young men. That has to be it, he reassured himself. I'm going to wake that bastard and tell him to call off the dogs.

He dialed Marcus' personal cellphone and waited. Ten rings later, a somewhat loopy voice slurred, "Yeah, what is it?"

"Did I wake you?" Bruck said, hoping that he had.

"Who is this?" Marcus screeched.

"Been drinking again, have we?"

"Ariel? Is that you?"

"Ah, my accent gave me away."

"Do you know what time it is?"

"What difference does it make, you're awake and, it appears, drunk."

A moment of hesitation and then, "Yeah, guess so. What do you want?"

"Your dogs are chasing my meat."

"Huh?"

"You know damn well what I'm talking about."

"Oh, that."

"Yes, that."

"I need absolute deniability."

"For what? You had nothing to do with the airport."

"My dead agent."

Bruck moved the phone away from his ear for a few seconds and realized that Marcus was truly drunk, otherwise he would never have mentioned the agent on an unsecured line. "I'll guarantee their silence on the matter," Bruck said.

"Not good enough."

"You do realize that you cannot touch an Israeli citizen?"

"I'd heard about that, but they're still Americans."

"Not for long, and by the time your dogs come running back they'll be bonafide Israelis."

Bruck could hear the sound of Marcus swallowing

something, alcohol, he'd guessed, and then he heard, "That's not the way we play this game."

"I hold the cards, Marcus. And if your people try to snare my citizens I'll have them locked up."

"You can't do that?" Marcus shouted.

"Watch me," Bruck said, and terminated the call with a big grin.

That felt good, Bruck said to himself. I'm going to personally expedite their request for entry under the Law of Return, and I'm going to do it immediately. That should put an end to the FBI's shenanigans. But that's not as big a problem as finding a home that meets my wife's requirements. She's pleased with the hotel, but I give her a few days of room service and then the whining will begin.

The secretary had just arrived and announced her presence with an overly exaggerated grin from just outside of the office. "Can I get you anything?" she asked.

"A noose, I'm ready to hang myself."

"You've maneuvered through worse in the past," she said, still standing by the door.

"I was younger," he breathed.

"Well, if there's anything I can do..."

"There is one thing," he interrupted, adding, "the two Americans, they're to be admitted under the Law of

Return, immediately. Make it a national security issue."

"But the forms?"

"My responsibility."

"Understood, I'll take care of it."

"And have Bina or Andrew inform them and find them a place to live," thinking, that damn hotel is expensive.

"What about security?"

"Assign one of our people to watch over them for the next seven days."

"And then they're on their own?"

"Pretty much, but we'll keep them on a short leash."

***

11 A.M.

Bruck had contacted a real estate agent to search for new living quarters. One of his trusted agents had accompanied the woman to view various small homes and high-rise apartments for the purpose of selecting a site that could be easily secured. Bruck knew that the ultimate decision would rest with his wife, but there were budget constraints to be considered, and single family homes with her required dimensions were cost prohibitive. That left a luxury, high-rise apartment building unit with two bedrooms. The cost was considerably above his stated maximum, but his wife and availability turned out to be the rate limiting factors. Since he'd been preoccupied with his official duties, he'd sent the Mossad agent to retrieve his wife to view the space.

"So, Motek, what did you think?" he asked, over the phone.

"You knew what I'd wanted, why did you show me an apartment?" she asked.

"We can't afford what you want."

He could hear a few sniffles, and with some degree of nasality she replied, "If you'd taken the job my father had offered we could have had it all," she complained.

"That was twenty years ago, Motek, and we'd agreed to make our own way."

"You would have been safe."

"Let's remain in the present, we need a place to live and the apartment is beyond our means as well. But, I'm willing to stretch the budget, so?"

"It was small, but nice—not too modern."

"What floor?"

"Top."

"A penthouse?"

"Yes, and there is the possibility of a garden, and the view is spectacular," she said, excitedly.

"What did you tell the realtor?"

She hesitated, and said, "I'd signed the contract."

"I'll have my people arrange to move our belongings."

He breathed a sigh of relief and lowered the phone to its cradle. At least that's out of the way, he thought, and even though I have yet to have seen it, if she's happy, I'll be happy.

Chapter Fifty-three

Friday

Shefayim Hotel

3 P.M.

Andrew Cosgrove had arrived at the hotel, knocked, and found the two men sitting in bed, eating potato chips and watching television. They'd gazed upwards when he'd entered, but otherwise had paid little attention to his presence, until he'd announced, "Good news."

"We get to breathe some fresh air?" George chuckled.

"Better than that, you've been admitted via the Law of Return."

"We're Israeli citizens?" Marvin said, jumping from the bed in his jockeys.

"If you want."

"What does that mean?"

"You're preliminary citizens, and you have three months to decide if you want to make it permanent."

"Great. When can we leave this place?" George asked.

"As soon as we find you suitable living quarters, but there's a catch."

"I was waiting for the shoe to drop," Marvin groused.

"It's not a big deal, but we'll be keeping an eye on you

both for awhile."

"But we're free to do whatever, right?"

"Within reason."

"I have a trust fund in the U.S., any chance I can tap into that?" Marvin inquired.

"Don't know, but I'll find out. But until then, you can use this credit card," he advised, handing it to Marvin, continuing with, "it has a five thousand Shekel limit, so budget carefully."

"How much is that in dollars?" he asked.

"On today's exchange," Andrew said, removing a smartphone from a pocket and tapping the keyboard, "fourteen hundred, twelve dollars and eighty-seven cents."

"Ugh, not gonna go very far."

Andrew shrugged and said, "I'll see about your trust fund. In addition, the Ministry of Immigration and Absorption will provide some assistance with living expenses, rent, jobs and so on."

"Ugh, work. I don't do work," Marvin bemoaned.

"Thank you," George said, frowning at his friend.

At that same moment in time, Ariel Bruck had been reviewing the statement that he'd received earlier that day from the commando who had returned to his unit unaccompanied. It was a lengthy written report that the man had hand delivered prior to the arrival of Andrew and Bina. His explanation had been sketchy, claiming that he'd been left to his own devices by his group leader, and that he had decided to return by himself.

Does he expect me to believe this crap, Bruck thought. Nobody leaves their unit, but his team leader will have to answer to this as well. And as he tried to imagine an alternative explanation, one that might suggest a more sinister motive, his desk phone came alive. It was the female member of the interrogation team that had been tasked with Seren Levin's inquisition. He grunted and lifted the receiver.

"Yes?"

"Sir, we have reached the end, the traitor has no more to give," she said.

"But he did give you something?"

"Yes."

"So?"

"It should be told in person."

"Come," he said.

Five minutes later both she and her partner were standing by his open office door, and he signaled for them to enter. The male interrogator closed the door and took a seat beside his partner.

"So?" Bruck asked.

"He was rock solid at first, but we turned on the heat and..."

Bruck grimaced, not wanting to imagine his supposed friend being tortured, and he cut the man short by asking, "What did he tell you?"

"The POF are looking to make a name for themselves, by any means possible. The missile attack had been part of that scheme, but there had been another, less visible plan that he'd been aware of."

"You're not auditioning a movie script, son, tell me what you've learned."

"They're after soft targets, the two young Americans that were with our commandos."

"Interesting, and what is it that they have planned?"

"The prisoner," he said, avoiding use of Moishe's name and rank, "had indicated a kidnapping. But he did not know if they were to be used for leverage, or if there were plans for a video execution."

Bruck spun around on his metal desk chair, the comical squeaking audible to all, stopped and mumbled, "ISIS wannabes."

"Sir?"

"I'll take care of it," he said.

"The rest of his confession was devoid of any valuable intel."

"Meaning?"

"Well, he tried to gain leverage by claiming that he is not alone."

Bruck's eyebrows furrowed, and he asked, "Did you pursue that possibility?"

"No, we thought he was trying to run out the clock, sir."

Bruck smiled, and with a sarcastic tone said, "Have you forgotten your training?"

"N n n o, sir," he stuttered," as his female partner remained silent.

"Where is he now?"

"The medical team is with him."

Bruck knew what that meant, and he felt a very brief pang of guilt, but Moishe's treasonous act had caused his rage to resurface, and he said, "You know what to do with him, I assume."

"We revoke his citizenship," the man said.

"You can dump him in the middle of Ha-Negev, for all I care, but not before I speak with him."

"If he survives, sir."

"And if not, you'd better be thinking about another form of employment. You may go."

Bruck took a deep breath and gathered his thoughts. If Moishe was telling the truth, there's another traitor among us, he considered.

He headed down the corridor to the oversized room that the medical team had commandeered following the missile attack. The windowed door was closed, but he could see two white coated individuals standing over a table, and gazed skyward, hoping for guidance as he entered.

The medical personnel immediately stopped what they'd been doing, a stethoscope sliding to the white tiled floor, and a female voice—a light blue mask covering the lower half of her face—asked, "Can we be of assistance, Director?"

"Who is that?"

"A prisoner," she replied.

"I need a moment with him."

"But his condition is critical, sir."

"Please wait outside," he ordered.

The two medical people left the room, leaving Bruck to stare down at the turncoat.

"Moishe, I know you can hear me. Who is your co-

conspirator?"

Moishe's body stirred on the gurney, and his swollen eyes opened a slit, while his equally engorged lips moved slightly, and he whispered, "Nobody cares."

"I care, Israel cares. Now, tell me," he demanded.

"I am loyal to myself, I'll take it to my grave," he mouthed.

"What has happened to the Moishe I'd thought I'd known?"

"We all have secrets."

"You know that I'll find that person without your help."

And then Moishe appeared to have found his voice, and he mumbled, "What's in it for me?"

"I'll let the doctors help you."

"And if I don't identify?"

"I'll make certain that the desert creatures devour your body piece by piece."

Moishe appeared to consider his options, his breathing quickening some, and he said, "I want exile."

"That I can guarantee," Bruck fibbed, as it was clear to him that Moishe's act, along with his knowledge of the inner workings of the Intelligence Service, and despite the restrictions dictated by the Israeli legal system, would require that he be treated with extreme prejudice—assassination.

"I have your word?"

"Yes," Bruck lied again.

"He is with the IDF."

"Name, I need a name."

"I don't know his name, but his unit has recently returned from New York."

A lightbulb illuminated in his mind, and Bruck began to wonder if the lone commando was the offender. He gazed down once more at his old friend turned enemy, and said, "This is the last time that we'll speak. Good-bye, Moishe."

Outside, the medical team asked if they could return to their patient, and Bruck shrugged. He watched as they walked toward the gurney and thought, what a waste of time for a dead man.

Chapter Fifty-four

Friday, January 19th

7 P.M.

The costly condo apartment had come furnished, and for the first time in many days Bruck experienced a moment of relaxation. He'd smiled inwardly during his wife's many complaints; the kitchen is too small, the oven is electric, the bed has a foam mattress, and so on. None of it mattered to him, and he'd simply said, in response to her colorful fault-finding, "You'll get used to it."

His agents had emptied their house and had brought whatever would fit into the new location. Of the many odds and ends that had been piled against one side of the living room was a small carton full of his favorite nighttime snack, red licorice. He snared a package, tore it open and inserted a Twizzler between his front teeth, as he walked to the open-air terrace. His wife had been calling from the kitchen, as she began organizing the cabinets and shelves, but he'd pretended to not hear her.

He took a deep breath and thought, oh Israel, how I love you. Even your air is sweet. But, suddenly, he recalled the threat that had been levied against the American ex-pats and his serenity dissipated like a deflating balloon. He swallowed the remains of his red treat and, with his back to the magnificent view, removed a cellphone from his front pocket and dialed Andrew Cosgrove's number.

"Are you decent?" Bruck asked, when Andrew answered.

"Yes, sir," he replied, despite the fact that he'd just walked naked from the shower.

"It appears that our young American friends might be in some trouble."

"What have they done?" he inquired, his wet feet slapping on the apartment's gray tiled flooring.

"Not them, the POF. It appears that they've been targeted. Where are they?"

"Should still be at the Shefayim."

"Go over there and move them."

"Where to?"

Bruck lowered the phone and considered various options, but in the end he said, "Bring them to headquarters."

"They won't be happy."

"They'd be happier dead?"

"OK, but what should I tell them?"

"The truth. They're on the POF's hit list."

"And when they ask how long?"

"I don't know, feel them out and tell them whatever they might find acceptable."

"You want me to lie?"

"You're a Mossad operative, improvise," he said, and terminated the call.

"We kill them, they try to kill us ... I'm tired of the game," he muttered, as he slid the glass door shut and entered the living room.

From his vantage point he could see his wife standing on a two step ladder, shoving small, spice containers onto the high shelves, and he called out, "Motek, leave that to me."

"I'm almost finished," she shouted.

"Leave the rest for tomorrow and let's go out to eat."

She stepped from the ladder, grinned and replied, "I was wondering when you'd ask."

A pair of agency bodyguards drove them to Cafe Noir, a favorite of the Brucks and many local residents. The agents had called ahead and a table had been set and waiting for the couple.

The bodyguards stood outside, while the couple ordered a bottle of Sassicaia—a costly Italian sangiovese— chose their favorite dishes and sat staring in silence at their dusky red filled glasses. Bruck took a sip of wine, swallowed and asked, "Can we make the apartment work?"

"Do we have a choice," his wife replied, more a statement than a question.

"Your safety is my biggest concern," he smiled, reaching across to grasp her hand.

"I'll get used to the elevator and the bodyguards," she announced, "but not having you by my side, wondering what dangers you're exposed to, I'll never become accustomed to that."

He nodded his understanding.

She took a thoughtful taste of the fruity wine and said, "Can you tell me about the explosion?"

He looked away for a moment, turned back to face her and replied, "I'm certain that the newspaper has covered it."

"Perhaps, but I would like to hear the truth."

He chuckled and whispered, "The usual perpetrators —it appears that I am not liked."

"Then they will try again," she murmured.

"Perhaps. But I am now on alert."

"If that's supposed to make me feel better..."

He cut her short by a squeeze of her hand, and cooed, "Motek, it is what I do, you knew that when we'd married."

"Should have gone with the butcher," she frowned.

"The short one with the potbelly?" he laughed.

The food had been delivered and they'd dined as if surrounded by an ocean of calm, the wine having burnished the crusty edge of fear and anxiety that hung over Tel Aviv's many inhabitants.

Suddenly, the two bodyguards came rushing to their table, grabbed each by an arm, and pulled them to a standing position.

"Bomb scare," the taller of the pair whispered, as he led the way out of the restaurant, to the surprise of nearby patrons who quickly followed thereafter.

"Here?" Bruck asked, still chewing on a piece of rare meat.

"Next door," the agent advised, as he ushered the pair into the waiting, armored SUV that quickly departed the area.

"Details," Bruck growled, from his seat in the rear.

"Young woman with a vest," he said, twisting in his seat, "we'd stopped her, but couldn't be certain that there hadn't been another."

Bruck turned to witness his wife taking a swig of the remaining Sassicaia from the bottle that she'd secreted from the table.

"Seriously," he breathed.

"I didn't get to finish my dinner, I wasn't going to leave this behind," she giggled, waving the bottle before his face.

He stared at her, grabbed the offered bottle, swallowed a mouthful, and asked, "Is there any food in the apartment?"

"Eggs, but you're doing the cooking."

***

9 P.M.

The newly minted Israelis had been spirited from their hotel room and driven to Mossad headquarters. The explanation for the hasty change of venue had not gone down well, and the two men were in a tizzy.

"This sucks," Marvin groaned, as they sat side by side on hard metal chairs.

"Would you prefer a pine box?" Andrew Cosgrove sneered.

"You could have upped the ante on our hotel security," George complained.

"Now you're a security expert," Andrew ridiculed.

"The big hole in the front of this building tells me that it ain't safe here, either."

"They won't try that again, we have missile defense."

"It didn't stop the first one," Marvin disagreed.

Andrew ignored his dig, and fiddled in his pocket for a stick of chewing gum.

"So this is where we spend the night?" George asked.

"Patience," Andrew warned, the gum cracking as he spoke.

A pair of rapidly speaking females passed by, and Marvin inquired, "Is this place open all night?"

"Intelligence is a 24-7 business," Andrew explained.

Marvin was about to respond, when Andrew's cellphone began to ring, and he walked several few away to take the call. When he'd finished, he returned and said, "You're being moved."

"Again?" George protested.

"The more we can obfuscate your location the safer you'll be."

"Where to this time?" Marvin droned.

"You'll know when you get there."

"I thought that the running would be over when we'd stepped off of the plane," George whined.

Andrew shrugged, as if to say, life is unpredictable.

One hour later, two unformed soldiers appeared before them. They were escorted to a military vehicle and driven off into the night.

Chapter Fifty-five

9 P.M.

Camp 1391

The two young men had been deposited at Camp 1391, an IDF base close to Tel Aviv. They'd been provided a single room containing two cots that had been reserved for VIP visitors, and they were in a sour mood.

"May as well be in prison," Marvin complained, as he kicked off his athletic shoes and stretched out on the rough, khaki colored fabric covering the bedsheet.

George grunted and replied, "Just another adventure."

"For you, maybe. But I had a life before the shit hit the fan."

"Yeah, I guess that I'm to blame."

"Not entirely," Marvin permitted, "I could have declined, but admittedly, I'd been bored."

"And if I hadn't gone to temple that night, we'd be sitting at the local pizza joint complaining about our shitty existence."

"Not me, my life was good."

"Oh, right, you have, or had a trust fund."

"It's still out there—just can't get to it."

"Is there an administrator?"

"Yeah, my father's attorney."

"Call him."

"Great idea. I'll tell him that I'm an Israeli prisoner, send money."

"I recall reading about an Israeli Bank in New York. Have him open an account in your name."

"Wait a minute, there's a branch of the Israeli Discount Bank in Aventura."

"But there's one small problem."

"Yeah?" he said excitedly.

"You have no way of contacting him."

"We can't stay here forever, and I'm sure there's a phone in my future."

"And then there's the issue of, I."

"Don't worry, I've got enough for both of us, that is, until you get a job."

"You're not gonna work?"

"Work makes me ill."

"How would you know, you've never had a job."

"I'd sold lemonade when I was seven, does that count?"

George chuckled, and walked off to the bathroom.

The two men had fallen asleep, secure in their new

surroundings. But at Midnight, they were awakened by a knock at their door. They bolted upright, waiting to see if it continued, or if someone had mistakenly arrived at their door. But the knock came again and George whispered, "Isn't it a bit late for visitors?"

"I would think so," Marvin replied.

Two more aggressive thumps on the door and George rose from the bed and opened it a crack. Standing in the narrow corridor was a vaguely familiar face.

"Can I help you?" he asked, while trying to recall where he'd seen the person.

"You're both in danger," the uniformed soldier said, gazing to the left and right, as if checking for uninvited guests.

"From whom?" he asked, suddenly recalling that the man had been the commander's New York van driver.

"Same as before," he said, avoiding use of the terrorist's label.

"You're saying that we're not safe on an army base?" he exclaimed.

The man shook his head in the affirmative.

"What do you suggest?"

"Get out."

"To where?"

"I know a place, but you'll have to hurry."

"Gimme a minute," he whispered, as he closed the door and turned to Marvin.

"What's up?" Marvin asked.

George put a finger to his lips, fearful that he could be heard through the closed door, and said, "Remember the van driver from New York?"

"Yeah."

"He's outside and claims that we're not safe here."

"Then we won't be safe anywhere."

"He knows a place."

"I'm not moving an inch," Marvin insisted.

"Something about him that makes me uneasy."

"Who sent him?"

"Didn't say."

"Ask him."

George returned to the door and cracked it slightly, but the solider used his booted foot to kick it open wide, striking George squarely in the nose. Blood gushed onto his chest and he grunted, "What the fuck?"

Marvin had scooted to the head of the bed, his facial expression a mass of surprise, and he shouted, "What the hell's going on?"

"I'm getting you out of here," the soldier sneered.

"Who sent you?" Marvin squealed, as George pressed a reddening towel against his nose.

"Not important, get moving," he barked.

"We're not going anywhere until we speak with Rafael, err, Andrew Cosgrove."

"I don't take orders from him."

"Then from whom?"

"Not your concern," he growled, grabbing the half-dressed Marvin beneath his armpits and lifting him from the bed.

From out of nowhere, George came up from behind the soldier and, with lightening speed, draped his bloody towel around the man's neck and dropped backwards to the ground. The soldier fell on top of his body and thrashed about, as George held fast onto the towel, tightening its grip on the man's throat. It had taken a few seconds, but Marvin jumped into the fray and further pinned the man down, while George managed to slither to one side, avoiding being crushed by the combined weight of the soldier and his friend.

"He's out," Marvin yelled.

George eased up on the garrote, leaving the crimson colored cloth draped over the soldier's face.

"You'd almost killed him," Marvin squawked.

"I got carried away."

"Think he's a lone wolf?"

"Well, he hadn't been sent by the Mossad," George advised.

"What should we do with him?"

"Use him for a footstool," George cackled.

"Funny, but he'll be awakening soon and all hell will break loose."

"OK, you take his head, I'll take his feet and we'll drag him as far away from here as possible."

"And you don't think he'll find his way back?"

"You wanna drown him in the toilet?"

"Be serious. We have no idea what's going on."

"OK, we move him and find a phone."

"And what, call a taxi?" Marvin said, sarcastically.

"I've got Rafael's cell number."

"You mean, Andrew Cosgrove, but maybe it was a burner."

"Worth a try," George croaked, as he grasped the solider by the ankles and began to pull.

They'd dragged the unconscious solider into a common area restroom on the opposite side of the building, and shoved his body into a stall. Due to the late hour no one else was about, and their attempt at concealment had gone unnoticed.

"He's gonna wake up," Marvin advised, as they stood just outside of the stall.

"We can still drown him," George said, with a serious tone.

"And end up in a real Israeli prison? Not on your life."

"Then we have to get off this base."

"I agree. But where to?"

"I vote for Mossad headquarters," George mumbled.

"Or, we could try to loose ourselves in the countryside."

George stared at his friend with an expression of incredulity, and said, "We're here because of the terrorists. You wanna make us an easy find?"

"OK, you're right. Let's get going."

"You might want to give some thought to how we're gonna get there," George suggested, as they left the restroom.

"A taxi?"

"Well, we still have the shekels, but getting off the base might present a problem."

They left the building and slithered off to the exit with catlike movements, avoiding the brightly lit areas and stopping every now and then to hide behind a parked military vehicle. The gated entrance was visible from their vantage point, as were the armed guards.

"I estimate a hundred yards to the gate," Marvin whispered.

"The problem isn't getting there, it's convincing the guard to allow our departure."

"We're not criminals."

"But we don't know what the Mossad has told them."

"I guess we're gonna find out," he said, as he began jogging in the direction of an apparently stunned sentry, with George following from behind.

"Halt," the guard called out, in Hebrew.

The two men, unable to comprehend the sentry's command, kept moving forward. The sentry, surprised by their unwillingness to obey, aimed her rifle at them and repeated her demand. They got the message.

"We don't speak Hebrew," Marvin advised, when he was within ten feet of the female guard.

"Where are you going?" she asked, the rifle still pointed at Marvin's chest, the second sentry watching from several feet away.

"We're leaving the base," he said.

"That's obvious," she barked, in accented English,

adding, "but where are you going at this hour?"

"We don't like the accommodations," George cut in.

The guard stifled a giggle, turned to her partner and said, "They don't like their cell," continuing with, "no one leaves the base after midnight."

"That rule applies to soldiers?" Marvin asked.

"Yes."

"We're civilians."

"Did you not understand the words, no one?" she growled.

"Our lives are in danger," George said.

"Welcome to Israel," she grinned.

Marvin gazed at his friend, exhaled, and said, "Well, we tried."

But the guard continued with her inquest, pressing on with, "Where were you going?"

"We'd been put here for safekeeping, but we don't feel safe," George explained.

"Who brought you here?"

"The Mossad."

She motioned for her partner to come closer, and she whispered something that the two men could not hear, then she turned and addressed them with, "Who is your contact?"

"Contact?" Marvin asked with a confused expression.

"Your control," she repeated.

"Wait a minute, we're not agents," George said.

"Then why are you here?"

"For our protection."

"I'll have you escorted back to your cell," she said.

"Cell?"

"This isn't a resort."

"Are you saying that this is a prison?" Marvin squealed.

"You didn't hear that from me," she whispered.

"OK, my contact is Andrew Cosgrove. He works for the director."

"I'll pretend that you didn't just try to escape, if you go back to your cell."

"What about calling my contact?"

"We don't accommodate inmates."

George flashed a worried expression at Marvin, and together they began to walk back to what they'd considered barracks.

Chapter Fifty-six

Saturday, January 20th

6 A.M.

Their escape attempt thwarted, George and Marvin had walked back toward the barracks, but once out of sight of the guards they'd taken refuge in the bed of a parked truck, where they'd spent the dark hours. But at the first sign of daylight they'd awakened to the sound of boots on the ground and approaching voices.

"We gotta go," George said, pulling on his now tattered sneakers and securing the laces.

"Sounds like someone has boarded the cab," Marvin noted, as the truck's engine came alive and the tires began to crunch on gravel.

"Let's jump out," George said, beginning to flip open the canvass tarp that acted as a rear door.

"Not so fast. Maybe this is our ticket out of here."

"We don't know where it's going."

"Anywhere off the base is good."

George relaxed, and dropped back into the depths of the truck's interior, where they'd remained inside, unnoticed, as the vehicle bumped its way over cavernous potholes, unpaved road and what they'd perceived as a shallow body of water.

"Where the hell are we going?" George mumbled.

"Better not be the desert."

"Should I take a look?"

"And if you get spotted by an accompanying vehicle?" Marvin cautioned.

"Shit. Not sure this was a good idea."

"At least the commando won't find us."

"We don't know that for a fact."

"What's the likelihood that he'd be driving this truck?" Marvin suggested.

"He was a driver in New York."

Marvin scratched his unwashed scalp, grimaced, and said, "OK, take a careful look out the rear. See if we're being followed."

George crawled to the hanging tarp and parted the dark green material by an inch. "Nobody back here," he advised, releasing the fabric and returning to his friend's side.

"What did you see?"

"A whole lot of sand and rocks," George explained, as the truck began to slow and come to a rolling stop.

"Take another look," Marvin said with urgency.

Without a word, George returned to the tarp and

stuck his head through the opening, returning quickly with, "He's taking a piss on the side of the road."

"But it's not the commando, I hope."

"Couldn't see his face, but he's a skinny dude, so, not the commando."

"OK, see any place outside where we could hide?"

"Not unless you're a scorpion."

"Shit. We're stuck here for the duration," Marvin complained.

"At least we're out of the prison."

"Gotta hand it to the Mossad. A secret prison is a great place to hide a pair of endangered expats."

"But no one told the warden that we're not criminals."

"We were in a room, not a cell. The base commander must have known."

"We'll, there are going to be a few red faces when they find out that we've skipped."

"Any thoughts about the commando's motive?" Marvin asked.

"Nope."

"I don't think we have to worry about him talking. After all, there's no way he could explain away the altercation."

"I wonder," George murmured.

"What?"

"We were probably safe in that prison, so why would he have insisted otherwise?"

"Good point. He wanted us out of there for some reason."

"Well, we've got bigger problems than that to deal with."

"Yeah, we have to somehow contact the Mossad to get us back to civilization."

The truck's tires renewed their noisy trek across the unpaved road, and the two men stifled their conversation. Thirty minutes later they began to hear the sound of mixed voices, and George peeked through a slit in the tarp.

"What do you see?" Marvin whispered.

"Looks like an open air market."

"But where the hell are we?"

"Who cares, let's get outta this truck and find a phone."

They jumped to the ground and ran behind a tent whose owner was selling fruit. Since they'd assumed that the driver had not been aware of their presence, they began to meander among the various stalls hoping to find one selling prepaid cellphones. And within short order they'd happened upon a seller of electronic gadgets.

"What language are they speaking?" Marvin asked.

"Isn't Hebrew, could be Arabic," George said.

A few prepaid cellphones—sealed in rigid plastic— were strewn about, mixed in with iPods, headphones and, of all things, an 8-track tape player.

"Ask how much?" Marvin said, holding a packaged phone above his head.

"I don't speak Arabic," George sneered, "ask him yourself."

Marvin approached the proprietor, who was seated on a low, wooden stool just outside of his tent, and asked, in English, "How much?"

The bald, toothless man smiled, and replied, "American?"

Marvin shook his head with a, yes.

"Fifty dollar U.S.," he announced succinctly in English.

"I have shekels."

The man's smile disappeared, and he rose from the stool with a grunt. "No dollars?" he questioned.

"Shekels," Marvin repeated.

With no fluent knowledge of the dollar/shekel exchange rate, Marvin assumed that he was getting screwed, but he peeled off the requested number of Israeli bills that he'd obtained earlier via a credit card machine and left with the cellphone.

"Did you ask what this place is called?" George said.

"No, was too busy getting fucked over by potato head."

"Maybe the phone has GPS," George said, as he tore away the packaging and removed the cellphone.

"Make the call," Marvin urged.

"Uh oh," George moaned.

"Now what?"

"Aside from the fact that there is no cell service out here, the battery is low."

"Then turn it off."

With some reluctance, Marvin walked back to shiny headed English speaker and asked, "Do you have a working telephone?"

The man grinned and, with his right hand, gestured to his left.

"What does that mean?" Marvin asked.

"City, that way," the man explained.

"Is there a bus?"

The man laughed, a few jets of spittle dropping between his bare, leathery, sandal covered feet, and he replied, "Want to buy camel?"

Marvin walked back to George and guffawed, "He wants to sell us a camel. But he did say that a City is to our left."

"Which city?"

Marvin shrugged, as if to say, I don't know.

"So we walk."

"Or hitch a ride, if one comes along."

"With our luck we'd end getting snared by the POF, so, no hitching."

"There is one other option," Marvin chuckled, as he nodded toward the military truck.

"You're kidding."

"The driver just left it standing there, unguarded."

"And that's our cue to steal it?"

"It beats walking I don't know how far."

"We'd just left a secret prison, you wanna go back there as an inmate?"

"Maybe Andrew will have our backs," Marvin pleaded.

"It's pointed in the wrong direction," George advised.

"So we turn it around."

"And the driver comes running, gun blazing, as we shuttle back and forth."

"We can back it up real fast and do one of those turns like you see in the movies."

"It's a damn truck, not your Porsche," George shrieked.

"If we walk we run the risk of either being spotted by our pursuers or dying from dehydration."

George exhaled loudly, and breathed, "OK, let's give it a try."

Marvin entered the cab, while George stood guard.

The key was not in the ignition, and after ransacking the truck's interior he was in a panic. But, ready to submit to failure, he gazed down at the floor and noticed a glint of sliver coming from beneath the seat, the key.

"Get in, and hurry," he called out, as the engine came to life with the characteristic rumble of a diesel.

"Can you drive it?" George asked, as he closed the passenger side door.

Marvin did not reply, but put the transmission in gear and began to accelerate in reverse.

"What the hell are you doing?" George screamed.

"Backing up as far as I can, out of sight of the market," he grunted, his head turned toward the sideview mirror.

"But you're gonna turn around at some point?"

"Plannin' on it."

"Wait. I see someone running from the market,"

George exclaimed excitedly.

"Big surprise, this thing is noisy."

"He stopped, not running anymore."

"No way he could catch us."

"Reinforcements from the prison base will," George advised.

"Remember, no cell service."

"And if he has a two-way radio?"

"We're fucked," Marvin agreed, slowing as the road widened, preparing to turn around.

"I don't recall any obvious turns, so if we stay on this road we're bound to pass the base."

"Keep checking for a cellphone signal, maybe we can contact Andrew Cosgrove before they see us."

"And if not?"

"We keep going and take our chances."

Chapter Fifty-seven

9 A.M.

Mossad Headquarters

Still unaccustomed to his new apartment, Bruck had endured a mostly sleepless night. His wife, on the other hand, had experienced no such issues, as her characteristic freight train snoring had proven.

Two giant mugs of black coffee had accomplished little for his nagging fatigue, and he was about to pour a third, when there was a knock at his partially closed door. He lowered the pot, took a deep breath, and called out, "Yes?"

"Sir, it's Andrew Cosgrove, can we talk?"

"Come."

Andrew entered with a brisk gait and, without asking, took a seat before the acting Director's desk.

"What is it?" Bruck said, his voice lacking in resolve.

"We have a small problem, sir."

"What else is new, go ahead," he said, resting his elbows on the desk, his chin cradled by the palms of both hands.

"The two Americans are missing."

"What?" he shouted, summoning a burst of energy.

"I'd had them transferred to Camp 1391..."

"You'd sent them to a prison," Bruck cut in angrily, as he rose from his chair and stared menacingly at his subordinate.

"It was the safest place I could think of."

"And you took them there yourself?"

"No, I had a pair of soldiers escort them."

"And they've escaped from our most secure site," he mumbled, shaking his head with disbelief.

"It appears so."

"It appears, or it is true."

"True."

"Had you installed the GPS trackers on their clothing as I'd ordered?"

"Yes."

"So where are they?"

"In a truck heading towards Tel Aviv."

Bruck, still standing, turned to face the wall that contained several commendations, ogled them for a long interval and then growled, with his back to the agent, "Where in hell did the truck come from?"

"They'd stolen it," he replied sheepishly.

Bruck began to laugh, at first a few hoots, but it quickly morphed into quasi hysteria. But he calmed and said, "Those two have more balls than most of my agents."

"Sir?"

"Find them and bring them to me—go," he ordered, his right index finger aimed at the doorway.

With Andrew out of earshot, and his office door now closed, Bruck considered the change of events. I should make them operatives, he joked to himself. No one has ever successfully escaped from 1391 but, then again, I assume that they had not been confined. Even so, there are guards and sensors everywhere—no one gets in or out unnoticed. But knowing that they'd been put there for safekeeping, why would they have bolted, he wondered. And do we have a problem at 1391?

He had assigned an operative, Hymie Ganz, to surveil the commando who'd left New York without notification, and he was now standing just outside of his office, waiting to be heard. Ganz, a forty-year-old, clean shaven native Israeli and closet alcoholic, stood by the door dancing from one foot to another. He'd been about to visit the restroom when the Acting Director's secretary had informed him that he was next in line to speak with the boss. But the night before he'd broken up with his girlfriend of ten years, and he'd gone on a bender ... his bladder was ready to explode. And just as he was about to ask to reschedule, the door opened and Bruck waved him in.

"Have a seat," he said, taking his place behind the desk.

"Sir," the man replied.

"What have you got for me, Hymie?"

"First, if I may, a question."

Bruck shook his head affirmatively.

"Had he been assigned to 1391?"

Bruck's eyelids shot open, and he stared at the man. "Absolutely not," he shouted, emphasized by a fist slammed against the desktop.

Ganz sat silent in response to the outburst, crossing his legs from one to the other.

"He's there?" Bruck asked.

"Was."

"How?"

"False documents, allegedly signed by yourself."

Bruck leaned back in the chair and wondered if he should have the man picked up, or if he should allow him time to reveal his true motive. Deciding on the latter, he said, "Keep him on a tight leash, figure out what he's up to."

"Anything else?"

A red flag rose before Bruck's eyes, and he suddenly

saw a vague and potential connection between the commando and the two Americans. "Do you know what he was doing at the prison?"

"No, sir."

"Keep him isolated."

"Sir?"

"I have reason to believe that he may be tracking a pair of recently arrived Americans."

"To what end?"

"That's for you to find out," Bruck snapped.

Without another word, Ganz shot from the seat like a supersonic projectile and headed for the men's room. Bruck scratched his head and wrote off the odd retreat to over-exuberance. He'd known about the man's drinking problem, but since Ganz had managed to keep his habit under wraps and out of public view, Bruck had refrained form addressing the issue.

My gut feeling had been on target with that solider, he said to himself, as he toyed with a yellow, number two pencil. Moishe had said that there was another, but I hadn't believed him. The interrogators should have put on the brakes when they'd seen him failing, but he's gone now. And having been all too familiar with that vindictive bastard's, at times twisted personality, I'm certain that he took some intel to his grave. But we'll get to the bottom of this cabal.

***

While Bruck contemplated the motive behind the two American's disappearance, George and Marvin were in the process of navigating their stolen truck onto a paved thoroughfare.

"Take your time, there's a lot of traffic and this truck is slow to accelerate," George warned.

"Don't you find it strange that the army hasn't apprehended us?" Marvin posed.

"Been thinkin' about that."

"I wonder if we'd been setup."

"For what purpose?"

"To keep us occupied."

George turned and gazed out of the passenger side window, thinking, it may not have been the army that had set us up, and said, "Look for a sign pointing to Tel Aviv."

"Uh, George," Marvin stuttered. "I think we're being followed."

"We just got onto this road, not possible."

"Tell that to the white SUV on our tail."

George craned his neck to look for the white car via the large, protruding sideview mirror, but since they'd been driving in the right lane, all he could visualize was a portion of the road. "I can't see it," he advised.

"Trust me, it's glued to our rear end."

"Maybe just an anxious tailgater."

"Do tailgaters carry short barreled rifles?"

"Shit," George shouted, adding, "I didn't want to alarm you, but I was thinking about your setup statement."

"Yeah?" he said, tentatively.

"The terrorists could be behind all of this."

"You think they've got Israeli soldiers on their payroll?" Marvin sneered, taking a sharp leap into the next lane.

"Money is at the bottom of just about everything."

"Well, right now we have to figure out a way to ditch the SUV."

"Still on our tail?"

"Like flies on honey."

"They're not gonna shoot at us in the middle of a highway," George reassured.

"They're terrorists, you think they give a shit."

"Yeah, maybe not."

"I've got an idea," Marvin grinned.

"I get nauseous whenever you say that, but go ahead," George urged.

"I'm gonna wait for a slight break in traffic and then I'm gonna hit the brakes hard."

"You could cause a pileup."

"Collateral damage, but the SUV, and hopefully its passengers, will have bloody noses."

"Go for it."

Traffic had been almost bumper to bumper from the time that they'd entered the highway, but for no discernible reason it had suddenly begun to speed up. Marvin waited until there had been several car lengths behind the rear following SUV and it nearest vehicle, and then called out, "Hold tight," as he literally stood on the brake pedal, causing the truck's rear end to fishtail from side to side. A wooden palate, that had been their resting platform when they'd stowed away in the truck while at the prison base, came flying out of the truck bed and smashed through the SUV's windshield. But Marvin had already accelerated away from the scene and had not borne witness to the white vehicle's decapitated driver, or the OTs-14 Groza (Russian made rifle) that had been ejected to the pavement.

"We in the clear?" George rasped, anxiously.

"For now."

Chapter Fifty-eight

Saturday, January 20th

1 P.M.

Andrew Cosgrove had reluctantly included his female partner, Bina, in the search for the Americans. And as they drove toward the highway that they thought to be traveled by the pursued truck, they began to argue about the use of equipment.

"Why did you use that old crap?" Bina said, referring to the GPS chips that Andrew had signed out of the armory from a box that had been labeled obsolete.

"They still work," he said, from his position behind the wheel of their unmarked vehicle.

"But they're unreliable," she advised.

"They're pointing us in the right direction now."

"You won't know that until you see the truck," she snapped.

"Calm down."

"What's gotten into you, you've changed," she observed, her nose pointed toward the passenger side window.

"Nothing's changed," he breathed, as he stopped at a traffic light.

"You've got a new girlfriend?" she asked.

"No, what makes you think so?"

"All those private phone calls."

"Personal stuff."

"You in some kind of trouble?"

"Cut it, will you."

"You're my partner, I need to know that I can depend upon you."

"Nothing's changed."

"What kind of personal stuff?" she pressed.

He allowed her question to hang in the air, and said, "The highway is just ahead."

"We gonna stop them or follow?"

"I'll try to flag them down, get them to follow us."

"We'll be pointed the wrong way to accomplish that."

"I'm not getting on the freeway, we'll wait near the off ramp."

As he pulled to a stop not far from the ramp, a cellphone began to buzz. Reaching into a back pocket, he removed the device and stifled the ringing.

"That's not your regular phone," Bina observed.

"It's one that I use for personal calls," he said.

"And you're avoiding the caller?"

"You might say that."

"So there is a new girlfriend," she gloated.

He ignored her tease, and was about to shove it back into his pocket, when it went off again. He stared at the LCD, grimaced, hit the talk button and said, "Not now," and terminated the call.

"Not the best way to maintain a relationship," Bina suggested.

"I'm not really into her," he lied.

"Military truck at our one o'clock," Bina indicated.

"I'm gonna head them off," he said, putting the car in gear and beginning to roll.

"Just make certain that it's them, we don't want to piss off the army."

The truck passed them doing thirty miles per hour and Andrew hit the accelerator, at first exceeding and then matching their speed, as he pulled alongside.

"Open your window, get their attention," he shouted at Bina.

Marvin had noticed her, and he gestured for her to follow to a parking area just ahead. Several minutes later the two vehicles came to a stop at the side of the road and rather than exit, Marvin and George waited for the Mossad operatives to approach, while the truck's diesel engine clattered away.

"Glad to see you," Marvin said, leaning out of the driver's side window.

"The Acting Director wants to see you both, right away," Andrew announced.

"The feeling is mutual," George shouted from the passenger seat.

"That's all you've got to say?" Marvin asked.

"What were you expecting?"

"An apology for putting us in that predicament."

"It was a safe place," Andrew explained.

Marvin gazed over at his seatmate, who advised, "Forget it, let's have the discussion with the Director."

"You all of a sudden don't have confidence in him?" he whispered.

"Remember, he put us there. So, no."

Marvin leaned back out of the window and said, "Give me directions to headquarters."

"Leave the truck and get in my vehicle," Andrew said, sternly.

"We can't leave an Army vehicle sitting here," Bina complained.

"We can and we will," Andrew growled, his demeanor transitioning to anger.

Bina walked back to their car and leaned against a

front fender with her cellphone in hand. Marvin had noticed the gesture, and it had added fuel to George's suspicion.

"I'd rather follow you," Marvin declared.

"I could arrest you both for theft," Andrew seethed.

And that's when Marvin, without a word of warning to his fellow Floridian, put the vehicle in gear and hit the accelerator.

"What the hell are you doing?" George shrieked.

"You were right not to trust him," he said, weaving back into traffic.

"He was only threatening."

"Bina had appeared really disturbed, and it'd looked like she was making a call."

"So?"

"I think she has an issue with his behavior."

"That's her problem, not ours."

Marvin ignored the statement and increased his speed. He had no idea how to navigate the streets of Tel Aviv to reach Mossad headquarters, but kept a lookout for familiar landmarks.

"There," George announced, anxiously, "we'd passed that building on the way to headquarters."

"You sure?"

"Definitely."

Marvin made a u-turn and headed down the designated street, but he suddenly became aware of Andrew Cosgrove's car tailing them from a short distance. "He's back," Marvin said.

"No surprise, but don't stop."

Fifteen minutes later, following a few wrong turns, they'd arrived at the Mossad building. Andrew Cosgrove came to a screeching halt alongside of the truck and growled, "Get out, now, get out."

"I don't like your attitude," Marvin, still seated behind the wheel, announced calmly.

"You're guests in this country."

"Correction, we're newly anointed citizens."

"That can change real fast."

"Look, we're here to speak with the Director, but we'd like Bina to take us to him."

She was standing a few feet off to Andrew's side and she called out, "My pleasure."

Andrew stalked off like an angry child, as Bina smiled and gestured for the pair to follow.

The secretary kept them waiting for ten minutes and then announced that the Acting Director was ready for them. She opened the door and motioned for them to enter.

"So soon you're making trouble?" Bruck chuckled, as the three stood before his desk.

"It's not their fault," Bina offered.

Bruck aimed an index finger at the only empty chairs and ordered, "Sit."

George offered a chair to Bina, but she shook her head as if to say no thank you, and he slid his body onto the metal chair alongside of his friend.

"Was that your first time in a prison?" Bruck grinned, taunting the pair.

"Yes, sir," George answered.

"Something spooked you, hadn't it?"

"A soldier had tried to force us to leave," Marvin cut in, avoiding the man's attempted strangulation.

"So you left anyway?" Bruck said, with a puzzled expression.

Marvin hesitated, as neither he nor George relished the idea of explaining how they'd dragged the man into the men's room, so he said, "We'd felt threatened."

"By the soldier?"

They shook their heads affirmatively.

"I'm assuming that it was a male, so had you ever seen him before?

"Yes."

"Interesting. Where?"

"He drove the commando's van in New York," George replied.

Bruck dropped the green, rubber anxiety ball that he'd been squeezing and leaned forward with his elbows on the desktop. "Had this soldier been with you at the time of the airport melee?"

"No."

Bruck gazed up at Bina, who was leaning against the back wall listening intently, and said, "I need to speak with you privately."

He rose from behind the desk, instructed the two Floridians to remain seated, and left the room with Bina by his side.

Outside, in the seclusion of a secondary office just feet from his own, he announced, "We have a security lapse."

"Sir?"

"The soldier that they'd spoken of has been on my radar. He may have been compromised by the terrorists."

"One of ours working with the enemy?" she repeated with surprise.

"Remember Seren Levin?" he said.

"He was..."

Bruck shook his head with a, yes.

"What are my orders?"

He took a few paces about the room, thinking that he now had enough to bring the commando down, and he was about to instruct her to locate and arrest the man, when he was struck by the absence of her partner. "Why is Andrew not by your side?" he inquired.

"That is a subject that I would like to discuss when you have the time, sir."

"This is the time, speak."

"He's been acting strange."

"How so?"

"Unexplained phone calls with an unauthorized cellphone, mood swings and irrational behavior."

"You believe him to be unfit?"

"Perhaps, but I'm wondering if there isn't something else."

"Oy," he breathed, "the agency is falling apart."

"Sir?"

"What are your suspicions?"

"Nothing distinct and clear, but my intuition is sounding an alarm."

"Instincts are good for an operative, but the law demands facts."

"Do I have your permission to surveil him?"

"You're asking to investigate a fellow agent?" he remarked, with astonishment.

"Something's not right, sir."

Bruck glared at her for a several seconds and replied, "Go with your gut feelings, you have my permission. But be discrete."

"And the solider?"

"Yes, bring him in by any means necessary."

"Do I involve Andrew?"

Bruck hesitated, and asked, "Can you locate him?"

"After today, I think that he'll respond to you better, sir."

"Understood, I'll handle it. And as for the commando, I'll arrange for backup. "

They returned to Bruck's office, where Marvin and George had been dozing in their chairs. Bruck smiled, as he passed them on the way to his desk. "Sorry to awaken you," he grinned.

"Sir," Marvin began, "what about our safety?"

"I hate to subject you to yet another prison, but for the time being you can stay in the cells downstairs."

"Seriously?" George perked up.

"It's safe, there's food, bathroom and shower facilities

and we won't lock you in."

Chapter Fifty-nine

3 P.M.

With the two Americans safely ensconced in the bowls of the Mossad headquarters, Bruck was saddled with the problem of ferreting out the bad seeds in his own organization. Bina had called in with the commando's approximate location and Bruck had dispatched a backup team of six. With any luck, he thought, the traitor will be behind bars within the hour. But what concerns me most is Andrew Cosgrove. He had been one of my most trusted operatives, privy to the agency's inner workings, and if he's gone rogue as Bina seems to suspect, whom else do I have to watch out for, he wondered.

He dragged his weary legs up onto the desktop and gazed at the ceiling. The slowly spinning ceiling fan blades were casting a flickering, mesmerizing pattern across his outstretched limbs and he was about to close his eyes for a brief and well deserved nap, when the phone came to life. He exhaled, a sign of exasperation, and reached for the receiver.

"Acting Director Bruck," he said.

"Sir, it's Bina," she cried out.

He bolted upright in the chair, his legs slipping from

the desktop, and asked, "You have him?"

"Not yet."

"Is that gunfire I hear?"

"Yes, it's coming at us from all directions," she advised, her voice catching at times.

His eyes widened and he shouted, "Where are you?"

"The outskirts of Haifa."

"Send me your coordinates and I'll arrange for air support."

"Too many locals, drone fire would be dangerous."

"Helicopters, they can rappel down for your support."

"Risky, there are shooters up high in the buildings."

During a moment of silence, Bruck could hear heavy breathing mixed with the intermittent rattle of rifle fire, and he racked his brain trying to conjure a solution. Agents on the ground know the situation best, he told himself, and he asked, "What do you need?"

"A way out."

"Anyone hit?"

"Not so far."

"Armored vehicles?"

"Yes, that might work. Send them, but hurry."

"Can you identify the perpetrators?"

"They're wearing Keffiyeh (Arab headdress).

"OK, I'll call the nearest base," he said, as he thought, *I should have allowed the army to take him down.*

For the first time since his own service in the military, he felt an icy bolt travel down his spine, as he tried to imagine the terror that Bina and her teammates were experiencing. To be trapped by incessant gunfire would frighten the Devil himself, he reasoned, as he reached for the phone and dialed Haifa's closest army base. When he'd finished conveying the dire circumstances to the base commander, he terminated the call and arranged for a drone to overfly the area to provide eyes on the battle zone. He took a deep breath, reached into a bottom desk drawer, withdrew a bottle of Johnny Walker Black and took a swig straight from the bottle. He dialed his wife, as his right had begun to quiver slightly, and told her that he might not make it home for dinner.

***

3:20 P.M.

Bina, and three of her backup team, had found refuge behind a parked delivery vehicle. They had ceased to return fire, as they were short on ammunition and did not wish to reveal their exact position. The shooters were still sending an occasional volley of bullets from two mid-rise apartment buildings located to their left and right.

"Can you estimate their numbers?" she asked of the man by her side.

"Hard to say. Either they're many, or they're moving from window to window to give that impression."

"Assuming that they're not changing position, how many do you estimate?"

"A dozen, maybe a few less."

"All of the gunfire is coming from the top floor..."

"Forget it," he interrupted, "they'd see us on approach to the building."

"You read my mind."

"We're stuck," he observed.

"So, either we wait for the cavalry, or we mount a counterattack."

"I'm almost out of ammo, and those of our team across the road are in the same predicament."

"So we go asymmetric."

"The commando that you're after is well versed in our tactics, I say we wait."

She lowered her head and groaned, "You're right, we wait."

One hour later, and wondering why the insurgents

hadn't tried to take them out by rushing their position, the rumble of an approaching Namer (Leopard), one of the few remaining armored vehicles of its kind, was heard.

"You hear that?" she said.

One of her team withdrew a pair of binoculars and exclaimed, "They've sent a fucking tank."

"Gimme those," another said, ripping the binoculars out of his hands and adding, "it's a Namer, some of us can fit inside."

"Those that cannot will walk behind it," Bina said.

"Do we draw straws?" the binocular holding man chuckled.

Ignoring his attempt at levity, Bina declared, "OK, we wait until it gets into position and then we run. Notify the group across the road."

A few rounds appeared to have been directed at the approaching personnel carrier, but the rifle fire ceased when the Namer came to a stop and its M2 Browning, .50 cal machine gun ratcheted upwards, its muzzle aimed at the top floor of one terrorist occupied building. Suddenly, a soldier's head appeared, and then his waving right arm urging them to run to the Namer.

To their relief, the Leopard had accommodated the entire team and it slowly departed from the area of conflict with its machine gun shifting aim from one targeted building to the other.

And as it bounced along the road, Bina turned to one team member and mumbled, "We've fucked up big time."

"Yeah, the asshole's in the wind by now."

Chapter Sixty

6 P.M.

The two Americans had reluctantly settled in to their new accommodations. And they were seated in one of the cells devouring large helpings of stuffed cabbage served on plastic dishes, when Bruck came by to check on them.

"How's the food?" he asked.

"Not bad," Marvin offered, with a full mouth.

"Yeah, compliments to the chef," George added.

"I have yet to arrive at a solution to your predicament," Bruck advised.

Marvin stopped chewing, shifted his gaze from the cabbage, and said, "Does that mean we're stuck here?"

"Bruck exhaled and admitted, "I'm afraid so, but it shouldn't be for too long."

"What about the commando?"

Bruck hesitated, scratched his scalp and then replied, "As they say on the American police shows, he's in the wind."

"Now we have to worry about him too?" George whined.

"How so?" Bruck asked.

The two Americans shot a glance at each other, and

George nodded an OK.

"We'd had a little incident with him," Marvin advised.

"Yes, you've already discussed his attempt to remove you from the prison," Bruck said.

"It'd been a little more involved than that."

"And you'd chosen to keep it a secret?" Bruck growled.

"We were afraid of what you might say, or do."

"Tell me what happened."

Marvin offered the details of the altercation, including the ineffective attempt at strangulation that had ended with the solider lying in a bathroom stall.

"You two never cease to amaze me," Bruck admitted, adding, "and neither of you have military training?"

"No sir."

"I may have to reassess my agent selection process," he laughed.

"Sir?" Marvin said, with a confused expression.

"Not your concern."

"And the commando?"

"He won't come anywhere near this place."

"Could we get some more of this?" George asked, holding the now empty, red plastic dish above his head.

Bruck shook his head, a sign of amusement, and with

a chuckle walked off.

"So that's it, we're Israeli prisoners," George moaned.

"Maybe we can bribe a guard with our shekels," Marvin joked.

"And maybe the terrorists will take up a new hobby," George hurled back sarcastically.

"I've been thinking…" Marvin began to say.

"That's never a good sign," George cut in.

"No, seriously, I'm wondering if staying in Israel is a good idea."

"You'd rather face the music back home?"

"Look at it this way, in the U.S. we might face legal issues that can be fought, but here we're targets for a bunch of maniacs."

"And it doesn't look like the lunatics are about to let us off the hook."

"So?"

"I think we should give it a little more time."

"Look around, George, this ain't exactly the Ritz."

"But the doors are wide open."

***

8 P.M.

Bruck had already informed his wife that there was no chance that he'd be returning home for dinner, or perhaps not at all that evening. He'd arranged to have a pizza from his favorite venue—Rustico—brought to his office, and he was halfway through the last slice with extra pepperoni, when there was a knock at his closed door. The secretary had already gone home for the day, and the agent who generally sat at her desk when the Acting Director was on the premises had taken a bathroom break.

Bruck wiped his hands on a well stained napkin, pushed the now empty pizza box off to one side of his desk, and rose to reply to the knock.

"Sorry about the mess up," Bina said, her hair askew, overlying several blood smeared forehead scratches.

"Come in, have a seat," Bruck said, continuing with, "tell me what happened."

"It was an ambush, they'd known that we were coming for him."

"By him, you mean the commando?"

Yes, she nodded.

"So we have another mole," he seethed.

"The backup team had not known about the target until we'd been on our way, sir."

"Then they're in the clear. Any other ideas?"

"Yes," she said, sheepishly, placing a small, metallic disc on his desk.

"A tracker?" he blurted.

"It's one of the new prototypes, sir. It can transmit voice for a short distance."

"Where did you find it?"

"Under the collar of my shirt."

"This is a shit storm," he shouted, banging a fist on his desk, causing the pizza box to slide to the floor, adding, "how could this have happened?"

"I've been racking my brain all the way here, and Andrew is the only possible source."

"So your intuition had been correct, Cosgrove has gone rogue."

"How shall I respond?"

"I'd like to say with extreme prejudice, but with the commando and Cosgrove in the mix I need some answers."

"So we bring them in?"

"Of course, but our recent attempt didn't go so well," he acknowledged, nodding at her abrasions.

"Sorry about that."

"But they'd been forewarned, and if I had to venture a guess I'd say that they've crossed into Gaza."

"I could organize a team."

"This is a national security issue, well within our purview, but I think it's time for the Army's special forces to get their boots dirty."

"Does the PM have to be informed, sir?"

"No, we do what we do to protect Israel."

"But with boots on the ground we could be giving Hamas a reason to bombard us."

"First of all, none of that is of your concern, and secondly, Hamas doesn't need a reason."

"I apologize for misspeaking."

Bruck grunted and shook his head, an acceptance of her regret.

"Try to put a call through to Cosgrove," he said.

"Our last conversation hadn't gone very well."

"Given our suspicions, he's likely to respond more favorably to a call from you than I."

"I'll try. But what if he's crossed into Gaza with the terrorists?"

Bruck shrugged, and said, "Cellphones work over there."

"I guess that I could pretend to be desirous of his good graces."

"If he responds, try to arrange a meeting ... here or there."

"I just had a thought, sir."

"Yes?"

"If his new associates get the notion that he no longer has contacts in the Mossad, he will be of little use to them."

"And that's why he *will* answer your call," Bruck smiled.

As Bina left the office, Bruck took a seat on the edge of his desk and starred at the pizza box lying on the floor. I wish that I could crawl into that thing, he thought. I should have been retired by now, vacationing with my wife and floating on the buoyant waters of the Dead Sea. But, no, I had to take the reins for the dead man who'd come before me. He gazed up at the ceiling and thought, why me, why me? A little voice in his head shouted back, "Because you're a schmuck."

Chapter Sixty-one

9 P.M.

The commander of Batar Dotan, an Israeli Defense Force base located in the Haifa district's Pardes Hanna-Karkur, had just settled in for the evening with a warm bottle of Guinness and a girlie magazine that he'd read so many times that the pages had begun to fray, when his bedside phone commenced to buzzing.

"Aluf mishne (colonel) Tamir Fetterman speaking," the gravely voice announced.

"Tamir, its Ariel Bruck."

Tamir lowered his beer bottle, sat upright at the edge of the bed, gazed at a wall clock, and said, "Nine o'clock, are we being invaded?"

"Not tonight, my friend," Bruck laughed, "but I need your help."

"The Mossad needs *my* assistance?" Tamir teased.

Bruck held his tongue, avoiding a sarcastic retort, and said, "It's a rather delicate matter."

"Sounds delicious, what do you need?"

"A special forces team."

"Oh, that's all?" he jeered.

"I know that we've had some issues in the past, but

can we put them aside for the sake of Israel?"

There was a moment of silence, and then, "Of course."

"Two Israelis have gone to the dark side, one of them is yours and one is mine. I want them back on Israeli soil for questioning and to face charges of treason."

"That sounds serious."

"It is."

"Why not send your own forces to retrieve them?"

That was a question that Bruck had hoped would not be posed, but he had no choice other than to respond with an on-the-fly fabrication of, "They're all otherwise occupied."

"You *are* busy, aren't you," Tamir taunted.

"No rest for intelligence gatherers."

"How soon?"

"Tonight would be good."

"You do know that operations of this nature require planning and good intel?"

"The intel I can provide, planning is up to you."

"Send me what you've got and I'll get back to you within the hour."

The call had been terminated, and Bruck sent off an encrypted copy of an aerial map depicting the last known location of the POF since the bombing of their prior hideout. When the machine had indicated that the data had been received, he pushed back in the chair and allowed his eyes to focus on the rhythmical movement of the desk clock's second hand. What I hadn't told the colonel was my reason for his involvement, he pondered. I could have easily organized a snatch and grab, and if it had gone well no one would have been the wiser. But I don't need the political headache that could be generated by the possible loss of operatives to the terrorists, the army is more suited for that scenario. We need better funding from those bean counting assholes, so the less notoriety the better, at least for the time being.

As an afterthought, he placed a call to Hymie Ganz, the operative to whom he'd assigned the task of investigating the rogue commando, and instructed him—without explanation—to stand down. And one hour and ten minutes later, true to his word, Aluf mishne Tamir Fetterman called.

"Working with only your map, I have cobbled together a team of eight," Tamir advised.

"Remember, I need the two turncoats alive," Bruck said.

"We'll do our best, but I can't guarantee it."

"I understand, that in the heat of battle shit happens.

But don't forget that one of them belongs to you," Bruck instructed, realizing that the army might feel the need to terminate the commando rather than suffer the backlash from a trial.

"We go green at midnight," Tamir advised.

"I'll be in my office waiting for your call," he advised, as Tamir hung up.

Just as he'd resigned to sliding his feet up on the desk and taking a nap, the telephone buzzed once again.

"Bruck here?" he droned, too tired to announce his full title.

"It Bina, sir."

"Are you OK?"

"Yes, thank you. I spoke with Andrew Cosgrove..."

"And?" he interrupted.

"He pretended to be at home, sleeping off a cold."

"And of course you knew otherwise."

"I'd already been to his apartment before placing the call—it'd been empty."

"How did you leave it?"

"I'd offered to come over with chicken soup," she giggled.

Bruck laughed, and replied, "Laced with cyanide, I assume."

"I'd rather fire my weapon into his skull," she hissed.

"That time may come, but for now, see if he calls back."

"Why would he do that when his phone can be traced."

"And if he uses a phone that cannot be traced?"

"He's already claimed to be at his home, a different phone would raise suspicion."

"Lack of sleep is dulling my mind—you're correct. He may not call back, unless he gets creative."

"Well, he's still Mossad, he can cross the border without scrutiny."

"Right, so you might find him back in his apartment shortly," Bruck said, realizing that the special operations team might get to him first.

"Should I set up surveillance?"

"No, it's almost midnight, get some sleep."

Without returning the receiver to its cradle, he dialed the number for a direct connection to the drone shack.

"This is Acting Director Ariel Bruck," he announced.

"Sir, Segen rishon (Lieutenant) Goldstein. How can I help you," a female voice inquired.

"Are you a pilot?" he asked.

"Yes, sir, I am tonight's driver."

"Do you have a drone near the following coordinates..." he asked.

"Within a kilometer."

"I need eyes on."

"How soon?"

Bruck checked his desk clock and replied, "Now."

"Can you lock onto my screen, sir?"

He swiveled to a lit computer monitor positioned off to one side of his desk and said, "I see green."

"Night vision, sir. OK, target should be coming up in less than sixty seconds."

"Remain on station until I say otherwise, unless you have a fuel issue."

"Roger that, sir."

Bruck terminated the call, secure in the belief that the pilot would follow his orders.

The drone's camera revealed a panorama at first, and then zeroed in on the targeted structure. In addition to its night vision capability, the camera could detect heat signatures, and as he sat transfixed by the image before his eyes, a handful of ill-defined, reddish orange points of light began to appear. The first to be observed had entered the field of view from behind the camera, and he presumed that they'd represented the special ops team. He watched as they slowly moved closer toward the target, stopping every now and then, before approaching its perimeter. Suddenly, what had appeared to have begun as an uneventful passage of roughly eight bobbing orange points of light turned into something unimaginable. The eight points had become twenty or more, from which emanated tiny, too numerous to count, flashes of red and orange. Shit, it's a firefight, Bruck said to himself. And then seven points of light began to move in the direction from whence they'd come. He moved to the edge of his seat, his pulse racing, as he realized that either the special ops team was in retreat, or they were being chased. I can't sit here and do nothing, he thought, as he reached for the phone and connected with the drone pilot.

"Goldstein?" he said, so stressed by the evolving scene that he'd ignored protocol by not using her rank.

"Yes, sir."

"Is the drone armed?"

"AGM-114's, sir."

He held the receiver close to his face, his heart racing, as he tried to arrive at a go, no go decision. And then, telling himself that the survival of the special ops team was more important than the capture of the traitors, and hoping that they were within the one story building, he asked, "Can you communicate with the boots on the ground?"

"Not reliably ... don't have their comms frequency, sir."

With the telephone still in hand, he scrutinized the screen. The retreating dots were no longer visible, but there still were occasional flashes that he'd determined to be gunfire. With his fingers crossed, he called out, "Send one to the target, send it now."

"Roger that, on its way," the pilot assured.

Sweat had begun to make his eyes burn, and he dabbed at them with the sleeve of his right arm. And just as his arm had cleared his face the computer screen went momentarily blank, followed by what the thermal camera revealed as dense flames. I hope they're out of harms way, he said to himself.

The flames continued, obscuring any other potentially visible activity, so he said to the pilot, "You can break off and return to your original grid."

"Yes, sir, turning away now."

"Good job, Segen rishon," he said, and terminated the call.

Twenty minutes later, following two gulps of Johnny Walker Black, the phone startled him and he lifted the receiver.

"Bruck here."

"It's Tamir, we had a mission failure."

"I know, we had a drone overhead."

"You do realize that you could have wiped out my entire team?" Tamir barked.

"Your men were in retreat—I had to act."

"Well, we did have one casualty but he'll survive."

"Let us both hope that the treasonous duo has been blown to bits."

Chapter Sixty-two

Sunday, January 21st

6 A.M.

Office of the Acting Director, Mossad

Bruck had awakened with a head and neck ache. He'd fallen sleep in his ancient desk chair and had forgotten to check in with his wife before closing his eyes the night before. And as he tried to massage the pain away with the palm of one hand, his eyes locked onto the angry face of Mrs. Bruck standing just inside his doorway.

"Motek?" he exclaimed, surprised by her presence.

"You were supposed to call," she scowled.

"There was a problem, I forgot," he grimaced.

She softened and walked toward the desk, sliding onto one of the metal chairs. "Your problem, has it been resolved?" she asked.

"You know that I cannot discuss such matters."

"Well, you're still here, so I can assume that it has not gone away."

"How did you get here?" he asked.

"Taxi."

He sniffed an armpit, grinned and said, "I need a shower."

"Come home, the shower works just fine."

He stared at her lovingly and replied, "I have some loose ends to deal with, but I'll be home shortly."

"I'm not taking another taxi," she instructed.

"No, of course not. I'll have someone drive you."

"What about food?" she asked.

"I'll get to it," he mumbled, as he rose and planted a kiss on her right cheek.

"You know, you're due for a day of rest."

"When the crazies take a rest, so will I," he breathed, as he reached for the phone and called for an agent to take her home.

The coffee pot was still hot to the touch, and he poured himself a cup of the now stale black liquid. It was bitter, but strong enough to awaken him to the fact that he did not know whether the missile had taken out Cosgrove and the commando. And then there was Bina, whom he had not informed of the prior night's mission. Hmm, should I read her in, or not, he wondered. If, for some strange reason, Andrew Cosgrove had not been present during the drone attack, or had managed to survive, he might still call. But she'd be royally pissed off to find out that he'd died during the attack and no one had informed her. So should I care what a subordinate thinks, he asked himself. No. I'm the boss, I do what is best for Israel, he reminded himself, as he took another swig of the nasty, black coffee. But what about me, what is best for me, he pondered. He yawned, dumped the remainder of the coffee into a trash can, and wandered off to the detainment level. Since the two Americans were still in his custody, he felt responsible for their wellbeing and guilty for not having given much attention to finding them a safe place to live.

He found them asleep in their respective cells, and he gently pulled George's squeaky door open to its extreme detent.

"Is it breakfast, already?" George yawned.

"Sorry, I have no food for either of us," Bruck chuckled.

"Oh, Director, I didn't mean to..."

Bruck smiled, as if to say, no problem, and offered, "How are you getting along?"

"Could be better."

Marvin, apparently awakened by the chatter, moaned, "This prison crap is getting old."

Bruck was about to address his concern, when a guard came running down the corridor and stopped one foot before him.

"Sir," he whispered, "we've got a problem."

"Explain?" Bruck demanded.

"Not here," the guard advised.

The two men walked off to a location that afforded them a degree of privacy and the guard, with animated excitement, said, "We've got a bomber at the front door."

"What?" Bruck shouted.

"He's surrounded, and bomb removal is on scene."

"What the hell are you talking about?" Bruck growled, pushing the man toward the staircase leading to the first floor.

The man took a deep breath, calmed himself to the point where he could begin to make sense, and explained, "Agent Cosgrove is trying to gain entrance."

Bruck glared at the man, waved his hands in the air in desperation, and ordered, "Get back to your post."

Bruck made his way to the entrance where a small crowd had gathered. The image of a male, surrounded by bomb protective gear attired personnel, popped into view as he slowly approached.

"Stay back, sir," one of his subordinates called out.

"Report," Bruck shouted, now standing twenty feet from the entrance.

"Man with an explosive vest, sir."

"Can you identify?" he asked, recalling Andrew

Cosgrove being named by the guard.

"One of our people, sir."

"Name?"

"Cosgrove."

Oh shit, Bruck said to himself. So much for crossed fingers. "Can you terminate without detonation?"

"No, sir. He's holding a deadman's switch."

"It keeps getting better," Bruck mumbled to himself.

"He's asking for help removing it," the man called out.

"Give him a radio."

Bruck watched as one of the bomb experts placed a radio in Cosgrove's free hand. He waited a few seconds and said, "This is Acting Director Bruck, I assume that you've changed your mind?"

He watched as Cosgrove's tremulous hand lifted the radio to his mouth and heard, "It's not what it appears to be."

"Really? From where I stand I see a traitor wearing an explosive vest at the Mossad's front door."

There was a momentary pause, and then, "I'm not here voluntarily, they're holding Bina hostage."

"Bullshit," Bruck said, while wondering if there could be any truth to his claim, as he removed his cellphone and dialed Bina's number.

It rang ten times more than acceptable with no answer. He redialed, and when there continued to be no response, he lifted the radio to his face and said, "Who's holding her?"

"The POF, they want revenge."

"Retaliation for what?" he seethed, all the while knowing the answer.

"For the missile attack that killed a lot of their people."

Too bad you hadn't been one of them, Bruck thought. "Are you being watched?"

"I don't know, but I sure as hell do *not* want to blow myself up."

Bruck lowered the radio and pondered the situation. Cosgrove is no longer as asset, he thought, but Bina is a horse of a different color. I have to get her back. He motioned for one of his agents to approach and ordered, "Take two men and check out Bina's apartment."

"Sir?"

"Cosgrove claims that she's been taken hostage—see if she's being held on site and call me. And alert the border."

He redirected his attention to the ongoing spectacle and watched as the removal team began their delicate invasion of the explosive's wiring harness. But as he watched, and due to the proximity of the bomb to the front entrance, several team members began installing a steel and Kevlar barrier around Cosgrove, for the purpose of minimizing any potential damage to their building, should there be a detonation. With his view obscured, Bruck withdrew to his office and waited.

Following an agonizing fifteen minutes, his phone buzzed.

"Bruck here," he said.

"Sir, Bina's apartment is empty."

"Any evidence to support the traitor's allegation?"

"There were some clothes strewn about, but I've seen worse in my own home."

"Anything else?"

"Well, there was one strange observation, sir."

"Cut the drama and tell me."

"Her Beretta was lying under the bed."

"She wouldn't have left her house without it. Go back and look for signs of forced entry."

"Sir, we'd checked, and there were none."

"Where are you?"

"One block away from headquarters."

"Stay away for now, the bomb is still active, but have communications ping her cellphone," Bruck ordered.

"Yes, sir."

Bina would never have left home without her weapon, Bruck reasoned. So either Cosgrove is telling the truth, or something else is in play, but what, he wondered.

Moments later a breathless agent ran to his office to inform him that the explosive vest had been removed and that Andrew Cosgrove was now in manacles and on his way to a cell.

***

8 A.M.

A old white van, with steam exiting from beneath its engine hood and marked with a baker's logo, pulled to the side of the road one kilometer away from the Israeli/Gaza border. In its rear compartment sat a bruised and seething Mossad agent—Bina Cohen—flanked by a pair of seedy, armed Palestinians.

The driver checked his sideview mirror and exited the vehicle, while the nervous, AK47 cradling passenger maintained a vigil for police. The heavily traveled road had been a poor choice, but the mission had been cobbled together rather hastily and the driver had had minimal experience with the Israeli side of the border. And as the driver leaned into the engine compartment, a police vehicle rapidly approached from behind, its strobing lights reflecting off of the pavement.

The driver motioned for the passenger to hide his weapon, but the man had either misunderstood, or had chosen to become a shahid (martyr), as he exited the van and dropped to a crouch, his rifle shouldered and aimed at the police vehicle's windshield. An instant later he opened fire with the AK on full automatic. One officer had been hit in his left shoulder, but the driver had managed to exit and return fire. Several of his rounds pierced the van's rear door, killing one of Bina's Palestinian guards and missing her head by inches. But as the dead guard slithered to the van's floor, his rifle fell, resulting in the discharge of a single round, a bullet that had struck his buddy square between the eyes.

Unaware of the van's occupant, the police officer had been aiming for the vehicle's visible, underbelly fuel tank. And a single round had found its way through the corroding metal vessel, resulting in a steady stream of gasoline running directly toward the kneeling Palestinian shooter. The officer fired at the line of fuel, just as Bina came flying out of the van's rear doors and hit the ground rolling away from the truck. Sparks from the bullet striking rock or pavement ignited the ribbon of fuel, reaching the shooter in a matter of seconds, and a short-while thereafter the fuel tank. The van exploded with a loud report and a burst of orange flames, its rear door landing on the police cruiser's roof. Bina had managed to roll off to the side of the road and down a shallow embankment, where she lie with her hands tied behind her back, the rope securing her legs having come loose during her escape.

She'd managed to chew through a flimsy gag and shouted to the second and newly arrived cruiser's occupants, "Down here, help me."

One officer cautiously approached, his weapon at the ready and she called out, "I'm Mossad, free my hands."

Chapter Sixty-three

Sunday, January 21st

1 P.M.

Bina sat—with three sutures sealing a forehead gash, two across her upper lip and a bandage covering her left earlobe—uncomfortably on the chair before Bruck's desk, desperately trying to return the smile offered by her boss.

"How are you feeling?" Bruck asked.

"I've been better, sir," she replied, through clenched teeth.

"You're due for sick leave."

"I'm not shutting down, there's work to be done."

Bruck took a deep breath and exhaled, while staring at his damaged operative, and said, "It appears that your intuition had been spot on. Cosgrove is in a cell downstairs."

"Has he talked?"

"He'd arrived strapped with plastic explosives, but claimed to have been on an off-the-books mission. Ring any bells?"

"No, sir. But as previously mentioned, he'd been acting strange."

"There is no plausible means of verifying his

assertion."

"He's a traitor," she bristled.

"That remains to be determined, but until that time he will stay locked up."

"And my abductors?"

"It appears that we've been engaged in a game of tit for tat, and unless we can terminate their existence, perpetuation will be futile."

"So it will go unanswered?"

"For now."

She narrowed her brow and suggested, "The POF are not aligned with Hamas, correct?"

"So it appears."

"Can we pit one against the other?"

"We'd need someone inside Hamas to get the ball rolling."

"I could volunteer."

Bruck laughed, and said, "They'd see you coming before you'd even left."

"But..."

"I understand your anger and eagerness for revenge, but neither side has gained from that approach."

"So we do nothing?"

"We wait."

"For?"

"An opportunity, either political or military, to arrive at a durable truce."

"And we allow the terrorists to disrupt our lives?"

"When we can inflict meaningful damage, we'll be all in."

A single tear trickled down her left cheek and she said, "I'll be ready when that day comes."

"Sadly, while we may have a hand in the eventual conflict, it is the army who will be on point."

She shook her head in agreement and rose to leave the office.

Bruck stared at the empty space created by Bina's absence, and thought, there goes a patriot.

The telephone buzzed, and since the secretary did not work on Sundays, Bruck lifted the receiver and announced, "Acting Director Ariel Bruck, how can I help you?"

"I'm returning your call. Do you know what time it is here?" a gruff voice demanded.

"Marcus, sorry for the hour, but it's important," Bruck apologized.

"The State Department is my day job, you should know that I have a life."

"I wish that I could say the same."

"What do you need?"

"Do you recall the Brooklyn terrorist incident?"

"I've tried not to."

"The two young American men are still here in Israel."

"So?"

"I need for your government to forget about them."

There was a pause and then, "To what end?"

"Should they decide to return to the States, I do not wish them to be pursued, by any governmental or local agency."

"That's asking a lot."

"Understood, but can you comply?"

"With our current political quagmire, I can't speak for the locals, but the government will look the other way."

"Thank you, I owe you one."

"You can count on that," Marcus said, and hung up.

***

3 P.M.

Following an abbreviated lunch, a call to his wife and a discussion with the guards in reference to the limited beneficial treatment to be afforded Andrew Cosgrove,

Bruck had come to a decision. And to that end, he marched himself down to the cells housing the Floridians and deftly avoided the area of Cosgrove's confinement. The barred door to Marvin's cell was wide open and he entered and stood by the edge of the bed.

"I need to speak with you both, so wake your friend and have him join us," Bruck ordered.

"This is his nap time, sir."

Bruck glared at him and he jumped from the bed and walked to George's cell.

With the two men now seated on Marvin's cot, Bruck paced for a few seconds, the thought of Bina having been kidnapped uppermost in his thoughts, and said, "You are not safe in Israel. The terrorists are out for your hides."

"What option do we have?" George interrupted.

"I've cut a deal with the U.S. State Department and I'm sending you back to the States."

"A deal?" Marvin said, the words drawn out slowly.

"They will not come after you," he advised, ignoring Marcus' warning about the local authorities.

"So we can go home as if nothing had happened?" George asked.

"I would suggest that you stay away from New York—go back to Florida."

"What about our Israeli citizenship?" Marvin asked.

"There will be no need for that."

"When do we leave?" George asked excitedly.

"There are a few details yet to be dealt with, but I will try to have you on a plane within the next forty-eight hours," Bruck instructed, as he turned and abruptly departed.

George watched as Bruck disappeared down the corridor, and when he was no longer visible he turned to Marvin and gleefully exclaimed, "We're going home."

"You buying his explanation?" Marvin asked.

"The terrorists are after us."

"And we know that because the Mossad has said so."

"You have doubt?" George asked, a thoughtful expression on his face, as he took a seat on the cot.

"Just considering various possibilities."

"And they are?"

"That they want us gone for another reason."

"Give me one plausible explanation."

"Maybe there is no deal with the State Department, and we're being used to pay a political debt."

"Hmm, we have only the Director's word for exoneration."

"Remember, while the Mossad are the good guys,

they're spies. And nothing is ever as it appears."

"Where the hell did you get that shit from?"

"I read."

"Any other scenarios where we get fucked?"

"Yeah, all of them."

"We don't have a lot of time to come up with an alternative."

"But we can walk out of here anytime we want."

"OK, let's look at what we know. Home might not be an option, and Bruck doesn't want us to stay in Israel. And there remains the possibility that he's correct in assessing the POF's hate for us."

"I say we go somewhere else."

"Passports ... we don't have our passports."

"And there's the first roadblock," Marvin groaned.

"What about the American Embassy?"

"If the alleged State Department deal is a hoax, the minute they do a search to create new passports they'll nail us."

"Like you said, we're fucked no matter what," George grumbled.

"I'm going for a walk."

"A perp walk?" George guffawed.

"No, up and down the corridor," he advised, as he left

the cell.

The short distance between his cell and the corridor's exit point had proven hardly enough to satisfy Marvin's need to burn off excess energy, and he turned a corner and traveled down a previously unexplored passage. There were cells like his own down each side, most of which were dark, with one exception at the very end of the hallway. Curiosity got the better of him and he approached slowly. Craning his head to one side to avoid discovery, he locked onto a disheveled male stretched out on a cot, his hair was askew and his face showed signs of an evolving beard. But there was something eerily familiar about the image and he ventured forward.

"Hello," he called out, at first softly, and when there had been no response, more forcefully.

The hobo apparent appeared to awaken from slumber, and his head turned toward the vertical bars separating his person from freedom. "Someone there?" a weak voice called out.

"What's your name?" Marvin asked, as he stood in the shadows.

"Who are you?"

"A fellow inmate," he said, despite the fact that he was free to come and go.

With some effort, the man rose to a seated position, squinted, and said, "Come closer."

Marvin hesitated, and moved to where his face rested less than an inch from the bars.

"I know you, you're Marvin, the American."

"Rafael?" Marvin exclaimed, with surprise.

"My name is Andrew Cosgrove, but Rafael will do."

"What the hell are you doing here?"

"I've asked myself the same question."

"No, seriously, what happened?"

"It's complicated."

"I've got time."

"The bigger question is, what are you doing in this place?" Cosgrove inquired.

"We're here for protection."

"From what?"

"The terrorists that are after us."

Cosgrove tilted his head to one side, as if trying to process the statement, and asked, "Which terrorists would they be?"

"The one's we'd traded fire with in New York."

Cosgrove began to laugh, but it quickly morphed into a raucous fit of coughing. When he'd calmed some, he said, "Bullshit."

"Excuse me?" Marvin exclaimed, clearly confused by Cosgrove's outburst.

"They're not really after you, they want the Acting Director."

"Bruck?"

Cosgrove shook his head affirmatively, adding, "And that's why I'm here."

"I don't understand," he breathed, while recalling his own words regarding spies and their motives.

"I can't reveal what I know, it's highly classified."

"You're a prisoner, how much worse could it get?" Marvin suggested.

"Good point. I'm going to assume that you know nothing about Israeli politics, correct?"

Marvin agreed with a nod.

"Rules are sometimes bent or twisted to achieve a desired result."

"OK, that means nothing to me, but go on."

"My intel had revealed that a deal had been struck to assist with the POF's takeover of Hamas, in exchange, the POF would begin to tear down the militant regime and transform it into an economic growth machine."

"Sounds too good to be true."

"Probably, but those in high places bought into the

idea."

"What happened?"

"Fell apart."

"Whose fault?"

"Take one guess ... OK, I'll answer, Hamas. They got word of the deal and came down hard on the POF for attempting a coup."

"So why are they after Bruck?"

"They'd concluded that the Mossad had set them up, and since Bruck is the Mossad, well, you see where that goes."

"And your involvement?"

"I thought that I could play peacemaker, but it'd turned against me."

"And you're here because?"

"The lunatics strapped an explosive vest around my chest and sent me to the front door, and to make certain that I would blow myself up, they'd kidnapped my partner."

"Shit."

"Yeah, big time. Have you heard anything about her, I'm really worried."

"No, me and George have been sitting in cells on the other side of this hallway."

"At least your doors are not locked."

Marvin remained in place, but kept silent.

Cosgrove inquired, "Was there something else?"

"You're a spy, right?"

"You might say that."

"We need passports."

"And I need a way out."

"Do you know someone who could create them?"

"If I did, and I'm not claiming that I do, it would be costly."

"I have a trust fund, I could have money transferred here."

"Well, it all moot, with me locked up."

"What if we could get you out?"

"It's not like in the movies, these are electronic locks that cannot be picked with a bobby pin."

"But the guy who controls them is down the hall."

"Sorry, but I don't think a blowjob would tempt him."

"Not what I had in mind," he laughed.

"OK, if you can get me out, I can arrange for the phony passports. But remember, you'll be risking criminal status. And the Mossad doesn't take kindly to the aiding and abetting of prisoners."

"Hadn't considered that."

"They'll hunt you down to the darkest corners of the planet."

"So we're all screwed?"

"If I can get out, and if I can prove my innocence, I'll make the escape assistance disappear."

"You can do that?"

"I said, if."

"Let me discuss it with George."

Chapter Sixty-four

2 P.M.

A guard had overheard the conversation between prisoner Andrew Cosgrove and Marvin. And he had quickly relayed the recorded exchange to his superior, who had fast tracked it to the Acting Director.

Bruck removed the flash drive containing the discussion from his computer, rose from his desk and turned towards a window. He gazed off into the distance and focused on nothing in particular, he was troubled. Could Cosgrove have been telling the truth, he wondered. He would have had no good reason to lie to Marvin. On the other hand, he most certainly knew about the detainment level's surveillance capability. Perhaps the conversation had been meant for my ears. But at least some of what he'd claimed makes sense. Certainly, the missile aimed at my office adds credence to that notion. So what do I do with him, he asked himself. And what about the two Americans.

The desk phone buzzed and he momentarily ignored it, but its incessancy begged for a response and he lifted the receiver.

"Bruck here," he said.

"It's Bina, sir. I need to speak with you."

"I'm listening."

"In person, sir."

He shifted his gaze to the desk clock, realized that his wife must be fuming mad for his remaining at the office on a Sunday, and decided to table the guilt. "I'll be waiting," he said.

Bina arrived twenty minutes later, knocked and entered.

"We couldn't have had this discussion earlier?" he asked, his words tinged with a hint of sarcasm.

"I'd arrived home, was making a pot of tea, when something popped into my head."

Bruck stared at her, as one might glare at a child who'd said something irrational, and asked, "What was it?"

"When the terrorists had me in their van, the driver and front seat passenger were arguing back and forth. I could only hear bits and pieces of what they'd had to say, and my Arabic isn't perfect, but I heard one of them gloat about capturing a Mossad agent and turning him into a bomb."

Bruck leaned forward, his elbows perched on the edge of his desk, and he said, "And you think that they were referring to Cosgrove?"

"I don't know of any other bomb laden operatives,

sir."

"What about your intuition?"

"I may have misinterpreted it."

He leaned back and thought, this could be the conformation that I'd been lacking. But she could be manufacturing the story to save her partner. "Do you have any proof?"

"They're dead, sir."

"You've presented me with a conundrum. If what you say is true, Cosgrove is innocent and should be free. But..."

"Sorry for interrupting, sir, but I now think that I'd been mistaken when I'd called him a traitor."

"And how do you propose that I verify your assertion?"

"You could free him on a provisional basis, freeze his security clearance and see what he does."

Hmm, she makes a good case, he said to himself, as he drummed the fingers of his right hand on the desktop. If the POF had considered him an asset, he pondered, they wouldn't have strapped him with Semtex, what good is a dead resource. Still, his actions had not been sanctioned. On the other hand, I had stressed individuality and independent thought for my operatives, but that was to apply to those agents who were to function in distant locations, outside of Israel, and crossing into Gaza hardly meets that test. But he'd never failed me in the past.

"OK, but before I allow the bird to fly, I want you to press him for information. See if you can reinforce your new take on him, and I'll be listening."

"When, sir?"

"Right now."

Bruck followed her down to the detainment level, but stayed behind and out of sight. The surveillance room was at the end of the corridor, and he stood behind the operator in the enclosed space with a pair of headphones resting against his ears.

"Bina, thank God you're OK," Cosgrove called out, as she approached his cell.

"Not exactly honkey dory, as they say in the States," she admitted, gesturing toward her sutures.

"But you're alive, that's what counts."

"What the hell were you thinking," she reprimanded.

He grimaced, rubbed a hand through his burgeoning beard, and replied, "You must have thought that I'd gone off the deep end, but I was not trying act aloof. I was fighting an internal battle, and in the end I did what I'd thought was best."

"For whom?"

"The Acting Director and Israel."

"It certainly didn't look that way."

"I guess."

"From whom had you obtained your intel?"

"About their plan to kill the boss?"

She nodded affirmatively.

"Wasn't the missile attack on the office proof enough?"

"No, you had to have had something more concrete."

"I have a conduit," he murmured.

"Louder," she urged.

"I have someone on the inside."

"Really. And you weren't going to share that with you partner?"

"Too dangerous."

"For whom?"

"Shit, Bina, I'll get her killed."

"So there is a woman," she crowed.

"Yes."

"And you've been doing the hokey pokey with the enemy?"

"She's not an ideologue, but her family members are."

"What have you promised her?"

"Nothing."

"C'mon, Andrew, no woman would risk her life for your schmekel (penis)."

"Alright, I'd promised to try and get her out of the country. And what's wrong with my schmekel?"

"Get rid of that silly beard, you look like a goat," she said, as she turned and departed.

Bruck met her at the staircase and advised, "I heard everything, and I'm not sure I liked what I'd heard."

"Which part, sir?"

"You know."

She exhaled, blushed and admitted, "It was just on one lonely occasion in New York, sir."

Bruck stopped in his tracks, his facial expression turned fearsome but he broke into laughter and said, "So his schmekel is nothing special."

Bina remained silent, as they marched up the staircase and entered his office.

"So, you are still convinced that your intuition had been wrong?" he asked.

"Even more so."

"I'm not happy about his woman, but she could be useful."

"Yes, you had said that you'd need someone on the inside."

"Inside of Hamas, not the POF."

"Will you free him?"

"In due time, assuming that he agrees to the use of the woman."

Bina had left the office with orders to remain at her residence until she'd received a medical clearance.

A weight had been lifted from his shoulders, as he no longer had to deal with the specter of a rogue agent, but the Americans were still a problem. It had become clear that the two Floridians did not trust his word, and had been conjuring up plans of their own. But despite the apparent fact that they were not POF targets, they could still be taken and used as bargaining chips, he'd reasoned, and that alone made their departure all the more pressing.

***

While Bruck contemplated the speedy exodus of his faux prisoners, Marvin had been in the process of initiating a second visit to Cosgrove's cell. And he'd found him lying on his back, asleep.

"Rafael, wake up."

Cosgrove stirred on the thin mattress and turned to face the barred door. "What do you want?" he growled.

"We're in," Marvin announced.

Cosgrove slowly rose to a seated position, scratched his chin and revealed, "I was just pulling your chain, everything we've discussed has been recorded."

"Seriously?"

"Scratch your balls and they know about it, kid. I can't help you."

"Shit, what are we gonna do?"

Cosgrove tilted his head and asked, "What's wrong with Israel?"

"You'd told us that the terrorists want us dead."

Cosgrove grinned, and replied, "Weren't you listening? I've already set the record straight on that topic."

"You're certain, they're not after us?"

"Yes."

"Then what the fuck are we doing down here?"

"Hell if I know."

Marvin, more confused than ever, turned on his heels and walked back to where George was waiting.

"Did he agree?" George asked.

"No, and it appears that we're in this shithole under false pretenses."

"Explain."

"He insists that the POF don't care about us."

George was about to let loose with a profanity, when Marvin slapped his palm over George's lips and pointed skyward. He then removed a ballpoint pen from his pocket and wrote, on the palm of his own hand, *they're listening*.

Chapter Sixty-five

Monday, January 22nd

6 A.M.

Mossad headquarters

Bruck had eventually returned home the evening prior and had received an earful from his wife. He'd consumed the cold leftovers that she'd silently shoved before him, before heading to the bedroom, leaving her husband to contemplate his life, present and future. And rather than face her wrath, he'd spent the night on the living room couch. At 5 a.m., he'd showered, dressed, scribbled a brief apologetic note for his still sleeping wife, and left for the office.

The secretary had yet to arrive, but a thoughtful agent had filled the coffee machine that sat upon the office credenza. He tossed his well scuffed, brown attache case onto a chair and poured himself a cup.

Today is decision day, he said to himself. I have to decide what I am going to do about Cosgrove and the Americans, whose distrust is a disappointment. But given the treatment that they'd received, along with the apparent misinformation, I can hardly blame them. As for Cosgrove, my actions had been justified, but it appears that however misguided his judgement had been, his intentions had been laudable. I will abide by Bina's suggestion and release him on a short leash.

After nearly burning his lips on the overly tepid coffee, he called down to the detention level and spoke with a guard.

"Have someone accompany the two Americans up to my office," he'd requested.

An agent appeared at his door thirty minutes later and deposited the two Floridians. Bruck gestured toward the pair of chairs at the head of his desk and they took their places.

"I understand that you do not wish to return to the States," Bruck said.

The two friends gazed at each other with an expression that said, *we've been busted.*

"We have our concerns," Marvin advised.

"And based upon your recorded conversations with agent Cosgrove, I recognize your confusion. However, it now appears that you have two options, Israel or the States ... the choice is yours."

"What proof can you offer that the U.S. government won't come after us?" Marvin asked.

"My word."

"Nothing in writing?"

"No."

"And if we stay here, the terrorists will leave us alone?"

"I can't guarantee it."

"We need to discuss it, but we'd like to get some fresh air," George offered.

"Across the way is the Sarona Market, there's a variety of food to be had there, but it opens at 9 a.m."

"We can walk out of here?" Marvin asked.

"Of course, you're not prisoners," he chuckled.

The two men rose cautiously from their seats, looked back once, and headed for the exit.

The Market was an eye opener, its ultra modern exterior conflicting with their mental images of the old world. Through the glass enclosed entrance they could see an interior expanse filled with colorful food displays and more. It was still roughly two hours before opening, so they sat down on the steps leading up to the front doors to consider the offered choices.

"Do we stay or go?" George mumbled, as if speaking to himself.

"We haven't seen enough of Israel to make an educated decision," Marvin suggested.

"Yeah, if the rest of the country is like this," he said, gesturing toward the market, "maybe we should stay."

"It's not just about modern buildings, there's the language issue, the terrorists just across the border and who knows what else."

"I'm hearing that you want to go home."

"Thinking about it."

"There's risk."

"Might be worth it."

"For you, with your trust fund dollars. But what have I got to return to?"

Marvin acknowledged his friend's indecision with a nod.

Three, very attractive young women, chatting away in Hebrew, slowed to a stop as they arrived at the steps. The taller of the trio smiled, her dark hair flowing as she giggled amongst her friends, moved forward and said something in Hebrew that neither George nor Marvin could understand.

"Tourists?" she repeated, in English.

"Sort of," George replied.

"What does that mean?" she asked.

"I'm George and my friend is Marvin," George replied, ignoring the requested explanation.

"My name is Carmel," she offered, turning and

grinning at her friends.

"And the others?"

"The blond is Eliana and the other, Golda."

"You here for the market?" he inquired.

"No, we walk every morning, different places."

"You're students?"

"No, we work across the road," she advised, nodding toward the Mossad's headquarters.

George laughed, "We just came from there."

The young women gathered into a huddle, and suddenly the English speaker turned and abruptly said, "We have to go."

They walked off rapidly in the direction from whence they'd come, leaving the two men somewhat confused.

"Did we offend them?" Marvin asked.

George shrugged and said, "Don't know, don't care, but if the rest of the women look like them I'm staying."

"Seriously?"

"Think so. There's nothing back home that I'd miss, and in Miami I'm just another jerk. But here, I could be a novelty."

"What about me?"

"Sure, I'd miss you, but you have your money to return to."

"That's cold, man."

"Yeah, guess it is, and I'm sorry, but it's time to grow up."

***

10 A.M.

Bruck had cleared his mind of the Americans, convinced that they would be out of his hair in the very near future. His secretary had arrived several hours earlier and he'd instructed her to have Andrew Cosgrove cleaned up and brought to his office. And at five minutes past ten a.m., an agent knocked on the doorframe and announced the prisoner's presence. Cosgrove entered and the agent closed the door, but remained just outside.

Bruck's expression was stern, and he said, without any added pleasantry, "Have a seat."

Cosgrove lowered his body onto one of the chairs before the Acting Director's desk and sat silent.

"I'm not going to rehash recent events, as it appears that your actions, however misguided, had been in good faith."

Cosgrove's face remained expressionless.

"I'm going to release you," Bruck said, adding,

"pending review."

"Review?"

"Yes. Your security clearance has been suspended."

Without warning, Cosgrove's face assumed a twisted, demonic expression, as Bruck was suddenly and unexpectedly assailed by Cosgrove's leap into the air and across the desktop. In the process, he'd grabbed Bruck's faux dagger turned letter opener and jammed it into Bruck's chest cage to the hilt. Bruck, caught by surprise, attempted to fight back, but the blade had punctured a lung and he began spitting up frothy blood, while trying to gouge Cosgrove's right eye with his fingers. The ex-operative held onto the letter opener and twisted, his face only inches away from Bruck's, his maniacal grimace adding to the macabre scene. Bruck's cries and the sound of the scuffle had attracted the attention of the agent waiting in the corridor and he came crashing through the door with his weapon aimed at the back of Cosgrove's head —he fired two rounds. A mist of red traveled through the air and coated everything in sight. He shoved Cosgrove's lifeless corpse to the ground and called for the medical team. Bruck slumped forward, gasping for breath, his eyes flared open like saucers as he attempted to speak.

"Save your breath," the Agent advised, as he

supported his boss, preventing him from slipping to the floor.

The medical team had arrived within minutes and had begun to administer first aid. A heavily guarded ambulance, its siren and lights blazing, was escorted to the nearest hospital, where Bruck's injury was quickly assessed and surgically addressed. His wife arrived following surgery and spent several nail biting hours outside of the recovery room, until the surgeon approached. With a well used tissue, she cleared the tears from her cheeks and waited.

"We had to remove a good part of one lung, but he should be OK," the surgeon advised.

"Thank you."

She turned to face the four agents who had accompanied Bruck to the hospital and repeated her thanks, adding, "You'd better start looking for a new director, Ariel Bruck is now retired."

"He said that?" one agent asked.

"No, those are my orders."

Epilogue

Bruck's recovery had taken longer than anticipated, several months to be exact, and a new acting Director had been assigned to his post. And while past events had continued to plague his sleep hours with disturbing nightmares, he was slowly becoming acclimated to retirement and his new hobby, the creation of a written memoir that he knew could not be published, given the classified nature of its contents.

Andrew Cosgrove had been buried in a closed coffin. Services had been brief, and the only visitor had been Bina, a reluctant attendee whose presence had been dictated out of a warped sense of camaraderie.

The initial and publicly announced motive for the attack on Bruck had been explained as a bizarre psychological derangement disorder related to a combination of ill defined factors. But the official, internal investigation had revealed that Cosgrove had indeed been a POF operative for an unknown period of time, and that the explosive vest scenario had been a gamble, perpetrated with the hope that he could further ingratiate himself with the Acting Director to gain stable access to closely held operational information. But in reality, numerous agency personnel had been left with a nagging sense of uncertainty, and the notion that Cosgrove's burst of rage may have been a schizoid reaction to the Mossad's rejection of his claimed allegiance to the agency and Israel, and that he had not gone rogue. In essence, they'd clung to the public explanation as the most plausible. Resolution would not be forthcoming.

No evidence of Cosgrove's alleged POF girlfriend had been revealed, but plans had been put in place to further discredit the terrorists in the eyes of Hamas and, for the weeks that followed, the POF had been observed fleeing Gaza like a flock of migrating birds.

George had dropped anchor in Tel Aviv. He'd spent many days seated on the steps of the Sarona Market, hoping to catch a glimpse of the woman who'd identified herself as Carmel. And on the eighth day of vigil, she'd crossed the road and stood before him. They'd had lunch in the market and their relationship had begun to build.

Marvin had returned to Aventura, spending his days on the beach, protected from the searing sun by a large umbrella. Both he and George shared their experiences via their cellphones and vowed to visit, secure in the painful knowledge that life would draw them farther apart. It was time, as George had suggested, for them to grow up.

THE END

www.ingramcontent.com/pod-product-compliance
Lightning Source LLC
Chambersburg PA
CBHW021833010726
47493CB00005B/1377